Secrets
of
Spring

Seasons of Jefferson: Book 3

JULIE SOLANO & TRACY JUSTICE

Visit us on Facebook:
www.facebook.com/jt.authors

Visit us on Twitter and Instagram:
twitter.com/jt_authors
instagram.com/jt_authors

ISBN-13 978-0-9863836-5-6

Other Books

SEASONS OF JEFFERSON

When Fall Breaks, Book One

The Dead of Winter, Book Two

Dedication

For our four children who inspire us every day.
Thank you for your unending support and understanding
throughout this exciting journey.

To our moms, who stoke the fire to keep us going.
Thank you for always believing in us.

To Dar, our biggest cheerleader and our ray of sunshine,
Thank you for being our soul sister.

To our extended families and friends.
Thank you for enduring the endless book talk.

To our loyal readers.
Thank you for hanging onto that cliff as long as you did.

We love you all.

This book is for all of you.

~In the depths of every soul lies a secret,
but rarely is it known by only one.

Prologue

SILENTLY, I STAND PEEKING AROUND THE CORNER INTO THE BIG, SHINY, metal kitchen. *The dinner party has just finished and Mommy and Daddy are having grown up drinks with all the fancy people in the ballroom. I don't think they'll hear me over the dancing music, or the loud lady who keeps laughing at everything Daddy says. The other kids are off playing hide and seek at the end of the long hallway. Not the one that leads to the playroom, but the creepy one with all the mirrors and old pictures of serious guys. I don't like playing there. It scares me how their eyes follow me when I walk through.*

I've left my friends long enough to try to sneak a chocolate chip cookie from the big, castle jar Nikolai showed me earlier. As I creep forward, my shiny, black shoes click on the tile, stopping me in my tracks. Checking behind me, I unbuckle the straps and slip them off to make sure I don't get caught. I lick my lips and wiggle my toes, readying myself to take that first step onto the black tile. That's when I notice something moving across the room behind the big island.

Ducking behind the wall, my eyes peek through the archway and follow the path between me and that cookie jar. I know I can get to it, but I have to be quick. Carefully planning my route, my heart jumps when I see the back of the big man in dress-up clothes. I try to see if he's one of Daddy's friends from the party, but I can't tell who he is in the dark. All I know is he's moving funny. I wonder why he's doing pushups on the wall. I tilt my head to study his movement. That's when I notice he's not alone.

A soft cry squeals from the front of him. When I hear the voice, I can tell she's a lady. It doesn't sound like she likes what he's doing. She's begging him to stop. I try to see what's making her so sad, but I can barely see them. Even after he pushes her away, I still can't see his face. He steps into the dim glow seeping from the hallway, but even then, all I can see are his black gloves.

Tossing and turning beneath a mountain of damp sheets, my muscles tense. Those gloves. They're the same ones that have haunted my nightmares for the last two years. I watch them again and again. Gripping. Grabbing. Strangling. Oversized hands, tangling through the long, brunette hair.

The lady speaks, "He's going to kill you when he finds me. You're not going to get away with this."

"He's not going to find out."

"He's good at his job."

"I'm better at mine."

Still trying to make out his voice, I struggle to keep my eyes closed. Maybe this time I'll figure out who he is. I remind myself to stay asleep. Just long enough to listen. To hear his voice. But it's too low. Too garbled.

"Don't. Please. I won't tell. I promise. My son. He still needs me." The lady cries as I watch her hair quickly swing from one side of his broad shoulders to the other. After her dark shadow finally separates from his, a scuffle breaks out between them. I hear her high heels screech across the floor, and watch as she kicks at his shins and pulls at his hair.

Dropping to my knees, I huddle against the archway and pray that he doesn't see me. That's when I hear a snap followed by a thump. Drawing my eyes downward, I watch her soft curls fall to the ground and splay around his shuffling feet. After a few well-placed steps, the gloved hands grab her lifeless ankles. Her hair slowly sweeps around the corner and disappears into the darkness. I pick up my shiny shoes and try to run, but my fancy tights cause my feet to slip out from under me. Crashing into the cupboard, the crunch of my little toe forces a whimper from my trembling body.

"Who's there?"

Like so many restless nights before, my mind works to escape the fear I've grown so accustomed to. For the life of me, I can't remember what happens next, but the same cycle ensues. I force my eyes open, lie in the darkness, and wonder what the hell I just witnessed; and why, for the love of God, I keep having the same dream over and over again.

Chapter One

Not Again

I REMEMBER IT ALL SO CLEARLY. THE NIGHT I AWOKE FROM THE recurring nightmare to the sound of my dad's muffled voice seeping through my bedroom wall. Something felt off about the way his words traveled through my room that night. Loud then quiet. Rushed then slow. He was a very composed man and I didn't hear him speak like that often, only when he was upset about something. Quietly, I slipped from my bed and tiptoed to the door. I pulled down on the handle without making a peep and pushed my ear against the sliver of an opening.

"Damn it. Not again." His growl accompanied the sound of a fist slamming against the tabletop. "It's only been three years!" His deep huffs shattered the otherwise silent summer night. "I know. I know. I get it. I just don't want to put them through this again." Another brief pause allowed me to focus on the nerves beginning to bundle deep in my core. "This is exactly what I was afraid of. Just promise me you'll put us somewhere safe this time."

Listening through the crack in the door, anxiety crept its way through my eleven-year-old body. Everyone had been on edge for days. My parents were exceptionally quiet, careful to talk only when they thought I wasn't listening. They had gone as far as to close the vineyard and send all the workers on a temporary vacation. The only ones left on duty were the guards who worked the security gate. My dad had never shut down his operation before, even when we were away on vacation. I couldn't help but wonder what was going on. That was until I overheard the phone call.

"Tonight? You're serious?" Desperation laced his voice. "You want us to leave it all behind? Our names too?" Pause. "So, we won't know till we get there." An uncomfortable silence filled the room. "What about Jenna?" His expression became more insistent as he spoke. "We can't change it again ... No. She's keeping it. There are thousands of Jennas." His volume rose and his words came out in a strong staccato. "Last. Name. Only ... She's just a kid. We'll take our chances."

I closed my eyes and swallowed hard when I realized what it meant. We were on the run again, and there was nothing I was going to be able to say about it. With the crescendo of footsteps approaching, I let my hand fall away from the door and scurried back to my bed. My parents' room was just across the hall from mine, so it was easy to hear when my mom spoke.

"Again? I thought this place was the one."

It was barely a whisper, but I heard it and knew. My life was about to take another turn. My friends. My sports. My school. Everything I had worked so hard to build in Napa Valley was going to be left behind.

"Should we get her up now or let her sleep a couple more hours?"

"Now! We don't have much time. They're on their way."

"I see."

"Brooks is sending a truck. It won't fit much. Just grab the things we can't replace."

I remember the surprise on my mom's face when she came into the room to find me already packing. I'd done it once before and I knew how it went. I was going to have to salvage what I could. The rest would be left up to my memory. The few remaining treasures

I had hidden in my closet were the first things I'd pack. There was no way I was going to leave them behind.

I opened my oversized suitcase and started shoving things in. My childhood photo album. The 35mm camera I'd gotten for my 6th birthday. My collection of nesting dolls. My pink and black catcher's gear. My baseball mitt and newly autographed Buster Posey rookie card. I pulled my most important belongings from my shelves and closet, running back and forth to the suitcase as fast as I could.

When I was finished, I stopped at my nightstand to pull out the real gem. A picture of me with my two best friends. It was the only picture I had left of Nikolai. My dad had taken the others when he caught me packing them last time. I couldn't let that happen again. I'd already given up enough of my past, and the people in it were not something my heart was willing to let go.

I was working frantically to wrap the framed picture and bury it beneath my gear when I heard his whispered voice drifting over my mom's shoulder.

"You're going to need a few clothes too. Not too many. We'll shop when we get there."

I had all I needed. I slipped my team hoodie over my head, threw a few sliders, t-shirts, and jeans into my suitcase, and zipped it up. I took one last look at my ladybug bedroom and flipped off the light. It took all the strength I had to tug my heavy suitcase down the hall where I sidled up next to my protective mom.

Gently, she pulled her arm around my shoulder. I said nothing when I felt the weight of her trembling chin come to rest atop my head. We swayed back and forth while my dad scurried in and out of the rooms, turning knobs, flipping switches, and gathering papers. Mom shushed me when I asked why he was turning the gas knobs. We weren't allowed to touch those.

We didn't stay long, only till we got the sign that it was time to leave. It was probably two in the morning when my dad got the message. Led by the light of his phone, he hurried us through the darkened house and into the garage where a black truck was waiting. As I crawled into the back, behind the big, bald man at the steering wheel, my dad gently pressed his hand onto the top of my head. "Stay down, princess," he whispered as the door closed and we began to accelerate.

After a few seconds, I heard a thundering boom and looked up through the rear window. I watched as a soft glow began to light up the sky in the distance. An eerie silence filled the cab of the truck, and at that moment I knew it was all gone. My memories, up in a burst of flames.

For what seemed like hours, we drove in the dark, only sneaking off to the side of the road long enough to answer nature's call. Not a word was spoken between the driver or my parents. Huddled on the floor behind his seat, I finally drifted off to sleep, dreaming of the little girl I used to be.

I climbed atop an old barrel and worked to find my balance. Peeking through a crack in the wooden wall of the wine cellar, I searched the courtyard for something to keep my eyes busy. Mommy was upstairs with the Au Pair teaching the older kids how to speak English, while Daddy had me down below with him telling the big man about the wine. I watched curiously as two boys, who looked to be my age, huddled just a few feet away. When they finally stood, they proudly glanced at the circle they had just drawn in the dirt outside.

In an accent that matched the big man's, the smaller brown-haired boy asked, "You want to go first?"

The boy with the blond hair nodded his head and carefully took the knife from his playmate's hand. Backing away from the circle, I watched as he took it by the blade, held it up to his nose, and released it into the air. It made a turn, but crashed to the ground with an unsuccessful thud. The boy shrugged his shoulders as the brown-haired boy bent down in the dirt and retrieved the knife.

"Let me show you." A serious look crossed his face as he stood, staring into the circle. I watched intently as he grabbed it by the blade and flung it over his shoulder. It twirled through the air, just like the other boy's, but this one stuck in the ground, right in the middle of the circle. A cheerful grin lit his face. He bent down, and drew a new line, then wiped the other one away with his small hand. The boys continued back and forth until the blond one was left with nowhere to move.

"Throwing knives. That's silly. I should teach them how to play baseball," I accidentally said a little too loudly.

"Baseball?" The big man laughed. "With my Nikolai?" I heard the humor seep through his thick accent. "What has baseball ever taught anyone? Now a good game of knives, that'll teach you something." His head nodded up and down as he spoke. "Weapon handling is a skill that can be used throughout one's life."

I pulled away from the wall and jumped down from the barrel to get a good look at the first man I'd ever met who didn't like baseball. I stared long and hard at his trousers, just to make sure I wasn't missing something. "Got any balls, mister?"

A scornful expression came over his face as he cleared his throat and stepped behind the workbench. My dad didn't seem too amused with my disrespect.

"Honey, apologize."

"For what? I just want to know if he has any baseballs. I want to teach the boys how to play a real sport."

The big man chuckled when he realized it was an innocent six-year-old question. "Why don't you go introduce yourself to Nikolai so we can get some work done in here? I'm sure he'd be thrilled to play with a little girl who likes to throw things."

Excited to get out of the dark cellar, I nodded my head and ran through the door to the play yard. There, the boys stood in place staring as I ran toward them with my pigtails bouncing and a huge grin plastered across my face. "Whatcha doin?"

The blond-haired boy looked me up and down and swallowed hard.

"Playing knives."

"Can I play?"

The second boy pinched his face into a scowl and replied, "This game is for boys."

Defensively, I pulled my hands onto my hips and huffed, "Oh, yeah? Well, my daddy says girls can do anything boys can do."

They looked at each other, then looked at me as they snickered. Suddenly, the brown-haired boy took his knife, held it up to his shoulder, and let it twirl through the air. After it swiftly landed right in the center of a circle he grinned, "I bet you can't do that."

I couldn't let on that his knife trick was awesome, rather I came up with something to let him know he wasn't all that cool. "What's the point of all that twirly stuff you do?"

"What's the point? Have you never played knives?"

"We play baseball in America."

"This is not America. It is Russia."

"Can I try?"

"Can you handle it?"

"Show me how."

"Watch."

Again, the boy took the knife carefully by the blade, held it up over his shoulder, and released it with a quick flick. For a second time, the shiny, silver streak twirled once in the air, and stuck down into the circle, landing right on its mark. I stood in awe, but couldn't let on that I was impressed by how the fascinating boy could stick a knife in the ground exactly where he wanted it.

"That's boring. Watch this!"

I looked around the play yard for a perfect target. My eyes came to rest on a stack of wine barrels over by the cellar door. Above the barrels, hung a round cork sign with funny letters I didn't recognize. On the cork, there was a picture of a castle that looked a lot like the front of the big house. Carefully, I took the knife from his hand, walked across the green grass and stood several feet in front of the sign.

Holding the knife carefully by the blade, I closed my right eye to zero in on my target. I flicked my wrist back and forth a couple times, just to feel the weight of the metal in my hand. When I felt good and ready, I released it, watching it sail through the air toward the big cork covered sign. When it stuck in the middle of the castle the boys cheered from behind me.

The last thing I saw before I awoke to my new life was the smiling face of my friend, Nikolai, in awe of his new American playmate.

Chapter Two

A New Start

THE JOSTLING OF THE BUMPY RIDE PULLED ME FROM MY DREAM. Realizing I was still curled in a ball on the floorboard of the back seat, I stretched my arms and tried to unfurl my stiff legs from beneath me. The warm sun beaming through the rear window cast just enough glare that I couldn't look up to see where we were. Stiff and sore from the night's expedition, I wanted nothing more than to pull over and take a break from the endless road.

When I tried to speak, the dryness caused by a night of panic and restless sleep, didn't allow for volume. I cleared my throat as I worked to make my voice audible. "Is it okay to get up now?"

An unfamiliar voice spoke from the front, "You're all good. We're in the clear."

Crawling up to join my mother on the seat, I couldn't help but notice the towering mountains and endless pine trees that blurred off into the distance. I rested my head against the window and took it all in. Gone were the road signs, freeways, and rush of traffic that I'd grown so accustomed to in the Bay Area. Aside from a few birds flying overhead, the land was motionless. There were no recognizable points of reference. No landmarks. No familiar sounds. In that moment, I had no idea where I was. It was a whole different world from the gently rolling hills and bustling crowds I was used to back home.

As the sun rose in the mid-morning sky, we finally turned onto a long, dirt road. I watched as a large herd of cattle followed a tractor across an open field. Wheel lines sprayed water that formed rainbows for what looked like miles. Off in the distance, a narrow river separated the farmland from the horizon. As I studied the landscape, fields, livestock, and dirt roads were the only visions to be seen. There were no houses, cars, or people anywhere.

When an old, wooden farmhouse finally came into view, the driver began to slow and pick up his cell phone. After a series of beeps, I could hear the ring echoing from the other end. The voice of a man answered.

"They're here?"

"We've got 'em."

"Let's play it safe. Bring 'em around back."

"Yeah, the barn."

The crunch of the gravel beneath the tires pulled my eyes down to the road. There, a sandy-haired boy was kneeling on the grass, playing with a yellow lab pup. As we pulled to a stop, he continued to play without taking notice that he had company. I couldn't see his face, but his size and the squeak of his changing voice as he called to his puppy told me he was not too much older than me.

"Wait here," my dad directed as he opened the door to slide out. An elderly couple had just stepped out of the old ranch house. As he made his way toward them, I bobbed back and forth behind the headrest of the driver's seat trying to get a better view. My curiosity was killing me. I could see my dad a few feet away, but what I really wanted was to hear what he was saying. I climbed to the front seat and leaned through the window just enough to hear the conversation taking place on the back porch.

"Mr. Mason, it's been a while. Nice to see you again." My dad extended his hand toward the elderly gentleman. "Thanks for letting us stay with you until the vineyard's ready. I appreciate your generosity."

"Well, our son-in-law filled us in. You'll have food and a bed for the night." He paused and lowered his voice, "Don't you worry. We've done this before. You'll be safe here."

Giving a thankful nod, my father waved us out of the truck. My enthusiasm to break free nearly left me in a heap on the ground. My mind didn't seem to care that my legs were still weak and wobbly from the long ride. Thankfully, I caught myself just before I hit the ground. Holding onto the bed of the truck, I stood in the heat of the morning sun and waited for my legs to find their strength.

The situation made it tough to know what to do. I didn't want to seem rude by not introducing myself to the old folks up on the porch, but I couldn't help but think of Dad's late-night phone call. He had argued with someone about my name. Was I still Jenna Greenwood? I decided it would be best to stay silent, at least until I had a better understanding of who I was supposed to be.

My mom must have sensed my unease. Protectively, she slipped her arm around my shoulder and guided me toward the back door. Drawn to the adorable pup, I glanced over to get a better look as we passed by. I'd always wanted a lab and had to stop myself from running right over and snatching him up. As I gawked in their direction, the boy's eyes began to narrow in on me. Shifting his attention away from the wrestling match, he set the puppy down and began to rise to his feet.

Quickly, I pulled my gaze away. I didn't know why he was looking at me like that, but the thought of any boy looking at me for any reason made me cringe. It was the summer I turned eleven, and during those middle school years, boys were gross and still had cooties.

"Hey!" I heard his hushed voice in back of me. Unsure if his *hey* was intended for me or his dog, I decided to focus on the path ahead and keep on walking. I wasn't about to embarrass myself by being friendly to a boy if I didn't have to be. My pace did not slow until the pitter-patter of feet rushed up from behind. "Jenna?"

Slowly, I turned to meet his gaze. In a hushed voice, I whispered, "Who told you my name? Do we know each other?"

"Jenna, it's me." He scratched the back of his head, "Don't you remember?"

I narrowed my eyes and studied the appearance of the adolescent boy. He was just a little taller than me, and his blue eyes smiled just a bit at the corners. The front of his dark blond-hair flared out in several directions, but it looked intentional and well-styled. From his cowboy boots to his rodeo t-shirt, I looked him up and down multiple times. But as hard as I tried, I couldn't place him. With my lengthened silence, disappointment grew on his face.

"It's me, Jenna."

I was confused. The boy seemed adamant that I knew who he was, yet I wasn't even sure who I was. It had been so much for me to take in. All of it. The phone call. The argument about changing names. The packing. My dad running around the house flipping switches and turning knobs. The fireball in the night. It all happened in such a flash. I hadn't wanted to forget anything, yet the craziness of it all had somehow made me forget everything.

I needed to remember, if only for the sake of the poor kid standing in front of me wondering why I didn't know who he was. My mind raced through the basic facts first, like what was left of my identity. I was an only child who still had my parents and my first name. Outside of my age and gender, that's about all that was left. But I did have a few belongings. I still had some clothes and a suitcase of everything that meant anything to me. Thank goodness for that suitcase. At least I had my catcher's gear, a few keepsakes, and my photos.

Thinking about those photos brought a grin to my face. Once more, I had managed to sneak in the framed picture of Nikolai, Mason, and me. They were the only real friends I'd ever had. It had been far too long since I'd seen them in real life. The last time the three of us were together, we were still missing our front teeth.

Staring intently at the boy who claimed to know me, I was determined to figure out how he fit into my past. The rise of his eyebrows and outline of his jaw did look vaguely familiar. Familiar enough that I began to make comparisons between him and the photos I'd snuck into my suitcase. There weren't too many kids my age in those pictures. That's when the boys from my cherished, framed picture flashed through my mind for a second time. The eyes, the lips, and the outline of the face began to match up with the boy on my right. Even their postures were the same. If I was correct, the face I was studying was a more mature version of my friend, Mason.

"Mason? Is that you?"

He nodded. "It's me."

Silence grew between us as we worked to take in how we'd both changed since we'd last seen each other. This time, I recognized his eyes. They still smiled, even when his lips didn't. He had grown several inches, and his big teeth had grown in nice and straight. The roundness of his face had faded into sharper, more angular features. Although he was barely recognizable in his transition from a boy to a teenager, as sure as the seasons change, I was standing in the presence of Mason Brooks.

It was hard to believe I was out in the middle of nowhere with one of my friends from a former life. Never, in a million years, did I think I'd see him or Nikolai again. A thousand questions flooded my mind. If only I could've gotten them out before I was interrupted by the old lady's voice.

"Mason, I'm sure Jenna's hungry. It was a long drive. Why don't you bring her inside and we'll get her fed?"

He tilted his head in the direction of the old farmhouse. "Never keep Grandma waiting."

I followed him into the kitchen where she pulled out an

oversized frying pan and set it down onto the stovetop. Then opening the refrigerator, she whispered under her breath, "Well, shoot, it seems we're out of eggs. Mason?" She peeked out from the open door. "Would you mind gathering a few from the chicken coop so I can get breakfast started?"

By that time, my mind was ready to explode with questions. "I'll help." I jumped down from the barstool where I had perched just seconds earlier. Following Mason out the back door, I came in close behind him, whispering into the back of his ear, "But how? What are you doing here? Where are we? How did you know I was coming? Is Nikolai with you?"

Mason began to chuckle, "You haven't changed a bit, have you? Still full of questions and still don't pause long enough to let a person answer them. If you slow down long enough for me to get a word in, I'll tell you what I can. I haven't seen Nikolai since I was eight."

My mind wandered back in time, struggling to find its way through my foggy history. I had often tried to think back on my days in Russia, but I could never recall an entire memory, just bits and pieces that came back to me in my dreams. Even those, were somewhat fragmented and didn't seem entirely real.

"Don't you remember leaving together?" Confusion shrouded Mason's face. The look in his eyes had me desperately searching my memories for the last time we were together. He looked away quietly, then muttered, "I forgot. You were asleep when we left. I tried to wake you up. I wanted you to watch the lights with me, but I couldn't get you to open your eyes." He looked back at me for any sign of recollection. "We were together when we came back, Jenna. They put us onto the jet in the middle of the night and sent us back to the states."

"Nikolai too?"

He shook his head. "No. Not Nikolai."

Again, I dug through my earlier memories, but nothing came.

"I don't remember leaving. I guess I was too young."

"I do." He looked at me again. "Probably because I was so scared. My dad put me on a plane with you and your parents. It was the first time I'd been apart from my family. I can't even begin to describe the look on his face when he sent me away. It haunted me the entire trip. I watched the lights, the stars, the clouds, anything to take my mind off of leaving. When we finally landed, my grandparents met us at the tiny airport and brought me back here to Jefferson County. You got on another flight with your mom and dad, and that was that. I never saw or heard from you or Nikolai again."

Mason stopped talking and refocused on the chicken coop in front of him. "Here, hold out your hands."

I held them out as he began to lay eggs in them one at a time. "Can you handle six without cracking them?"

"I thought you knew me." I smiled. "These hands are like magic. Stack 'em up."

When we got inside, the adults had all gathered in the living room. I could tell by the quiet murmur that things had turned serious. If I could just sneak a little closer, maybe I could find out the truth about what was going on. Quietly, I set the eggs on the counter and tiptoed to the edge of the wall. My mom was talking just loud enough that I could barely make out what she was saying.

"Do you think they're old enough to handle this?"

"I don't think there's any way this is going to work without telling them. At some point, it's safer for them to know than not to know. I think we're finally at that point, honey."

Mason and I looked at each other. The curious expression on his face let me know that we were thinking the same thing. We needed to get in there to find out exactly what it was safer for us to know than not to know. The problem was, they would stop talking the minute they knew we were listening. They always did. Mason obviously didn't know my parents as well as I did. "Let's go see what they're talking about," he whispered and gently tugged my arm forward.

Just as I'd suspected, the minute we walked into the room everyone stopped talking and looked up at the two of us. As I glanced around, I noticed a new face had joined the circle. I had not seen him for years but recognized the dominating man instantly.

"I see you two have become reacquainted," he nodded with a friendly smile.

As soon as I smiled back, I looked to Mason. "My dad," he confirmed.

"Why don't you two come on in and sit down?"

There was noticeable tension when we crossed the threshold from the kitchen into the living room. The adults had filled all the available chairs that lined the perimeter of the room. My parents sat close on the couch, while Mason's grandparents and father sat separately in an eclectic group of armchairs. Mason pulled an old, piano bench into the circle for me. After directing me to sit, he stood so close behind that I could feel his presence against my back. As I looked around the circle of somber adults, my mom slid her hand over my dad's knee. He began to speak.

"Jenna, Mason." He looked at us individually as he addressed us. "I know it was a crazy night, and you're probably wondering what's going on. There's a lot we just can't tell you right now. I don't want to get into it. Sometimes things are better left unsaid. It's safer."

And there it was, another bogus line to keep me from the truth. I felt the heat rise in my face as my anger began to grow. Thinking about what I had gone through in the past twelve hours had my heart racing. I had been shaken up in the middle of the night and forced to pack a handful of possessions. If that wasn't bad enough, I watched my house explode before my eyes, then had to travel curled up in a ball on the floorboard until we reached safety. All of this with no explanation. In a matter of hours, my life had spun out of control and I had no say in any of it.

As the vision of my life exploding before me replayed in my mind, my anger ignited to fury. What kind of a situation had my parents gotten me into? Why did my life have to be flipped upside down because of it? Sometimes things are better left unsaid? The fact that they couldn't give me answers made me even more upset. I was so agitated that I couldn't hold it back anymore. I didn't care if I was in somebody else's house. Losing control, I began to shout, "Why is everything always such a big secret? You can't just pull me out of my exploding house in the middle of the night and then not tell me why! What's going on? Who am I? For all I know, I'm not even Jenna Greenwood anymore."

"Shhh."

"Careful."

"Oh, dear."

Voices sprouted up from all sides of the room. Mouths dropped, and eyes popped wide, "Honey, please don't use that name again."

It didn't seem quite fair that they could make such a life-changing request without telling me why I could no longer use my own name. I was going to get answers, even if I had to throw myself on the ground and cry. Before I resorted to those tactics, I decided to start with a deliberate threat. One that they knew I would make good on. "I refuse to use a different name unless you tell me why!"

I continued with the threat that I would tell every teacher in school and anyone I met that my parents made me change my name. That was unless they told me exactly what type of danger we were in and how it came to be. By the time I laid out my demands, I had pushed my parents into a corner. My mom looked at my dad with desperation. They knew I wasn't willing to keep a secret for them if I didn't even know what that secret was. After staring at me for what seemed like minutes, Dad turned to Isaiah, "You're the expert on this, Brooks. How much can we say? Your son is at risk of exposure too."

"Me?"

Mason's dad looked back at mine. "We don't have a choice any-more. Once you leave the ranch, these kids must hide any connection they have. It's a small county. Their paths are going to cross. They need to know why they have to pretend they've never met. It's the only way to keep them safe. Keep us all safe."

Mason and I sat in silence as our parents began to explain why we had to keep quiet. It was a long and complicated story, one that I could barely understand. My parents had met the Brooks in Russia, where Isaiah worked at the American Embassy. It was a time when they had put a halt on Russian adoptions and Isaiah worked tirelessly to push mine through. They spent hours together, working through deals and expediting paperwork. He used every connection he had to make it happen. That's how my parents had become such good friends with them, almost like family.

While the three of us were living back in the states, my dad received a phone call. Isaiah needed a favor, and though it may have been dangerous, there was no way my dad was going to let him down. He needed him to go to work at a Russian vineyard for a guy by the name of Sergei Vasiliev. My dad knew it was a risk to be the eyes and ears for Brooks, but the contract was enough money to set us up for life, and again he owed it to Isaiah. All he had to do was ride out the length of one visa. That was three years back in Russia. My dad would spend that time teaching Vasiliev the craft of winemaking, where to get the finest ingredients, and how to distribute the wines worldwide.

According to Isaiah, it was at a time when Russia was in poor relations with the rest of the world. As well as putting a halt to all adoptions, there was an embargo placed on imports to Russia. There was no way to transport or sell the wine legally. Somehow, using my dad's connections, he and Vasiliev found a way to get around it. With the help of my dad, Sergei had found great success with his highly rated wines, something that would have been impossible without my father or his network.

Something went wrong before his contract was up. It happened the night we left with Mason. My dad wouldn't tell us what it was, or the exact reason we were in hiding, but whatever happened back in Russia had caught up with us again. Mason and I, being their children, were at greatest risk for retaliation of Vasiliev and his men.

The thought of being a target of such a powerful man had my inner alarm blaring. Though I'd had very few interactions with him, he seemed nice enough. He gave me cookies out of the big castle jar and let us play hide and seek in his movie room whenever Dad was busy working. It didn't make sense that the same man who had shown me such hospitality could hunt me down just a few years later.

I wondered if Nikolai was okay, but I didn't ask. I was scared to hear the truth. What if his dad was such an evil man that there was no longer a Nikolai? I'd heard enough. Knowing the risk, it made sense that the story of our past couldn't resurface in our new home. If a connection was made between Mason and me, it would put us all in danger. It would be far safer to take the new names and new life being offered to us, and never look back. We made a pact that day, that no matter what, we would keep our pasts a secret from the rest of the world.

We were out of the city now. Hidden in the thickly forested mountains of Jefferson County. It was the same place Brooks had tucked his son away all those years ago. We were likely in the safest place in the world. Off the radar. Isolated. Free from danger.

Chapter Three

You're not in Napa Anymore

MASON'S DAD DEPARTED SHORTLY AFTER HE ESCORTED US TO our new home. He was still deeply involved at the embassy, and it was time for him to head back to Russia to carry on with his business. Before he left town, Isaiah assured us that as long as we stayed true to our new identities and avoided all ties to our former lives, we were safe. That included keeping my connection to Mason as quiet as possible.

Our new home was the perfect place to rebuild what we had lost. The secluded property was located just over the mountain, thirty minutes east of the grandparents' ranch. There must have been a lot of strings pulled to find such a magnificent location. It was hidden on the outskirts of a small town, tucked deep in a valley with little to no activity aside from the wildlife that roamed the open fields.

Evidently, Isaiah's strategy for hiding our family had changed. When we fled Russia years earlier, we were relocated to the city. It was a place we could blend in with many faces while getting swept up in the commotion of endless activity. He had gone the opposite route this time. In our new location, there was no traffic except for the crew who had come to install the gates. The only faces I'd seen in days were those of Mason's family and the security crew.

The lack of activity would prove to be a huge adjustment for all of us. In Napa Valley, it was hard to find time to spare. Between school, sports, shopping, and friends, there was never a dull moment. Here, the only form of entertainment was rocking upside down on the hammock while listening to the security team tell stories about their weekend *fishing* expeditions.

It didn't take my parents long to notice the environment was making me a little stir crazy. Maybe it was the way I was trying to climb the hallway walls like Spiderman, but when they walked in on me three-quarters of the way to the ceiling, they decided to take me on a short drive. I was never one for sitting around and it was time to take me into town to check out all the new opportunities for adventure.

Just minutes from the bottom of our long driveway, I was excited to discover a YMCA. With its large windows and metal siding, it looked different than any facility I'd seen before, almost as though it had taken up residency in an old bottling plant. Still, it was a great prospect for sports clinics or maybe even finding a summer camp to attend.

Deciding we'd check that out later, we continued to make the ten-minute drive into town. Soon, we discovered it wouldn't take long to learn our way around the place. There were only a handful of main streets, all aligned in a grid layout. My first impression was that we were in a ghost town. Antique hitching posts were cemented into the sidewalks along the historic street. At one time they'd probably held the horses for the residents, miners, and merchants. Surprisingly, the buildings were all still standing and fully occupied. It was interesting, the way they had been painted every shade of the rainbow. I wondered how they stayed open for business when there were no cars or foot traffic to be seen.

As we continued through the historic district, I noticed an abundance of second-hand stores, an abandoned barber shop, and an old Chinese restaurant. The only sign of life was a stray cat that sat just outside a big, red door. Turning the corner onto the next street, I was excited to spot a movie theater. It was disappointing when I realized it had been shut down. Its windows were soaped over so I couldn't look in to see what I was missing.

When we came to the last street, I was a bit confused. The recession must've hit the town hard. None of the stores seemed to match the design of the buildings. The old logos had bled through the fading paint, revealing the original shops and what was probably a more prosperous time in the old, mining town. There was a charter school inside of an old furniture store. A burger joint inside of an old fifties-style car garage. A tribal office inside of an old Pizza Hut. And my favorite, a church inside of an old liquor store. I couldn't help but think of how hermit crabs abandon their shells for new ones throughout their lives. That was obviously how this town ran. In and out.

When my dad finally pulled into our garage, we all sat silently until I bravely asked, "Not to be ungrateful for our safety or anything, but where the hell did Mr. Brooks move us?"

"I believe they call it the armpit of America," my dad chuckled, barely getting out a full laugh before my mom slugged him on the arm.

"Honey, you can't be so negative. I'm sure there are a lot of great things about this little town. Let's focus on what we can do to make our stay here … comfortable. By the way, I did see a Walmart."

It was that conversation that brought us to the realization that our future was a blank slate. We'd never lived the country life and it was exciting when we began to view our new location as a gift. Jefferson County could be one great adventure, just waiting for us to grab hold and take the ride.

Chapter Four

Livin' the Dream

THROUGHOUT THAT FIRST WEEK, WE STRATEGIZED A PLAN TO create our dream lives. Dad would rebuild his vineyard, keeping distribution local. He didn't want anything fancy, just something that was big enough to keep himself busy with limited staff, and small enough to stay under the radar. As for my mom, Brooks would fix the name on her teaching credential, so she could apply for a language arts job at one of the county's schools. They would both have the opportunity to do what they loved again.

My dream was to find a new softball team, but that wasn't a year-round option in our small town. When I was the only one left without a plan, my parents decided it would be in my best interest to join the summer swim team. I hated the idea of getting up at the crack of dawn every morning and jumping into freezing cold water, but it was the only sport aside from golf that was available in June, and my hybrid baseball swing wasn't pretty.

My parents wouldn't take no for an answer. They insisted it would do me good to meet some of the local kids before I had to go to a new school. I put up one hell of a fight, but finally caved when I got an offer I couldn't refuse. If I agreed to swim for just one summer, my dad promised to build me a baseball field on the back side of the property. The words barely left his mouth before it was a done deal. Thank goodness I agreed. The pool deck was where I met my best friend, Kaitlyn.

The first week of swim practice was an eye opener, for sure. I got to see exactly what it looked like to be an athlete in a small town. Since I had no experience with competitive swimming, the coach started me out in the baby lane. That would be the lane where kids still used kickboards and hung on to the lane lines to avoid certain drowning. It was impossible to swim a full lap in the jungle of flailing six-year-olds. Every two strokes I found myself tangled in little arms and legs.

At one point, I could sense that I was being watched. Frustrated, I was hoping it was the coach there to save me from the insanity. When I stopped mid-lane to check it out, there were two girls on deck looking at me through the corners of their eyes. One was whispering behind her hand while the other was snickering. Obviously, they were laughing at me.

Ready to quit on day one, I pulled myself out of the water and headed straight for the coach. I needed her to know that even though I had never swum competitively, I was by no means a lane-one bobber. I was an athlete. A competitor. I was not made to be the butt of the mean girls' jokes. Thankfully, Coach Della agreed that she would find me a better lane assignment at the next practice.

That afternoon, I tried to convince my parents I didn't want to go back, but they told me I'd already committed, and it wasn't a choice. My only alternative was to prove I was worthy of a better lane. The next morning, I showed up bright and early before the rest of the team arrived. Della was there waiting to see what I could do. Thankfully, I'd had a lot of private lessons as a kid and knew how to swim all the strokes she asked to see. It was a quick test. After exiting the pool, I was met with a huge grin. "Well, you were definitely in the wrong lane yesterday. Let me think about where I want to put you. I'll have it figured out before practice starts."

Thanking her, I walked across the deck and waited on the wooden bench at the far end of the pool. I watched quietly as the messy haired teens began to drag themselves across the deck. Most of them had just gotten out of bed. They were still yawning with remnants of drool crusting the sides of their mouths.

Eyeing my new teammates, I was instantly drawn to a girl about my age. She jumped up and down, flapped her arms, and rolled her neck round and round. Nobody seemed to be approaching her, possibly because she was so focused on what she was doing. I could tell she was one of the serious ones. Judging by the way the girls were mocking her, she probably got a lot of crap for it. She was exactly the kind of friend I was hoping to find.

I focused on her movements, trying to commit them to memory. If I could imitate the best, I might pull off the false impression that I knew what I was doing. If nothing else, it could help me avoid being laughed at again. As I rose from the bench, the pitter-patter of feet drew my eyes away from her. Standing before me were the two snickering girls from the day before. They were wearing smirks on their faces and holding their hands behind their backs. "We brought a welcome gift for you."

I couldn't imagine what they had for me, but I decided to play along. "Thank you. I think."

"We thought you might need these." Each girl brought an inflatable duck floatie from behind her back and handed it to me. "It looked like you were struggling yesterday. We borrowed these from Tiara's baby sister."

Deciding not to dignify the insult with a response, I graciously accepted the floaties and thanked them. "Anything we can do to help," they giggled.

As I dropped the floaties on my towel, the coach hollered to the three of us to get over there. Summoned by Della, the girls turned their backs to me. With a hint of amusement, she boomed from the other side of the pool, "Behind the blocks ladies. Chelsea, you're in lane three, Tiara, you're in five. Jenna, you take four."

It was the first time I'd ever stepped up on a block. The steep incline and the nervous shaking in my legs made it hard to stay on the thing. I barely saved myself from the humiliation of falling in when the coach's booming voice shouted right behind me. "I want to choose the best lane for our new swimmer." She clapped the floaties she'd picked up from the deck and winked. Then she called to the serious girl, "Hey, T! Want to come help me judge which lane would be the best for Jenna?"

The thought of her watching me swim was a little intimidating. My first race from the block had just turned into an exhibition. I could only hope I didn't embarrass myself. As I stood there biting my nails, the girl called T walked up behind me and whispered, "Go get 'em." Then, she snapped my back strap for good luck. Both girls huffed when they saw the gesture. I knew right then, they didn't like her any more than they liked me.

"Swimmers, take your mark," Della's voice rang out. Imitating the actions of the two veterans, I looked left and right and dropped to the block. "Get set." They pulled in tight and I copied. "Go!" I knew what that meant. I was off.

It was just my luck that the moment I hit the water, my goggles flipped. Though they were wrapped around my cheeks and stuck under my nose, there was no way in hell I was going to let that slow me down. I was an athlete. Not made to lose. It wasn't in my nature to go down without a fight. I buried my head and went for it. If nothing else, I'd make sure I was close. I decided not to come up for air until my lungs could no longer take it. When I hit the first wall, I stopped briefly to throw my goggles. Immediately, I turned for my second lap. When I felt the wall within reach, I kicked in hard and searched for my opponents.

After I resurfaced, the first thing I heard was laughing. Thinking I must have embarrassed myself, the blood rushed to my cheeks. Unable to look up, I buried my face beside the gutter and blew air from my mouth and nose. That's when a rush of water flowed over my shoulders and caused me to choke on my bubbles. Realizing that the tsunami of waves was from the girls coming into the wall, I looked up to find T and Della suppressing their laughter.

When I finally caught my breath, my focus shifted to the coach, who was still holding the duck floaties. "Can I have those?" I asked. With a shrug and a puzzled grimace, she tossed them down to me in lane four. Grinning, I looked left and right. "Nice race ladies. Looks like you'll be needing these more than I do." Then I shot each of them a floatie and exited the pool.

Amusement laced Della's expression as she assigned us our new lanes, "Jenna, you're in lane five."

"Chelsea, Tiara, down to lane four. T, when you get a minute, take Jenna to the deep end. I want you to teach her flip turns and that trick you do to keep your goggles on. I think we might have a new freestyler for our A relay team."

As the girls' faces morphed into grimaces, T looked on like she was watching her favorite television comedy.

"I'd be happy to, Coach. Jenna, come with me."

As we walked over to the deep end, she laughed. "You know you're in for it, right? You just got them demoted a lane."

I nodded, knowing full well I'd just started a war. I'd played sports for a long time. I'd met girls like Chelsea and Tiara before, hell-bent on making sure they were at the top of the pecking order. I'd also met girls like T, humble about their talent, and willing to sacrifice recognition in favor of kindness toward their less-skilled teammates. I liked that quality, and from what I'd already experienced, I knew this quiet girl named T was my only real shot at a friend on the team.

The mean girls were no match for me, athletically or socially. They'd learn where they stood against me soon enough. But something told me if I came off as arrogant, a friendship with the nice girl wasn't going to happen. I decided to act concerned. "What have I done?"

"You just drew a line in the sand. Nobody beats those girls and lives happily ever after."

"Should I be worried?"

"Just watch your back."

Something told me Kaitlyn had gone through her fair share of being pecked at by Chelsea and Tiara. From the few minutes I'd spent with her, I could already tell she didn't deserve it. I knew one thing for sure, it wasn't going to happen on my watch. From that afternoon on, I made it my mission not just to watch my back, but hers too.

And that's exactly what I did over the next six years. From embarrassing training bra displays hung across our lockers to our names being slathered across bathroom stalls, together we battled the forces of Chelsea, Tiara, and the rest of the girls we later nick-named the kitty crew. Though their attacks were relentless, we met each one with a fair and just response.

Filling their sports bottles with toilet water and their hairbrush-es with food coloring were just a couple retaliatory tricks we had up our sleeves. When it came to our masterful defense, the kitty crew would learn over time that they'd met their match, especially when we teamed up with Kaitlyn's twin brother Caden and his best friend Brody. Using their unparalleled charm, they helped us with everything from feeding the girls toothpaste-stuffed Oreos to car-amel onions on a stick. Let's just say our alliance was a dominant force throughout junior high and into high school.

As it stood, the best thing my parents ever did was to force me onto the swim team. Though it wasn't my favorite sport, my time on the pool deck that summer helped define the role I would play in my new life. I was to be Jenna Bailey, Jack of all sports, best friend to the Woodley twins, and the ringleader for justice. For the first time in my life, I was happy. Surrounded by a small group of friends and setting backfires against evil, I was truly living the dream.

Chapter Five

The Smile that Changed my World

I T WASN'T UNTIL OUR JUNIOR YEAR, THINGS REALLY STARTED TO CHANGE. We were no longer chained to the small group of rivals who had once dominated our every action. Our world expanded with the gift of smartphones and new sets of wheels for all of us. We had our licenses now, and the fierce boundaries of this small town were no match for our will to escape it. Our stomping grounds had grown to include all six-thousand-plus square miles of Jefferson County. Lakes, mountains, rivers, and forests were all a part of our natural playground.

At first, the boys' new-found freedom took them away from our circle. Their overactive hormones led them anywhere the kitty crew went. Usually, that meant wild, after-game parties, or any other number of frisky escapades the girls could entice them into. Kaitlyn and I avoided that crew the best we could. We set out on our own adventures to new swimming holes, mud bogs, high mountain lakes, and anywhere else we could find country boys.

Our world had expanded, but with it, so did the risk of accidentally stepping into the danger zone. Tucked away in my safe, rural vineyard on a hill for the past six years, I had become quite complacent in the way I moved through life. The dullness of the town had always kept me out of trouble, so I didn't need to give a second thought to where I was going or who I might run into. It wasn't until spring of my junior year when I wanted to cross the boundaries. I realized my freedom wasn't like everyone else's. My freedom was determined by the secrets I could keep.

I remember it all too clearly, the first time I sidestepped the truth in favor of keeping a date with my friends. Running late from softball practice, I had narrowly escaped my parents. They were increasingly determined to keep me on a short leash and I needed to start getting creative to lengthen it. That night, in order to pass my mother's security screening, I fumbled through some story about an optional batting practice. In reality, I had told Kaitlyn and the boys I would meet them at a rodeo out in the valley. It wasn't a promise I wanted to go back on.

Driving out to the Pleasure Park had me on edge. I'd never been so bold as to leave town on a lie. The entire ride, I teetered back and forth between going through with it or turning the car around and heading back home. Making things worse, the valley was the one place I'd been told to avoid. As I fought my conscience, I realized that it was a command given to me in middle school, a time when all kids need protection. I was older now and highly capable of navigating questionable situations. Feeling confident, I decided that orders were meant to be lifted. It was time I gave myself a little more freedom. I'd been in the county for years and had always felt safe there.

As I pulled into the parking lot, I took a deep breath to release my anxiety. I hadn't yet made it to the grandstands when Kaitlyn found me and dragged me toward the chutes. Ecstatic that she had met a gorgeous cowboy, she couldn't pull me back there fast enough. It was hard to hear all the facts through her squealing, but I managed to pick up on the basics. He was a tall, dark, and handsome bull rider named Pistol. Though it was difficult to tell by the way she jumped up and down as she spoke, he'd left her weak and bubbly inside.

Earlier in the day, Kaitlyn learned that Pistol had been wanting to meet her since his little sister's swim meet. His first bold move was to dedicate his eight-second ride to her. They'd been hanging out all afternoon. She was so captivated by the thrill of it all, that she wanted to hook me up with a cowboy of my own. By the time she'd found me, she had already chosen her single, rodeo buddy for me to meet. She claimed he was the perfect match.

Excitedly, she dragged me back to the gate where there was a whole row of Wrangler butts, 10-gallon hats, and numbered shirts lining the top rung. There were no faces, but it was an incredible view. As we approached the contestants, her strength and speed intensified. "You've got to meet this guy. He's a friend of mine," she lifted her eyebrows, "You've probably heard about him."

"Slow down. You're making me nervous," I panted as I slowed my feet. I couldn't imagine how I would've heard about her rodeo friend. Outside of a wisecrack here and there about Brody, Kaitlyn never talked about guys at all. "And, how would I have heard of him? Does he play baseball?"

"No. He lives over here. He's Brody's cousin." Reading the confusion on my face, she continued, "I've known him forever. I can't believe I've never thought to introduce you two. This is going to be perfect!"

The last thing on my mind as I left for the rodeo that afternoon was meeting a cowboy. All I wanted to do was break out of town and have a good time with my friends. Cowboys weren't ever really my type, but as Kaitlyn tugged me toward the row of tight Wrangler butts and contestant numbers, I began to rethink my position. They were indeed hot specimens.

As we approached, I was surprised when she reached up and backhanded Brody on the rear. "Hey, Brody. Where's your cousin?"

Looking pleasantly surprised, he turned around and glanced down with a playful grin. "Hey, T," he jumped from the gate, pausing a moment before he rubbed his seat where she had just smacked him. "You should probably watch the spanking. We wouldn't want to make your new man jealous." He scanned the arena behind us then looked at Kaitlyn. "Where is he anyway? I figured he would've carried you off into the sunset by now." His smile grew wide when he continued, "If he doesn't step it up, he's going to miss his chance to hide you from the competition." His eyebrows danced up and down on his forehead to let her know that he was said competition. I'd never seen him so blatantly flirtatious with her. It was fun to watch her reaction.

Kaitlyn's face flushed as she quickly took a step back and changed subjects. The interaction was just the confirmation I needed. I had suspected for a while that he had a thing for her. The fact that there was a new man in the picture was prompting him to step up his game. Interestingly, she wasn't taking the bait. She played it off like she didn't hear him, but stumbled with her next words, "So, where is he?"

"Pistol?" Brody asked.

"No, your cousin."

"He's putting his gear away. Wait just a sec. He'll be right back."

Again, he flashed his dimpled grin. It made me smile to see the new chemistry between the two of them. I wondered if it was just me, or if they'd noticed it too. Kaitlyn's whisper snapped my attention away from studying Brody.

"There he is!"

When I caught the six-foot-plus silhouette of a cowboy walking our way, my heart jumped anxiously. The sun beaming behind him made it difficult to see. I had to look down momentarily to clear the blind spot that had just burned into my eyes. Within seconds, the darkness faded, and my vision traced a path along the ground, following the sound of clanking spurs. Suddenly, the rattling stopped. He was standing in front of me when my line of sight traveled up the starched, blue jeans, north to his button up shirt, and right into his eyes.

"Holy shit," were the only words I could draw from my mouth. After that, I damn near swallowed my tongue. The look on his face mimicked exactly what I was thinking. Looking at his surprise was like looking in a mirror.

"See, I told you. You're speechless," Kaitlyn whispered in my ear.

There was no way I could let on, and I knew he couldn't either. The sweat began to build in my palms as we slowly made our approach. My eyes locked instantly on that face. The one any other girl would never be able to resist. Except for me. I had been ordered to avoid it. It had been six years since my heart jumped like this. Since the last time I looked into those very eyes. I knew full well we were not allowed to be seen together. Especially not in public. Giving me a small nod as he looked knowingly in my eyes, he held out his hand and shook it. "Nice to meet you. I'm Mason Brooks."

Kaitlyn looked at me, wiggling her eyebrows up and down. I wrapped my arms around my waist, trying to calm the twisting. I knew to Kaitlyn, my reaction would come across as nervousness, but in reality, it was alarm tearing through me. I wasn't even supposed to be at that rodeo. I had snuck away, feeding my parents that ridiculous story about another practice. And there I was over in the valley, a place I had been warned to stay away from. It took everything in me to collect myself and act like nothing was wrong.

Taking a deep breath, I half whispered, "Nice to meet you, Mason." I shook his hand hesitantly, giving a slight nod. Touching him even briefly, shot fire through my veins. It was all too much. The fear. The deceit. I had to disconnect from reality for a second.

Pulling away, I looked toward the arena, where a cowboy was currently flying over the top of a bull. Hiding the truth from my friends made it hard to look any of them in the eyes. Rather, I chose to cast my gaze downward. The silence was becoming awkward. I had to fumble for something to say. "It looks hard. You ride often?" The boys began to snort laugh, tipping me off to my accidental suggestive humor. "Sorry, that didn't come out right."

"Whoa there," Caden chuckled, "Go easy on him. You two just met."

Heat began to fill my cheeks. "Livestock, I mean. It looks hard to ride bulls." I covered my eyes with my hands and took a deep breath.

"Oh, a lot of that is up to which one you're riding," Mason replied. "Sometimes it's harder than others." He pulled his lips into a closed grin and pinched them tightly to trap his silent chuckle, knowing he had just played into my blunder.

I had no response. Completely mortified at where my mind took me, I waited for someone to come to my rescue. Anyone. After an awkward moment of silence, a hand wrapped around my upper arm. "Guys, we'll be back in a minute. I need a second with Jenna." Thankfully it was Kaitlyn, who was giving me some time to get myself together.

We walked to the back of the grandstands where she began to question me, "So, what do you think? He's hot, right?"

Hot? All I could think of was how hot my ass would be if my parents found out I was hanging out with Mason. It could jeopardize everything. "He's okay."

"Okay? You couldn't even speak back there."

"He's just not ... what I was expecting."

"What were you expecting? Cuz the boy is right up there with the Hemsworth brothers. You've heard the girls talking about him, haven't you?"

"Well, I've heard, but I didn't really pay too much attention. I always fade out when the word "cowboy" is mentioned. I don't know. I'm sort of into athletes. Like the kind who wear baseball pants, not starched blue jeans. I ... I don't think he's my type."

She looked me up and down, studying my face. With all the adrenaline that had just exploded inside, I was hoping to hide my signature blush. Likely, that wasn't going to happen with Kaitlyn.

"You're just embarrassed, aren't you? Don't worry about mixing up all your words. You're frazzled."

Frazzled? My forbidden past had just blown up in my face. "Oh, you have no idea."

"It's natural to be nervous around guys like Mason. And you've got to admit, there's nothing hotter than a Wrangler butt."

A small giggle escaped me. She did have a point.

"Are you okay now? We should get back. I just heard them announce saddle cow. The boys are in that event."

I needed to get through the rest of the night without messing up. It was hard to stomach the fact that our worlds had finally collided, and it was all my fault. But something told me, it was time I figured out how to navigate my life with Mason being a small part of it. After all, though it did shock the hell out of me to learn of it after all those years, he was Brody's cousin. It was highly likely that our paths would cross again. We'd been thrown back together by fate, and it was up to us to figure out how to keep our past a secret. I would keep him at a distance. That was it. I convinced myself that I could do it. We could do it. I'd just follow Mason's lead. I forced a smile, took a deep breath, and said, "Let's go!"

Thankfully, as we walked back to the chutes, Kaitlyn didn't speak another word about me hooking up with Mason Brooks. The lack of pressure made it easier to enjoy the saddle cow event. It was super exciting watching Mason and Brody pair to make the fastest team in the event. Mason's timing was perfect on the cow. It didn't get too far from the gate, and once he jumped off, Brody flew out to help grab the saddle. They were back in a flash, slamming it into the back of the chute. It was a flawless effort. Unlike the other teams, they didn't trip, fall, or stumble their way across the entire arena.

We had watched through the opening of the rails, excitedly cheering on the boys. There we waited for awards to wrap up. After they were handed their shiny, new buckles, we climbed the rungs to congratulate them. With big smiles and all-around hugs, a sudden flash from my right had me turning my head.

"Smile for the camera!" A giant lens had zoomed in on the four of us. *Click. Click. Click.* It was the rodeo photographer, capturing the roundup on camera. "Raise your buckles, boys!" *Click. Click. Click.* "Okay, let's make this one look good! Put the pretty girls in between you!" We shuffled across the rail to the inside and leaned into the boys. *Click. Click. Click.* "Closer. I need to get all of you in the frame." Mason's hand slowly wrapped around my upper arm and gave it a comforting squeeze. I knew it was his way to reassure me that everything was going to be okay. That's when I allowed myself to relax. Snuggled under his arm, a new calm came over me, and a genuine smile grew on my face. I finally felt the security I'd been missing out on for years. The security that could only come from being next to my oldest, dearest friend. *Click. Click. Click.*

Breaking the Rules

THAT WAS THE LAST TIME I SAW MASON IN PUBLIC. OUR NIGHT AT the rodeo had become a distant memory. Blurred into the background of spring storms, softball practices, games, and a never-ending mountain of school work, I was too busy to get over to the valley, let alone hang out with my friends. Even Kaitlyn and I had taken to texting in order to communicate outside of class. It was the last week of May. School was nearly out, and I was studying for finals when my phone alerted me to a text.

Kaitlyn:
It sucks your parents won't let you have any social media accounts. The Jefferson Roundup has the cutest pics ever!

Me:
You'll have to show me next time we get together.

Kaitlyn:
Too bad we're all so busy. That could be retirement. Can't you just sneak an account already?

Me:

Nope. You know how my parents like their privacy. They don't think I need to broadcast my life.

Kaitlyn:

There's ways to make it private so only your friends can see your stuff. You're really missing out here. You should see the one of us behind the chutes with those *H *O* T* Cowboys.

Me:

I'll think about it. Maybe you can just download some and text them to me?

Kaitlyn:

Yeah, uh, I'll work on that when I get a minute. Gotta study for my honors chem final. See ya when I see ya! Miss you. :)

Me:

Miss U 2! <3

My overbooked schedule sucked. I sat in my room thinking about all the stuff I was missing due to my restriction from social media. Maybe Kaitlyn was right. If I could just figure out a way to set up an account without my parents finding out, at least I could see what was going on in the outside world. I suddenly had an urge to get on my laptop and check it out. Maybe I could just tinker around a bit and see what I could find while staying anonymous. When I reached the site, I was disappointed to find a login page. I had to have an account to see anything. There was no way I could set one up. My mom taught at my high school. She would definitely find out.

Growing frustrated with my situation, I fell back into the

mountain of pillows and stared up at my ceiling. Everyone else seemed to have a life. Or at least they had social media to pretend they did. Even as busy as Kaitlyn was, she still found time to check out the local scoop and chat online. My mind reeled with indignation. Why was I the only kid in Jefferson County barred from social media? Damn. If spring wasn't so busy, it wouldn't matter anyway. I could actually live in the real world, talk to people, see my friends.

It was almost as though spring had become my rival. Not a season, but an opposing force meant to stand between me and any kind of social life. I started to laugh as I painted a picture of Spring in my mind wearing catcher's gear and holding a stack of books. She was the fundamental brick in a barricade with a "No Trespassing" sign nailed smack dab in the middle.

It was a ridiculous thought that I'd conjured. Spring as a real person, an evil rival who barred me from the fun zone. That's when it hit me. I laughed to myself when I realized that I could use the name Spring as an alias to create a fictitious account. Why not? People did it all the time. I sat up and looked at the login page once again. Still hesitant, I tapped my fingers on the keys. If I dared to create one, I promised myself I would shut it down as soon as school was over and I got my life back.

Without another thought, I went in to sign up. I'd settled on using Spring as my last name and my initials, JB, for my first. It seemed anonymous to me, and it was easy. Nobody questioned me. I didn't need a license. No proof of who I was. It was great. All I had to do was plug in my email address and a couple other insignificant details and hit "Sign Up." Nobody could track the information I'd entered. It wasn't even real. I was certain everything was going to work out perfectly.

When I hit *Enter*, everything went black and suddenly flashed a welcome page. The sudden disappearance of the screen had left my heart racing, but the sweet victory of looking at my first account quickly erased the momentary panic. As I gawked at my new page, the first thing that popped up was the opportunity to find friends. Other than adding Kaitlyn, I wasn't so sure I should go there. I decided to wait a minute and upload a profile picture so she would know who I was. I chose one I thought only Kaitlyn would recognize. One where I was mostly shielded by a face mask and catcher's gear.

The minute I had my picture up, I decided to add her. I shot her a friend request which was immediately accepted. A few more suggestions came up. They were girls from my team. What could it hurt? I decided to click on them too, just so I didn't look like a loser who had only one friend. Again, the girls accepted immediately. Within five minutes, I had added fifteen new friends. It was an addicting high. I didn't know it was possible to make that many friends so quickly.

My friending activity was interrupted when the chime of my phone sent me leaping from the bed. For as much fun as I was having, I was also keenly aware that I was breaking my parents' rule. Not just any rule. A cardinal rule. I could only hope it wasn't my mom telling me that I'd been caught. Relief hit when I saw it was Kaitlyn again.

Kaitlyn:
Smooth. Haha. JB Spring? Nice. LOL!!!

Me:
Shh. You know we need to keep this quiet. My parents can't find out. Is there a way to make this stuff private?

Kaitlyn:
Just go into your account settings and click that only your friends can see your stuff.

I began to scroll around trying to find my account settings.

Search. No. *Post*. Not on your life. Except for the little camera, I couldn't make sense of the icons at all. I was just about to hit *More* when my mom's voice drifted through my bedroom window. The thought of her catching me in the act of navigating my new social media account had me a little frantic.

"Jenna! Jenna!" her insistent call jabbed at my composure.

Stumbling over the keyboard, I quickly replied to Kaitlyn's last text.

Me:
Thanks for the help with the privacy thing. I'll figure it out in a bit. My mom is calling. Gotta go!!!

I closed my laptop and ran out the back door to find my mom standing beneath my window. She was with Mr. Pine. That was a new one. Except for Kaitlyn's mom, none of my other teachers had ever visited the vineyard. I couldn't help but wonder if I'd done something wrong. *Nope, not in science*.

"Hey," I greeted curiously, "everything okay?"

Mr. Pine nodded and shined his signature grin.

"Jenna, the boys need to use our baseball field for a few days. A pipe broke under theirs and it's completely flooded. I said they could practice here until they get it fixed and it dries out a bit."

Instantly, the smile melted from my face. It was hard to hide the irritation I felt about the situation. Sharing *my* field with the entire varsity team was a lot to ask. They were the same guys who forced my softball team to take the crappy field out by the ag building last year because it was too far from their locker room. Pine had some nerve thinking he could bring his gorillas to overtake my field. Not to mention, it broke all my rules. Nobody was allowed to play there without me. I literally had to press down on my thigh to stop myself from stomping my foot.

I could tell my mom had picked up on my attitude when she

raised her eyebrows as she spoke, "You know how important practices are right now. These boys are in the running for league this year. It's only a few days, honey. Now, go show Mr. Pine to the field. Oh, and give him the spare key to the equipment shed. They'll need to be able to get to the bases and chalker ... you know, stuff like that."

Not only were they using my field, but they were using my equipment too?

It was tough to stifle my annoyance. The look on my face, accompanied by the forced breath through my nose, wasn't lost on either of the adults.

"We'll take great care of your field, kid. You can even come supervise if you want to."

"I'll be at my own practices, but thanks."

"That's right. I heard you're quite a catcher ... Pickle, isn't it?" He laughed at the nickname my team had given me. "Well, if you get a chance to stop by, please do. I appreciate you giving up your field for a few days, Jenna. Really. It'll mean a lot to the boys when they hear we have a place to practice."

The compliment from Pine, lightened my mood a bit. It made me feel good that he'd heard about my catching. I resigned myself to the fact that I didn't have a choice in the matter anyway. I didn't want to look like an ass. Not to mention, Mr. Pine was in control of my final chemistry grade. "But only for a couple days." I accidentally ended my thought out loud.

"Deal."

On the way down to the field, I explained how I got my nickname. My solid record of making outs when players were in a pickle between third and home, spoke for itself. As intrigued as he was by the story, it was nothing compared to his reaction to my field. His breath hitched as he stepped over the foul line and onto the diamond. I could tell he was in awe of the perfectly manicured grass and freshly dragged infield. My parents had a special landscaping crew to take care of the grounds, and one of their responsibilities was to keep the grass mowed and the infield in pristine condition.

"It's so perfect. You even keep it lined?"

"Well, the vineyard crew and their families join me down here all the time. We like to play games just before dusk when it starts to cool off."

"I see the infield has just been dragged too."

"Well, the last thing my parents need are broken ankles and toothless employees. We try to minimize bad hops, you know?"

Mr. Pine looked like he was in heaven, standing on my field, surrounded by our vineyard. "Just like field of dreams," I detected his soft whisper.

Referencing one of my favorite movies I replied, "Guess it's true. If you build it, they will come," I held out my hand, offering the key to the shed. "Take care of it, huh, Coach?"

"You've got my word."

"Just a few practices, right?"

"I'll take care of it, Pickle. Don't worry."

I turned away and slowly trudged back up the hill, trying to remember who exactly was on the baseball team. Who would be to blame when I found my equipment out of place or a divot in my grass? The softball field was where I spent all my time. I never got to watch the boys play. It might be fun to watch them. Maybe I'd sneak down if I got off practice early. Just to see if they were worthy of playing on my field.

As I walked the path daydreaming about the possibility of working my way into one of their practices, I'd barely noticed I was back at my room. I was so distracted handing over the key, I'd nearly forgotten I'd just opened a new social media account. A rush of excitement hit me when I logged on and saw I was up to twenty friends with several new requests waiting for a response. I found it odd that even a couple members of the kitty crew, who were never friendly to me at school, had requested my friendship. After thinking about it for a couple seconds, I figured it would improve my street cred if they showed up on my friends list. I went ahead and approved all of them. *Up to thirty-seven. Not too shabby for the first hour.*

"You doing okay with all of this?" my mom asked as she peeked through my door. At the first sound of her voice, I slammed down the cover of my laptop. Thankfully, she hadn't seen me on the internet. "Before you answer that, you might want to take a look outside," she snickered as she stepped back into the hallway.

Curiously, I stood up and walked to my window. A herd of ball caps and well-fitted baseball pants were jogging down the path. I pressed my face against the window screen, straining to recognize who would be invading my field the next few days. Caden was leading, of course. He knew where he was going. But I hadn't realized Jacob, Dawson, and Brandon were all on the team. Then there was Eamon, Timmy, Lane, and Michael. Those boys were a riot. *Baseball players, huh?* As they disappeared over the rolling hill, a deep cough drew my attention toward the ground below.

"Ahem."

When I glanced down, round, blue eyes and a dimpled smile, were looking back at me.

A tiny rush came over me when his plump lips spoke, "Jenna?"

Clearing the lump in my throat, I answered, "Hey, Ty. What're you doing down there?"

"Watching you check out my teammates," he chuckled. "Hey, I'm running a little late. Can you point me to the field?"

The field. Staring at those lips. I almost forgot where it was. "Uh, straight down that path," I gestured.

"Thanks," he winked as he took off at a quick jog.

With my forehead pressed to the window screen, it took me a second to realize why I was having trouble remembering to breathe. That's when it hit me that Ty Connelly was at my house, under my window, talking to me.

As my mind worked to commit my new favorite interaction to memory, I couldn't help but wonder why he needed me to point him to the field if he had just seen me staring at his teammates. I wondered how long he had been under the window watching me. Had he intentionally made himself late so we could talk?

Standing at the window, staring out toward the field, I found myself trying to calm the swarm of butterflies that Ty had just unleashed in me. It was then that I realized maybe, just maybe, sharing my field with the boys wasn't going to be such a bad deal after all.

For three school weeks, they came. Fifteen days of pure baseball heaven. Several times when they stayed late, I snuck down to the field and hid behind the dugout to watch. As resistant as I was at first, I quickly warmed up to having them play on my field. I was impressed with what I saw and learned a lot from listening to Coach Pine. I wanted nothing more than to grab my mitt and join them, but I held myself back.

Hidden from view, they didn't know I was watching. I had become addicted to all of it. Speed. Accuracy. Jumping. Diving. Sliding. Baseball was hardcore. I loved this sport more than anything in the world, and it was apparent that these boys had the same heart for it that I did. I had found my people. If only they knew they were my people. What I wouldn't give to play with them, rather than hide behind the dugout.

Secretly, I wanted them to keep coming back. Tied up in my own two-hour practices, I tried to make theirs run longer by organizing snacks and drinks. I had them delivered to the dugout each day before practice. I even had Roger, my dad's gardener, drag the field every night, so they couldn't start until at least four o'clock.

That way I assured myself that I could catch at least thirty minutes of their practice. Thirty minutes of the hottest pitcher this side of the Atlantic.

My efforts did not go unnoticed. Every time one of the guys saw me in the hall at school, they made sure to show their appreciation. They even named me their honorary mascot. The extra attention I got didn't go over well with the kitty crew, but I sure had fun with it. And let's just say, the more attention I got, the more I made sure to show the boys my support.

I'll never forget the day Timmy popped me up on his shoulder and carried me down the hallway. Some of the players bowed and others cheered as we passed by. The only ones who didn't find the fun in it were Chelsea and Tiara. They rolled their eyes and turned away, whispering.

Preoccupied as I watched their reaction, I was startled when Ty stepped out from behind his locker, raising his hand to stop Timmy. "Hold up."

I focused on his hand. The same one I'd been watching for days. Every time it pitched. Every time it hit. Nothing it did went unnoticed. As a matter of fact, nothing about him went unnoticed. Nothing. Not the solid lines beneath his snug jersey. Not the way the muscles strained in his forearm at the release of a pitch. I studied his every move. Not like a stalker, but as a girl who was thoroughly impressed by his talent. He was pure baseball perfection. There was nothing about him that didn't ignite a fire inside of me every single time he came into view.

"You know you're going to have to come watch us play, right?" he grinned. *If he only knew I'd been watching him for weeks.*

I peeled my eyes away from his hand and forced them to look at his mischievous face. Seeing him in that baseball hat with his sideways grin damn near stopped my heart. But, I wasn't about to let on that every time I was within feet of him, my body ceased to function properly. I fought the urge to jump off Timmy's shoulder and into his arms. Convincing myself to breathe, I came up with something that sounded confident, not desperate. I reached down deep and found my voice. "You know my games are the same time as yours. You're gonna have to make playoffs in order for that to happen."

His response was quick and assured, "Oh, it's gonna happen. You can count on it."

Just then, Timmy began to lose his grip on me. I don't think he had intended to carry me so long. He grabbed my legs tightly and popped my slipping butt back up on his shoulder.

Watching his struggle, an amused look grew on Ty's face, "Mind if I take over for a sec? We need to have a chat about how to get this girl to a game."

"If you insist."

"Oh, I do."

I tried to control the slight tremble in my hand as Ty slipped me onto his shoulder. "Steady there, princess. I've got ya."

I was anything but steady. I wondered if he could feel the tug of the tsunami that had just crashed inside of me. As we moved away from Timmy, the crowds began to part again.

"Stand back, coming through, got my ..." he paused and looked up, "What position do you play, anyway?"

"Catcher."

"Interesting." His voice boomed through the hall again, "Got my catcher here."

"Looks like someone needs to come to one of my games too. You didn't even know what position I played."

"Well, until two weeks ago, I didn't know I cared. Are you any good?"

My frenzied nervous system betrayed me again. I couldn't silence my gulp, "I guess you're gonna have to come watch to find out."

There was a moment of silence as we continued walking down the hall. He cared about what position I played? Had I heard him wrong? He bent down gently and slid me back to the ground. Before he'd even risen to his feet, I was surprised when he spoke again, "Got an idea. Clearly, we aren't going to be making it to each other's games. So, sometime this summer we'll have to meet down at your field so you can show me what you've got."

I studied his face, unable to tell if he was being serious. Was he setting up a baseball date with me? I looked around to see if I was being Punk'd. He stared at me for a second more before he continued with what he thought might be his most convincing persuasion, "Don't worry, I'll go easy on you."

My heart momentarily hitched. *Go easy on me?* "Why would you need to do that?"

A small chuckle broke through his response, "You know, you're a girl. You're used to big balls and slow pitches."

It didn't take me long to return his insult, "Then I shouldn't have a problem playing with you." His eyebrows drew together as though he was trying to read whether I was joking. The thing was, I wasn't sure if I was joking either, and it might be a while before I figured that out. Did he think softball was less of a sport? Or that I was less of a player because I was a girl? I knew one thing, nobody insulted my game. Not even a baseball god like Tyler Connelly.

Ty grew quiet, as we stopped in front of my fifth-period class, "I'm sorry. I didn't mean it like that," he shook his head finally realizing we were getting nowhere fast. "So, about getting together to play this summer ..."

"Yeah, uh, see ya when I see ya."

"Got it."

That was the last real conversation I had with Ty that season. Their field was back up and running. Since my energy was no longer spent watching the boys practice, I invested the extra effort into my own team who kicked ass, by the way. We won league. Practices ceased. School came to an end, and I gained a new interest. Summer camp.

Chapter Seven

Making a Splash

"YOU'RE SERIOUSLY DOING THIS?" KAITLYN WHINED. "WHO'S going to take your leg of the relay?"

"Kait, I just want to do something different this summer. You know how much I love working with kids."

"Yeah, but, you've been doing summer swim with me since we were in seventh grade. Who's going to push me? This is going to suck without you." Her pouty lip began to grow, "Besides, there's barely anyone left in our age group. You're leaving me alone with the twelve-year-olds."

Guilt wasn't going to work this time. I'd made up my mind and there was nothing that was going to stop me. I loved the outdoors and I wanted to experience a normal summer in the wilderness. Rising at the crack of dawn every morning just to kill myself with 3,000 meters of torture in freezing, cold water was not something I was willing to endure again.

"It'll be fine." I grabbed her by the shoulders. "Go get all those damn medals you love collecting."

"You love collecting them too," she sulked.

"Yeah, but I love living life more. Besides, I've already signed up to be a counselor at Kelsey Creek Camp."

Clearly disappointed in my decision to quit the summer swim

team, Kaitlyn let go of her hold on me.

"Look," I set my hand on her shoulder, "you love swimming and I love you. It's the only reason I've kept it up as long as I have. It's the only way I get to spend time with you in the summer. I'll do high school swim with you in the fall. It's just, I want to do something *I* love this season," I confessed.

Kaitlyn breathed out a deep sigh, "Not swimming?"

I shook my head, "Not swimming."

"Okay, but two months without my best friend? That's an eternity. Promise me you'll keep in touch. Send me pics of you doing you. I want to see all the stuff this camp has to offer that swimming doesn't."

"Can't. No computers or cell phones allowed. I'll keep a journal and fill you in on everything when I get back." I stuck out my pinky. "Promise."

She tightened her pinky around mine. "It's gonna be a long ass summer without you, ya know."

"You'll get by," I smiled and gave her a hug. "I've gotta pack. Six weeks is a lot to get ready for." And ready I was. It would be my first summer doing exactly what I wanted to do. Being exactly who I wanted to be.

I'll never forget that first night at camp. I had nothing dry to wear. Not of my own anyway. My mom had just pulled away when I realized she left me at the wrong entrance. The only way to get up to the lodge was to take the steep, dirt path or to cross the rushing creek. Not wanting to carry my forty-pound bag up a mile-long hill, I decided to chance it.

Peeking through my armload of gear, I found a small path of protruding rocks that cut through the creek. I set my foot onto the first one and pushed it back and forth to make sure it was stable. When it didn't move, I stepped out to begin my trek. The first two rocks were okay, but by the third I was a bit unsteady. My duffel bag was heavy and trying to carry my sleeping bag and pillow in the other arm threw me off balance. Wobbling side to side, I managed to get my footing on rock number three. Rock number four, I wasn't so lucky. The slippery surface had me sliding across the creek-bed into the splits. With no control of my overloaded arms, I landed with a splash. Despite the bruise I could feel forming on my right butt cheek, I began scrambling to get back on my feet.

It was just my luck that somebody was nearby. Not only was it my fate to begin camp soaked, but also humiliated. "Damn. That looked like it hurt." A concerned voice broke through the sloshing water that roared from behind, "Are you okay?"

Balancing my bedding above the water and flailing to grab my bag before it drifted too far down the creek, I couldn't manage to catch a glimpse of who was talking, but instantly, I was drawn to his soft yet husky tone.

As I grabbed onto the bag he spoke again, "I'll get that."

I watched the waterfall cascade before me as my duffel bag lifted from the water. Then a tanned forearm reached out toward me, "Your turn."

Embarrassed, I kept my eyes on the bed of rocks beneath me. "I'm okay, thanks. I've got this."

"You sure? At least let me help you with your sleeping bag."

Nodding, I loosened my hold as it slipped away from me. I pressed my newly freed hands into the slimy creek bottom, but still couldn't seem to get myself flipped over and back on my feet. "This current is deceiving." I slipped again. "Maybe I should've taken the long way."

Just then, his two heavily muscled calves returned from the shore and bent down in front of me. "What would be the fun in that?"

Trying to recognize the familiar voice, I dared to let my eyes travel up to see my rescuer. My eyes scanned past his khaki shorts, then up his Jefferson t-shirt, right to that handsome face. At first sight, a burst of adrenaline fired from my chest with enough heat that I could've sworn the water around me began to boil.

"Jenna?" he laughed. "It's you?"

I felt my face flush when he came down into the water and knelt before me. "Ty? Uh, what're you doing here?"

"I'm a counselor ... but it looks like my job description just changed to lifeguard," he smiled. "Here, let me help you up."

Weak from fighting both the current and the exothermic reaction my body was producing, I no longer had a choice. I reached up as his warm hand wrapped around mine and sent an instant wave of goosebumps up my arm. Gently, he pulled me to my feet and helped me find my balance. With a little stumble, his hand came to rest on the small of my back. Then holding me firmly, he escorted me through the rushing current.

As we walked, he took on a joking tone, "My campers are usually eleven or twelve. What made you decide to camp with us this summer?" I looked at him just in time to catch his lips curling into a sideways grin.

"Funny." I paused before I answered him. "Lucky for you, I'm not one of your campers. I'm actually one of the counselors."

Humor laced his voice as he lifted his face toward the heavens. "Lord have mercy!"

"What?" I giggled.

He shook his head as he chuckled, "Looks like my job just got a little bigger, that's all." Then he pulled me into him and helped move me toward the shore. "Welcome aboard, counselor."

As he grinned down at me, the twinkle in his eye told me he was pleasantly surprised that I was there. It was an exhilarating moment for me, knowing I would have the opportunity to get to know Ty outside of school. As I focused on the warmth of his arm wrapped around my shoulders, I had to thank fate for delivering me into the perfect hands. It was confirmation that I'd made a great decision. I wasn't losing a summer of swimming, I was gaining a summer of new memories. This was just going to be the first of many. Taking it all in, I watched as he raised my soaking, wet duffel bag to eye level. I pinched my face into a grimace as the waterfall dripped from the bottom. He shook his head chuckling in reply, "There's no way I'm leaving you alone with seven campers for six weeks."

Hoping he wouldn't change his mind about that, I stuck out my pinky. "Promise?"

It didn't take him long to think about it. My breath silently hitched as he wrapped his warm pinky around mine. "You've got my word," he grinned. I couldn't help but notice that he held on a little longer than he had to. "Now, let's go get you into some dry clothes. I have an extra sweatshirt in my cabin you can borrow."

His offer had me beaming inside. As I walked toward the cabins with Ty, I knew my summer was going to be one for the record books. A hot, private lifeguard with closet privileges. What could be better than that?

Running late after struggling to make his oversized sweatshirt with no shorts look somewhat modest, I made my way into our orientation meeting. I looked at the group of twelve, who had already packed tightly into a circle around the campfire.

Quietly, I snuck in from behind, trying to go unnoticed. Still, I could feel all eyes on me. "You can sit here." I glanced toward the voice. A handsome blond, who looked to be in his early twenties, patted the ground next to him. "You look cold. I have a blanket."

I smiled and sat down as he pulled the blanket over our laps.

Waiting for the director to begin, I looked around at the different faces. Five other girls, sporting various college logos, were scattered among the guys. There was the blond beach boy who was sharing his blanket with me, followed by a hipster, and a couple country boys in ball caps and t-shirts. Though every guy in the circle seemed worthy of getting to know, my eyes settled on Ty. He sat directly across from me, chatting with a brunette who was wearing an "Oregon" hat. Her beauty was obvious from across the room, and she seemed to laugh at everything he said. They'd probably been counselors together before. Watching how comfortable they were with each other, I knew right then that his pinky promise to me would soon be forgotten.

Pulling my curious gaze away from the two of them, I focused on the center of the circle where our director, Marcus, stepped up to give us the rundown of the program. We went over everything from cabin mascots and skits to the final talent show. He stressed how important it was to follow the schedule in the handbook. If we messed up or deviated from the plan, it would throw off the entire program. I couldn't help but feel a little stressed. There was so much to do and remember, I hoped I could live up to his expectations.

As if all the activities weren't enough to keep track of, Marcus followed his instructions with the list of counselor rules. I fixated on his intriguing British accent as he directed, "No campers without a counselor, anywhere or anytime. No cell phones. No computers. No drinking, smoking, or physical contact with another counselor ... under any circumstances!" At the mention of the last rule, I became keenly aware that surfer boy's knee had been firmly resting against mine up until that moment. He pulled away after the rule was announced, leaving me to believe that the knee-to-knee contact was no accident.

At our movement beneath the blanket, I looked up to see Ty's brow pinch together. His eyes slowly traced a path across the blanket and up toward my face. When our eyes met, he quickly looked away, leaving me to wonder if I'd just imagined he'd been watching me. Logic told me he hadn't been. There was no way he was studying my movement when he was so obviously engaged with Oregon girl. Watching *her*. Talking to *her*. Laughing with *her*. The sudden urge to jump up and plop down between them caught me by surprise. I had to fight myself to stay put next to surfer boy.

I wondered if that was what jealousy felt like. Madness? Frustration? Impulsivity? Wanting to jump up in the middle of a serious meeting to sever the obvious connection between the guy I was so clearly attracted to and the girl who stood in my way? I didn't do jealousy. Something had to be wrong with me. I refocused on Marcus and tried to ignore the insanity brewing inside of me.

The rest of the meeting became a blur as I worked to shift my attention away from *them*. I made small talk with the surfer guy, who I later found out was named Leif. He was nice enough, but his surfer lingo was lost on me. As he spoke about hunting for barrels, I tried to look interested, but my eyes kept drifting back to Ty. Each time I looked across the circle, his glimpse was there waiting. Then like repelling magnets, our glances would bounce away almost instantly. I began to find humor in our watching game. It was almost as though we were having a silent ping-pong match of who could look at whom without being caught.

When the meeting ended, we all stood up and walked in a cluster away from the outside meeting area. Frustrated that surfer guy was attached to the back of me, I sped up. I'd just sat through an hour-long orientation with him. All I really wanted to do was talk to Ty. Or at least be near him. I couldn't help but worry that based on our blanket sharing status, he might have thought I was interested in Leif.

I had to talk to him. From the moment I found out he was at camp, he had found his way into my every thought. I needed to make sure we were still good, and it was clear that I had no interest in the surfer. I wanted Ty to be my guide through the whole coun-selor thing. After all, he'd pinky promised he wouldn't leave me alone. As the mass of counselors began walking down the trail to-ward the cabins, I weaved in and out trying to get within whisper-ing distance. My heart raced as I drew nearer. "Ty!" I tripped as I spoke his name.

Turning around just in time, he caught me as I stumbled into his arms. "Watch that root. It's gotten me a couple times too." He looked me up and down for a moment, "Did you need something?"

What I needed was to let him know *he* was the one I wanted to share a blanket with, but that's not what came out. "I was just trying to ask if you wanted this back." I tugged at the neck of his bulky sweatshirt.

A curious look crossed his face as he scanned the oversized sweatshirt that drowned my petite frame. Then continuing to hold me tightly, he looked down at me and smiled, "Why don't you hang onto it for a bit. I kinda like the way it looks on you."

A surge of warmth exploded from my chest. Mingling with the chilly air, it forced a slight shiver to make its way through me. I tried to hide my reaction, but it was just enough that Ty felt the small tremor. "Chilly?" he whispered. Then pulling me in closer he grinned, "I have an extra sleeping bag I'll set outside your cabin door. I'm sure yours is still a little soggy, and as much as I'd like to break the rules and share mine, it'll still be a part of me keeping you warm."

And with that whispering smile gleaming against the backdrop of the lighted trail, for the slightest moment in time, I forgot all about Oregon girl.

Chapter Eight

Choose Wisely

IT WAS MY FIRST NIGHT AT CAMP. LYING IN BED RESTLESS AND ALONE, I closed my eyes wanting nothing more than to push away the unsettling silence of the night. The kids weren't coming until morning, which left me ten solid hours to think and plan. The problem was, I couldn't. I couldn't think about anything but the smell of his cologne drifting up from beneath the covers. The scent was so strong, it was almost as though he'd intentionally doused his sweatshirt in it before he loaned it to me. Was cologne his alternative to doing laundry, or did he want to mess with my sleep schedule? Regardless of the intention, the woodsy scent drifting up from his sweatshirt lit a warm fire in my chest, causing my breath to hitch and my insides to tighten nervously.

Between the eerie silence of the empty cabin and my racing heart, it seemed like hours, before I finally drifted off to sleep. Back to the relentless nightmare. In the complete darkness and solitude of the woods, the haunting images were more vivid than ever.

The gloves. The lady. The horror. They were all back. This time, with a vengeance. I leaned against the door frame, wrapped my arms tightly around my knees and curled into a ball. Peeking through a small gap, I watched as a white streak passed by the kitchen island. "Son of a Bitch,

Sobaka," a deep, accented voice growled at the dog, as simultaneously, a big, black shoe gave him a swift kick across the floor. I covered my mouth, trying to keep my terrified squeal from giving me away. "You scared the shit out of me. Go!" he directed, as the door that led outside closed behind them.

Seconds later, I found my way to my feet, carefully opened the back door and peeked through the crack where I saw him leave. Long, brown curls flowed over his shoulder. He walked slowly, placing one foot steadily in front of the other. "Don't go with him!" my inner voice screamed at the little girl who was hiding in the kitchen. Fire. Pounding. I hated it where they made the barrels. "It's scary down there!" But it was too late. My heart raced as they disappeared into the cellar. Though my voice had warned me to stay away, my tiny feet couldn't help but follow the trail to check on the brown-haired lady.

Knock. Knock. Knock. I heard the steady thump as I inched my way down the stairs. I had to help her. I didn't want her to be alone. Knock. Knock. Knock. I always cringed when they pounded in the staves. It was so loud. Relentless.

Again my heart raced as the pounding got louder. Knock. Knock. Knock. "Jenna!" How did he know I was there? I pulled back against the wall and froze in place. Knock. Knock. Knock. "Jenna?" I strained, listening to who was saying my name. Whose voice was that? It didn't sound like him. "Jenna. Open the door."

Open the door? Hell no, I reasoned, starting to realize I was coming out of my sleep.

"Open up."

At the final thump, my eyes popped open and I looked around. The glow of the moon cast enough light that I could see I was back in the cabin. I thought if I got away, the dreams would go away too. No such luck. My breathing quickened as I tried to pull air into my constricted lungs. As I worked to calm myself, there was a shuffling sound outside the window. Quickly, I curled into a protective ball and brought the covers up to my chin. The worst part of the nightmare was the after effects. It always amplified my nervous system to full throttle.

Knock. Knock. Knock.

"Who's there?" I gasped.

"It's me, Ty. Open up."

Lowering the covers, I swallowed the lump that had formed in my throat and sucked in a deep breath. "Be right there." I had to pull myself together before I opened the door. I didn't want Ty to see me in my post-nightmare frenzy. Pulling my hair into a ponytail, I wiped the sweat from my forehead and grabbed a piece of gum. Then steadying my shaking hand on the knob, I opened the door.

"You alone? I thought I heard you talking to someone," he whispered.

"Yeah, uh, just having a little nightmare," I giggled. "I've been told I talk in my sleep sometimes."

"You okay?"

"I am now. What're you doing here? It's the middle of the night."

He opened the door wider and pointed over his shoulder, "Initiation time for you newbies! Let's get this over with."

"Right now?"

His eyebrows drifted up his forehead, "If you want your counselor's kit, we have to do this before morning."

"Counselor kit?"

"Yep. All of our stuff. Talking sticks. Bandanas. Award supplies. All of it."

"Who else is going?"

"Mariah, Leif, and us."

"Are they out there waiting?"

"Not yet. Leif and I battled at rock-paper-scissors for partners."

Trying to hide the confusion, I grimaced, "How'd you end up here?"

"Well," he grinned, "I won." He paused as he studied my face for a moment, then continued, "He's grabbing Mariah."

"Mariah? Isn't that the Oregon girl you were so chummy with at the orientation meeting?"

"Yeah ... and?"

"So, why are you partnering with me?"

Pausing momentarily, he smirked, "She's not the one I wanted to see blindfolded."

Blindfolded? I couldn't help but wonder what I was about to get myself into. My slack jaw bounced wordlessly as I tried to see through his mischievous eyes into his scheming brain. The look on his face told me to let loose and have fun with whatever it was that he was about to get me to do.

A shuffling sound grew louder as I watched two silhouettes appear from behind the back corner of my cabin. As they moved closer, I could see it was a scowling Leif with giggling, blindfolded Mariah.

"Got her." He grumbled at Ty, "You ready?"

Grinning from ear to ear, Ty pulled out a handkerchief and dangled it before me. "You in?"

I breathed in hesitantly, trying to play it cool. I hadn't let anyone blindfold me since playing "Seven Minutes in Heaven or Hell" in eighth grade. It was the junior high basketball tournament and Kaitlyn and Caden were housing an entire team from Mt. Shasta. We were having a pregame party, getting to know each other. Everyone thought it was such a great idea to use blindfolds. The boys would go in one room and the girls in the other. Brody would draw names and blindfold each partner before bringing them to meet in the closet.

Looking around at the basketball team, I figured, "Why not get my first kiss out of the way with one of these good-looking basketball players?" Never once did I think they'd dare to partner me with *him*.

Because it was so dark in there, my senses were heightened to his delicious smell. I breathed in his Phoenix-scented Axe. Locked closely and surrounded by big pillows and blankets, he gently pulled me onto his lap. *Smooth*, I thought. At least I got someone who knows what he's doing. Not breaking the voice recognition rule, he whispered confidently, "You sure you wanna do this? I'm good if you are."

I'd wanted to get my first kiss out of the way for a while. Playing it with a stranger, I knew if I messed up, at least I'd never have to look at him again. Seven Minutes was the perfect learning opportunity.

"Lay it on me, big guy," I whispered.

He chuckled as his heat moved in closer. "Okay, here we go." As I felt his breath on my cheek, I took in the scent of his bubble-gum toothpaste. Then his soft lips came to mine. He led each step of the way, making sure to teach me exactly what to do. Softly parting our lips and brushing our tongues, I could tell he had braces too, but it didn't matter. I will never forget the arousing combination of Axe, bubblegum toothpaste, and his warm, soft, perfect lips. My heart raced as my first kiss fulfilled every junior high fantasy I'd ever had.

Seven minutes of heaven. We never parted once until the time was up. Disappointment filled me when they knocked on the door to get us out. I heard them giggling. Hesitantly, I slipped off my blindfold, excited to see my new Prince Charming. As the door creaked open and the light shined in from the hallway, it lit the smiling face of my blindfolded partner. I froze at the sight of him.

"Holy Shit!" I screeched. He flinched at my voice, swiftly tearing the blindfold from his eyes and scrambling from beneath me. Horror struck both of us when we saw who we'd been kissing. My seven minutes in heaven had just turned to seven minutes of hell!

"I'll kill him!" Caden screamed as he pulled me off his lap and raced toward a hysterical Brody. "She's like my sister, you asshole!"

he screamed as he chased him up the stairs. I kinda felt bad for Brody when Caden got a hold of him. I heard scuffling and then a slam.

"It was just a joke!" Brody's chuckling voice came to an abrupt halt, just before I heard the pop.

His black eye only took about two weeks to heal completely, and they both came to terms after Caden clobbered him. Brody realized the error of his ways and agreed to never set us up like that again. I still laugh when I think about that game, and how damn Brody pranked us into what is technically the best kiss I'd ever had. Thank goodness Kaitlyn stepped in and finally got us to talk about it. As we awkwardly giggled through that first meeting, we promised to never, ever speak of the kiss again. Ever.

The dangling bandana Ty held in front of me pulled me from my memory. Thank God Caden wasn't there. Nothing could be worse than kissing my best friend.

"Okay," I grunted. "Tie it on me." I turned my back to Ty, swooning as he carefully swept my hair away from my neck. He took his time, gently lifting the strands into place. It was a slow and deliberate process. Having his hands in my hair sent chills across my sensitive skin. I wrapped my arms around my waist as my tummy contracted. With each stroke, I had to remind myself to breathe.

Just as my fatigued nerves were about to give out, I felt him whisper into the top of my head, "Don't want to get any strays in that knot." Finally, I felt the bandana secure at the back of my head. Disappointment filled me when his hands dropped away, but a warm rush replaced the void of his touch when he leaned into me and whispered, "All set." It didn't take me long to figure out that there was truth in what they say about taking your sight away. It heightened the senses. Standing near him, I could feel his warmth, his closeness, and even the slightest brush of his body against mine.

As I waited for my instructions, the lingering feeling of his hands moving through my hair raised goosebumps from my neck through my crown. The warmth of his fingers slipping beneath the bandana to check its snugness set me on fire. When he whispered again, "Don't worry, you can trust me," I had no doubt that I was in good hands.

The cool night air gently blew across my face as his hands rested firmly on each of my shoulders. "We're about to hit an incline. There are some wooden footholds here. I'll tell you when to step up." Cautiously, he pressed gently into my back as our steps became smaller and more intentional. "Step up," he whispered, as he slid his hands down my arms and held me a little more tightly. When I began to take the first step, I felt his open palms slide beneath mine. "Hold on," he advised. When my hands felt him beneath me, I deliberately curled my wanting fingers around his. He reacted with a tight squeeze. Focused only on our secured hands, I hadn't even noticed when I cleared the first foothold.

"Good." I shuffled five steps forward. "Up," he whispered again. "You got it. You're doing good." Five more steps. "Now." I lifted my foot, barely catching it on the foothold. Before I could fall forward, his arms came around my waist. "Got ya. It's okay. You're doing good." He helped me adjust my balance. "Only two more." We shuffled a few more feet. I felt the corner of his mouth against my ear as he whispered, "Step up." His warm breath lit a fire across my skin. Between the gentle night breeze, his firm grasp, and whispers against my cheek, my strength began to crumble. "It's okay. We're almost past this. I've got you. No need to be nervous."

"Why do you think I'm nervous?"

"I can feel it."

I knew damn well that he was right. I could feel myself trembling from the tickle of his breath and his warm, strong hands. I wasn't ready for him to know he was the cause. I giggled and nervously fumbled for a cover. "Not nervous, just cold."

A sharp, "Hmph," accompanied by the feeling of his grin against my ear was a sure sign that he wasn't buying it. He came in closer again, "I can help with the chills, you know."

"Oh, really? How?"

He turned me around to face him. I could feel his firm chest next to mine. We stood motionless for a few seconds. I hoped he couldn't feel what he was doing to me as I stood gently against him, chest to chest.

After mustering the courage, I whispered, "What are we doing?"

"I'm going to give you a ride." He took my hands and guided them around his neck. "Hop up."

As I clasped my hands behind his head and allowed him to ready himself for the weight of my jump, I began to count.

"One, two,"

A voice suddenly boomed from behind us, "Hands off, Connelly!"

Leif?

"Rules are rules, you know. No touching allowed." I swore I heard him say. "Especially not her," but I couldn't be sure over the sound of my disappointment sliding off his chest and slamming down into the ground.

"It's okay. We're here," Ty whispered into my ear. "You can take it off now."

We had reached the top. When I slipped the blindfold from my eyes, the voices I had heard on our approach began to attach themselves to faces. There was a group of counselors sitting around a fire. They looked to be passing around some sort of plate.

"You made it!" Mariah sang, as she skipped her way across the open meadow and sidled up next to Ty. "We've been waiting for you." Not wanting to invade their space, I took a step away. Clearly, they had some kind of history and I wasn't going to get in the way of it.

"Hey, Mariah," he greeted cheerfully, taking her under his arm. "How was your hike with Leif? Did you guys get to know each other at all?"

"Eehhh, it was a little quiet. And rushed. It kinda felt like he was in a race to get up here. He actually tripped me twice. He didn't slow down until we could hear you two." She looked over at me and back at Leif. Sounding a bit worried she questioned, "Is he okay in the woods by himself? Seems like he might have been scared."

Another grin made its way across Ty's face as his eyes bounced back and forth between Leif's big feet and my curious expression. "Nah, it's not the woods that he's scared of." Mariah slowly bobbed her head up and down like she knew what he was talking about.

"Oh, got it," she said quietly as she turned away and walked back toward the fire.

Once Mariah had disappeared, Ty stepped into me and nudged me with his arm. "Why are you all the way over here? I don't bite."

But she might. I couldn't help but think that Mariah was probably already upset about Ty choosing to partner with me. I didn't want to do anything to make things more uncomfortable.

"Connelly, get your counselor over here. We've got an initiation to take care of."

Unexpectedly, his arm wrapped around my shoulders as he guided me over to the circle and pulled me down onto him. The sudden contact with his firm lap sent an instant pang of pleasure through my core. It warmed me instantly. It was a good thing the director wasn't there or we'd have been in trouble for inappropriate contact.

I looked around instinctively to make sure we weren't going to get ourselves in trouble on night one. "Where's Marcus? I thought this was a mandated camp activity."

"Oh, no. Nobody knows about this but the counselors. It's a secret. A fun activity we came up with to get to know each other better. Since the guys are always stuck with the guys and the girls with the girls, this is something we can do to mix things up a bit. It makes our camp experience, uh, interesting. Plus, it'll give us a fun camp activity we won't need approved by the director."

"You know how this goes, Connelly. Have her grab a fortune." He took the plate that was being passed around the circle and held it up in front of me as though he was serving me a plate of fine hors-d'oeuvres. Upon closer inspection, it was a pile of fortune cookies.

"Pick your poison. It's up to you." I turned in his lap so I could see him. "Choose wisely," he smiled.

I felt uneasy as I stared down at the plate and took a cookie. Then spinning back to face him, I held it up, "What is this all about?"

"This, my dear, is a plate of adventures. Inside each cookie is the hiding place of a counselor's kit. Every destination has its challenges, but they're all pretty fun and relatively safe … and as luck has it, you got the best partner." He held his hands out and wiggled his eyebrows.

"Wow, lucky me," I lifted my brows and tilted my head as I giggled at the sight of him trying to sell himself.

He looked at the cookie I'd chosen and grinned as though he already knew what it said inside, "Yep. Lucky you."

I held the fortune in my hand until all of the cookies had been handed out.

"On the count of three, crack them open," Gwen, one of the senior counselors, commanded. "One, two, three."

When I cracked the cookie, a piece of paper exposed itself. Unlike regular fortune cookies, it was a strip of paper with a special handwritten message.

Out in the pond, beyond the shore,
your gear awaits, now go explore.

His head tilted back as he started to laugh. "Oh, Jenna. Do you know where that is?"

"Not a clue. Do you?" I asked incredulously.

"Well, I did help come up with all the hiding places. I just didn't think you'd actually draw the toughest one to get to." He chuckled again. "You just can't stay away from the water today, can you?"

I wondered what I had done, but Ty sure seemed to be getting a kick out of it. "We'd better get going. This could take a little longer than most." He took me by the hand and pulled me off the ground. "Let's do this."

Chapter Nine

Night Vision

"WHERE ARE WE GOING?" I ASKED TIMIDLY AS TY TOOK my hand and dragged me away from the light of the fire. "I can't see."

"Don't worry. It's a full moon. Give your night vision a chance to adjust." I could hear the amusement in his voice as we continued shuffling away from the crowd.

"I'm probably wrong, but isn't the trail that way?" I pointed toward the back side of the lodge.

Again, amusement laced his voice as he chuckled, "Well, the pond is sort of off the beaten path. If we're gonna get any sleep at all tonight, we're gonna have to take the shortcut." Again, he tugged at me until he felt me walking with him, only letting go when we had to start using our arms for balance. Moving deeper into the pasture, the mud began to squish between my toes. That's when I realized I may not be wearing the appropriate footwear for a boondock adventure.

With each step, I sank deeper into the mushy ground, finally losing my flip-flop to the muck. I slid my foot around the slop to feel for my shoe. Without footwear, I wasn't going anywhere, but it was becoming increasingly clear that Ty was still on the move. The dark figure of my guide grew smaller and smaller as the distance grew between us. Still working to find my shoe, I began to wonder if he even knew he was leaving me behind. Panic began to grow as I watched his silhouette fade from view completely.

At the thought of being abandoned out in the middle of a field, my heart rate quickened. I looked around to make sure there were no wild animals lurking nearby. Nothing seemed out of the ordinary. Intentionally, I slowed my breathing to calm myself, figuring maybe by the time he reached the pond he'd realize I was no longer with him and he'd come back to look for me.

"You still with me?" his distant, baritone voice carried from up ahead.

"Back here," I giggled nervously, trying to hide the fact that I was freaking out. "Stuck in the mud."

No response. I didn't even hear movement. The silence was deafening. The void lasted long enough for me to begin questioning if he was simply going to abandon me out there in the dark. Maybe he was just going to grab the kit and find me on the way back. I'd be okay with that.

Or maybe I wouldn't. Alone was not my favorite thing. Especially not in the middle of the night with terrifying predators roaming through the nearby forest. Thoughts of black bears, coyotes, and mountain lions began to plague my mind. The search for my shoe became frantic. I took a step back thinking maybe it was behind me. As my foot hit a dip in the ground, it slid beneath me, causing me to teeter in the slick mud. My flailing arms shot out, momentarily helping me regain balance.

"Looks like you could use some help."

Suddenly, I felt his hands wrap around my waist. His unexpected touch caused my weight to shift. Again, my foot found the uneven ground and began to slide away from me. As I lost balance, I grabbed at his collar, trying to save myself from the impending humiliation of a mud bath.

"Whoa, whoa, whoa," he choked out, bending forward as

we both toppled over. It was such a blur that I couldn't process quickly enough what was happening. Before I knew it, I was flat on my back, trying to replay the events that put me there. I'd heard a splash, hit the ground with a cold, wet thud, and felt his heaviness pressing down on top of me.

The reflection of the moonlight off the puddle lit his grinning face. A small groan slipped from his smirking lips as his hands came down on each side of me. I felt his weight shift only slightly as he rested comfortably on my trembling body.

As his chest pressed into mine, I felt the echo of his chuckle move through both of us. Not seconds later, his breath tickled my cheek as his face began to move in closer. The silence between us grew. Even the crickets stopped chirping as we stared into each other's eyes. I couldn't help but wonder if he was going to kiss me. I'd imagined it, but I wasn't quite sure I was ready for it.

I was frozen, not knowing how to react to Tyler Connelly lying on top of me in a puddle of mud. My heart raced. If he was ever going to try anything with me, it was going to be right then. I studied his movement carefully as he lifted his hand from the muddy ground and moved it toward my face. Before I could move or dodge his advance, his finger swiftly came down on my forehead and I felt a stroke of mud being painted from my hairline to the tip of my nose.

"Gotcha!" he laughed as he peeled his chest from mine.

That's the moment I realized I did want him to kiss me right then and there. His warmth peeling away from mine was disheartening. I was frustrated with myself for thinking he might have actually wanted to. I knew deep down that he wasn't into me in that way. He was just trying to have fun and I had read too much into it. To hide the disappointment, I forced a laugh and asked, "Did you just paint mud on me?"

Still pinning me to the ground from the waist down, he chuckled. "What if I did?"

Quickly, I came up with my next move. "Don't you know what war paint does to a girl?" Then without another word, I grabbed him, wrapped my leg behind his knee and flipped him onto his back.

With his eyes open wide and staring into mine, he laid still, stunned into silence. We looked at each other with amused expressions slowly growing across both of our faces. My instinct to pull his lips to mine was so strong that I knew I had to break away before I made a fool of myself. Abruptly, I jumped up and held out my hand.

After helping pull him to his feet, the warmth of his gentle grasp wrapped around my shoulders. My breath hitched at his touch. He eased me into him, and I felt his grin against my ear. "You're one tough cookie. Remind me never to challenge you to a mud wrestling match. By the way, I found your shoe, Cinderella," he whispered as he handed me my muddy flip-flop. "Put it on and stay close to me." As I bent down to slip on my shoe, his hand slid down my back, never losing contact.

When I stood, he gently took my muddy hand and laced it through his bent elbow, linking us together. "There." Satisfaction painted his voice. "You can't get away from me now." I had been holding my breath since the moment he'd laid his hands on my shoulders. I reminded myself to relax as he began to tug me forward.

My senses heightened as the night darkened along a thickly forested area on the path. Tucked under his strong arm, I could feel the rhythm of his heart, my body moving in and out with the rise and fall of each breath. As we walked gingerly through the meadow, each time I sank into the soft ground, he was there tugging me back into him. The steady rhythm of me sinking and him saving me had me dazed. I didn't even notice when we'd escaped the dark forested area and the moonlight had begun to light the path toward the glistening water.

My sole focus had been on the heat of his sculpted body pressing into mine. Watching him out on my ball field last spring, I'd had a few short-lived fantasies about holding onto him like this, but always dismissed them almost immediately. Ty wasn't the kind of guy who would hook up with another athlete. I'm sure his taste ran more along the lines of "Miss Teen." As a matter of fact, I'd never seen him with any girl in our high school. He was probably holding out for the next Sports Illustrated supermodel. I was sure she'd be interested.

I couldn't help but fixate on the fact that the boy of my dreams was holding onto me. In the dark. Just the two of us. I could feel my body temperature rise. The thought of Ty steadying me with each misstep began to overtake my senses. I had to remind myself to stay calm. To breathe. *It's just Ty. Ty? Most wanted senior. Second to none. No biggie.*

As we walked, I couldn't help but question how I'd ended up playing leading lady in my biggest fantasy. Alone in the woods with Ty? I would've never had the nerve to pair myself with him, and that night, not only were we partners, but he had just grabbed my hand and slipped it through his arm so he could take care of me. I hoped nobody woke me from that gift of a dream. When the cool breeze reminded me that I was indeed awake, I found myself overwhelmed and unable to speak. The only way I could figure to break the uncomfortable silence was to fake a few stumbles. Maybe that would kick start a conversation. Each time I teetered, I was met with his strong arms and a knowing chuckle.

"You still playing ball this year, Jenna?" he asked with amusement laced in his voice.

"Yeah, what makes you ask?"

"I've never known a catcher who can't stand on their own two feet."

I should've figured he knew I was faking the clumsiness. I could've shown my slight embarrassment, but rather, I decided to play it cool with my admission. "Oh, I can stand on my own two feet ... when I want to."

He paused and looked at me contemplatively. "Interesting," he chuckled. He opened his mouth and closed it again, shaking his head. A small grin grew across his lips. Then after a beat, he said, "Well, you're gonna have to find your balance, cuz we're here, catcher girl."

He pulled me toward the water's edge. The night brightened as the full moon reflected on the water. I looked around, wondering where the kit could possibly be.

"You've done this before, right?" I asked.

"Sure have."

"So, where is it?"

"Out there," he grinned, pointing at the big climbing structure with a diving board. It sat in the middle of the pond. There was no way to get out there other than a kayak or to swim.

"Seriously?"

"Yep, hope you brought your swimsuit."

I hadn't worn my swimsuit and I wasn't about to drown under his heavy sweatshirt. I wasn't sure if I wanted to strip down to my lacy hipsters and bralette. They did sort of look like a bikini. I would be covered... somewhat.

After thinking it through, I decided to let him make that decision. "Would it bother you if I just wore what I sleep in?"

"You brought your pajamas, but no swimsuit?" he laughed.

"Kind of," I batted my eyelashes as I studied his questioning face. I was glad that it was dark outside so he couldn't see the pink blushing in my cheeks. Lord knows the heat was rising all over my hesitant body. The sudden feeling of modesty was new to me, but for some reason, I wasn't sure I wanted to reveal my moonlit body to the guy I'd been crushing on all year. "Maybe you should, uh, turn around for a second."

"I guess, but you know I'll probably see you anyway, right? I mean, I'm not gonna send you out into the middle of the pond alone."

"Point taken." I began to slide his sweatshirt over my head, working up the nerve to reveal myself. *Suck it up, buttercup.* And there it went. The sweatshirt came off and so did the shorts. I stood there no longer hiding Victoria's secret. Silence filled the brisk air as I stood looking down at my feet. I wasn't ready to see his reaction. Nobody had ever seen me in my underwear. Well, no boys had ever seen me in my underwear. Not in the dark. Not under the moonlight. I started second guessing my decision. After all, Ty was the most popular guy at school. I'm sure he'd seen plenty of girls both in and out of their underwear. I moved to grab my sweatshirt from the ground when his hand suddenly came to mine.

"Leave it," he gulped.

When I looked up, our eyes met. Our faces were so close, yet I could barely hear his whisper, "I like your pj's better than my old, ratty sweatshirt." He grinned as his gaze wandered from my feet back up to my eyes. "I think those will work just fine for what we're about to do. You ready?"

He took me by the hand and walked me to the shoreline. "We're gonna have to be a little careful here. We haven't quite gotten it set up for the campers yet. The kayaks are still locked up and I don't have the key. We'll have to swim out there. How are your skills?"

My mind flashed to all of the swim medals hanging on my bedroom wall back at home. Apparently, he'd been too busy with his own sports to follow swim team. "I'm okay … I guess."

I watched as an idea appeared in his eyes. "Wanna race?"

It seemed he'd given me a green light to show off a bit. I couldn't let him know that I was about to make him eat my bubbles. I put on my contemplative face and acted worried. "Is that really fair? I mean, look at you, and then look at me."

"Oh, I'm looking. You've got plenty of muscle working for

you." He pointed at my abs.

Adrenaline shot through me as I realized once again that I was on full display. A swimsuit was one thing, but my undies were something else. I wanted to get in the water and quick.

"Okay. I'll give it a shot. Just to the tower?"

"Yep. First one to climb the ladder to the top wins. You're starter."

We moved to the water's edge and readied ourselves to race. "On your mark, get set, go!"

I could feel his splash next to me as I focused on the tower and submerged myself into the chilly pond. As soon as the water was deep enough to swim, I took off in a full sprint, burying my head and kicking with all my might. Swimming blind, it seemed like I was never going to get there, but I wasn't about to let him win. I pulled and kicked until I couldn't help but raise my head enough to peek at where I was.

I was about two strokes from the finish when I heard a yelp behind me. I stopped and looked toward the shore. Ty was treading water about fifty yards back. "Alright, you win!" he choked out.

Calling to him, I panted, "I forgot to tell you, softball's not my only sport. I also play basketball. Oh yeah, and I swim varsity!" I giggled as I gave two breaststroke kicks to the tower and pulled myself out of the water. Shakily, I climbed the wooden ladder and made my way to the top, jumping up and down to celebrate my victory. "Okay, it's cold up here. Let's get this over with." I shouted down to him. "Where is it?"

"Lifeguards' chest!" he gargled as he made his way toward the structure.

I kneeled in front of the box and peeked my head in, patting around for anything that felt like a kit. When I was sure I had it, I pulled it from its hiding place and set it on the ground next to me. Still panting from the race, I decided to sit for a moment and catch my breath. I turned around and leaned against the chest, waiting for my heart to calm down and for Ty to join me up top.

As I heard him approach, I slid my back across the wooden side to shift to a less awkward position. That's when I felt it catch. The back of my bralette. As I tried to pull away, I found myself stuck to the trunk. If my bra had a clasp, maybe I could have undone it real quick and released myself before he got there. No such luck. It was sports bra style and there was no way out.

He showed up just when I realized I wasn't going anywhere. His breathing was heavy when his head appeared at the edge of the tower. "I see you found a seat. Mind if I join you?"

"Sure, I don't think I'll be going anywhere for a bit."

"You seem to be in great shape. You'll be ready to go in a few minutes, I'm sure."

"Oh, I'm ready to go now. It's my pj's that won't let me."

A quizzical look grew on his brow as he turned to face me. "What do you mean?"

I leaned forward, showing him the gap between me and the back of my bralette. It was obvious he was trying to hold back his laughter, but it seeped through when he chuckled, "Looks like you've gotten yourself in a real pickle."

My hands came over my eyes as I began to laugh too. "Yep, Pickle's my middle name."

"Pickle," he repeated. "Isn't that what they call you out on the ball field?"

"Yeah, I'm pretty renowned for getting caught up in pickles. Not usually this kind, but, you know."

"Well, guess what catcher girl? From now on, when I call you Pickle, it's gonna take on a whole new meaning," he grinned as he looked me up and down. "How do we get you out of this one?"

"I think I'll have to slip it over my head. It doesn't have a clasp."

"I'll just, uh, step down while you do that."

Grinning from ear to ear, Ty pushed himself up and tiptoed backward to the edge of the structure. Then with a slight nod, he disappeared down the ladder. "Let me know when you're out of your pickle, Pickle."

I wiggled and tugged trying to get that thing over my head, but I just couldn't seem to get out of it. By that point, I was freezing and desperate. I knew I was going to have to get his help. "Ty?" I finally forced out.

"Yeah?"

"I think I need your help."

"I can see that," he chuckled, peeking back over the edge of the tower.

"You've been watching the whole time?" If I wasn't stuck, I think I would've stood up and smacked him. But then again, looking at his impossibly adorable face, maybe not. "Sorry I'm taking so long."

"Oh, I'm not complaining. Take all the time you need. It's not often a guy's lucky enough to find himself in this sort of situation. What can I do for you?"

"I can't get it off. You've got to come help or we'll be here all night."

"Help take that off," he coughed. "Of you?" He put his hand to his forehead and spoke to himself. "Of course off of you. What am I thinking?" As he made his way to my rescue, the deck beneath me bounced with each footstep. "Let me get a closer look." He kneeled beside me and set his hand on my shoulder.

"Lean forward a bit." I did as he asked. "Looks like you're caught up on the latch. What in the world?" he said to himself as I felt his hand come down on my back. Goosebumps rose across my skin as I felt his trembling hand gently work at the lace. Then leaning into me he whispered, "Pickle, I really do think you might need to take this thing off. I can't get it."

"Promise you won't look."

"Pinky swear." He held his pinky out to mine, and for a second time that day, I made a pact with my rescuer. He smiled down at me, and for some reason, I knew he was telling the truth. I watched him closely as he helped me slip out of my top. "Hold your arms up and slide toward the ladder," he directed. Then looking away, his strong hands came to my ribs and found their way to the lace. Again, I felt the goosebumps rise on my skin at his trembling touch. "Am I doing okay?" he asked, gently working his fingertips beneath the lace.

"You're doing great," I whispered, hoping his well-placed hands would continue their straight path up the sides of my body and not find themselves wandering into uncharted territory. As I slowly slid across the deck, toward the ladder, I inhaled at the release and the feeling of the cool night air on my bare chest. Peeking up, I could see he was still looking away. The boy had kept his promise.

"Okay, Jenna. I won't be able to loosen it from the trunk until I can look at what I'm doing. Maybe you can climb down and wait in the water till I get it free."

I couldn't believe my good fortune in partners. Who knew Jefferson High's most wanted jock was such a gentleman? Not many guys would've handled that kind of vulnerable situation the way he did. Especially not smoking hot, star athletes. As I shakily crawled down the ladder, my heart about burst. That's when I knew Ty Connelly had me, hook, line, and sinker. He may not have wanted me, but he had me anyway.

Within seconds his victory cry pulled me from my daze, "Got it!"

I stared in awe as I watched him come down the ladder with my top in one hand, and the plastic bag carrying the counselor's kit in the other. Standing on the deck, he looked up at the full moon. "Since I'm not allowed to look," he twirled my bra around his finger, "you're gonna have to come get it."

I could barely move as I watched my new favorite lacy bra turning around and around on Ty's finger. I swore I'd never wash it again if I could help it. Then I took a deep breath, blew the bubbles out of my nose and resurfaced to grab my top from his hand.

"Let me know when you're dressed," he laughed and cannon-balled over my head.

I slipped it on and swam back to him. We met at the water's edge, where he helped pull me onto the shore. That's where we sat for a moment to catch our breath. There were no words spoken. Just silence. I looked out over the water, taking in the serenity of the moonlit night.

"Jenna?"

"Yeah?" I looked over at him, as I watched his eyes slowly scan my body.

"I sure am glad we rescued that top."

"Yeah?"

"Yeah, it looks a lot better on your chest," he pointed up toward the tower, "than the one up there."

I didn't know how many times a heart could stop in one day, but by the time those words left his lips, I was pretty sure I was a dead girl walking. If I made it through that summer camp without having a massive heart attack, it would be a miracle.

The experienced counselors were right. After that first night when we mixed up and paired with a partner, there was no more inter-action with the guys. We were separated at all times. Aside from stolen glances during campfire circle, I barely had a chance to speak to Ty. Sure, every once in a while, he'd brush past me in line at the dining hall and ask, "How's it going, Pickle?" And each time, either Leif or Mariah would come between us and let us know just how urgently we were needed at our tables.

It seemed that this was the neediest group of kids the camp had seen in years. Between patching up scrapes, stopping food fights, phone calls to parents, and keeping our campers from getting lost along far-off trails, we barely had time to interact with one another. I kept my promise to Kaitlyn and wrote in my journal. When the time came to share, she'd be sure to know just how much I'd been secretly pining over Ty Connelly.

I'd made bullets of every single interaction we had. The way he rescued me from the creek on the first day. Our trip to the pond to retrieve our kits. The way I always rerouted my campers past Cabin 8, just to try to catch a glimpse of him doting over his kids. Lucky boys. What I wouldn't have done to be one of them. At one point I was ready to hurt myself, just so he could patch me up the way he did for them. It was a good thing I wrote it all down for her because by the time my head hit my pillow each night, I was out like a light. Even if I could've kept a phone, I would've been too exhausted to text back and forth about my summer saga.

Exhaustion became my friend. For the first time in years, there were no nightmares. No flashbacks. The only thing that drifted through my dreams each night was Ty. His presence at camp had been my cure. And though I was almost certain he had eyes for Mariah, I had definitely developed eyes for him. I was going to have to suck it up though. Camp was over, and so were my chances with him. It was time to go. My mom had pulled up to take me away. As I packed my gear into the back of her car, I looked over my shoulder. He was standing across the road with her, obviously telling her goodbye. I swallowed the lump in my throat as I slammed the lid of the trunk.

"You leaving, Pickle?" he shouted to me from across the road. "Come tell us goodbye, at least." Goodbyes were not my thing, especially not when I was attracted to one-half of a couple that I was supposed to say goodbye to. I knew if I got too close, she'd read the attraction all over my body. Slowly, I sauntered across the road, resisting my irrational urge to step in between him and his girlfriend to break up their impending embrace. As I neared the couple, I watched him take her in his outstretched arms. "Not so long next time, huh, cuz?"

"Thanks for getting me the job this summer," she hugged him quickly and released him as she turned and walked toward me. "It was nice to meet you, Jenna." She held out her arms. "Have a great senior year."

Confused by the revelation, I hugged her back and whispered, "Thanks."

She nodded with a grin and climbed into her car. With a quick honk, she drove off, waving through her window.

I turned toward Ty and questioned, "Cuz?"

"Yeah. Mariah's my cousin. She wanted to get out of the Pacific Northwest for the summer, so I got her a job down here. Guess I never had a chance to tell you," he chuckled. Then pausing momentarily, he looked at me. The sunlight caught his eyes just right, causing me to damn near lose my breath with their dazzling shade of blue. "So, I'll see you around at school this year?"

Looking into his eyes I grinned, "Not unless I see you first." No sooner did the words come out, then adrenaline spiked through my chest. My impulsive slip had me searching for a way to make sure he knew I was joking. I wiggled my brows, trying to break the new intensity of his gaze.

A contemplative look came over him, as a smirk grew on his lips. "Come here, you." He took me into his arms and squeezed me. "This was fun. And I fully intend to see you at school this year, Pickle. Till then, stay out of trouble, huh?"

At the mention of my nickname, heat rose in my cheeks. I nodded and smiled as he released me. Slowly, I lifted my hand and waved goodbye. Hesitant to leave him, I shuffled my feet across the road back toward my mom's car. So, Mariah wasn't his girlfriend. He was unattached. The more I thought about it, the more it stunned me that he had called me to *him*. *He* had chosen to wrap me up in his available embrace. I focused on my arms, where his hands had seconds ago seared their warm touch. I was going to hold onto that memory until I could get him to do it again. For the first time in my life, I couldn't wait till fall. School couldn't come soon enough.

Chapter Ten

Notified

THE FIRST THING I DID WHEN I DROPPED MY STUFF IN THE DOORWAY was run to my phone. I gave it a quick kiss as I hit the home button. It was a great summer, but I missed my best friend more than anything in the world and needed to call her to catch up. When the home screen popped up, it was filled with messages and notifications. Glimpses of blue and green social media and message icons flashed before me, but they disappeared as I accidentally hit the home button again. I wasn't too worried. I'd try to remember my login and check that stuff later.

Me:
Kait? You around? I'm home. I miss my best friend.

I waited for a few minutes, but there was no response. Not wanting to waste time, I decided to go back and look at all of my notifications. My phone had blown up with summer messages from acquaintances who obviously didn't know I was away at camp. I had invitations to bonfires, rafting trips, and pool parties. All of which sounded like they would have been fun, but I wouldn't have traded my summer at camp for any of them.

It took me a while to read and respond to messages that needed my attention. As I responded to texts, I kept staring at my laptop. I don't know why I was so hesitant to check the social media notifications, but knowing it was a secret account made me reluctant to see how big of a mess I'd let pile up while I was away. If it had gotten too out of control, it was going to be tough to hide from my teacher-mom. Clearly, I had done something wrong. I knew my parents were completely opposed to me having online accounts, and now that a full summer had passed, I couldn't remember why I'd let myself break their rule. What a dumb move. As my eyes bounced back and forth between my phone and laptop, the guilt ate at me. After little contemplation, I decided to go in and delete my account.

I readied myself as I plopped down on the bed and slid my laptop in front of me. It wasn't too hard to remember the password. It was just my name and jersey number. When I typed it in, my home page flashed up and I went straight to the notifications. I was surprised to see how many friend requests had piled up over summer. I guess more people recognized my picture than I thought. Maybe it was because Kaitlyn had added me to the Jefferson High Swim team group. After all, I had gotten a few friend requests from people I'd met on other area swim teams. I also noticed half of the baseball team had requested me. I giggled, thinking that was because of the profile picture of me in my catcher's gear. I never intended it to attract baseball players. I just wanted a picture that only close friends would recognize. One where you'd have to know my eyes. As I went through the new requests, I began to lose my enthusiasm for deleting my account. How could I abandon all those people who wanted to be my friend? My finger hovered over the delete button as I looked at all of my new friends. That's when I saw a tiny picture of Ty. It was a friend suggestion. I thought maybe I'd just go check it out real quick before I deleted my account. When I clicked on his name my breath hitched. I didn't know it was humanly possible to be that good looking. My eyes focused on his profile picture. It was a shot of him in his board shorts, giving a smaller brown-haired boy a piggyback ride. I instantly recognized the background as Kelsey Creek Pond and the boy as one of his campers. It was that cute little kid named Aiden.

I knew he must have recently uploaded the picture. It was probably from our last rec time. As I scrolled down, I saw a new album. The first few pictures showed groups of kids down at the pond. I decided to click on +8. Eight more pictures popped into view. As I clicked on them one by one, I caught sight of myself in the background of a few of them. They were pretty cute. One was me helping Aiden into a kayak. In another, I was clipping Trey into the harness on the zip line. The last one I saw was me helping Megan jump from the diving structure. That's when I noticed the caption beside the picture. "Best memory of summer camp happened right up there." My heart stopped. A little burst of adrenaline rushed from my chest. That was our spot. It warmed my heart to read that I was one of his favorite memories from summer camp.

I focused on the lifeguard stand and debated whether to download the pictures before I deleted my account. I couldn't help but wonder if he'd be able to see if I downloaded them. I had no idea how the whole social media thing worked. I thought maybe he'd get one of those notifications that said a creepy stalker, who's not your friend, just downloaded your pictures. I grabbed my phone.

Me:
Kait!!! Where are you? Social media question. Need help.

Ten minutes passed as I scrolled down Ty's page waiting for an answer. I learned a lot about him in those ten minutes. I saw snapshot after snapshot of Aiden and wondered why he had so many pictures of the little guy. I thought he was just another camper, but I finally realized Aiden was his little brother. His little brother who he seemed to adore more than anyone else in the world. In one picture, he was on his shoulders after a baseball game. In another, Ty was standing by the dugout coaching him as he stood at the plate.

As I continued to scroll, I was surprised to see a photo of them together in the hospital. Aiden was lying in the bed and Ty was sitting by his side. The caption read, "Here we go again. Bravest boy I know." When I clicked on the comments to see what was wrong with the little guy, one read, "Praying for a cure." Under it, Ty had responded, "He's getting the insulin pump soon. Things are looking up."

I scrolled back up to the top of the page where I'd seen the album. Obviously, Kaitlyn was away from her phone. I was going to bite the bullet and download that picture and then delete my account. I knew way too much. I felt so invasive. Ty hadn't even told me about Aiden and now I knew everything. I felt like a stalker. I should have never known such personal issues without being told face to face. Not to mention, I wasn't even his friend on social media.

I clicked on the picture of me with Aiden and hit download. Instantly, a new friend request popped up. I jumped when I clicked on it. It was Ty. The timing was uncanny. I couldn't help but wonder if he could see me on his page downloading all of his photos. Had he caught me? I knew I couldn't respond right away. I had to talk to Kaitlyn. I picked up my phone and called her number.

"Hello?"

"Where are you?"

"I-*gasp*-just-*gasp*-got out-*gasp*-of my 500 Free."

I cringed at the memory of what twenty laps of racing felt like. "Oh, you're at Championships. Sorry, Kait. Do you have enough breath for a quick question?"

"Yeah."

"Can someone see when you download their picture?"

"What are you talking about?"

"My social media account," I gnarled through my teeth, trying not to let my mom hear me.

She snickered. "Glad you're home safe, and I have a feeling there's more to this story, but I'll wait."

"I'll fill you in later. So can they see or not?"

"Nope. You're safe. Download away."

"Thanks, Kait. Call me after you're done with High Point."

"Sure thing."

After we hung up, I decided to accept his request. I mean, who in their right mind would have turned down a friend request from Ty? Not me. I clicked "Accept" and a celebration banner declaring I had 100 friends floated across the screen. I couldn't help but feel a little proud of myself. People liked me. As I stared at the balloons making their way up the page, I decided that maybe I wouldn't delete that account after all.

Chapter Eleven

Peek-A-Boo

ETWEEN BACK TO SCHOOL SHOPPING, HIGH SCHOOL SWIM PRACTICE starting, and hanging out with my squad, the last few weeks of summer were a blur. It wasn't until I hit the pillow each night that I had time to think. Time to dream. Time to slip back to the uneasiness I had felt before camp. In the stillness of the night, the reprieve from my angst had slipped away. Once again, the nightmares I had repressed through summer resurfaced.

The first nightmare came the day I got the friend request from a man I did not know. I chuckled at the profile picture of him in a furry walrus hat, and couldn't help but wonder where he got his fashion sense. I clicked on his photo trying to get a better view. At first, I thought he might be a relative, or even one of my parents' cousins. He seemed to be about their age. I clicked around a bit until I found a photo album titled "On the Job." I couldn't believe it when I saw a stack of wine barrels. My heart jumped when I realized he must have been one of my dad's friends or co-workers. I hadn't thought of my parents' acquaintances finding out about my account. I quickly deleted the request and slammed the laptop closed.

The panic stirred something in me that must have affected my dreams that night. I was back in the long, dark passage wearing the little, ruffly dress and tights. I heard footsteps coming down the hallway. Quickly, I grabbed my nesting doll from the shelf and ran with it as fast as I could. As the footsteps quickened, I found the room with the long curtains that hung behind the big, black piano. I slipped behind the drapes. Trembling and holding my breath, I saw the big, black shoe next to the piano bench. Just then, the doll slipped from my hand, hit the wooden floor, and cracked open with a thud. Instantly, the gloved fingers wrapped around the curtain and tugged it open.

"Found you!"

I woke to a puddle of sweat.

"It's okay, Jenna. I'm here," my mom's voice wrapped itself around me.

Heart beating, and eyes wide, I looked up at my mom. When she sat down beside me, she pulled me into her. "Are the dreams back?"

As I leaned into her, all I could do was nod in response.

"I was in the kitchen when I heard your cries. Do you remember this time?"

"Only that there's a guy. I can't ever see his face, but he's so scary. He knows who I am." I swallowed hard. "Mom, he found me."

I felt her breath hitch beneath my cheek. Her arms tightened around me. "I think it's time," she whispered. "We've got to get to the bottom of this. These nightmares can't go on forever."

I shook my head, feeling defeated. This was never going to end. "There's nothing we can do. You can't control your dreams."

"There's something that's causing them and we're going to figure it out. We're going back to Dr. Isabelle."

I remembered the small office that suffocated me each time I walked through the doors. The leather couch. The chocolate walls. The smell of peppermint. The thought of going under made me uneasy. I didn't like the idea of not having control. No control over what I said. No control of what I did. No control over what I remembered. "I don't want to be hypnotized again. I hate what it does to me. Don't you remember how bad my nightmares were during the last set of treatments?"

"You're older now. We always said if they didn't go away we'd try again when you got to high school."

I fumbled for excuses to avoid a new round of hypnotic treatments. I didn't want to go back to a shrink. "I don't want anyone to know I'm crazy! I have friends now! You have friends now! They'll find out!"

"We'll come up with a story. Nobody needs to know."

She paused for a moment. I could tell her mind was reeling. My mom was going to come up with a way to cover for me.

"Idea. The Woodleys are trying to get us to go to Mexico. I'm sure we're going to have a hard time getting passports. Dad and I were looking over the stuff we need to take to the post office. We noticed our names aren't on your citizenship documents. We've gotta get that taken care of. This is perfect timing to get it fixed. If anyone asks or says anything, we can tell them we're down in Sacramento working on fixing your citizenship paperwork from the adoption. How's that?"

I thought about it and it made sense. I could totally use my citizenship as a cover. It sounded believable enough. I decided I would try hypnosis one last time. If I didn't, the cycle of nightmares might never end.

The recurring dream had haunted me all morning. I knew I needed to shake my mood. Trying to cover my exhaustion from lack of sleep, I overzealously bounced up next to my best friend who was headed toward the music room. I didn't want to say anything, but the funny stench coming off of her clothes had to be addressed. She told me how she'd just been tripped by Chelsea and landed in the garbage can. Chelsea was relentless when it came to Kaitlyn. I didn't know why she was so mean to her, but I'd been going to battle with Chelsea for years trying to defend my best friend. Even Kait's mom had to go to the police about the cyberbullying she'd inflicted just last spring. I felt bad about her smell but tried to make her feel better by telling her the latest Chelsea break-up rumors.

That's when I spotted Ty on the far side of the quad. He was walking toward the parking lot. I stopped mid-sentence, "Oh my gosh, I've gotta get across the street to the gym. It's weightlifting today and I'm gonna try to sneak a peek at Ty through the locker room door before I go to P.E." I hadn't yet told Kaitlyn about my summer crush on Ty. Not even about initiation night. Interestingly, she'd been hanging out with Brody a lot lately and we hadn't fully had a chance to catch up on boy talk. It was time to let her know the details, but not here. I winked, knowing I'd let her in on my secret during practice. "I'll catch you after school and we can go to practice together." I took off, not giving her a chance to question me.

Running across the street to the gym, I was extra careful not to let Ty see me. Slipping into the locker room, I threw on my running gear. It was pacer day and as soon as I was done seeing Ty, it was time to break my own school record.

After slipping my shoes on, I made my way through the maze of lockers to the back entrance. The back door to the girls' locker room happened to be connected to the short hallway leading to the boys' locker room. It was a known fact at Jefferson High that it was off limits to go that way. We'd been warned since freshman year that locker room mingling was prohibited under any circumstance. I couldn't help it. I hadn't seen him since camp, and now that my eyes had caught sight of him, I was addicted. It was as though we were connected by an invisible elastic band. It really wasn't my fault. My heartbeat quickened as I was tugged against my will. I knew full well if Coach Cowley came out of her adjacent office, I'd be dead.

I found myself peeking through a slat in a blinded window. It was cracked open just enough to see the color of skin, but not enough to make out who it belonged to. I had to get a closer look. I took a deep breath, dropped to my knees, and began to crawl down the hallway, only looking over my shoulder once to see if anyone was watching me.

As I peeked my head into the open doorway, I spotted him right away next to a corner locker. I couldn't believe my luck. It was him and a few other guys from the football team. They were chuckling about something, but I couldn't make out what they were saying. I could only focus on Ty's athletic physique. My jaw dropped at the sight of his six-foot frame standing in his black Abercrombie boxer briefs. They hit near the top of his muscular thighs. My stare roamed from muscle to muscle, stopping just above the V that invaded his waistline. Forcing my eyes to leave his chiseled abs, my sight was fixated on his perfect face. His warm complexion, olive skin, and dark brown-hair were a rare combination of perfection. His face was nearly shaven, with just enough stubble to make him look like less of a boy and more of a man. Even at a distance, I was drawn to his captivating grin and smiling blue eyes.

The slamming of a locker near the sidewall snapped me back to reality. The volume of banter that I'd heard earlier as I cautiously crawled down the hallway had stopped. The silence was almost deafening as I froze at the open doorway. At one point, I swore my heartbeat could be heard across the room. Just as I thought I was going to collapse from panic, I heard Ty speak.

"You guys know much about Jenna Bailey?"

Did I just hear my name? Focusing on his mouth, I tried to read his lips. A new twinkle in his eyes and a devious grin registered on his face.

"Why are you asking about her? Did something happen?"

"Nah, I ran into her a lot this summer and I kinda liked what I saw."

"I'm sure you did." Blake started belly laughing as he set his hand on Ty's shoulder. "I tried to date her last basketball season and she blew me off. Says her focus is sports, not dating. Hate to tell you, but she's out of your league, dude."

I almost laughed out loud. He had to be joking. I was not out of his league. He was out of mine. Without realizing it, I began to lean forward. I had to hear more.

"We'll see about that." His glance drifted down to the doorway where I kneeled looking up at him. "I'm not afraid of a challenge," he winked, looking down at me.

His eyes remained fixed on mine as he closed his locker door. I felt the heat rise in my cheeks. The devious grin that had plagued his face just a few seconds earlier grew into a knowing smile. I'd been caught. I wondered how long he knew I was there. Jumping to my feet, I sprinted back to the locker room and hid there for the rest of the period. My heart raced as the image of his grinning face that accompanied his flirty words kept playing back in my mind. He liked what he saw? He wasn't afraid? *I* was a challenge? For Ty? I had to pinch myself to make sure I wasn't dreaming.

Chapter Twelve

Snubbed

I WANTED TO TELL KAITLYN EVERYTHING. ABOUT THE NIGHT AT CAMP. About stalking Ty's social media. About getting caught looking at him through the locker room door and hiding out for the rest of the period. I tried to call. I tried to text. She never answered. She was so preoccupied lately that I was starting to feel like she'd forgotten about me. She didn't even show up to practice on time. I waited to meet her like we'd talked about at school, but I didn't want extra laps for being late.

As I joined the stretch circle, a loud screech drew my attention toward the fence. It was just a flash, but I saw Pistol's truck pull away in a loud roar. I couldn't believe she was ignoring me to spend the afternoon with *him* again. I couldn't stand that jerk. I'd been working for weeks to try to talk her out of dating him, hinting about the rumors I'd heard. The rumors that he was a pretty big drinker and when he hit the bottle, he also hit on every girl in sight.

I looked up from my butterfly stretch to see her walking down the sidewalk with Brody. His arm was draped over her shoulder and she was leaning into him. Was she still with Pistol? I was confused by the intimacy of her tucked under his arm. Maybe she *had* listened to my warnings. Perhaps while I was away at camp, I'd missed how much things had changed over summer. Based on the screeching tires, I was thinking Pistol didn't like the change. I tried not to get upset about her tardiness, but by the time she finally passed through the dressing room and skipped out on deck, I could barely look at her. By that point, I didn't care which one of the boys she'd stood me up for. I was too frustrated with her ignoring me to question it.

Listening as she apologized to Coach Hendryx, I tried to move my towel away, but I wasn't fast enough. I spotted her feet next to mine. Since there was nowhere left to go, I turned away from her and struck up a conversation with McKenna. Kaitlyn may or may not have tried to talk to me, but I wouldn't have known. It was going to take a few laps before I was willing to listen.

I don't know if I was more upset that she was withholding secrets, unavailable to catch up, or that she'd left me alone with the new exchange student who seemed to pay far too much attention to the cut of my suit, and too little attention to the actual sport of swimming. He'd shown up the first day of practice wanting to take on the challenge of learning a new sport. Apparently, he was on the diving team at his school in France. He searched for a team at JHS, but the only sport he was interested in involved water. Lucky us, he found our Jefferson High Swim Team listing after Kaitlyn made a group on social media. If only she'd made that group a few weeks later he would've been running cross country or something. Crap. It was just one more thing I could throw in her face when she was finally available to talk.

Personally, I thought he was just there to watch the swimsuits. Rather than practicing, he spent most of his time bobbing at the end of the lane, trying to cop a feel whenever we'd go in for a flip turn. Not to mention, he was such a great diver that the one time we asked him to show us a trick off our diving board, it resulted in a huge belly flop and six inches of water lost from the deep end of the pool. He said our board was too low to pull it off.

We were only a few days into practice, but so far the flopping

Frenchman alternated between Kaitlyn's and my lanes. After ditching me for the boys, I made sure he was in hers that day. I ran and jumped in lane 7 with McKenna, forcing him into lane 8. I figured I'd let Kaitlyn deal with that nipping shark for a full practice. That would teach her not to stand me up and show up late again. Some captain she was.

By the time I got through the practice, I was barely cooled off. In fact, I stormed out front where I saw Caden waiting by his truck. Kaitlyn was still swimming so I jumped at the opportunity to figure out what was going on with her. Obviously, *she* didn't have time to tell me. I marched up to her twin brother and demanded answers. Practically spitting my words, I told him how she'd stood me up. How she'd been ignoring me and wouldn't answer my calls or text me back. How I thought she was possibly ditching me for his best friend.

I asked what the deal was with Pistol and Brody. Clearly, she was keeping something from me. He was holding her in a way I'd never seen before. That's when Caden told me what had happened and how Brody was just being protective. Apparently, Caden was driving around the corner just before practice when he pulled up on Pistol getting a little rough with Kaitlyn. Brody had just stepped away after giving her a ride to practice. Seeing them together had thrown Pistol into some jealous outburst. Clearly, Pistol had assumed the same thing I did, that there was more than friendship brewing between those two. But according to Caden, they were friends. That was it.

I felt like a big ass when Kaitlyn came through the glass doors shaking and teary-eyed. She dragged her feet as she slowly made her way down the sidewalk to Caden's truck. Looking at her slumped over and weak, I couldn't help it. I caved and threw my arms around her shoulders. When she began to cry, I was disappointed in myself. Not only had I ignored her, but I made her swim with the Daemon for a full practice. Clearly, I'd added insult to injury. Not knowing how to fix what I'd done, I held her silently as her tears streamed down over my shoulders.

I was thankful Caden was there. He always knew how to lift his sister's spirits when I couldn't. Wanting to fix her day, he came up with a plan. That night, he and Brody were supposed to bale hay out in the valley. He called Brody to get the okay, and then invited us to go with them for a little after-work bonfire. I wanted nothing more than to right my wrong. No questions asked, I accepted on the spot. I hadn't realized where they were baling.

Instantly, my relief turned to concern when I found out they were working at Brody's cousin's ranch. The very one I hadn't been to since the night we left our home in Napa. When I heard we were headed to Mason's, I almost backed out. There was no way I could explain to my friends that I'd known Mason since I was little and our families were deeply connected. That Isaiah Brooks was the only reason any of us were still alive. For all my friends knew, I'd only met Brody's cousin one time at the rodeo. There was no way I was going to put my family at risk by blowing our cover over one bad day at the pool. If I decided to go, I knew that night I'd have to give the performance of my life.

I contemplated what to do the entire ride home. As much as I didn't want to tell my mom where I was going, I knew I needed her input. She would have to be part of the decision. Living in such a small county, my parents were bound to find out that I was out at the ranch, especially if Mason's grandparents saw me. I didn't have to tell her I'd already hung out with him over the summer. That could be my little secret. However, now that all of us were driving and one of my best friends turned out to be his cousin, it was inevitable that mine and Mason's paths would cross. They couldn't keep us apart forever. My parents had to know that, and under the circumstances, there was no getting around it that night. I had already promised Caden that I'd go. We would just have to be careful.

I rushed home, where I found my mom correcting papers at her desk. "You have a minute?" She nodded and spun around in her office chair.

"Sure, hon, what's up?"

I took a deep breath and decided to start the conversation by telling her how bad Kaitlyn's day was. By the time I finished telling her about the French exchange student, Daemon, her extra Fly set, and her emotional breakdown outside of the pool, I had softened her to the idea of letting me go. When I sensed she was almost ready to cave, I assured her that I wouldn't tell Kaitlyn or Caden that Mason and I knew each other. Nobody else would see us together. She was pretty apprehensive. Finally, she agreed to let me go, sending me off with a reminder that I had to be home at a reasonable time. We had a counseling appointment down in Sacramento the next day.

Counseling. Ugh. It plagued my mind the entire time I got ready. I was nervous and antsy about going under hypnosis. The last thing I wanted was for my nightmares to intensify. I grabbed my laptop and headed up to the pool to wait for my friends. I couldn't think of a better way to take my mind off of the appointment than checking my emails and messages before I left for the weekend.

I decided to start with social media. I saw notifications that I had been tagged in a bunch of photos. When I followed the link to see what they were, it took me to the Jefferson Roundup page. I'd almost forgotten Kaitlyn told me about those. Remembering I had an account, she must've just tagged me in them. I loved seeing the pictures of my friends competing. The candid of the boys after saddle cow was priceless. Brody had taken one for the team as the cow had relieved himself down the side of his head. The cameraman was clearly in the right place at the right time to catch that one.

It was a lot of fun reliving the memories of that night. Fun until I saw the close-up of Mason and me standing side by side on the rung of the fence. A lump began to form in my throat as I clicked the forward arrow. Picture after picture of us during the awards ceremony came into view, and I was tagged in every one of them. I swallowed the lump as I thought back on the conversation I'd had with my mother just an hour ago. I had promised her that Mason and I wouldn't be seen together in public. Yet there we were in full color, smiling for the camera.

What would happen if the wrong person saw those photos? My parents would definitely find out that we had been together at the rodeo. As I studied the images, I realized we were recognizable to anyone. I could've kicked myself for being so careless. I nearly started hyperventilating as I reviewed the pictures of Mason and me.

I had to fix it but had no idea how to get them off of there. Searching for what to do, my eyes were drawn to the likes. There weren't too many, so I dared to hope that I was okay. As I clicked on them one by one, I scanned the people who had reacted to the pictures. Most of the likers were my friends. Except for one. As I went back and checked each picture, I saw his face at the bottom of each list. The same face I had laughed at a few days ago for his odd fashion sense. The guy that had friend requested me, the one with the furry hat.

Jumping when I heard the gravel crunch beside the pool, I slammed the lid of my laptop and looked up to see my friends. Trying to cover my unease, I took a deep breath, swallowed and worked to slow my heart rate, but my voice came out a little fast and squeaky. Assuring my friends that I was fine, I rose to my feet and told them we'd better get moving.

The ride to the ranch was mostly a blur. I tried to crack jokes about some lame bet the boys made to get Kaitlyn to jump from the bridge and how it was never going to happen. I hope my words made sense. The jokes were all I could do to distract from the fact that my thoughts were a million miles away, tormented by the possibilities of what mine and Mason's exposure might mean for our families.

At some point during the drive, my stomach did a few extra somersaults when Kaitlyn mentioned that I needed to take a look at the pictures she'd tagged me in and that she'd also added me to the swim team page as an administrator. She seemed so happy about sharing the benefits of social media with me that I couldn't tell her to remove the tags and take me off the stupid swim page. It was a good thing we were pulling up to the bridge. I needed a minute to think. To figure a good way out of this mess without exposing my past. The Woodleys meant way too much to me. As dangerous as it was to have me as a friend, I didn't want to lose them. I wasn't about to say or do anything to scare them away.

I made my way down the steep slope of the hill and slipped into the cool water, watching as Caden and Brody worked to coax Kaitlyn off the bridge. There was something different in the way Brody was with Kaitlyn lately. Gentle, protective almost. It made me think back to the summer at camp with Ty. The way he guided me through the field. Took care of me during the scavenger hunt down at the pond. Made sure I was safe. There was a tiny pang in my chest, yearning for the magic of summer to come back. The warmth of Ty's arms. The safety of his hands.

The loud splash brought me back to reality. Brody had actually gotten Kaitlyn to take the leap. As they resurfaced together, their silhouettes appeared in the moonlight, so close I could barely tell where one ended and the other began. I almost swore they were about to kiss when Caden came up behind them. The shadows quickly parted, and I knew it was time to go. Time to have a private chat with Mason. I had no idea how to make it happen, but if I was going to keep my sanity, I needed his help. There was no way around it.

Nervously, I popped off with jokes the entire way to the ranch.

For some reason, my friends weren't laughing. Either there was something going on that I wasn't aware of, or my uneasiness had stripped me of my usual wittiness. As we slowed down, the gravel road lit by the glowing windows of the old ranch house came into view. Hiding the fact that I'd been here before I asked, "Is this it?"

In reality, not much had changed. It was just as we'd left it six years earlier.

Mason bounced up to the truck, smiling, as he greeted Brody and Caden. They exchanged a few words before he started giving orders on how to get out to the field. There was a four-wheeler and Ranger available to get all of us across the wide expanse and over to the river. I pretended I was excited that Brody and Kaitlyn would be riding solo on the four-wheeler, but I really needed to catch a private ride with Mason. Plastering on my fake charm and flirty humor, I jokingly sidled up against him and whispered in his ear, "We need to talk. Bad."

Mason winked at me and then looked to Caden, "Hey, pal, would you mind sitting in the back to hold the gear? Can't seem to find my bungees."

Thank God he was a quick thinker. Being out at the ranch, a flood of memories had my terrors resurfacing. I could almost feel my eleven-year-old-self, huddled on the floorboard watching the flames as they engulfed my home, driving for hours to safety, and finally ending up at this very place. The memory reminded me now more than ever of why I was such a mess. How could I have exposed us like that? Was it worth it?

I was practically trembling by the time Mason sat down beside me. The dipping of his seat slid me into him. "Are you okay?"

"Not really."

"Just a few more minutes and we can talk," he looked down at me as he whispered. As he turned the key, the engine roared to life. It was a hearty buzz. The loudness of it would surely mute what I had to say to him. There was no way Caden could hear us when I began to speak.

"I did something really stupid," I finally spoke.

"Something stupid, huh?"

"Really stupid." I took a deep breath. "I opened a social media account."

"Seriously, Jenna? Why'd you go and do something like that?"

I watched as he looked away. His shoulders raised and lowered as he took in and exhaled a deep breath. "Tell me more."

"I guess I wasn't thinking straight. I didn't think anyone would know it was me, I guess. I just felt isolated. Left out. And I wanted to see the pictures."

"Pictures?"

"Of us at the Roundup."

"Us? As in us?" He pointed back and forth between himself and me.

I nodded silently.

"Jesus, Jenna. You're kidding me. There's a picture of us together?"

"That's why I needed to talk to you."

He took a deep breath. "Show me."

I took out my phone as Mason pulled over. "Hey Caden, I'm gonna need you to grab that wheel line and push it against the fence for me. It's blocking the gate.

"A little help, lazy ass?" he chuckled.

"You can handle it. It doesn't take too much muscle. Anyway, the Ranger's pulling funny and I'm gonna take a look while you're moving it."

Thankfully, Caden didn't question him further and headed out toward the wheel line.

He looked back at me. "Show me, quick."

I opened my page and showed him all of the tags.

"JB Spring?" he laughed. "Is this you?"

"Yeah."

"Don't worry. You kind of look like a little boy here," he joked. "Nobody who doesn't know you is going to think this is you."

"So, you're not worried."

"Not from looking at this picture. Your catcher's mask is blocking everything but your eyes. It doesn't even have your name. We're fine."

I took a deep breath as I studied my JB Spring page. I didn't even remember what had me so worked up in the first place. I guess the fact that I broke my parents' rules had me on edge. "So, we're still safe?"

"Jenna, I've had to sacrifice my dad almost my whole life for our safety. That has to be worth something. I know he's still working hard on his end to keep us hidden and protected. He's not going to let anything happen to us."

"Are you sure?"

"I promise."

Right as I tucked my phone back in my pocket, Caden walked up behind us, "Did you get it fixed?"

"Yes, sir. Everything is just fine." Mason looked at me and winked. "Do me a favor, Caden. Tell this girl to relax. It's all fixed now. She's freaking out about nothing."

"You heard him, Jenna. Now let's get over to that river."

The rest of the night brought peace to my social media stress. Knowing I was safe, allowed me to take my mind off my worries and help Kaitlyn with hers. We got to spend the time we needed to heal our earlier tension and talk about upcoming homecoming plans. We chatted a bit about Pistol, and then moved on to the feelings I saw developing between Brody and her. A little later in the evening, it was clear that Caden had also picked up on those feelings and he wasn't happy about it. The boys bickered and baited each other all night, which was rather entertaining to watch. It wasn't until Mason noticed I was stoking the fire with poison oak, that the two boys let up and we all went home. But, that's a different story.

Chapter Thirteen

Revelations

IT WAS ALMOST UNBEARABLE THE ITCHING I ENDURED ON THE RIDE down to Sacramento. Despite the blisters that were forming on my face from inhaling the poison oak, my mom insisted that I wasn't going to miss that appointment. The dreams had resurfaced, and I was finally at the age when we might be able to figure out more about them. Trying to distract myself from the impending doom of hypnosis, I hid in the backseat scrolling through JB's page to see what was happening in the world of Jefferson High.

It was homecoming week and there were a lot of photos to look at. Many were of my classmates building the senior float down at Nora's ranch. From the looks of my news feed, Peyton was developing a little something for Caden. It was obvious that he was the prime subject of her homecoming album. Every picture she posted had him front and center. Caden holding a paintbrush. Caden dressed up for Duck Dynasty day. Caden's jersey number. The Caden photos went on and on. That's all he needed. To hook up with one of the founding members of the kitty crew.

As I continued scrolling, there was a notification that Chelsea was going live. I clicked on the banner and put my earbuds in to watch intently. From the looks of it, she was gunning to take Brody to the homecoming dance. Watching the news feed of her talking with Tiara made my blood pressure rise instantly. I'd been hoping for days that Brody was Kaitlyn's chance to finally break free of Pistol, but when Chelsea held up the animal print bra she planned on having him autograph, I figured my plan was ruined.

I continued to watch the video when my eyes were drawn to the background. Ty had just walked behind the float and stopped to talk to the sweet flag girl whose name I couldn't remember. He was shaking his head, no. From their movements, he seemed to be politely declining her invitation to the dance. That's when one of the football players appeared beside him, looking as though he was giving Ty a hard time. The live video stopped. I couldn't believe Chelsea's timing. She'd left me on a cliffhanger. I stared at my phone wanting more. I needed to know what I was missing.

Over and over, I replayed the video to see if I could hear what Ty was saying, but his words were barely audible. After several attempts at re-watching, I could almost make out, "Not afraid of a challenge." Instantly, my thoughts raced back to the day at the locker room. The day I was caught on my hands and knees, spying on Ty.

Did he really just say he wasn't afraid of a challenge? Or was I rearranging his words into something I was hoping to hear? Either way, the heat rose in my cheeks.

"We're here," my mom turned and looked over the seat as I closed the app on my phone. "Are you ready?"

"You know how I feel about this, Mom. I hate what it does to me. I'm scared the nightmares are going to get worse. Do you think you can come in the room this time?"

"Well, honey, you're old enough now to make your own decision about that. I can go in with you if you want me to."

Knowing my mom would be by my side made me feel a little more at ease. It had always just been me and my counselor trying to make sense of what I was seeing and feeling. Maybe if my mom could actually hear the details of my memories or dreams during a session, she would be able to make connections. Connections that perhaps I wasn't able to make because I was so young when these nightmares started happening.

We trudged our way into Dr. Isabelle's office. Greeted by the warm chocolate walls and the smell of peppermint, I plopped down on the couch and threw my arms around my waist. My anxiety began to intensify as I thought back on the last time I was there. I was eleven then. Right before we left Napa. All I could think at that moment was here we go again. I was glad my friends didn't know I was crazy and my mom had come up with that adoption passport stuff to cover for the insanity that was Jenna Bailey.

As I sat and waited for the receptionist to call my name, my mind spun through all the nightmares. I wondered if anything new was going to surface. Perhaps something that my subconscious had chosen to forget? As I dug through the files of my memory searching for anything that could be causing my nightmares, my mind stopped. Followed by my heart. I realized I had a secret that I didn't want to be revealed. Not in front of my mother anyway. It was my social media page. The new worry began to eat at me. Maybe I wouldn't let myself fully go under. Or maybe I would un-invite my mom to the session. I had to protect myself. I didn't know how I was going to go through with it.

It was too late to think about it. My name was being called and it was time to go back to the leather couch. My mom stood up beside me and asked if I still wanted her to go. It took me a second before I agreed to let her come along. When we got in the room, I sat down and started talking with my therapist. We talked about what I'd been up to since we last met. How things were going with school. With friends. Before long, I was completely at ease with my counselor friend.

"So are you ready to relax and talk a little more about these dreams of yours?" she asked after we caught up. I nodded as I reclined on the couch with my mom sitting in the chair next to me.

Dr. Isabelle began telling me a story about the beautiful vineyards of my childhood. Before long I was in a completely relaxed state and ready to talk.

"Do you see it?" I heard her voice. "Just over there? Do you see the house?"

Nodding, I looked over to the big, brick castle. I found myself pulling out from behind the barrel and making my way toward the heavy, wooden doors. Not wanting anyone to know I was there, I padded across the dirt path, tiptoed up the stairway, cracked open the door and snuck inside. I was in awe. It was just like I'd remembered it. The big, beautiful kitchen, the shiny floor, and the castle cookie jar. Even the familiar voices traced their way down the hall and found their way into the kitchen. I heard the music playing in the background and the laughter of my friends seeping through the walls of the playroom.

"What do you see?" I heard Dr. Isabelle's voice.

"I'm back there. Back at the castle. Standing near the vineyard. I hear my friends playing. I can hear the party music. I even see the castle cookie jar." I giggled, "I still want one."

"Go ahead. You can get one. Nobody can see you. You're safe. Untouchable."

Her reassurance allowed me to cross the floor and make my way to the island. I'd never actually made it to the jar in my dreams, but I was older now. Bigger. Stronger. Braver. If I was ever going to make it, this was the time. I was just about to reach for the jar when I heard scuffling and looked across the room. I flinched at the shock of his sudden appearance.

"It's okay, Jenna. You look a little surprised. Can you tell me what has your attention?" Dr. Isabelle's soft voice entered the scene.

I shook my head, not wanting to make a sound, then drew my finger to my mouth to quiet her. The last thing I wanted was for him to hear me. I'd spent my whole life hiding from him. I couldn't believe I was stupid enough to cross the floor in the open. How could I have let her lead me there?

"Remember, you're invisible. Nobody can see or hear you. You can talk to me. You're safe."

Though her voice seemed loud enough to wake the dead, he didn't seem to notice. Maybe she was telling the truth. Everything felt so real, appeared so vivid, but maybe she really couldn't see or hear me. Ready to make a run for it if necessary, I cleared my throat. Yet it didn't seem to affect the scene playing out near the wall.

"Talk to me, Jenna. What are you looking at?"

Again, I cleared my throat. "I see *him*. He's just there, against the wall." I pointed toward the kitchen wall. The one that held the door that led to the outside. "He's got her with him. They're arguing about something."

"Do you recognize either of them? The man? The woman?"

"I can't see either of their faces. His back is turned to me. He's blocking her face."

"Jenna, you know you're safe, right? They can't see you."

I nodded.

"I want you to walk across the floor so you can see who they are."

Typically, I wouldn't have been that brave, but the way Dr. Isabelle spoke to me, had me relaxed and at ease. I slowly left my place behind the big island and made my way across the floor. As I walked, the intensity between the man and lady grew. The arguing turned to silence as he pushed against her, slamming her into the wall. "Stop!" I screamed, but he continued his assault.

"Are you okay? Is he hurting you?"

"It's not me. It's her."

"Who, Jenna? Can you see their faces?"

"I need to get closer."

Tiptoeing across the room, I approached the outside doorway. As I stood shielding myself with the thick, velvety curtain, a vision of me running from Nikolai flashed through my thoughts. That's right, I remembered. Nikolai lived here. We used to play hide and seek in this wing of the castle. I looked again around the big room. The voices were still bouncing through the hall. Laughter. My friends. I looked back over at the cookie jar, and then down at my tights and ruffly dress. What in the world was I doing in that dress? I would never hear the end of it if Kaitlyn saw me like that.

A thud drew my attention back over to the two figures moving awkwardly against the dark wall. It was then that I realized what I was watching. It was the same scene from my nightmare. The night of the big dinner party. The one where our parents got all dressed up and talked about wine and other things I really had no idea about. They sent us all out to the playroom. Me. Nikolai. And our other friend. Mason. It was Mason. He was there. At the party.

"Jenna, what is it? What are you looking at?"

"I think I'm in Russia."

I heard Dr. Isabelle talking, but it wasn't to me. Whatever it was, it wasn't important. Her voice faded into the background as I focused my attention on the couple. I could see her face now. Her round, tear-filled eyes pleaded with him to stop. Her shiny, brown hair flowed over her shoulders. She was a beautiful, petite woman. Her flawless skin was the color of peaches. She seemed so familiar, yet I couldn't place her. I studied her face, trying to make sense of why it looked so familiar.

Fixating on her pink lips, straight white teeth, and trembling voice, her face suddenly jerked from view. He stepped in front of her once again, blocking her from my vision. His breathing deepened as his figure began to move wildly. There was garbled mumbling, a soft cry, more scuffling, and a bone-chilling snap. Instantly, the beautiful woman fell to the floor.

Again, I screamed in horror and tried to run to her. To help her. Stronger, braver than I ever thought I could be, I jumped in front of him and yelled, "Leave her alone!" He walked over the top of me, dragging her lifeless body straight through me.

"Stop this!" I heard my mom's voice in the distance. "Stop this now! Look at her."

"One more minute. Give her another minute."

"Jenna, tell me what you're seeing."

"It's him. The man in the black gloves. He's dragging her out of the kitchen. She's not moving!"

"Dragging her? The lady? Do you know him? Can you see where he's taking her?"

"I don't know who he is. No matter how hard I try, I can't see his face, only those black gloves. But he's trying to take her to the alley. He's having a hard time. The fringe on her dress is caught on the door jam."

"Remember you're safe. They can't see you. Go to them. See if you can get a closer look."

I stood over the top of her limp figure, taking a deep breath before I dared to peek down at her once more. She was still stunning, even in her lifeless state. "She's gorgeous. Tiny. Dainty like a sprite, except with soft features. Look at her chiffon dress. It's embellished with sparkly silver beads. It shimmers like a disco ball." I kneeled and tried to hold onto her wrist to see if I could find a pulse. When my fingers slipped through the phantom image, I noticed a braided band. It was a rugged bracelet that was in stark contrast to the outfit she was wearing.

"Weird."

"What's weird, Jenna?"

"It doesn't go with her outfit. She's dressed so elegantly, but her bracelet just doesn't match."

"You can see her bracelet? Can you describe it?"

"It looks like something you'd find at the county fair. Not something you'd wear to a dinner party at a castle." I studied her bracelet until it slipped from view. "He's moving her again."

"I'm going to give you a pad of paper, Jenna," Dr. Isabelle spoke. "I want you to sketch the bracelet before you forget what it looks like."

That would be easy, I thought to myself. It looks just like the brand out at Mason's ranch. Nonetheless, I took the pad of paper and effortlessly sketched the two crescent moons, one perpendicular to the other.

When I handed the pad back to Dr. Isabelle, a gasp and a whisper sounded from the corner of the room. "I know that bracelet." It was my mom's voice.

"Olivia." There was a pause. "Oh, my God. This makes so much sense. She was there. She saw. This isn't a dream. Wake her up. Wake her up. Now! She can't see this."

"Cinda, whatever she's looking at has already happened. It's trapped inside of her mind and we've got to get it out so we can work through it. Trust me on this. We've got to let her finish."

"Jenna, you said he's moving her. Can you see where they're going?"

I shook my head. "I don't want to follow them. I already know where he took her. I hate it down there."

"How do you know where they went?"

"I watched him take her there last time."

"Last time?"

"The night of the party. I followed him. Nobody knew. I didn't tell anyone. I thought that's why we were hiding. If I told anyone what I saw, I knew he'd find me and I'd end up just like her."

"Just like her?"

"Down in the cellar. Stuffed in the wine barrel."

Chapter Fourteen

Covering Our Trail

I T WAS A CRAZY WEEK LEADING UP TO HOMECOMING. BETWEEN THE intense sessions with Dr. Isabelle and my parents sneaking off to the den for private talks and phone calls with Isaiah, my mind was wrecked. I had no idea that all those years my nightmare was a real memory, trapped, and screaming to be heard. I had actually witnessed the murder of Mason's mother. It was a revelation for all of us, and as desperately as they'd tried to solve the mystery of her disappearance, not even my dad or Isaiah had known about Olivia's last moments.

Working with my parents and therapist, we pieced our memories together to make a complete picture of a very real, shared nightmare. There was a small crowd that night at the vineyard castle. All the ladies were dressed in heels and gowns, scattered about the room sipping champagne, while the men sat around the table smoking cigars, talking about how and where they were going to bootleg the wine. They were negotiating a deal I couldn't begin to understand. Not that any of us kids were given the chance to listen.

We were all sent to the playroom. While I found my way to the heirloom nesting dolls that stood about my height, Mason and Nikolai messed around with his Polaroid camera. They laughed and laughed as they took shot after shot of me climbing in and out of the dolls, moving about in my party clothes. They thought it was hilarious that my mom had dressed me in ruffles and lace. They'd never seen me wear anything but overalls and tennis shoes, clothes I could play ball and throw knives in.

"Very funny, boys!" I grunted as Nikolai handed me a stack of pictures, topped with one of my bloomered bottom crawling into the sarcophagus-like doll. I rolled my eyes, annoyed as I fanned through the ridiculous photos. Then to hide them from the light of day, I stuffed them inside one of the dolls. Boys. They could be very obnoxious if you hung around them too long. I needed to get out of the playroom so they'd stop taking my picture. That's when I decided to go get one of the cookies from the castle jar.

Meanwhile, over in the ballroom, drinks were flowing, the music was getting louder, and voices were beginning to permeate the walls of the castle. Some happy and laughing, others not so much. As the party escalated, my mom noticed Olivia wasn't around. Wanting to include her in the conversation with the other wives, she went to ask Isaiah if he'd seen her. That's when they began looking. At first, they thought she'd simply gotten swept up in the crowd, but as more time passed Isaiah became frantic. Olivia had been gone far longer than she should have been. She wasn't answering her phone and she wasn't in any of the common areas. He knew disappearing in the midst of the company they were keeping meant something was seriously wrong. Those were dangerous people who knew how to get anything and everything they wanted.

That's why Isaiah was there in the first place. He was working undercover on a bust. His knowledge was limited, so he had reached out to an old friend, my father, for his expertise in the wine business. His sole purpose was to work alongside the head winemaker, Sergei Vasiliev, known to me as Nikolai's dad. My dad's work with Sergei would allow Isaiah access to inside information, and help legitimize his involvement at the vineyard. The government paid my father a handsome sum of money to assist Isaiah and help keep his cover. Though they told him the job came with a risk, and the less he knew the better, it was more dangerous than he could have imagined. Little did he know that it was no minor sting. He was actually working within the Russian mafia.

Perhaps Isaiah's cover was blown that night. Maybe not. Either way, he knew if we remained in Russia, Olivia wasn't the only loved one who would disappear. With little time to explain that we were in imminent danger, he pulled my dad to the side and told him the job was over, to collect Mason and our family and leave through the cellar exit. While we packed into the car and sped away, Isaiah continued to race through the hallways of the castle in search of his wife.

We took Mason with us that night, to the safety of his grandparents. At the time, we had no idea that my dad's connection with Isaiah would have led to such a large target on all our backs. Especially mine and Mason's. Isaiah stayed back, working to find Olivia and protect us by covering our trail. Despite his best efforts, he never found her. At least after my revelation, he would know the truth. I could give him that much.

As I sat thinking through our therapy sessions, I finally understood my past. Why I had to live like I did. Why I had to change my name. Why we had to hide. Stay off social media. Why I couldn't be like my friends. The secrets. It was all for our protection. It made so much sense after therapy. After the nightmare revealed itself as reality.

I'd always been resentful when I should've been grateful. Grateful for my safety and the fact that my family was still a family. My suffering was minimal compared to what the Brooks had endured. Mason had tragically lost his mother at the age of nine and was ultimately handed over to his grandparents for all our safety. He knew why his father was never around. Not because he didn't want to be, but because he couldn't be. He never complained about the hand he'd been dealt. I had so much respect for him. For his sacrifice.

Pondering everything Mason had gone through, I felt foolish about my resentment toward my situation. Because I'd fully learned about my past and how lucky I was to exist, I was finally at peace. I was ready to move on and become the person my parents and the Brooks family had allowed me to be. For the first time since I could remember, I felt like embracing the creation of Jenna Bailey. I was ready to close the door on my old life. There was no need to ever look back. It was time to take full advantage of the gift I'd been given. The gift of freedom to live in the safety and wide-open spaces of Jefferson County.

Chapter Fifteen
I Don't Dance

I PULLED UP TO MY HOUSE AND RAN IN TO GRAB EVERYTHING I NEEDED to get ready. I'd been so busy with therapy, training, and embracing my new life, that I hadn't made many plans for Homecoming. I was still hung up on Ty, and even though he'd accepted a blind date with some girl from the valley, I couldn't wait for the dance. It was my chance to show him I wasn't into Daemon and he missed out by believing that silly rumor.

After avoiding the nightmares for nearly two weeks, I felt and looked alive again, glowing even. I wanted to debut the new me, and maybe if I was lucky, steal a dance or two away from that valley girl.

The anticipation of the evening was killing me. That hadn't been the case until recently. When I heard Ty was going with someone else, I almost considered ditching Homecoming altogether. But once the spirit of homecoming week actually arrived, I was thankful I'd gone dress shopping with Kaitlyn. Standing in front of the mirror, I held up the flowing, coral gown with the heart-shaped bodice. It was the absolute perfect dress to catch his eye. I was thankful Kaitlyn decided not to buy it, though I knew she was going to look hot as hell in her little, black dress. I'd make sure to fix her up so she out-shined her slimy date, Pistol. He wasn't worthy of her, and I was determined to make sure he and everyone else knew it.

Checking the clock reminded me that I was due at her house. I sprinted out the door, yelling to my mom that we would send her pictures of us getting ready. I felt a little bad to skip the whole pre-homecoming photo shoot, but seeing as I didn't have a date, and she'd likely drop in as a staff chaperone later, I was okay with it. There was no time to waste. I tossed my dress in the back seat of my VW Beetle, along with my huge Barbie case of makeup. It was going to be tricky to cover up the last of our remaining poison oak rashes, but I had full confidence that after my last trip to Ulta, I could do it.

I had to be there with my best friend on such an important night. We both had something to prove. She wanted Pistol to see her the way he saw all his rodeo princesses, and I wanted Ty to notice me as more than the rookie camp counselor and the jockette in a ponytail. He crossed my mind a million times as I straightened and curled Kaitlyn's hair and moved onto mine. I could barely contain my smile as I thought about the way his mouth curled into a grin when he caught me spying on him in the locker room, and the way he could barely look away last summer when he helped me escape from the lifeguard stand. Remembering the feeling of his warm fingers against my skin shot a tingly burst of adrenaline through my chest.

"You're awfully quiet tonight. Everything okay?"

"Great!" I piped in a little too enthusiastically.

"You've been a little … distant lately. Like your mind's a million miles away. Are you sure?"

It was true I'd been a bit secretive and even distant. I hadn't let Kaitlyn in on anything I'd gone through. I knew I could never tell her about Olivia or Mason. Not that I would, even if I could. I'd closed the door on all that days ago, and I wanted to leave it shut, sealed, and barricaded for the rest of eternity. I dismissed the fleeting image of a chained, Russian castle door. It wasn't the reason I was being quiet anyway. I had one thing on my mind, and one thing only.

"Just been thinking about someone."

"Someone … Really? Could this someone be the center on the football team?"

I took a deep breath. "How'd you know?"

"Seriously?" she laughed, "You blush every time you're within a fifty-foot radius of the guy."

Thinking about Ty leaning up against his gym locker as he caught sight of me down on my knees had my hormones jumping again. I still couldn't help but wonder if his friends knew I was there. My throat went dry. "Let's not talk about it, okay?"

"Okay." Looking a bit disappointed, she pulled her lips together. For a brief moment, she opened her mouth as though she was ready to say something but closed it again. We sat silently for a second until she finally decided to speak up. "Hey, listen," her voice was soft. "I'm not trying to be an ass by reminding you, but in the dressing room, didn't we hear that Ty's going with Pistol's roping partner, CJ?"

I nodded, fully aware that Ty had another date. But from the sounds of the dressing room talk, she wasn't going for him anyway. Agreeing to a blind date with my crush was just an underhanded way to get to Kaitlyn's two-timing boyfriend. I had been gushing over him for months. There was no way I was going to let a blind date with some calf roper get in my way. Even if she was rodeo royalty.

The fact that my best friend and I needed to knock out the same girl lit a fire in me. I was going to bring my A game and help Kaitlyn bring hers too. I finished painting my lips a berry pink, then pinched them together before finalizing them with a loud pop. "Perfect," I smiled. "Game on."

Her eyes widened. "You do look smokin' hot. Do you have a

plan?" Kaitlyn's eyebrows danced menacingly on her forehead.

"Shh." I pulled my finger to my newly, plumped lips. "I don't want to jinx it."

Taking one final glance in the mirror, it seemed we were set. Kaitlyn's hair was in long, blonde waves that stood in beautiful contrast to her little, black dress. Though she didn't know it, she'd been perfectly designed to outshine her slithery boyfriend.

I shimmered in my bedazzled, flowing, coral gown. My long, loose, curls cascaded over my shoulders, hitting me just above the small of my back. I had to say, it was the best hair and makeup I'd ever given myself. I was nearly unrecognizable without my running clothes, athletic gear, and my hair tied back.

We were taking turns straightening each other's dresses and snapping a few photos when we heard voices down the hall. As much as I didn't want to see his face, I knew it was time to hand my best friend over to that snake of a cowboy. All I could do was hope for kindness. I didn't want to see my Kaitlyn hurt, but something told me with Pistol, hurt was inevitable.

I thanked the Woodleys for letting me get ready at their house, stopped on the front porch to snap a selfie for my mom, and then jumped in the VW. Turning up my jam on KSYC country radio, I sped away from Kaitlyn's and headed straight to the gym.

I was blown away as I stepped through the doors of the lobby. The decorating committee had transformed the entire gymnasium into a football stadium. Stepping onto the green AstroTurf, I scanned the room hoping to see Ty. No luck. It was still early. Even the DJ was still setting up.

As I sat down on one of the benches that had been brought in from the field, my belly began to grumble. It reminded me that I hadn't eaten dinner. With no date to worry about, I hadn't even thought about eating. I guess that was one downfall of going stag. I wasn't into doing the whole five-star dining thing alone, so I opted out altogether. Again, my stomach grumbled as I headed over to the food table. Scanning the spread, there wasn't a lot of substance there. Some juice, chips, and a few plates of cheese and crackers. Just as I readied my hand to dive into a helmet of nachos, I felt someone brush by me.

"I zee you're here a little early," he whispered over my shoulder.

I closed my eyes and gulped as I turned around to see our exchange student. Noticing that he'd worn the same form-fitting tux he'd donned for the homecoming court, I tried to shake the image of Willy Wonka standing before me. It must've been a French thing. Haute couture for men, I supposed. Forcing a smile, I reminded myself to be nice. It wasn't his fault that his wish had turned into the rumor that kept me from being there with Ty. I had to forgive him. After all, the poor kid was in a new country with no friends, and sadly alone at his only American homecoming dance.

"Hey, Daemon. I see you made it to the homecoming dance."

"Wouldn't mizz it for zee world."

As much as some poked fun at it, I found his accent kind of endearing. Not that I would've ever admitted that to anyone.

"You're here early too, huh?"

"Well, I helped decorate and wanted to zee people'z reactionz. Do you like it?"

"It's fantastic." My belly grumbled again.

Daemon's eyes widened as the groan of my stomach penetrated the room. "Are you zure these chipz are enough for you? It'z ztill early. We could go grab zomezing. Pizza?"

Pizza actually sounded perfect. It was quick, close by, and I knew it would give us plenty of time to get back to the dance before the crowd rolled in and the party picked up.

"Why not?" I grinned. "How does TJ's sound?"

"Oh, TJ'z! I love zheir taco pizza. And zhey have my favorite eightiez video gamez. We can play while we wait. I have a boatload of tokenz." He shoved his hand in his pants pocket and jingled some coins. "I'll pay if you drive." It didn't take any more thought.

I was always up for TJ's pizza. Especially if somebody else was willing to foot the bill.

Daemon really was a strange character. As soon as we jumped into my car he began fiddling around under the passenger's seat. Apparently, the tokens had slipped from his pocket when he squeezed his six-foot-something frame into my tiny VW. As he alternated between digging under the seat and shoving his hand back in his pant pocket I had to ask, "Is everything alright down there?"

"Zhust gazering my coinz."

"I could pull over and help if you need me to."

He chuckled. "Oh, no. It'z all taken care of now. Let'z go eat."

After we ordered, he took me on a tour of the arcade. Jingling the coins in his pocket, he playfully pulled me toward Ms. Pac-Man. "Play me?" he asked excitedly. He stood on the left, tugging me into his right side. I died in no time flat. His game continued. He made it all the way to the melons before he insisted that I took over his joystick. That's where I solidified my lack of aptitude in the gaming world. I was eaten by the ghosts almost as quickly as I took over.

Next, we jogged to Missile Command. "You zhould probably juzt watch zis one," he winked. Intensity grew in his eyes as I watched him target and shoot. Destroy. Kill. "Record time!" he cheered, "My dad would be pizzed! I zhink I just pummeled hiz top zcore!" I couldn't help but giggle at his enthusiasm for the shooting game and how he was so happy to beat his dad.

By the time he was done blowing everything to smithereens, my heels were taking their toll on my inexperienced feet. "Are you ready to sit down yet?"

"One more! Zhis one'z my favorite," he grinned as he pulled me over to Pole Position.

"Zit with me. It'z fun." He patted the seat as I squished in beside him. "I had zhis one when I was little."

I gazed at him incredulously. "You had the sit-down arcade Pole Position?"

"My parentz were ... buzy. Zhey kept me entertained wiz big toyz." He tilted his head and smiled, "Buckle up!"

After dropping the coins into the slot, the game began. Again, his vision was glued to the screen. It was quite a sight, his large frame squeezed into the compartment that held the driver's seat. Though I was basically on his lap smashed up next to him, it wasn't quite as awkward as I thought it would be. He smelled nice enough, and my focus was more on the screen and my aching feet than his crazy tux and odd accent. I had to hand it to him, he was pretty coordinated, zipping around all of the obstacles at top speed. "Anozer top zcore!" he laughed as he pulled through the finish line. It was kind of cute how excited he got over the video games. In the end, he turned out to be one hell of an eighties gamer.

Dinner wasn't too bad either. The pizza was delicious as always, and once I got past the accent, Daemon was pretty decent company. Unlike my other guy pals who basically talked sports scores and which player was being traded to which team that month, all of Daemon's questions showed interest in me. My childhood, my life at school, where I'd been, where I wanted to go after graduation.

He made it so easy to open up that I had to remind myself that certain pieces of my childhood must remain dead and buried. It took a little sidestepping and creative thinking, but aside from the little, white lie about being born and raised in the great State of Jefferson, our chat centered on my post-Napa life. He almost looked confused when I told him I'd always lived there. Maybe I wasn't the best liar, but it was the best I could do to avert his line of questioning. The conversation moved on quickly when I tried to shift the focus to him.

"Turnabout is fair play. Tell me about your childhood."

"Boring. Like I zaid earlier, my parentz were very buzy. I played with a lot of big toyz," he smiled. "Enough about me, I want to know about you," he filled his mouth with pizza and stopped chewing only long enough to say, "I'm here to learn about America. If you want to know about me, you'll juzt have to come vizit me in my country."

I laughed, "Fair enough."

By the time we left for the dance, I felt like I'd been visiting an old friend. Surprisingly, I'd genuinely enjoyed my chat with him. He was a good listener with questions I'd never been asked. What were the challenges of having a mom as a teacher? How did I get involved in so many sports? What were my favorite vacation spots, the places I'd traveled and sights I'd seen? He was especially fascinated by my life at the vineyard. He hoped I would give him a tour, so he could see a real-life American vineyard before he went back to France. The conversation flowed so easily, it was oddly refreshing. As we drove back to the dance, I thought maybe he was going to make an okay friend after all.

"Zave a danze for me?" he asked as we re-entered the gym.

Not wanting to give him the wrong impression, I quickly answered. "Check with me in a while. The guy I'm supposed to meet might not be willing to give all this up." I winked as I raised my hands in the air and twirled around in a circle.

"You've got a point," he winked as he bowed his head toward me and walked off into the distance.

I watched him for a minute as he made his way back toward the drink table. About mid-gym I caught sight of Kaitlyn dancing with Pistol. She looked super stiff and uncomfortable. I decided to run over to see if she needed help escaping his tentacles. Choosing to shock her away from his evil grasp, I ran up behind her and poked her sides. "Gotcha!" I laughed. "So, are you having fun yet?"

She looked at me like I already knew the answer. I had to save her. "Hey, Pistol, I heard someone spiked the punch." I knew he'd go check it out if alcohol was involved. When he looked toward the kitty crew gathered around the large thermoses, he grinned, "Be back in few."

I listened to Kaitlyn as I eyed the slimy creep making his way toward the large, yellow cooler. Daemon had made his way over there too. He was near the food table when I saw Pistol lean into him. I hoped he wasn't being an ass, making fun of his suit or something. I was of a mind to walk over there and tell him to back off when I noticed the two of them looking friendly. Pistol filled a cup and handed it to him. They were laughing.

My focus didn't stay on the two of them long. My eyes were drawn to Pistol's roping partner, CJ, the girl who managed to lasso my crush for the night. She definitely wasn't giving Ty the same kind of attention she was giving Pistol. I felt the angry heat radiating between my best friend and me as we watched her ride Pistol's thigh like a mechanical bull.

After a few minutes, he slithered back to where we were standing. He had a cup of punch for Kaitlyn and a phony story about how long the line was. I sensed she was done with his line of crap and was ready to let him have it when I heard "Pop, Lock, and Drop It" blaring over the speakers.

The crowd poured onto the dance floor. When I saw a solo Ty moving with it, I couldn't resist following him out. Pulling my attention from T, I made my way to Ty's vicinity. I had to get him to notice me among the crowd of other girls.

Watching him intently, I snapped my fingers and jumped to the beat. As loud, giggly, and bouncy as I was, he didn't seem to notice. After working that angle for a couple minutes, I knew I wasn't going to get his attention. Not without seeming desperate anyway. I needed a hook. Something that showed him I was a way better time than the rodeo queen. That's when I grabbed Caden. We'd been a dancing duo for years, and I needed him to help me get noticed.

"I need help," I held out my hand to him.

He jerked his head, "Whose ass do I need to beat?"

"Not that kind of help." I laughed. "I'm here alone. Dance with me?"

His eyes shifted to Peyton. "I'm a little busy here."

I could see he was working it with Peyton, so I knew it would take a little convincing. "Cadennnn. Tell her you'll be right back. We're going to check out those huge speakers and make sure they're safe to dance on."

He took a deep breath and rolled his eyes.

"Come on. You'll be her hero. We're gonna get the party started. You can grab her when we're done. You'll thank me for this." That time I grabbed his hand and tugged it.

He leaned into Peyton and then let me pull him out to the floor. I was thankful he caved, but still found myself trapped in a crowd of taffeta and tulle. I needed visibility.

"Lift me up!"

He laughed at my insanity but grabbed me by the waist and easily flung me onto the big, boxy speaker. When the crowd roared, he jumped up onto the speaker next to me, drawing even more attention. All eyes were on us then, and for the first of several times that evening, we found ourselves twerking for a newly energized gymnasium.

Between movements, I studied the crowd. Peyton watched with an amused smile on her face, and finally motioned Caden to come down and dance with her. Deciding maybe it was time to step aside and let somebody else have the stage, I let Caden lift me down after him. As I soared above the crowd, my gaze caught Ty's. He'd definitely been watching our show. Even at a distance, I saw his dimple pop as a smile lit his face.

Still, we continued to dance solo, keeping just enough distance to feel each other's nervous energy. From the corner of my eye, I watched as one girl after another approached him. Each time they walked away without a dance, his eyes found mine. And each time, a flirty smile lit both of our faces. I still wasn't brave enough to be one of those girls. I wasn't up for being turned away by Ty. If he wanted to dance with me, he was going to have to be the one to make it happen.

I decided to go check on Kaitlyn. She'd been away from the dance floor for a while at that point and had just come back through the lobby door. She was with Brody, and they'd asked me to request a country song for them to dance to. Pumped that she wasn't dancing with Pistol, and even more excited to get back over to those speakers, I ran to the DJ and requested "Country Girl Shake it For Me."

When the music began, so did the best show of the night. Kaitlyn and Brody twirled, whirled, and flipped their way out onto the dance floor. I'd never seen them dance like that before. The crowd was going crazy. From atop the speaker, I caught sight of Pistol watching them. His face twisted into a grimace. I continued to track him, worried about his wrath coming down on two of my best friends' heads.

Rather than staying to watch their whole show, he stormed back to the corner of the room where again, he made his way to Daemon. Dateless at Homecoming, I think he'd made it his job to monitor the food table for the night. By the looks of it, our unsuspecting exchange student got an earful. Maybe I should've danced with him. Poor guy. But, I sure did get a lot of satisfaction out of watching Pistol finally get a dose of his own medicine.

I was giddy as I watched Brody toss Kaitlyn over his shoulder and head over to the photo booth. Practically cheering, I began jumping once more on the speaker. That's when I felt his eyes on me. I knew I had his attention that time. I looked over, instantly knowing the direction where he stood. When neither of us looked away, I noticed his dimples begin to pop again. I could see them, even from a distance. His smile widened as he held my gaze, and after the longest five seconds of my life, he lifted his finger and motioned for me to come over to him. My heart just about leaped from my chest as I contemplated his invitation. Finally, I got up the nerve to walk to him. He spoke no words, but his charmingly expectant face begged me to ask him to dance.

"Shall we?" I held out my hand.

"I knew if I sent enough girls away, the right one would show up eventually." He closed his mouth and grinned. Then lifting his eyebrows, he added, "You know, Miss Jenna, I don't like to dance, but I've got a special one in me that I was saving just for you."

He took my hand and led me out to the floor where we danced and talked for what seemed like hours. For not liking to dance, the boy had moves. With the exception of the very impressive dance by Kaitlyn and Brody before they left the building, I felt like we were center stage for most of the night. Homecoming passed like a fairy-tale ball, complete with those little Fairy-Godmother sprinkles that zapped me each time he grabbed my hand and pulled me out to the dance floor. It had been a long time since I'd actually been close to him. It was almost torture knowing that when the clock struck midnight, that scene of our fairy tale would have to come to an end. I could only hope that there would be more scenes in the very near future.

Chapter Sixteen

Here's to Sister Jenna

THE REST OF THE WEEKEND PASSED WITH NO WORD FROM TY. IT seemed my fairy tale had come to an end at the stroke of midnight. So preoccupied with laughing and dancing the night away, we had missed our opportunity to exchange numbers. I looked for him at school the next week but had to resort to stalking him online. Thankfully, he'd posted something about traveling down to Stanford for his brother's insulin pump training. Hopefully, we could catch up when he got back.

So much had happened that week, that I was too preoccupied to feel the intensity of disappointment. My focus had shifted to protecting my best friend. The night of Homecoming, someone had broken into Kaitlyn's room and left her with a couple of unsettling surprises. They had taken a picture of her and Pistol from the wall, torn it up, and decapitated the teddy bear he'd won for her over the summer.

Of course, she thought it was Pistol. We all did after the way she humiliated him with hers and Brody's five-star dance performance. Everyone knew he wasn't someone to be messed with, especially not when he was drinking. Clearly, he'd been doing that a lot.

He constantly sent her crazy texts and pictures. It was to the point where none of us wanted to leave her alone.

His stalking came to a head the night of our championship swim meet. Pistol, drunk and out on the prowl, attacked her when she didn't accept his advances. Brody found her unconscious, lying in her driveway with a torn-up shoulder. I'd never seen my friends more horrified.

Since she'd been released from the hospital, all of us made it our mission to protect her. Being part of the security team kept me distracted from the fact that I hadn't seen or heard from Ty for a week. Though he was still gone from school, I thought he might try to get a hold of me. Any discouraging thoughts, in that regard, were quickly knocked out by calculus homework and the start of basketball. Our grueling fall term had come to an end.

Thankfully, the weekend had come, and it was time to cut loose at T's and Caden's birthday party. Caden and I kicked things off with a bang. His Auntie Macy and Grandma Sandy wheeled down a couple huge thermoses of apple cider to supply the party. They'd neatly labeled them "Alcoholic" and "Non-alcoholic" just to make sure there was no underage drinking. We decided to pull an innocent gag and remove the sign from the spiked cider, joking that nobody liked to be labeled an alcoholic. We figured without the signs, we had permission to drink as much as we wanted.

The cider packed a pretty good punch. By the time my first solo cup was drained, I'd gotten a bit warm and tingly inside. It was just enough of a buzz that Caden and I were at ease playing superhero without feeling stupid. We flew from the bales and chased each other in circles around the barn. When Brody and Kaitlyn finally made their appearance, we decided they were just a little too sober for an eighteenth-birthday party. We made it our job to loosen them up with the spiked apple cider.

A few cups in, I felt light headed and knew it was time to slow down. Brody had just pulled Kaitlyn to the dance floor, which gave me the break I needed to go check out the party snacks. I knew if I wanted to last all night, I needed to knock down my growing buzz.

Soaking up the alcohol with food was a great idea. My mind began to clear as I wolfed down some ribs and corn on the cob. The ever-growing crowd came and went from the table, picking at the cakes and pies. I was just about to head over to the photo booth, to visit Peyton, when I heard that voice. The only one that could put my heart on pause from twenty feet away. I looked over to see him walking through the barn door. My eyes traced his long, lean body. Boots, Wranglers, T-shirt. Ball cap. I gulped as my gaze fixed on his chiseled jaw and moved on to his perfect smile.

A firestorm of emotions began to flicker. God, he was hot. But apparently, he was uninterested. I hadn't seen or heard from him all week. Apparently, I wasn't worth the challenge after all. He could have probably messaged me online if he wanted to. He hadn't even tried. At least he hadn't caught sight of me ogling him from the food table. Not wanting to embarrass myself, I turned away and began to fill another cup of cider.

"Jenna!" I jumped as a hand came down on mine, stopping me from pulling the lever to the thermos. "I've barely zeen you zince our homecoming dinner. How are you?"

Startled, I held up my empty cup, "I'll be better once I get this filled."

"I've got zomething you might like better." He patted his backpack which seemed to be fully loaded with bottles and flasks.

"Really? Better than Auntie Macy's spiked cider?"

"Have you ever tried a, how do you call it in America, Purple Hooter?"

I couldn't help but laugh at the name. "Purple Hooter?" I took a look at the fizzy, purple liquid that flowed through the hose of his hydration pack. Then he pulled it from his lips and stuck it in my face.

I wasn't about to drink from the tube that he was sucking on. I'm sure the disgust registered on my face as he spoke again.

"Here, I haven't drunk from zhis one yet," he began to tug a silver flask from his backpack.

"Jenna, do you have a minute?"

My body ceased when a soft baritone voice wrapped itself around me from behind. Oh, hell. That voice. Unable to hold the barrel of blood that had stopped in my chest, my heart slammed to the ground. The smile fell from Daemon's lips as he caught a glimpse of Ty standing behind me.

"Zhees buzy," Daemon twitched, seemingly annoyed at the interruption.

But I couldn't help it. As rude as it was to turn my back on our conversation, I was drawn to Ty like a child to candy. Slowly, I turned around to meet his amused gaze.

"Sorry," he grinned, pointing back and forth between the two of us. "Did the two of you come here together?"

"Zo, what if we did, you zhealous?" Daemon snapped.

There was a moment of pause before he answered. "Maybe … a little." Surprised by his response, my breath hitched, leaving me speechless.

Ty watched me struggle for words when a small snicker found its way from his pinched lips. Looking back at Daemon he joked, "You're not a very good date. You missed something." He turned to grab a napkin from the table and held it to the corner of my mouth. "Here, let *me* get that for you."

His twinkling eyes studied me as he gently cleaned the barbecue sauce from my lips. "You never called."

"I was supposed to call you? You didn't give me your number."

The playful grin grew on his face. "I didn't know you wanted it."

"You should've asked."

"I'm asking now."

The flirtatious banter had my cheeks flushing when Daemon cleared his voice. "I can zee you two are buzy. I'm going to go make

130

myself vizible over zhere. Come zee me when you want to try my hooterz." He held up the silver flask as he walked out to the field and sat down on the bed of an old, green Ford. I couldn't help but notice him looking over his shoulder at us, as he continued to sip from his hose.

"You up for trying his hooterz?" Ty chuckled.

"Depends."

"Really?"

"You got something better?"

Ty looked around the barn. His eyes stopped when they landed on the stack of hay bales holding a keg. "You ever done a keg stand?"

"All the time."

He looked at me incredulously. He knew I was bluffing.

"Prove it."

"Let's go."

Ty grabbed my hand and led me over to the keg. Reeling from his unexpected touch, the effects of the spiked apple cider that had momentarily settled, began to reignite. Maybe it wasn't the alcohol. It may have been the natural high I got every time I was around him. Either way, I was ready to saddle up my partner and get phase two of the party started.

Entranced by his touch and the energy of the crowd around me, I hit a new high. I didn't care where I was or who was watching. New basketball contract or not, I was going to do anything Ty wanted to do. Looking around, I figured why not. All my classmates were doing the same thing. If one of us was going down, we were all going down together.

Ty went first. He wanted to show me how it was done. He didn't need any help. It was crazy how well he could balance on his own, almost as though he was made to stand on his hands. Next up, he handed me the tube. "Let's see what you've got."

"I'm not a gymnast like you. A little help please."

131

I put my hands on each side of the keg as Ty gently maneuvered my feet up against his shoulders. Leaning into him, I began to drink as the crowd sang, "Here's to Sister Jenna, Sister Jenna, Sister Jenna …"

By the time they'd gotten to the chugga lugga part of the song, I'd already downed more than I'd anticipated. Though I'd just filled my belly, I couldn't help but feel empty when he released me to come back to the ground. We took turns waiting in the long line. Chatting in between chugging.

"I didn't know you could drink like that."

"There's a lot you don't know about me."

"Oh, Pickle. I know more than you think."

"Tell me one thing." I paused for a moment trying to get my dizzy brain to think, "Something that's not public knowledge."

"Your hair smells like apple pie." He started to chuckle before coming in to whisper in my ear, "and sometimes you hang out on lifeguard stands … topless."

The heat rose in my face when I thought back on the night of the scavenger hunt. The night Ty had to help me out of my bralette. I laughed and smacked him playfully, "Funny."

"More like, sexy." He grinned, changing the subject almost as quickly as the words left his mouth. "Alright, last one for you. Then you've reached your limit."

"Oh, really?"

"Well, maybe it's my limit for you. But I don't need to get you out of any more pickles, Pickle. Up you go."

He grabbed my feet and propped me up again. I was snorting and giggling when I noticed an upside-down Peyton and Kaitlyn headed my way. Call me crazy. Maybe I just liked the feeling of his hands around my ankles or the way he held onto me as I rested against him, but I wasn't ready to give up that firm grip just yet.

"Hey, Jenna, come get a picture with Kaitlyn and me before you pop all the blood vessels in that beautiful face of yours." It was

Peyton. She must've thought I was getting a little too tipsy.

"Just a second, ladies," I lifted one arm and pointed toward the dance floor, hoping Ty would grab on just a little tighter. I pointed out each member of the kitty crew, cracking jokes about their armpit sweat, wedgies, and anything else I could come up with to stay next to him a little longer. By the time I ran out of people, I had worked myself into such hysterics that I finally slipped out of his arms and crashed to the ground. "Catch you in a bit." I waved at Ty before slipping my arms around the girls' necks so we could head over to get our pictures taken.

The girls and I continued the party over at the photo station. We drew quite a crowd as we did stunts, pyramids, and even took a few live action shots for the camera. I was really starting to feel the buzz when Peyton and Kaitlyn wandered away to meet their boys. I scanned the crowd looking for Ty. When I didn't see him, I slipped outside to get some air, a stone's throw away from the party. I headed over to take a seat on a bale of hay near the corrals. Sitting there, I gazed up at the night sky. All the stars seemed to have tails. Were they stars or meteors? I couldn't tell looking through my beer goggles.

"Zhere you are!" The hay crunched as he sat down beside me. "I bet you're ready to try my hooterz now."

Knowing it was the end of the night, and that was probably going to be my last drink, I gave in. "Sure, Daemon. Why not?"

Excitedly, he pulled out his flask, popped the lid, and held it to my lips.

Surprisingly, it was really good. The grape soda concoction flowed easily down my throat. It was like nothing I'd ever had before.

"Wow, you weren't kidding. That stuff's incredible."

"Go ahead. Have zome more. I made it juzt for you. I promize I didn't drink off it."

We sat there for a minute. "You know, you're not so bad," I

laid my head on his shoulder and began to ramble freely. "I mean, some of the swimmers think you're weird. And you do aggravate us in the pool. And the farting, jeez. I almost died on the bus ride to the championships meet. But really, when it's just you and me and the stars, you're kind of sweet." I patted his knee. "You're good company. And you smell nice."

He interrupted with a laugh. "Zhank you. You don't smell so bad eizer." He laughed again and mumbled, "Zometimes I zhink I might even like to take you home. You know juzt to introduze a real American girl to my family. I don't zhink you're what they would exzpect."

"What would they expect?"

"Well, not zhis. You're zo different. Funny! Look, I took zome picturez of you when you were doing your pyramidz."

He opened his phone to show me the pictures he'd taken of me and the girls. The glare of the bright lights against the darkness of the night, in combination with my spinning head, had me so dizzy I couldn't look.

Maybe Ty was right. I should've stopped with the keg stand. "I think I might throw up. Can you send them to me and I'll look at them later?"

Lit by his phone, I watched the smile grow on his face. "What'z your number? I'll zend zhem."

I pulled out my phone and stared at the screen. "I don't know right now. I never dial my own number. I really don't feel too good."

"Here, give it to me. I can do it while you rezt. Why don't you lie down for a minute?"

Without further thought, I handed him my phone, then laid across his lap while he fiddled with the numbers. As I watched him alternate between phones, my eyelids grew heavy. The comforting sound of cars pulling in and out, along with the rise and fall of Daemon's chest, lulled me into a dreamy state. Before I knew it, I was dreaming of another boy. The one who reminded me just how often I got myself into pickles.

I awoke to the sound of voices.

"Whoa. Hold up. I'll take her from here, big guy."

I recognized that voice. It was Mason. Where was I? I slowly opened my eyes to see gravel moving beneath me, yet it wasn't my feet traveling across it. That's when I heard him again. "Where are you going with her?"

"I waz juzt taking her to my truck to let her rezt."

It was Daemon. It took me a second to realize he was carrying me over his shoulder. Looking down at the back of his shirt, I would recognize his French fabric anywhere.

"Thanks for your help, pal, I'll take it from here. Come here, Jenna." Mason held out his arms. I watched as Daemon's eyes opened wide. There was a moment of silence. I swore I felt tension rise in his neck as he stiffened beneath me.

Quickly, Daemon dropped his head, and looked away from Mason, stammering in a whispered bellow, "Are you zure? I can take her home. Zhe's not feeling well."

"No, no, no, buddy. I don't know you from Adam. I'm not sending her over that hill with you or anyone else. There's been way too much drinking going on here tonight."

I felt him pull me from Daemon's hold. "She can rest at my grandma's house."

"Your grandmother. Zhe livez here?"

"Yeah, this is my place."

"I zee."

Breaking the awkward lull in conversation, Mason finally began to walk away with me. "Well, thanks for your help."

"Any time," Daemon softly grunted as he walked back toward the barn dance.

That's when Mason leaned down and whispered, "Jenna, Jenna, Jenna, what were you thinking? Who was that guy?" I felt the shift in his stride as he piggybacked me toward his ranch house.

"It's okay, old friend. He's my French foreign buddy. We were having fun. I'm just trying to live a little."

Mason shook his head. "Now, listen here, girl. I want you to live. Just remember to be careful while you're doing it."

Chapter Seventeen

Weak Signals

THREE WEEKS WITHOUT MY PHONE OR HUMAN CONTACT OUTSIDE of school or basketball practice was the punishment I endured for my drinking binge at the party. I had nobody to hang out with anyway. The boys were serving hard labor at the vineyard, and Kaitlyn wouldn't come out of her room. I didn't blame her one bit. Our terrible decision to get drunk at the birthday party had left her vulnerable when she needed us most. As it turned out, while we were all partying, Pistol found a way to get Kaitlyn alone out in the tack room. Nobody knew how long she fought him off, but according to Peyton, the part she witnessed was pretty brutal. Thank God she had the mind to stay sober that night. It was her quick thinking that helped rescue Kaitlyn before things went as far as Pistol was trying to take them.

It took three weeks to get Kaitlyn to come out of her room. We had just begun our Thanksgiving break and things were starting to look up. To put some distance between us and the hellish weeks we had endured, our families decided to take a road trip out to Forks of the Salmon, a small river community about an hour off the grid. They thought it would be good for us to get away for a while.

The Woodleys met us at my house. Trying to beat a forecasted storm, we quickly headed over the hill to Dotty's hamburger joint where we met Mason, Brody, and their parents. The cabins had been in their families for years, and they had invited all of us to spend the holiday with them. As we pulled into Dotty's, I noticed a vaguely familiar man sitting on the picnic table chatting with the Brooks. His dominating appearance peaked my curiosity.

"Who's that?" I asked my mom.

"Don't you recognize him? That's Isaiah."

I thought it kind of looked like him, but he'd taken on a gruff appearance. He was heavier, harder looking, and had grown a stubbly beard. And as much as I wanted it for Mason, I never expected to see him back in Jefferson. He was supposed to be out of the country protecting him. Protecting all of us.

"Is everything okay? I thought he was working in Russia."

"He's not back for long. He came to talk to Mason about some developments that came after hearing about your, uh …"

"My very true nightmares."

"Yes, honey. He's decided it's time to tell Mason that Olivia," she sighed, "won't be coming home."

I couldn't help but think of what that terrible news was going to do to him. "That's going to kill him, you know. Does he have to do it now?"

Before she answered, she looked away and took a deep breath. I could tell she was holding out on me, but wasn't ready to get into a deep discussion right there in the middle of Dotty's parking lot. "Jenna, all you need to know is there are reasons for everything Isaiah does. Now, I'd imagine he must get back before anyone knows he's here. If he wants to tell him in person, it can't wait."

"I still don't get it." I shook my head, irritated that Mason still couldn't have his dad after all those years. "This place is barely on the map. There's more cows than people. Nobody knows we're here. Why can't he just come home for good?"

"It's not that easy, sweetie. Like I said, Isaiah will know when it's safe to come home. Until then, we just have to send our prayers and appreciate the sacrifices he's made to keep us all safe."

Not wanting to hang out in the parking lot for one more minute, I snapped, "What're we waiting for? It's time to hit the road!" I wanted to catch up with my friends, without our parents listening ears.

Smothered by all the blankets and pillows in the back seat, my mom must've decided I needed something to take my mind off my impending suffocation. That's when she handed my phone over the top of the seat. "Thought you might want this back."

"Thanks." I looked down at my signal to watch the three bars fade to one. "Not sure I'll be able to use it." I stared out the window and noticed the mountains had begun to close in on the sides of the road. They were growing by the second, which told me cell service would be hit and miss from that point on.

"Exactly." My mom pulled down the visor mirror and winked. "Extended punishment. I charged it for you."

I opened my messages to find one lonely text that was dated two weeks earlier.

(364) 627-2017:
Got your number from Caden ~ hmu if you want to hang out ;)

Could it be? The name wasn't in my contacts, but I didn't want to look like a fool if I was wrong. Quickly, I texted Caden before we lost cell service.

Me:
Who did you give my number to?
(Read)

Caden:
What're you talking about?

Me:
Who's (364) 627-2017???

Caden:
Not sure. Let me check.
(Read)

Me:
How often do you give out my number, jackass???
(Read)

Me:
Answer me!!!!
(Read)

There was no response. I checked and rechecked my messages until I was at zero bars. What perfect timing to lose service. It wasn't my intention to avoid him. It wasn't a choice, I'd been grounded for three weeks. Ty and I had no classes together. My teacher-mom made me eat in her classroom at lunch. She drove me to school every day and waited until I was done with practice to take me home. And because of my drunk escapade, I still hadn't gotten his number at the party. Not that I would have been able to use it anyway. They had stripped me of all forms of communication.

Because of the severity of the situation, my parents had gone extremely hard on me. There were only a few times when I was lucky enough to catch a glimpse of Ty during our two-minute passing periods. If that was his text waiting on my phone, I could see why he wouldn't make eye contact. He had been waiting on a response that never came. He might have been up for a challenge, but a challenge was different than ignoring him completely. There were too many other girls willing to step up to the plate.

When we finally pulled up to the cabin, I jumped out of the car and went straight to Caden. "You didn't respond."

"That's cuz I wanted to see you all pouty by the time we got here," he mocked my lower lip and chuckled.

"You're a great friend," I snarled.

"Yes, I am."

"If you're so great, then tell me."

"Tell you what?"

"Who'd you give my number to?"

"You can't text him back anyway. No cell service."

"So it is him." I hid the underlying smile trying to force its way to the corners of my mouth.

"You're right, Jenna. Or should I say, Pickle?" he laughed.

Playfully, I shook my head and growled at him. I knew I was supposed to act mad that he was messing with me, but deep down I knew he'd done me a favor by giving Ty my number. In reality, there was a glowing ball of warmth in the pit of my stomach. It lit me up inside to know Ty had my number and he actually used it. It didn't take long for my delight to turn to anxiety. Two weeks was a long time to ignore a text. I looked at my phone again. Still no bars. I needed to find a signal. My thoughts were quickly interrupted when my dad walked up behind us.

"Jenna, Kaitlyn. Come help us put away the food."

Before I headed inside I looked back to Caden. "I can't believe you never told me."

"I can't believe you never asked," he smiled with his big grimace-emoji teeth.

Shaking my head, I shoved my phone in my pocket. "Payback's a bitch, you know," I winked as I looked over to Peyton who was twirling herself up in a blanket like spaghetti on a fork. He didn't have a chance to respond when my dad started shouting for us again.

"Kaitlyn! Jenna! Now!"

I couldn't believe it had only been two minutes since we'd pulled up, and they'd already assigned us kitchen duty. With no luck, I tried to push Ty to the back of my mind as I scooped up a box of supplies and headed to the kitchen with Kaitlyn. I popped open drawers and shoved boxes into the cupboards as fast as I could. There was only one thing on my mind. I needed to finish my job so I could go find some service.

"Jenna, slow down!" My dad barked out as the salt shaker crashed to the counter and spilled all over a plate of hot dogs. "What the hell are you doing out there anyway?"

"Hurry! We'd better get this off before your dad takes these out to grill," Kaitlyn laughed as she dipped each link in water and wiped it off with a napkin. As she worked to clean the hotdogs, I moved onto something a little safer. Or, so I thought. As I began to set the apple pie on the counter, it slipped from my hand and splattered all over the floor.

Kaitlyn stopped what she was doing. I could see she was a little concerned when she put her hand on my shoulder and asked if I was okay.

Bending down to clean up the mess, I looked up at her and muttered through gritted teeth, "I'm fine."

She kneeled next to me with her box of disinfectant wipes. "I hope so. Cuz if you get any less fine, we're not going to have any food left for our Thanksgiving dinner."

"I guess I'm just in a hurry."

I didn't look up but watched as the disinfectant wipe came to a halt. "I'm not buying it. There's nothing out here to be in a hurry for. No basketball. No television. No deadlines. Something's going on with you. What is it?"

I paused long enough to look her in the eyes. It was obvious I wasn't going to get away with not telling her what was distracting me.

"Alright. Alright. I haven't had my phone for three weeks. On the way over here, I noticed an old text from someone asking if I wanted to hang out."

"And?"

"Caden just told me it was Ty. That was two weeks ago. I've ignored him for two weeks now, without knowing it."

Kaitlyn grimaced as she processed what I'd just said. "You haven't replied to Ty?" Her lips squeezed into a line before she spoke again, "for two weeks?" She clicked her tongue a few times as her eyebrows crawled up her forehead. Then she took a deep breath before shaking her head, "That's it." She took the broken pie out of my hands. "You need to go. He's not a two-week kind of guy."

"What? Where?" I looked around.

"Up on the hill. Follow the trail past the creepy cabin. There's service up at the corrals."

Too focused on the cleanup to respond, I continued to scoop the apple pie from the floor into the tin.

"What are you waiting for, another two weeks? Go text him." She pulled the tin from my hands. "I've got this. Now go."

I gave her a thank you hug and took off looking for any sign of a signal. As I walked up the muddy trail nearing an old, screened-in cabin, my thoughts focused on what I was going to say in my text. I stared at the screen, hoping to see even a hint of cell service. Not watching where I was going, I missed a protruding tree limb and tumbled to the ground. Stunned from the sudden fall, I sat silently and concentrated on the whistling wind picking up around me.

That's when a creaking noise drew my attention to the cabin. It almost sounded like a rocking chair rolling over an old, wooden deck. As I looked up at the dark, eerie haunt in the middle of the woods, goosebumps lifted from my arms. It looked like it had been abandoned years ago.

As I rolled over to push myself back onto my feet, I swore I heard the crunching of leaves out in the mist. "Hello?" I called. "Anybody there?" There was no answer. My imagination was starting to play tricks on me. I thought about going over to take a look inside. That's when I caught sight of the back end of a deer sputtering away, nearly losing its footing on the slick, wet leaves. It must have been looking for food before winter blew in. Poor thing. From the chill in the air, that was going to be any minute.

The thought of hungry animals trying to find food in the middle of nowhere had me on edge. Not wanting to meet up with anything more ravenous than a deer, I scrambled to my feet. The last thing I needed was to see a mountain lion's teeth up close. I decided to jog up to the corrals. Needing to strengthen my signal, I climbed up the rungs, plopped down to catch my breath, and pulled my phone from my pocket.

Staring down at the screen, I memorized his number. As I did so, I had to think hard about what I was going to say if he did answer. I didn't want to mess up. Not only had I ignored him, but I had a reputation at stake. I wanted to sound sincere, not desperate. Everyone knew I wasn't the kind of girl who couldn't live without a guy. What they didn't need to know was I would've made an exception for Ty. Finally, after staring at the screen for ten minutes I came up with something.

Me:
Hi

As I waited for his answer, I stared up at the sky, watching the fluffy snowflakes begin to float down from above. It was beautiful sitting up on the hillside in the brisk, snowy air, watching a thin layer of snow accumulate around me. There wasn't another soul in sight. The only sound was the rushing river. It was well out of view from the corrals, but I could still hear it from where I sat and waited.

I doubted he'd text back. Two weeks was a long time to make someone wait for a response. He'd probably forgotten he'd texted me by then. I was sure he didn't even know who the random "Hi" was from. I was sure his phone was filled with *"Hi's"* from all kinds of girls, girls who actually responded when he asked them to hit him up.

The wind picked up and whipped my ponytail across my face. My hands began to sting from the chilly air. I was ready to give up and head back down the hill when my phone chimed. I looked down to see his text.

Ty:
Hi?

Me:
Hey. I just saw your text.

Ty:
No kidding. I just sent it. Who's this?

Me:
It's Jenna. Sorry, I thought you had my number.

Ty:
Oh hey, Pickle. I don't add contacts until after the fifth text.

Me:
Really?

Ty:
Yep. It's kinda one of my rules.

Me:
Well, this is my fifth text. You gonna add me or what?

Ty:
Hey, listen. I'm tied up right now. Don't mean to be rude, but I've got to run. Family emergency.

It pretty much went as I suspected it would. Tied up? I'd have to remember that excuse. Maybe in the weeks following Homecoming, he ended up with CJ after all. I mean, aside from a few keg stands which I was too drunk to enjoy, we'd never really gotten back together. I cringed at the vision of her hog-tying him on the living room floor. From the icy, cold blow-off, I could tell it sure wasn't me he was into. Who was I kidding anyway? Me having a thing with Ty? I actually laughed when I thought of the reality of it. I didn't even make his contacts.

There was no use dwelling on it. I'd already blown it. I couldn't even keep him on the phone for a sixth text. After a few minutes of re-reading our conversation, my frustration turned to indifference. I wanted the trip to be fun. After all, I had five friends waiting for me down at the cabin. I was determined to shake it off, and fast. The least I could do after the last few weeks was make sure the six of us had a good time.

I jumped down from the corral and headed back toward our cabin. As I stepped down, I could've sworn I heard a second set of footsteps crunching in the snow behind me. Hoping it wasn't that mountain lion that I'd imagined, I began to pick up speed until I was jogging down the hill past the creepy cabin. Somehow, it looked different as the sun began to sink. There was almost a glow to it. At some point during our visit, I knew I had to take a look inside. My curiosity was killing me.

Chapter Eighteen

A River of Troubles

THAT FIRST NIGHT THE SIX OF US HAD A GREAT TIME AS WE SAT around in a circle enjoying a nice Thanksgiving dinner. We had our parents in stitches as we worked overtime to one-up each other on how terrible our post-birthday-party punishments were. We could tell they were proud of themselves for making their point that teenage drinking would lead straight to hell. They were right. It did. Three weeks of it.

There was only a brief lull in our conversation when the story telling shifted from us to Grandma and Grandpa Mason, who romanticized about their crazy days out at the Forks. We could tell they'd had a few sips of my dad's vintage wine when they started opening up about some of their teenage shenanigans out at camp. We all smirked at Brody and Mason when their grandpa told us how he used to sneak Grandma off at night to play "hide and seek" under the full moon. Or, when they got a little older, how he coaxed her into a little moonlit skinny dip. He swore he wouldn't look, but said when he "accidentally" caught sight of her silhouette, it sealed the deal on his decision to marry her. I could tell Forks of the Salmon was a magical place to them, and remained so even after they were married and had children of their own.

Grandpa carried on with the story of how they started bringing

Olivia out when she was just a little girl. He got a kick out of how she turned "roughing it" into the high life with just a little creativity. Apparently, she would devise scavenger hunts to see what kinds of goodies she could get all her little friends to swindle from the other campers.

"She was such a smart girl," Grandpa smiled. "She always did know how to harness the power of persuasion."

As Grandpa spoke, Isaiah grew quiet. I could tell he'd heard those sweet, childhood stories many times through the years. As long as Olivia had been gone, he was still suffering a deep hurt from the loss of his beautiful wife. When he looked up toward the ceiling, the room grew still. We decided to give Isaiah some space. Figuring we heard enough about the good old days, we decided to head outside for some fresh air and a chance to make some stories of our own.

Thinking about the adventures they must have had back in the day, gave me the brilliant idea to play *Truth or Dare*. That game always seemed to bring a good rush of adrenaline and excitement. It took a little convincing, but all the friends decided to go with it. The game was interesting, to say the least. So much happened as we revealed unspoken truths and took on crazy dares. Brody hung from the middle of Mule Bridge. Kaitlyn and I came clean about the poison oak we'd infected half the school with. Caden confessed his undying love for Peyton. And the funniest thing of all, Mason ended up adding a seventh friend to the party. Marissa, the girl from the cabin down the way. Everything was fun and games until the final challenge, when Kaitlyn was dared to go investigate creepy cabin by herself.

I felt kind of sorry for her. I knew she was already jumpy from everything she'd gone through. I couldn't blame her. Two sneak attacks by Pistol in the same month would've had me skittish too. I decided that Peyton and I would go with her. Heck, I'd been dying to look inside anyway.

When we got to the porch, I volunteered to climb the ladder first to look inside. I knew it was Kaitlyn's dare. She was so nervous, I was happy to go first and check it out. I wanted to make sure things were safe before letting her go through with it. Once I'd made up my mind, she couldn't stop me.

"I've got this," I convinced her, as I climbed to the top of the ladder toward the loft. When I got to the top rung, I had to pause. I swore there was something in front of me. It was a light-colored mound, but I couldn't make sense of what it was. "I think I see something, Kait, I need light. Give me your phone," I whispered.

I grabbed the light from her hand and shined it toward the mound before me. When a mattress covered in blankets came into view, the phone was suddenly smacked from my hand, blinding me right where I stood. I couldn't see, but I swore I heard shuffling as I abruptly jumped from the ladder to the floor.

I grabbed the girls and we barreled down that hill as fast as we could. My heart hadn't run a race like that since the night we left Napa. I didn't know who or what we'd encountered at that cabin, but it left all of us girls scared out of our minds. The boys tried to convince us it was a raccoon, but that didn't make sense considering the force that hit the phone from my hand. Adrenaline junkie or not, I'd had my fill of the woods and was ready to go home.

Little did I know that the attack on the phone at creepy cabin wasn't going to be the scariest part of the trip. The next morning, we had to get up early for Christmas tree cutting. What was supposed to be a fun day playing in a winter wonderland, turned out to be the worst nightmare we could've ever imagined.

We'd just finished dragging the huge Douglas firs down the hill, when we got close enough to the vehicles to notice something was wrong. The windows had been smashed out of Caden's truck and our stuff was all over the ground. The fact that his gun was missing, sent on into a full-on panic. Left in its place was an empty bottle of Jack Daniels. It was no secret that was Pistol Black's drink of choice. He had been after Kaitlyn since their break-up, and it was obvious he was ready to inflict his hell.

The nightmare escalated from there. Despite Caden's missing windows, we loaded into the vehicles and headed back to the cabins. Most of us squished into Brody's jeep, but Peyton braved the cold and rode with Caden. She didn't want to leave him alone. Just a little way down the road, we knew we were in trouble when we saw Pistol's red truck headed straight at Caden on the narrow, icy highway.

We tried to follow but had to slow and duck when we heard gunshots. Huddled in the backseat of the car, I could've sworn they were coming from the side of the road. Before my mind could process what I was seeing and hearing, I watched Pistol's truck wrap into Caden's, pulling both vehicles over the embankment.

The scene that unfolded before us will be forever seared into the darkest nightmares of my mind. When we jumped out and looked over the cliff, Caden's truck was nearly submerged in the river. The cab was crushed. I couldn't imagine how either of my friends would have survived.

We all rushed toward the scene. Caden, who was blue and covered with blood, was on the riverbank shrieking in pain. I stayed by his side while the others ran to see if they could get Peyton out of the truck. I knelt over him, trying to keep him calm and manage his shock. He was conscious for a while. Long enough to cry out for us to help his girlfriend. That's when I heard the truck release, and watched the swift current carry it downstream. I swore all hope was lost when Caden went limp.

I'll never forget the agony of that moment or the tragedy of that season. Thankfully, Caden and Peyton survived. Likely, neither of them, or any of us for that matter, would ever be the same. All of us were ready to see the end of fall.

The tragedy at the river would shatter our innocence and infuse us with a new set of nightmares. Nightmares, that without a shadow of a doubt, would change the very core of who we were and how we would navigate the rest of our senior year.

Chapter Ninteen

Secret Crush

THOUGH FALL WAS LIKELY THE WORST TIME OF ANY OF OUR LIVES, there was some good sprinkled throughout that season. It was actually in the midst of one of the darkest times that I found a glimmer of light. I was sitting in Caden's hospital room praying for his and Peyton's recovery when I realized I needed a stronger connection. I was too distracted by the beeping machines, visiting nurses, and the clanking of medical carts to focus on the serious talk I needed to have with God. I decided to go to the chapel where I could find solitude, and quite possibly He might hear my pleas a little more clearly.

The dark room with the soft light from the glowing candles invited me in. I made my way to the front of the chapel, near the statue of Saint Francis. Wondering how to even begin to pray for my friends, I sat down in the pew and stared up at the altar. Images of their conditions plagued me.

Caden was barely able to get out of bed while he was recovering from a dislocated elbow, liver lacerations, and severe hypothermia. Kaitlyn had been released. Miraculously, she had only suffered hypothermia after heroically pulling Peyton from the river. However, she was psychologically shredded. She blamed herself for everything that had happened at the hands of her ex-boyfriend.

Utter devastation surrounded my entire circle of friends. The only thing I thought might help the situation was to ask God for His help.

As I sat there, prayers for comfort and healing poured out, one after the other. But when I was done, I had to wonder if I could have done anything differently. Helped more? Been more protective? Overcome with emotion, I could no longer keep the tears from escaping. The images of the accident ran in a loop repeatedly. My first vision was Caden's smashed, submerged truck. Then his bloody, lifeless body. Next, Kaitlyn, and the way she braved the icy river to rescue Peyton. Finally, the helicopter that lifted them far up into the snowy sky. It all replayed again and again as I prayed over and then reflected on each of my affected friends and their parents.

I had just said, "Amen" when I heard the crescendo of footsteps walking up the aisle. Hoping to camouflage myself, I leaned forward and buried my face in my hands. The last thing I wanted was for anyone to see me upset. I didn't deserve to cry. I wasn't the one lying in the hospital bed on the verge of death.

That's when the wooden bench creaked beside me. Glancing to the left, I caught sight of blue jeans, barely touching the fabric of my paisley leggings. Slowly, I drew my eyes up an athletic frame to see the face of my visitor. My heart skipped a little when I saw it was Ty. As he studied my demeanor, his expression began to show concern.

"You okay?" he whispered as he gently set his hand on my leg.

I wiped the tears from my eyes and nodded, yes.

"I heard about the accident. I'm so sorry for all of you."

"Thanks," I sniffled. "Did you come to see Caden?"

"Well, actually, I was here because my little brother had to spend Thanksgiving down in pediatrics. But I plan to go visit him."

My voice was still muffled with sadness, but I was able to ask, "So, you're here for Aiden? Is everything okay?"

"It's his diabetes. He got sick just before Thanksgiving and we couldn't get his blood sugar to come down. Thank God for the upgraded insulin pump. It can read his blood sugar now. They've extended his stay while the specialist works with him. I've been coming in during my parents' work shifts. You know, learning how all this works so I can fill them in on whatever they miss."

"Are you doing okay with all of it? Diabetes. Insulin pumps. That seems like a lot to take on for a high school senior."

"I wouldn't want it any other way. I love that kid. If anything ever happened to him, I don't know what I'd do."

"You're a good big brother." I thought about how responsible it was for him to take over for his parents when they had no choice but to work. I didn't know too many guys my age who had that much dedication to a sibling. "I guess you really have been tied up."

My innocent statement must have reminded him that he'd kind of left me hanging with his last text message.

He shook his head. "I never texted back, did I?" He grimaced, "Sorry."

Thinking about how dismissive I felt after his last text, I was disappointed in myself for thinking he had probably hooked up with someone else. It was to be expected, and rather touching that he would put me off for his sick brother. The residual tears from my earlier cry began to trickle down my face. I shook my head and pulled my sunglasses from my bag. I didn't want him to see that I was hurt when I thought he was ignoring me.

"It's okay." I lied. "I haven't thought about it. I was kind of tied up too."

I was still quietly sniffling through our conversation when he wrapped his arm around my shoulder and pulled me into him. The sincerity of his hug tugged at my heart. Nestled against him, knowing he cared about my pain, completely unraveled my defenses. I'd been holding it together for too long.

"You don't have to be strong all the time. It's okay to cry." His words induced another wave of tears. "This must've been so hard on all of you," he whispered. He hugged me tighter and rested his chin on the top of my head. "Everything's going to be okay. Our friends are in good hands. This is a great hospital."

I didn't know how long he held me. It could've been minutes. It could've been hours. I just knew that it was the first time I'd felt at ease in a very long time. When the tears finally dried, I collected my thoughts. How selfish I'd been to hoard his attention the entire time we were in the chapel. Obviously, he was there for a reason. My focus shifted to his little brother. I remembered how cute he was at camp the previous summer and I felt bad that he was in his room alone. "You should probably get back to Aiden."

"Yeah, no telling what kind of trouble he's gotten himself into by now," he grinned.

"How long will he be here? I'd like to stop by to say hello."

"Today's his last day." He paused momentarily, allowing an idea to light his face. "Hey, you can come with me, if you want." He stood and held out his hand as he pulled me to my feet. "It might help take your mind off Peyton and Caden … and I know Aiden would love to see you." A smirk played on his lips as he leaned over and whispered, "Don't tell him, but I think he has a secret crush. He still has a picture of the two of you pinned to the roof of his bunk bed."

"Well, in that case, let's go make a little kid's day." Walking out of the chapel, I smiled, knowing exactly where that picture was taken. It was on stage the night of the talent show. I'd called him up to introduce him, giving him a hug as I handed over the microphone. He sang "Camp Granada." It had to be the cutest rendition I'd ever seen.

I didn't want to visit him empty-handed, so I pulled Ty into the gift shop before heading to Aiden's room. We looked around for a minute before I found a stuffed black lab and a small box of sugar-free chocolates.

"He'll love it," Ty grinned.

He was right. Aiden's eyes lit up when he saw his brother walk through the door.

"I brought you something," Ty smiled, pulling me out from behind him.

In an instant, I watched his face flush red. He buried his head under his blankets and peeked up over the top of his pillow. His muffled voice found its way through the stuffing, "Where'd you find her?"

"You can come out now, Aiden." I giggled. "I'm not going to bite you. But I know someone who might." I plopped down beside him and jammed the little, black dog into his side, tickling him wildly with his snout.

Aiden broke into a fit of giggles and finally crawled out to say hello.

"For you," I held out the stuffed puppy. "You think you can name him?"

Donning his best thinking face, he wrinkled his nose and pinched his lips together. "Help me."

It took a second, but I finally had an idea. "Well, usually you name an animal after something or someplace you love."

He looked at me and smiled.

"Got it."

"What?"

"Kelsey Creek Camp."

Ty chuckled. "You can't name a dog Kelsey Creek Camp. How would you ever call him? Come here, Kelsey Creek Camp." He patted his thighs, "Come here, boy."

"How about, Kelsey?" I suggested. "You can make Creek his middle name and Camp his last name. That way you don't have to use them when you call him."

Aiden nodded his head. "Hi there, Kelsey." He ran his hand over his new stuffed lab.

I watched him play for a minute before I realized I'd better get back upstairs and check on Caden. "Well, I'm glad to see you're doing better, kiddo. I have to go visit another friend now, okay?"

As I moved toward the door to leave, I looked over my shoulder at Aiden. I was happy to see the smile the new, stuffed puppy put on his face.

Ty met me over in the corner and whispered, "Thank you. You really made his day."

"Anytime."

He looked back over at Aiden, who was flying his new puppy through the air, "I'm sure Kelsey's going to keep him busy for a while."

I smiled, knowing that all of us were going to be busy for a while. "Listen, it's gonna be a pretty busy season. I might not see you much. It looks like we've both got a lot going on."

"Yeah, with my parents' work schedules, I'll be on Aiden duty when I'm not at basketball, or pre-season training."

"Yep. And I've got basketball and Caden. He's going to need me to get him through this whole mess. He's in pretty bad shape."

"Ah, Caden." The tone of his voice and the look in his expression told me that he thought Caden and I were more than friends. It was true, we were more like family. But our friendship was a lot deeper than I had time to get into. I couldn't explain that yes, he was just my friend, but he was also my priority. And he would continue to be until he was healed. I smiled at Ty, unable to correct his assumption.

Finally, he spoke. "Guess I'll see you when I see you?"

Nodding, I offered, "Text if you need me. I'm always happy to help with that little guy."

"Guess it wouldn't hurt to add you." He took out his phone and opened the screen. "Oh, looks like I already did," he winked. And that was the way Ty Connelly crawled his way back into my heart to hibernate for the winter.

Chapter Twenty

Shattered

JUST AS I'D THOUGHT, WINTER WAS NOT ONLY BUSY, BUT FULL OF trials. When I wasn't stumbling through school work and basketball, the rest of my time was spent trying to get Caden through the devastation of Peyton leaving. I vowed to myself that I would bandage the heartache she'd unintentionally inflicted and step up to be the best friend he needed.

I must admit, the time I devoted to him wasn't purely selfless. My circle of friends was where I found my security. It had been several weeks since the devastating events that took place on the river, yet the investigation seemed to be never-ending. Discrepancies in what we had seen, or thought we'd seen leading up to the wreck, made it tough to piece everything together. We knew there was a gun and there were shots fired. But, none of us could figure out where they came from. Something just didn't add up. Pistol's truck had ended up in the ravine, not far from Caden's. He still hadn't been found. None of us knew whether he was dead or alive. Thinking he still might be out there armed kept us all on edge.

We felt like we were under some type of cosmic microscope. Even I felt a sense of being watched. At school. Out on the court. In my bedroom at night. I despised being alone. All of us did. Sticking together was the only thing we could do to take our minds off the insecurity and hurt we were struggling with. I'll never forget the first night we decided to go out in public together after the accident. It was at Lyda's Christmas party.

We could sense all eyes were on us as we walked through the door. We were a bit apprehensive, but we wanted to get our feet wet and see if we could handle being out in a crowd post-accident. We knew rumors had been flying about Caden and Peyton and their potential breakup. Other hot topics were the "Pistol, Kaitlyn, and Brody Triangle," the accident, and Marissa, Mason, and me as the supporting cast. We knew they'd embellished the story for their entertainment and none of us were ready to give them the truth.

Knowing we were trying to keep the night low-key, Lyda had agreed to hide us away upstairs in her open loft. That way we could look down at the gathering, but we were somewhat removed from the crowd. At first, we were having a great time. Everyone was getting friendly. We got a kick out of watching people snap pictures of Santa Benny playing with the ornaments on Charity's and Cindy's ugly sweaters. Seconds later, my eyes were drawn to a group of football players from the south county. They had smuggled liquor bottles under their letterman's jackets. Seeing that booze had found its way to the party, we knew we had to either lay low or leave. After the hell we'd just been through, we had definitely learned our lesson about drinking

That's when my buddy, Daemon, made his way up the stairs. It was funny how he always wound up near me. Especially at parties. It seemed alcohol gave him the courage he needed to engage me in conversation. My friends joked that they thought it was because he'd developed a little crush on me. They'd seen how he watched me in the hallways, at games, and probably why he'd asked to be the statistician for our basketball team. I didn't want to give him the wrong idea. There was zero attraction on my end, and I still had dreams of Ty hibernating deep in my heart. But, I couldn't help but be kind. I knew what it was like living in a foreign country. I kind of had a soft spot for the guy.

Sitting on the arm of the couch, I overheard him talking to Lyda. She was guarding the upstairs so nobody would come and invade our space.

"Ve are just looking for ze bazzroom," he pleaded, desperation in his voice.

She must have let him through because the next thing I knew he was bent over the top of me.

"Could you hold zis for me, please? It'z really good. I haven't touched it yet, so you can drink some if you'd like."

He handed me a brown bottle with no label. "Go ahead. I'll be right back. Try it."

Caden looked at me incredulously. "Is it just me, or does that guy's accent change every time I'm around him?"

I did notice he was getting clearer with some words. "He's just getting better at English. That's all."

After he left for the bathroom, I popped open the lid, curious as to what I was holding. I set my nose down on the opening and began to inhale.

"You're not drinking that, right?" Kaitlyn asked.

Pulling it away from my nose, I answered, "Not on your life."

It smelled strongly of Kahlua, which I was sure was fine, but it led Kaitlyn, Caden, and me to a brief conversation about the dangers of taking drinks from people at parties. And boy was I glad that I hadn't taken a drink because just as I was smelling the bottle, a flash made me turn my head. It was Tiara with her phone camera. It was pointed right at me. All I could think at the time was that she'd better hope her stolen picture was not of me holding that bottle.

She turned her back on me and continued taking pictures. That's when my attention was drawn to Daemon, who had just knelt beside me. "Did you try it? It's really good."

I shook my head, no and handed it back to him.

"Try some. I inzeest," he whined and shook the bottle under my nose.

That's when Caden stepped in. "Dude, she said no. Back off." His voice faded to a mumble. "Little gnat. Always swarming."

I could tell Daemon was disappointed as he stood up and turned away. Then looking back over his shoulder, he grumbled, "Maybe later, huh?"

Once again, I found myself defending the poor kid. I knew all he wanted was to find American friends. Apparently, alcohol was the way he made them. Well, at least that seemed to be his tactic with me.

As I watched Daemon head back down the stairs, I caught sight of Mason and Marissa who had just come through the front door. It wasn't seconds after they made their way into the house that Peyton appeared right behind them. We were all shocked, when seductively, she drew her arms around Mason's neck and whispered into his ear. It was heartbreaking to watch Caden's face as she tugged Mason under the mistletoe and laid a kiss on him that none of us would ever forget.

That was where the party ended for us. After that night, Peyton refused to see Caden. Not that he didn't keep trying to change her mind. The one time I finally caved in and took him to her house, it was horrific. I should've known that day was going to be hell when I realized my wallet was missing. Knowing I had all kinds of private information floating around out there, had my stomach turning. If any of my cards got into the wrong hands, my entire family could be in grave danger. I had to shut everything down and quick. My father was irate. Though it was a tough situation to downplay, I wanted to follow through with my promise to Caden. He needed me to take him over to Peyton's to deliver the Christmas gift he'd gotten her.

I should've taken the missing wallet as a warning that it was a cursed day. Things didn't get any better from there. We both battled trepidation, knowing the last time we'd seen her, she was kissing Mason. I dropped Caden off at the front of the house and watched him make his way up the driveway. After sitting in the car for what seemed like an hour, I finally decided to go inside and check on him. That's when I caught sight of one of the most heart-wrenching scenes I'd ever witnessed. Peyton's appearance had severely declined. She looked like a creature from The Walking Dead, screaming as she threw things from one end of the room to the other. The way she demolished his Christmas gift ripped my heart out. We both knew that moment was the end for Caden and Peyton. It was the last time we saw her that winter. She never returned to school. We later learned that she was suffering from post-traumatic stress, and Caden was one of her triggers. Thank God her parents sent her away for the help she needed.

Chapter Twenty-One

Zero to Hero

THE WEEKEND HAD COME TO AN END. AS THE ALARM PULLED ME out of a restless sleep, I convinced myself to get out of bed. After all, Christmas break was only two weeks away. All of us wanted desperately to get back to normal, work through our assignments, finish off our winter sports season, and start a fresh, new year. We simply wanted to make life good again.

My principal, however, had other ideas in mind. I was sitting in Mr. Pine's science class when an office aide handed him a red slip. He glanced at the note for a split second before his eyes met mine. "Jenna?" He held it out to me. Hesitantly, I sauntered to the front of the room and took the note from his hand, double checking to make sure it had my name on it. I knew I was in trouble when I noticed the box checked "Principal's Office Immediately".

Looking over at Caden, he mouthed, "What did you do now?" Nervously, I shrugged before scurrying out the door. As I walked down the hallway, my mind replayed reel after reel of the past couple week's footage. My missing wallet didn't have anything to do with school, so I knew it wasn't about my so-called irresponsibility. I didn't cheat on any tests. I hadn't cut any classes. Maybe the school cameras had caught me spying on Ty in the locker room. For all the possibilities, I couldn't come up with one good reason for getting a "Principal's Office Immediately" slip.

Surprised to see them sitting there, with anger dominating their expressions, the first people I saw when I entered the office were my parents. I must've done something terrible because they wouldn't even engage me with a simple "Hello." My mother slid her hand down her cheek and shook her head, displaying her embarrassment at having a child like me attending her school. My father completely ignored me, choosing instead to take a business call. Silence permeated the room. Each second that ticked by felt like an hour. Finally, the principal opened his door and waved us in.

"Have a seat," he said as he grabbed a paper and slid it across the shiny, wooden desk. "Do you recognize this?" It was the current season's athletic contract.

I nodded, acknowledging that indeed I did recognize the paper in front of me. Looking up at him with confusion, he tilted his head and asked, "Do you remember signing this contract, Miss Bailey?"

I nodded again as I studied the contract. What else was I supposed to say? I didn't know why we were all there looking at my signature on a piece of paper. Again, dead silence. My parents sat and watched me, pulling in air, exhaling loudly, and shaking their heads. Clearly, everyone was extremely disappointed with something I had done, though I still had no idea what it was.

Finally, after much anticipation coupled with a rising blood pressure, he decided to let me off the hook. Intently, I watched as he slowly turned his computer screen in my direction. There it was. A picture of me at Lyda's party sniffing the brown bottle Daemon had asked me to hold. Damn Tiara. She had snapped a picture of me after all. On top of it, she had posted it on social media. No wonder my parents were fit to be tied. Shaking my head, I pinched my lips together and balled my fists. I was going to kill her. But that would have to come later. Right then, I had a way bigger mess to deal with.

I uied to explain what had happened. Unfortunately, the more

I spoke, the worse things sounded. Whether I drank or not, I had clearly violated the contract's stipulation that I could not be at a party with alcohol. After the birthday party, my parents didn't believe that I hadn't consumed any. And looking at the picture in front of him, neither did the principal. I wasn't going to smooth talk my way out of it. I knew the fate that was about to be handed to me. I was going to be kicked off the basketball team. That was a given. I couldn't expect leniency because my mom was on staff. If anything, I was going to be made an example of. Could that year get any worse? I doubted it. Hopes of making Championships were shot. I was devastated.

What I didn't expect was to run into the person who would come to my rescue. After my harsh sentence, I wandered down the hallway in a daze. I could barely concentrate on where my feet were taking me. The blur of students who buzzed past me were all walking in the opposite direction. I bounced off their shoulders like a pinball, hitting them one by one, as I made my way through the lunchtime rush. I could feel the tears stinging the backs of my eyes, ready to escape with each hit. Finally, a set of strong hands softly grabbed my shoulders and held me in place.

"You okay?" he asked. It was Daemon. He could tell I was upset. "Come wiz me to the library? It'z quiet there." Not wanting anybody to see me cry, I nodded and followed him to the north side of campus. Thankfully, they turned off all the lights and left the building unlocked during lunch. Daemon led me to the far corner, where we sat quietly until he decided to speak. Leaning into his lap, he placed his chin on his hands. "We can just zit here if you want, Jenna. But, I've never zeen you zo out of it. You can talk to me about it. I promize to be a good liziner."

I looked at him for a moment. It was sweet that he would take me there to shield me from my classmates. He must've picked up on the fact that I didn't want anyone to see how embarrassed, humiliated, and angry I was. Maybe French guys were more sensitive.

Touched by his concern, I found myself confiding in him about everything that had just happened. "I'm off the team," I began to cry. "It was the party. Tiara took pictures of me holding your brown bottle and posted them on social media. It looked like I was drinking."

"Oh, no. Zis can't happen. I watched you. You did not drink it." Silently, he sat there with me through lunch, listening as I told him about the picture and the talk I'd had with the principal and my parents. When the bell rang, he held out his hand and pulled me to my feet. "Don't worry about a zhing. I will handle zhis." His face took on a serious expression as he walked me to my next class and headed straight to the office.

There was no way I could focus on the three branches of government right then. I was too busy dwelling on my own laws and judgments to worry about how the country handled theirs. I agonized through the next fifty minutes, worrying about Daemon. Poor guy. He had no idea how things worked in America, and how strict they were about underage drinking. He should've been sitting through that class learning about law and order, checks and balances, rather than wasting his time trying to get me back on the team. My slimmest hope was that if he couldn't save my position, he'd at least be able to save my reputation. When class ended, he was standing outside the door. A small grin played on his lips. "I've got zome newz."

I was back on the team. Daemon had talked with the principal and athletic director and delivered one hell of a story. Though he put himself at risk by admitting he was also at a drinking party, he managed to save his spot on the ski team and was still able to keep his position as our basketball statistician. Maybe they showed leniency because he had limited time to enjoy his American experience, but I was surprised that the administrators bought his story.

He'd explained how he'd grabbed an unlabeled bottle from the drink table and asked me to see if I could tell what it was. He wasn't familiar with American soft drinks, but he was thirsty and wanted to make sure it was not alcohol. He went on to explain that none of us wanted to drink; we were just there to hang out. He also told them that thankfully I'd saved him from certain death. He was allergic to the rum in Kahlua and I was the one who told him it wasn't root beer and not to drink it.

Hearing his story match the one about me just smelling the bottle must have convinced them that I was telling the truth. He also told them that our group was hanging out away from the rest of the party. We were just upstairs watching, like in a movie theater.

That afternoon, I was called back to the office for a reduced sentence. Though I was still reprimanded for being at the party, I was only benched for one game. Not only was Daemon my new hero, but the entire basketball team embraced him. He had saved our championship season. Soon he walked the halls of Jefferson High, enjoying his new popularity among the girls on the varsity basketball team.

Chapter Twenty-Two
Homework on a Friday Night?

FRUSTRATED, I STUFFED MY BACKPACK UNDER THE BLEACHERS AS I headed onto the court for pre-game warm-ups. I had been struggling with an assignment Mrs. G had given us in English class, and it was taking me every spare second to try to figure it out. My family tree, aka the toughest assignment I'd ever been given, was turning into a real challenge. My parents had never spoken much about family, likely because we'd been in hiding nearly my entire childhood. We weren't in contact with any relatives. I'd heard mention of their names here and there, but the reality was, I didn't even know where my aunts, uncles, or grandparents lived. My parents were always so resistant to talking about it, I was afraid to ask. I was literally getting sick from the stress of trying to remember even the tiniest details such as their names.

"Hey, Jenna," a voice drew my attention away from the warm-up circle forming down on the court. "I know I already offered, but I'm really hoping you'll let me help you whiz that project zhiz weekend." He pointed toward the bleachers where my bag rested. He must have seen me struggling. The project was due Friday, and still, all I had on my paper was lines with blank circles. I didn't know where to begin. I was ready to make it up. Maybe I'd just use Mason's family tree. His were the only grandparents I knew anyway. I shook the thought as soon as it entered my head. I was genuinely curious about my family. Who they were. Where they were from.

Again, Daemon's voice reclaimed my attention. "I know you've been having a tough time wiz it. I zaw you ztruggling up there." I felt the color drain from my face as I stood listening to him. "Look, I'm really good at trazing people'z rootz. I have Zeze pre-made templatez I can help you uze. It won't be zo bad. I promize."

Pre-made templates sounded good to me. There he was coming to my rescue again. It made me feel bad about how cold I was to him during swim season. I'd cracked sarcastic remarks at his expense and filled my lane with swimmers so he couldn't get in it. At the time, I just couldn't get past the ridiculous antics he used to try to get my attention. Pinching, flat tires, hanging on the lane lines like a pool shark waiting to attack. I didn't know how to deal with it back then. Nobody on the swim team was a Daemon fan. My personal friends still weren't.

I knew if I was going to let him help me on my project, I'd have to come up with a cover story. I didn't need anyone giving me a hard time about hanging out with Daemon. Though I'd grown kind of fond of him, my friends had not. Caden and Brody were completely put off by the way he always seemed to be lurking in the background.

We all knew he had a little crush on me. They didn't want me encouraging it. But I didn't see the harm in being nice. He would be going back to France in June anyway. It wasn't going to hurt me to give him a little innocent attention. Besides, I owed him. He'd put his own sports season on the line for me. On top of that, he was willing to get me through the toughest assignment of my life. If it made him feel good to help me with a little project, I was more than willing to give him that satisfaction. I'd just tell my friends I had to house sit or something.

"Sure," I smiled. "You can help me." A wide grin grew on

Daemon's face. "My place this weekend? I know you wanted a tour. We'll kill two birds with one stone."

"I can't do it Zaturday. I have a raze down in Mt. Shazta," he paused as a contemplative look grew on his face. "But, we could do it tomorrow night?"

"Tomorrow? You're willing to give up your Friday night for me?"

"Of courze. It'z a date."

I knew I'd have to straighten out the date thing with him later. Right then, I had to get out on the court and throw the ball around with the girls. Even though I was benched for the game, I wanted to get my team pumped up. We were one win away from Championships. Being suspended the game before was horrible timing. Maybe I couldn't be out there to help them, but I was determined to keep their spirits up and let them know I was cheering them on.

After the pre-game pep talk, I took my seat on the bench. It was not a position I was used to watching from. The whistle blew, and chaos ensued. I could see it from the start. Their rhythm was off. With an inexperienced point guard, communication was practically non-existent. The girls kept looking over to me. I could see their deep sighs from twenty feet away. As I suffered the torture helplessly from the sidelines, I leaned into my lap and rested my chin on my hands.

"Rough game," the familiar baritone voice found its way to my ears. "The team's really hurting without their number one."

It was Ty's voice. We hadn't spoken much since the hospital, when I told him I'd be focusing on Caden, but the thought of him close enough to whisper in my ear stirred the dormant crush that I had tried to put to rest. Slowly, I turned my head to look back at the handsome baller sitting kitty-corner to me. He was in uniform, ready to play the next game.

"It sucks. I know. I had to do it once … worst minute of my

athletic life," he chuckled.

"One minute, huh?" I laughed. "What'd you do? Break a shoelace?"

"Something like that. But it still hurt, nonetheless." After donning his sad puppy dog face, his eyebrows drew together, "So, what's got you riding the bench?"

I was silent. I didn't know how to answer his embarrassing question without looking like a dumbass.

"Sorry, you don't have to tell me."

"It's okay. I was at a party. I shouldn't have been there."

"Ah. Well, live and learn, I guess."

I raised my eyebrows sarcastically and looked over my shoulder at him as he continued, "You know, you should really learn to find some more wholesome things to do than go to parties."

"Really? Like what?"

"Well, movies. Those are always good."

"Movies, huh?"

"Yep. There's a good one playing tomorrow night if you want me to show you how wholesome they can be."

After a couple weeks limited to hallway smiles and a few coy gestures, I couldn't believe he was inviting me to watch a movie with him. Of all the luck, it was on Friday. That was the night Daemon was supposed to help me on my project. It took everything in me to gracefully decline his invitation.

"I wish I could, but I've already got plans."

"Really?"

"Daemon's going to help me on that English project."

"Homework on a Friday night? Ouch." I could almost see his wheels spinning before he muttered softly, "And I thought I was running second to Caden?" His forehead wrinkled as he scratched the side of his head. Then sounding sincerely confused, he continued, "Well, priorities are priorities."

I could not let him go on thinking he was my second choice.

Especially not to Daemon. My mind raced for something that didn't sound desperate. "There's this thing." I blurted. "In Mount Shasta."

"Yeah?"

"It's this whole town celebration, charity scavenger hunt thing. It's super wholesome. You should go with me. It's next weekend."

"I'll check my calendar."

Just then the buzzer sounded. It was the end of the third quarter. Ty looked over at the scoreboard and then jumped from his seat, "Uh, gotta go," he half grinned. Just enough to pop that heart-stopping dimple. Before he headed off to the locker room, he held up his hand in front of me to give me a high five. As our hands met, his fingers wrapped around mine. Then tugging me into him he whispered, "Don't get down. It's not too late for a comeback." A swift streak of electricity zapped through our tangled hands to the tips of my toes. In record time, his ten-word pep talk had re-ignited the feelings I had been stifling.

He pulled away, grinning mischievously as he released his hold on me. I could barely breathe from the firestorm of hormones his touch ignited. He was hot as hell. Especially in his basketball uniform. I pursed my lips and pulled in a deep breath. It was all I could do to stop myself from melting into a pool of sweat right there in the bleachers.

I couldn't take my eyes off of him. Rather than heading to the locker room, he made his way down the bench to Coach Bennett. He looked over at me and smirked. I studied his expression, wondering what he had up his sleeve. The next thing I knew, he was leaning into Coach. As he bent down behind him to whisper in his ear, he eyed me from over the top of his shoulder. We locked eyes. Again, my heart clenched as he playfully winked and headed off to the boys' locker room.

Not ten seconds later, Coach called me over, "Bailey, get in there."

"Seriously?" I mouthed.

"Now's not the time to question me, kid. I need you."

"But … my suspension."

"Bailey. We don't have time to discuss this. Get in there and fix this game. Championships are on the line."

I wasn't going to argue about it any further. My blood was pumping and I was ready to go. Knowing Ty had convinced Coach to put me in filled me with confidence. I ran over to the score-keeper and waited to be subbed in. Excited for my eight minutes, I bounced like a little, red, playground ball. Infused with Ty power, I knew I could jump higher, run faster, defend harder, and shoot more accurately than I ever had.

Every cell in my body was on heightened alert. The first thirty-seconds out, I stole the ball and made a fast break, beating everyone down the court. I was in for the lay-up and it was good. The crowd roared and started chanting my name. It must've rattled the opposition because with the chanting and stomping, they started to fall apart. My lay-up was followed by two Bears turnovers. I snagged the first one and passed it to our post, Sammi, who had no problem banking it for an easy two. The second was scooped up by Nora. Immediately, I set up a screen while she cut in from the rear and made it to the hoop.

Clearly, the girls were beginning to find their rhythm. Another series of brilliant defensive plays left the Lady Bears scoreless in the fourth quarter. The gym was crowded. Fans who had started to pack up and leave, stuck around to watch the newly energized battle. We had fought our way back from a twelve-point deficit and now, only two points separated us. There was no way I was going down without a fight. That game would mean the difference between League Championships or playing second fiddle to the Bears again.

We were battling a full-court press when I got the ball for the final play. It was up to me to get it into the right hands, but I was finding it exceptionally difficult to move the ball at all. Nobody could seem to get open. We were down to just seconds. Between the blaring of the pep band and the screaming of the crowd, my nerves were on fire. I had to shake the distractions. I knew I had to stay calm, so I didn't blow it for the team. I took a deep breath and centered my focus up court. Realizing my options were limited, I decided to attack. Gritting my teeth, I looked over at Nora, my number two, and whispered, "Game on!"

Thankfully, we'd been playing together since we were kids. She knew we were about to make heads spin. A smile crossed her face as she made a cut around her defender. I passed her the ball, but within seconds, it was back in my hands. We completely had them off balance with our quick, sharp passes. I knew the clock was running down. I could rock layups, but when it came to threes, things got a little dicier. It was a gamble, but Lilly and Bailey couldn't seem to get open. Two girls from the south county, Grace and Lexi, had a definite height advantage and were setting a hard press. It was up to me to act quickly. The risk was one I was willing to take. The seconds were ticking. I was down to four … three … then without further hesitation, I set my feet and put it up from the three.

Time seemed to stand still as I watched the ball soar through the air. The arc looked to be a little flat, which left my heart hanging mid-air. After the hard-fought battle to come back, was I about to hand our team its first loss? I almost couldn't bear to watch it. It was no swish, that's for sure. The ball came down on the rim and circled with a velocity that I swore was going to send it flying right out the gym door. The crowd stood silently, watching it circle, circle, circle, circle. Finally, it began to slow.

It seemed like a full minute, but the reality was, it took three seconds for the ball to make its decision. As the buzzer began to sound, the ball dropped through the net. It was a three! The crowd went wild. Though it was a one-point lead, it was a win. The team ran on court circling me for a victory celebration. The Miner Fight Song blasted through the gym. There were tears and high fives exchanged by all the teammates. Needing to catch a breath, I crawled out from the huddle of girls and made my way to the outer circle. That's when I saw him standing in the varsity line-up with a small grin decorating his face. It was Ty. He made sure to let me see that he was watching me.

As we jogged off the court, and the varsity boys jogged on, he slowed for just a second. Long enough to let me know he'd checked his calendar. "It's a date, Jenna," he shouted as he ran past me with his team. Just loud enough so that everyone could hear. Including Daemon.

Chapter Twenty-Three

A Date With Daemon

PULLING SWEATSHIRTS OFF THE HANGERS AND TOSSING THEM around my room, I worked to make things look a little less tidy than usual. I bounced on my bed to untuck the sheets and mess the perfectly placed comforter and throw pillows. Then blowing out my cherry blossom candle, I fanned the wick, hoping the smoke would smother the sweet air. Typically, I liked my room to look like it came straight out of a Pottery Barn catalog, but not that day. I didn't want to give Daemon the impression that I was putting in extra effort or trying to set some kind of hopeful mood. Having a vineyard as a backdrop, I had to work extra hard to make things seem as unromantic as possible.

The reality was, I struggled with the thought of being alone with Daemon. I knew he had a little crush on me and as much as I needed his help, the last thing I wanted to do was lead him on. I almost changed our meeting to someplace a little more public like the coffee shop, but it was too late. He had just texted and reminded me that I'd promised to give him a tour of the vineyard on our date. As soon as he hung up, I called our foreman Roger and begged him to hang around for some overtime. I wanted some of our staff on hand to intervene and help me out in case things got awkward.

"Hey, Rosie?" I peeked my head around the kitchen wall to

our beloved chef. "Could you cook up something quick tonight? Preferably something on the messy side? I've got this, uh, person coming over and we might get hungry."

"Person, huh?" Amusement lit her face, "Oh, a special someone," she playfully winked. "You know you don't have to be shy about dating. We all did it. It's gonna happen sooner or later."

The bile rose, and my cheeks quivered at the image of Daemon as a romantic date. Though by that point, he had softened me to the idea of being his American buddy, there was no attraction. "He's not a date. He's more like a ... tutor," I finally responded. Then contorting my face into a mildly repulsed grimace I paused, hoping Rosie might understand my lack of romantic interest in our guest. In case my intentions weren't clear enough, I added, "Thus, the messy dinner."

After a few seconds, she nodded in understanding. I had to hand it to Rosie, she was great at the cooking game. She was quick to come up with the perfect entree. Not thirty seconds after opening the fridge in search of a quick meal idea she giggled, "Got it! One rack of overly saucy ribs headed your way, sweetie."

Just before she headed into the pantry to find the ingredients for a perfect side, I added, "Oh, and could you stay for dinner? Sometimes three *is* company." Thankfully, our ever-accommodating chef knew exactly what I needed and agreed to be our third wheel for the evening.

About an hour later, I received a call from the security gate telling me I had a guest. Arriving the exact minute he said he'd be there, I knew it was Daemon. I told Roger to send him on up. It surprised me to see he had driven himself. Maybe he had a little rebel side to him after all. I peeked through the slats in my blinds as I watched him get out of the little, black Peugeot. He was wearing a black and white striped sweater with a black jacket and red scarf tied around his neck. He even wore a little, black beret. I giggled at his cliché appearance. He must have wanted to give me the full

French experience that evening.

I continued to watch as he bent over and fiddled in his car for a bit before finally slipping his way up the walk. He didn't have to knock. As soon as he passed the security cameras near the front entrance, a buzzer alarmed to let me know he was there. When I opened the door to greet him, the smell of cologne singed the hair in my nostrils.

"How did you know I waz here?"

The stench of black licorice was overpowering. I had to turn my head and take a deep breath before I could answer. "I saw you coming up the walkway." Trying to hold in my cough, I glanced over the top of him at his car. "You drove yourself?"

He looked over his shoulder, "Yez. I wanted to take my time whiz you tonight."

"You can do that? I always heard you weren't allowed to drive while on exchange."

"Caught me," he laughed. "Zzhhh, don't tell anybody. I znuck zhe car out. My hozt family iz gone for zhe night. Zhey probably won't notize." His eyebrows wandered up to his forehead. "Oh, I almozt forgot. Zheze are for you." He pulled out a dozen long-stemmed fire and ice roses. "I know I have zome competizion. Hopefully, zheze will zeal the deal."

Competition? My mind searched for what he was talking about. That's when my thoughts landed on Ty. The basketball game. Though I didn't know if they were going to lead to anything, my feelings for him were getting stronger than I wanted to admit. I would definitely have to set Daemon straight before the end of the night. But for a couple hours, I owed it to him to be a good sport. He'd done so many considerate things for me. Homecoming dinner. Hanging out at the birthday party. Saving my spot on the basketball team after the Christmas party. It wasn't going to hurt me to play nice. I took the flowers from his hand and gave him a one-armed hug. Patting his back, I whispered, "Thanks." Unable to look him in the eye, I stared at my feet as I walked him into the house.

"So, this is the foyer," I waved my arm, displaying the entrance. "What would you like to see next?"

"Zhe good ztuff. I'd love to zee zhe whole operazion."

"You've got it."

I guided Daemon through the house and down the path to the warehouse. That's where we found Roger waiting for us. Roger was my favorite of the vineyard employees. He was in his early twenties, was a treat to look at, and had a hilariously dry sense of humor. Not to mention, he had a huge soft spot for me. I'd asked him earlier if he might be able to give Daemon and me the grand tour from the Ranger. He was off for the weekend and I knew it was going to take some convincing to get him to stay late. Thankfully, that little, soft spot helped. It didn't take much to get him to cave to my begging, especially when I convinced him that it was too cold and icy to walk the grounds. The real hook was when I asked him to be my secret saboteur and make sure that no matter what, things between me and our visitor remained platonic. He seemed pretty excited about that job.

The smirk grew on Roger's face as he looked Daemon up and down. I could tell he was just as entertained by the French attire as I was. Then scratching the side of his head, he walked over to my dad's coat rack and grabbed a set of gloves and jacket. "You might want to bundle up. This isn't your typical vineyard tour," he laughed.

It had gotten pretty chilly the past few weeks. Watching Daemon dress in my dad's outerwear drew my attention to the frigid air. I tugged my hoodie down over my frozen ears as we walked down the icy path to the shop where we stored the heavy equipment. When we got to the ATV, Roger insisted that Daemon sat shotgun. I took my seat in the back. It was obvious that he wanted to sit next to me, but I convinced him that he couldn't miss the view from the front. I'd seen our little slice of heaven millions of times and I wanted him to have the full experience. It was beautiful the way the sun glistened on the frosted vines. It was like our own winter wonderland.

For the next half hour, we drove around the entire vineyard, stopping at various sites so Daemon could get a better look. It was interesting the way his face lit up as he studied the frosty plants, holding them close to his eyes and running his fingers along the vines. "It'z interezting to me that you're able to grow grapes in zhiz climate. It'z zuch a tricky thing to do." He almost sounded like he knew what he was talking about. "And you've got Syrah, Merlot, and Pinot Noir. Who knew?" Roger and I looked at each other in amusement. I giggled quietly at the thought of him trying to impress me with his knowledge of grape varieties.

"So, cold." I blew into my hands. "Do you mind if we go inside?"

"I'd love to see zhe zellar. Can you take me zhere?"

At the cellar, Daemon admired the craftsmanship of the barrels. He picked up various tools almost mimicking the exact actions they were used for. Next, he ran his fingers up and down the bottles of wine, almost as if to memorize their labels. When Daemon finally peeled himself away from the wine and started to sidle up next to me, Roger cleared his throat.

"Well, kids, we'd better get back before Rosie sends a search party after us. I'm sure she's holding dinner up at the house." Roger had the Ranger started before either of us could get another word in. "Hop in."

He did a great job on his mission to keep things platonic. While I sat in the back seat blowing warm air into my hands, he talked to Daemon the rest of the ride about the growing season in Northern California and the limited varieties we could keep so far north. I could hear the fascination in Daemon's voice as he hung on every word. In no time, we had pulled into the driveway at the main house.

"How was it?"

"Marvelouz. You Baileyz really know your ztuff. I would only change one zhing."

"What's that?"

"I zhought we might have a little alone time out at that bazeball field of yourz." It'z zo beautiful out zhere." He looked over the seat at Roger. "It'z a zetting meant for two."

There was only one place at the vineyard I was not willing to take him. My field. I was saving that for someone special. Thankfully, I didn't have to say anything. I could read the response brewing on Roger's face. He glared over his shoulder at Daemon. His expression reminded me very much of the one Caden often used on him. The one that told me he'd decided this kid was an irritating gnat. Sarcastically, Roger raised his eyebrows and smiled, "Not on my watch, son. I'll let Rosie know you're headed in for dinner."

"Rozie?"

"Our chef."

"I zhought we were alone tonight."

"Oh, we're never alone at the vineyard." I wanted to make it clear that my home was not the place he'd be getting any one-on-one time with me. I needed to get his mind off romance and onto the real reason he was there. "I Icy, let's get in there and work on that project."

"Well zince this plaze is crawling with people, could we at leazt work zomeplace private? I can't zhink in too much chaoz."

"I can arrange that," I smiled. As we walked past the kitchen I shouted, "Hey, Rosie, we'll be in my room!" I hoped that would tip her off to monitor the cameras and step in if I needed saving. Making sure to leave the door open, I showed him to my messy room. He glanced around, pursing his lips as his eyes bounced from one covered piece of furniture to the next. "Maybe we can go zit by zhe fire."

His bouncing eyebrows indicated that he was ready for a fire-side romance. I, however, was not. After clearing it of my sports bra, I pulled a stool next to my desk. "You can sit here." I patted the cushy seat, before plopping down onto my own. "Sit."

When I opened my laptop, Daemon handed me a glittery, pink thumb drive. "For you."

I'm sure amusement lit my face as I asked incredulously, "This is yours?"

Watching the glittery, pink flash drive shimmer as I turned it back and forth to catch the light, he chuckled. "I made it for you. It'z for your project. It'z got the templatez on it."

"Thanks, Daemon. That was very thoughtful." I powered my laptop on and waited for the welcome screen before slipping the flash drive into the USB. Instantly, a million numbers and letters flashed across my screen before it went blank. I slapped my hand over my chest, and gasped, "Oh, my God. I think it just ate my hard drive!"

"What? Let me zee it." He pulled the computer from my hands and typed in a series of commands. "Zhis haz happened to me before whiz new storage devizes." He continued to type quickly. Watching his fingers fly across the keyboard, I had to hand it to him. The guy was a programming genius. He handed me back the computer with a family tree template on the screen. "It'z az good az new. Juzt zome glitch."

For the next half hour, Daemon worked with me, asking me questions about my parents' names, where they were from, their siblings. I was careful with the information I knew. Unable to an-swer many of his questions, I got quiet. Clearly, he could see me struggling.

"Sorry, some of this stuff's kind of private."

"It'z okay." He stood up and walked around my room, pausing to pick up the lone, childhood picture of my friends and me. Gently shaking the framed picture he held in front of him, a distant look grew on his face. "Ztart whiz your own houze. Look around. You'll find more anzwerz here than you might zhink." The picture must have sparked some kind of inspiration. Immediately, he set it down and rushed to the laptop.

He bent over the top of me and started typing as he talked. "I have zhis site I uze. You can uze it too," he smiled, pulling up an ancestry site he used for his own family tree. Once he showed me how to obtain public records and plug my findings into the tree, he assured me I could take it from there. He looked at me with a knowing smile, "I muzt uze zhe bathroom. It might take a little while. I'll be back." The look on his face told me he was going to try to give me some privacy.

He wasn't kidding about taking a little while. By the time he returned, I had more names, birthdates, and cities of origin than I could've hoped for. Using my mom's maiden name and what I knew about her city of birth, I found her parents and grandparents, just enough information about her side of the family to fill in six more bubbles on the family tree. I was fascinated to discover that all the men were in the military and buried throughout Virginia and Maryland. Looking through the census and other public records was kind of interesting, but I didn't have time to dig any deeper. I could do that later. All I needed was enough to complete my project.

Oddly, when I plugged in my dad's name, a lot of his tree was already built. Someone in his family must've been into genealogy because it was all laid out there for me. All I had to do was transfer it onto the flash drive. "Thank you, some distant relative! I'll have to study up on you later," I whispered as I copied and pasted the information into the template on the flash drive. All I wanted to do was get those names and stats saved so I could develop the project later, alone, with nobody looking over my shoulder.

"How did you do?"

A huge smile plastered my face as he came back through the

door. "I have enough for the project!" I exclaimed.

"Did you uze my templatez?"

I nodded excitedly, "It's all here!" I held up the flash drive.

A smile lit his face as he scooped me up in a hug and swung me around. "I knew you could do it!" Then he slid me down to the floor, as he continued to stare into my eyes. Looking down at me, his grin spread from one side of his face to the other. Then in slow motion, he leaned into me, lowering his lips to where they nearly met mine. Thankfully, I had just enough flexibility in my back that he couldn't reach his target before we were interrupted.

"Dinner!" Rosie hollered, ringing a cowbell as she walked through the door.

Startled at the sound of the piercing bell, Daemon hopped back and released me from his hold. Scarlet-faced and breathing heavily, he was clearly flustered. Rosie walked in behind him and mouthed over the top of his head, "Yikes," then added with volume, "Let's move along now, kids. Nobody likes cold ribs around here."

When we got out into the kitchen, she asked if I'd help her with the serving. She pulled me into the pantry, where the walls were thick enough so we couldn't be overheard. "Who is this kid?"

"I told you. He's just a friend. Well, more like a tutor."

"Well, I don't like him."

"Rosie, you've seen him for like thirty seconds. You're not giving him much of a chance."

Concern grew on Rosie's face. "Did you know he was in your dad's den earlier? When I asked him what he was doing, he said he was looking for the bathroom."

"So?"

"So? He was inside the room behind your dad's desk. Most offices don't lead to a bathroom, child. I say he was up to something. Snoopy, little bugger." She paused for a minute waiting for my response.

I couldn't help but feel protective over Daemon. He was just there trying to help. And who knew how houses were designed in France? I didn't. "Actually, he was being sweet. I think he knew I was struggling with my project, so he was giving me some space. I actually appreciated it."

"Jenna, space or not, he was snooping around your dad's bookshelf."

"Maybe he wanted to look at the vineyard books. He seemed really interested."

"Possibly, but it's still not polite to go through another person's things."

"Maybe looking through someone's bookshelf is not rude in France. Maybe it's a sign of intelligence. He might actually like to read, Rosie."

Finally, with a goading grin, she said, "You sure are defending him for this not being a date."

"Look, he's always been super sweet to me. He comes off a little awkward at first. I think it's just a cultural difference. He's nice. You'll see."

"You could be right. Just be careful. Don't trust every boy who shows up at your house with cheap cologne and flowers."

"Got it," I smiled, picking up the potato salad and carrying it back to the dining room. "He's just my tutor," I smirked. Poor Rosie. She's from that paranoid generation. The one that has a hard time embracing cultural differences. Thankfully, I was being raised in a world that did. Daemon wasn't a bad guy. Just a guy that I wasn't into as anything more than a friend. Which reminded me. He just tried to lay one on me.

Stopping abruptly, I remembered to thank Rosie for saving me. Just before I opened the door, I turned my head and whispered, "Oh, I almost forgot. Thanks for saving me from the kiss with that cowbell. I didn't know we owned one of those things," I laughed. "That was a close one."

"Yes, it was. Don't think you're out of the woods yet. I have a feeling he's going to try again before the night's end. I'll keep my eye on him."

After her warning, I made dinner as unromantic as possible. I had sauce from one ear to the other and made sure to smile every time I felt the beef dangling between my two front teeth. I smacked my potato salad and let the butter from the corn on the cob drip from my fingers. Rosie seemed rather entertained as she sat in between the two of us watching my show. There was no way I wanted him to come close to me, let alone try to kiss me again. I made myself as greasy, buttery, and disgusting as possible. At the end of the night, when he came in again for a thank you hug, I let out a belch. He backed up quickly as I patted my stomach. "Rosie's some cook, huh?"

"Yez, um, zome cook," he said as he bowed his head and backed his way toward the door. "I zink I'd better go now. How about next time I chooze zhe plaze? Huh?"

"About that, Daemon. Thanks for helping me with the project. You are such a sweet friend, but I'm kind of interested in someone else right now. I think he kinda likes me too. Maybe we could do a group thing sometime, huh?"

His face flushed red as he nodded. I knew he was trying to cover his disappointment with a forced smile. "Zoundz good. I'll be zeeing you." Then he headed out the door and left without looking back.

Chapter Twenty-Four
Rumor Has It

THE WEEK FOLLOWING MY STUDY DATE WITH DAEMON WAS UTTER chaos. Pistol was still missing. Some recent developments in the investigation, along with news articles regarding suspicious activity near the cabin at the Forks, had us cautious, jumpy, and on high alert. We had no idea when or where Pistol might pop up again. Since Kaitlyn was at the greatest risk, Brody spent every waking minute with her. Caden had attached himself to me, convincing me that it was in our best interest to stick together. We'd never been so dependent on each other, guarding one another whenever we weren't in the security of our home.

Since his healing arm still wouldn't allow him to drive, I was Caden's personal chauffeur for the winter. I didn't mind it at all. Knowing he was by my side made me feel safe. Not to mention, he was hilariously entertaining, and I loved spending time with him. The only problem was, our showing up everywhere together had rumors flying, including the one that Caden dumped Peyton for *me*. As we walked down the hall together each morning, the backlash of whispers and snarky comments did not go unnoticed. We both knew it was leaving a kink in our dating lives, but the side effects of our alleged "thing" was something we were willing to put up with. Our safety was more important than people having a misconception about us being "more than just friends."

Aside from my Caden duties, I was bogged down with studying for finals, I had to finish the heritage project, and basketball practice ran late every night. The one thing in my favor was my nightmares had been nonexistent. By the time I hit the pillow each night everything went black, only to be awoken, what seemed like minutes later, by the annoying alarm. By the week leading into Christmas vacation, I felt like I was living inside a washing machine stuck on spin cycle. Wake. Drive. Work. Sleep five minutes. Repeat. Let's just say, I didn't know my head from my tail.

It was the morning my project was due, when I realized just how disorganized living on spin mode had left me. I needed to get to my mom's classroom a little early to print out the research paper and charts I'd made for my assignment. With my gym bag hanging from one arm and a piece of toast sticking out of my mouth, I scrambled to get out the door. Thank goodness I'd left my binder with all the rest of my stuff inside the car. I didn't have time to get all that together too. Running late, as usual, I pulled up in front of Caden's house to pick him up for school. He threw his backpack over the seat and began to gather the pile of papers he was about to sit on.

"Can you set my flash drive on top? It has my heritage report on it."

Caden scanned the console and dash before he shoved his hand between the backrest and seat. "Don't see a flash drive." He kneeled on the ground to continue his search of the floorboard. Shuffling papers, he chuckled as he pulled odds and ends from under the seat. "Looks like you got a loose wire here." He held up the end of what looked to be a stereo wire.

Frustrated, I straightened my arms and pushed my head into the backrest. "Can we look at that later?" If we didn't leave in the next two minutes, there was no way I was going to make it to my mom's class to print everything Impatience laced my tone, "In a hurry here." Annoyed at my lack of appreciation, he stood up and huffed, "Still not seeing it. Maybe you should help me."

It was a sparkly flash drive for goodness sake. It couldn't be that hard to find. "Ohhh. I forgot it's hooked to my lanyard and house key."

"I just checked this entire side. I didn't see a lanyard or house key either."

"Oh, come on," I mumbled to myself more than to Caden. I was about ready to slam my head into the steering wheel. "It's pink and glittery." I slid out of the car to search my side. "I just had it."

"Like this morning?" he asked.

When I stopped to think about it, I realized it had been a couple days since I'd used my house key. By the time I got home from basketball every night, my parents were already home. I'd been so relieved to finish the report mid-week. I hadn't even thought about the flash drive till I went to print my report and found out we were out of ink. Crap. I kneeled on the ground and felt around the floorboard.

Caden paused, looking up at me, "What the hell's that smell?"

From the driver's side, all I could smell was strawberries. "My air freshener?"

"If peanut butter and Fritos is your scent, I guess so." He continued to rifle through my stuff. "This place is a shit hole. What've you been doing in here?"

"My car's been my closet this week." Jokingly I added, "You could be smelling my sweaty, practice jersey or my gym socks. I haven't had time to do laundry."

"Smells more like peanut butter."

"I thought so too, but all I've eaten in here is a cranberry turkey wrap," I held up the wrapper and crumbled it into a ball.

He plugged his nose as he went in further, "It's definitely peanut butter and Fritos."

Caden crawled out, set the pile of work on the back seat, and plopped back down on the passenger's side. "We'd better go. It's not here." Then looking over at me he questioned, "Hey, you haven't been leaving your car at the gym, have you?"

"Yeah. It's been late practice this week and I don't want to walk over to the high school in the dark. You know, with Pistol and everything. You remember what he did to your sister that night in your driveway."

"Yeah, good job for being smart, but just so you know, you need to keep this thing locked. Kaleb's car was broken into this week, and so was Shelby's."

"Crazy. Thanks for the warning."

We drove for several minutes in silence before Caden threw me for a loop with an unexpected question. "By the way, how did you figure it all out? The project, I mean. You were so stressed out about it last week."

My heart stopped a beat. I knew I had to come up with something fast. I guessed a half-truth would work. "I spent a long weekend with this website I found out about."

"Yeah, where'd you find out about that? I could've used some help with mine too."

"Just a pop-up ad. I clicked on it, and voila. I don't even remember what it was called now."

An incredulous look grew on his face. It almost seemed as though he knew I wasn't telling him the whole story. However, I knew it was in my best interest to leave Daemon's name out of that one. Caden had already warned me multiple times about his unhealthy crush on me. I knew he would give me crap for encouraging it, even though I wasn't. Thankfully, Caden didn't question me further. If he had, I knew I wouldn't be able to keep the truth from him.

Thinking of all the ways I'd discouraged his advances on our study date left me quiet the rest of the drive. I could defend myself if Caden pressed it. Actually, he may have gotten a kick out of my dinner theatrics. I was happy with the way things turned out. I was nice and hospitable, but by the end of the night, he knew where he stood. I was into someone else. Daemon and I were just friends, plain and simple.

As I pulled into the parking lot, my focus shifted off Daemon. Looking toward the senior hallway, my uneasiness grew as I realized I had to face Mrs. G. Thinking about the fact that she'd already extended my due date once, made me feel even worse. The bottom line was, there was no way I could get the project done without that flash drive. Everything was on there. I was going to have to ask for a second extension.

Things went downhill once I got inside. Seeing I was nervous to speak with Mrs. George, Caden put his arm around my shoulder to comfort me. As we walked down the hall, he whispered into my ear and told me that everything was going to be fine. Then he cracked a few jokes to take my mind off the growing nausea in the pit of my stomach.

As we were cracking up over the last one, I spotted Ty walking toward us. Naturally, when our eyes met, I smiled at him. His reaction wasn't so warm. That's when I realized how things must have looked from across the hall. I watched as Ty's eyes roamed the length of Caden's arm right up around my shoulder. My heartbeat quickened as he began to walk toward us.

"Can I steal your girl for a sec?" Ty's voice was low and serious.

Caden lifted his arm from around my shoulder. "Guess so."

I grimaced at my best friend for doing nothing to clarify that I was not his girl. The rumors didn't matter to me when it came to Caden's fan club, but when it came to Ty, that was another story. He smirked at me as he watched us walk across the hall. We stopped at the edge of the lockers where we could chat privately.

Silently, he looked at me for an uncomfortable length of time. Was he waiting for an explanation? Because as far as I was concerned, I didn't owe him one. He'd never committed to me. From what I knew about high school dating, telling a girl "It's a date" as you ran out onto a basketball court, did not prohibit said girl from walking down the hall under the arm of her best friend. "What's going on?" I finally asked defensively.

His answer seemed forced, like he didn't really want to talk to me. I was right. Just like everybody else at Jefferson High, he thought I had a thing with my best friend. And the fact that my best friend was also one of his buddies had likely caused him to change his mind about going on a real date. He'd probably been looking for an excuse to break it off all week.

I had just opened my mouth to let him off the hook when Ty cut me off. "I'm not going to be able to make it tomorrow night."

And there it was. I knew going to the dash with my elusive crush was too good to be true. Every time I started to let myself like him, something slapped me across the face and reminded me that when it came to us, it just wasn't going to happen. Smothering my disappointment, I tried to act casual.

"No biggie," I shrugged, nonchalantly. "I've got plenty of guys to go with."

"Yeah, I see that," he looked over at Caden, who had just turned the corner into Mrs. G.'s. I'd expected him to call me out on watching him come around the corner, but instead his tone turned to disappointment. "It's just, I've got family coming."

It was no secret that Ty was an experienced dater. He'd broken half the hearts at Jefferson High. I'm sure he'd readied himself for a flood of tears, and also prepared himself with an explanation to help dry them. Well, his "disappointment act" wasn't going to work on me. I was determined to meet his crap with a good dose of indifference.

"No need to explain," I smiled and began to walk away. Looking back over my shoulder, I replied, "Gotta go. I'm meeting with Mrs. G. Like I said, it's all good. Have fun with your," I shined an exaggerated smile, "family." To emphasize my lack of sadness, I put a little bounce in my step as I skipped off.

The truth was, I felt like I had just been punched in the throat. I had been looking forward to my date with Ty for an entire week. I'd fantasized about us holding hands, racing through the streets, me dragging him to the Christmas tree lighting, and sipping hot chocolate under the snowy sky. I wanted us to get our pictures on Santa's lap, and maybe even find some mistletoe. It was going to be the perfect first date with the perfect guy.

Only Ty wasn't the perfect guy. Not a real one anyway. He was just some silly fantasy I had to get over. It was never going to work with him, especially if he was willing to believe the stupid rumors. Visiting family was a lame excuse. He could have at least been a little more creative. Who needed a smoking-hot jock anyway? Not me. I was ready to cut his face out of my Christmas fantasy date and replace it with the pile-of-poo emoji.

By the time I slipped into class, almost everyone was already seated. I could see there were only two open seats, but explaining why my heritage project was missing couldn't wait. I had to talk to Mrs. G. about the flash drive. I hadn't said a word when she held her hand up and stopped me. "No worries, Jenna. Your boy, I mean, Caden already explained everything."

Caden winked as I looked back at him and whispered, "Seriously?" I couldn't believe he'd been perpetuating the ridiculous notion that he and I were a thing. He even had Mrs. G. believing it. Shaking my head, I thanked her for extending my deadline till after Christmas. Then turning to find one of those empty seats, I noticed the only one left was next to Daemon.

"Hey," he smiled, "I juzt heard you talking to Mrz. G."

"Yeah, all that work for nothing."

"Oh no, it'z not for nothing. I zhink I can help you whiz your problem."

"Haven't you already done enough? You wasted an entire night with me for no reason."

"Oh, no. You're never a wazte of time. I can get it all back for you."

"Really? How?"

"I'll juzt vizit zhe hiztory on your computer and get it back for you. No problem. You will zee. Juzt let me know when and where and I'll be zhere."

I couldn't help but wonder why the guy was so good to me. "Even if it's during break?"

"Ezpezially if it'z during break."

Relief came over me. "I don't know why you keep helping me like this, but thank you. So much, Daemon. Really. I owe you."

Chapter Twenty-Five

Excuses, Excuses

I WASN'T GOING TO LET TY'S OBVIOUS BLOW-OFF RUIN THE FIRST weekend of my Christmas vacation. Not being the kind of person to sit around and feel sorry for myself, I came up with another plan. I asked Caden if we could go to the Night of Lights Christmas parade together, and maybe afterward team up for Dash to the Pole. Knowing I could kick serious booty when it came to all things scavenger hunt, he happily accepted my offer. Thinking back on my earlier conversation in the hallway, I found it interesting that Caden would replace Ty as my date after all. I knew half of our high school celebrated Christmas in Mt. Shasta. Our teaming up was likely to fuel the rumors, but to me, the charity dash with my best friend was worth enduring the gossip.

With no four-wheel drive available, Caden's parents were gracious enough to drive us. Pulling into the downtown area, we found the roads were blocked off and the crossroads were bustling with traffic. Fire trucks, antique cars, and beautiful Clydesdales, all adorned with Christmas lights and festive trimmings, moved slowly into their starting positions. Because the drive was slow going, it had left the Woodleys late to check into their station. Coach insisted that Caden drop them off at the checkpoint and park the truck down at his store.

Even though he knew his dad was in a bind, Caden refused. That was my first inclination that something was up with him. He'd had me drive him everywhere for weeks, but I'd never thought much of it. I knew he was still favoring his arm after the accident, but somehow his resistance to helping his dad didn't fit his personality. I'd seen him endure pretty severe injuries in football, but he'd never babied his wounds like that before. He had always been tough and resilient, defying doctor's orders in favor of four-wheeling, snow-mobiling, or anything else that required motors and speed.

That's why his reaction to Coach surprised me. I sat and listened as Caden tried to talk his way out of driving through town. When his father wouldn't take no for an answer, the color drained from his face. His adamant refusal had me questioning if there wasn't more to his resistance than an arm injury.

Finally, he caved to his dad's pressure. When his parents got out, we slid into the front seat. He sat and watched them walk into The Fifth Season, the sporting goods store where they were stationed. After a minute, a horn blasted behind us. Knocking Caden upside the back of the head, I tried to spur him to move the truck. I wondered why he continued to block traffic with so many people trying to move into position. Ignoring me, he continued to watch his parents walk into the store. The second they were out of sight, Caden turned and handed me the keys.

"Here."

"Here?"

"You've got to drive."

"Seriously, you really don't want to drive your dad's truck? I thought you lived to drive this rig."

"I'm not feeling so good. It's my arm."

Knowing that I couldn't get into a full-on battle at the stop-light, I played along. I needed to get us out of there. "Well, if you don't want to, I have no problem."

Caden slid across the bench seat, pulling me over the top of him. He set me in front of the wheel and took a deep breath as he looked around at the blur of movement in front of us. The way he lifted me with ease and plopped me in the driver's seat assured me that my suspicions were correct. His arm was not the reason he wouldn't drive.

Once I was in the driver's seat, things began to make a little more sense. The congestion was terrible. I could see where Caden might have been hesitant to drive. It had only been a month since his accident. Between the snowflakes coming at warp speed under the street lamps, the bright lights from the parade, and the people buzzing through the streets, even I was a little dizzy.

I pulled into the parking lot at Coach's store. That's where we met Brody and Kaitlyn. The minute we saw them, I could tell she was unsettled. I thought maybe in the midst of the large crowd, her anxiety over Pistol was flaring up. Or not. The way she stared us down as we sat side-by-side on the bench seat, made me question if I was wrong.

Maybe it wasn't Pistol. Perhaps she was just as tired of defending rumors about Caden and me as I was. The one thing I did know, was I'd find out what was wrong with her soon enough. She wasn't one to keep anything from me. We slipped out of the truck as they approached. Kaitlyn continued to study the two of us, finally huffing, "We'd better get up there."

We knew trekking five blocks to the starting point would be slow going. We'd likely miss registration for the dash if we couldn't find a ride. Thankfully, as we neared the diner, we spotted a caroling truck ready to take off. As it slowly lurched forward, Caden and Brody jumped up, extending their arms to help us onto the moving truck. Kaitlyn grabbed Brody's hand, and without thinking, I clutched Caden's. He hoisted me with ease, pulling me into his arms.

Standing together as he steadied me, I noticed Kaitlyn had the same fiery glare. I was going to be pissed if she started believing the rumors too. He had simply wrapped his arms around me until I gained my balance. Kaitlyn knew we were just friends. Best friends at that. At least we had been since she and Brody had nearly become recluses. They're the ones who left Caden and me out in the open world to protect each other.

As I studied her angry face, I realized she wasn't looking at me after all. Her eyes were glued to her brother. Well, more to his arm. That's when I realized why she was so upset. He had tugged me onto the flatbed with his injured arm. Kaitlyn had noticed his slip.

"I'm telling." She scowled at Caden.

"You're telling? Are we six now?"

My mind drifted as Kaitlyn began to argue with her brother over his arm and how he'd been keeping his recovery a secret. After watching the way he flung me onto the truck bed, we both knew that he had been suffering more than physical damage. No wonder he'd been allowing everyone to think we were together all winter. It was his way of keeping me as his personal chauffeur. If he'd let on that I wasn't into him, surely Ty would have taken me away. It all made so much sense.

Clearly, he needed help. Knowing I would come up with a way to talk to him about the benefits of counseling later, I let Kaitlyn take that battle. The middle of a Christmas caroling truck was not someplace I wanted to get into it. As the Carol of the Bells got louder, so did their argument.

Finally, Caden covered his ears and began to sarcastically bellow, "la la la la, la la la la … ding dong, ding dong …" mocking the elderly singers during the chorus. He wasn't going to listen to his sister one more second. I knew he was completely done with the argument, with the ride, with everything, when he snarled, "See you later," and bailed from the truck.

I stood there looking after him, as Caden disappeared into the crowd. With the glare of the lights and loud music, my eyes could no longer track him. Bobbing up and down and side to side,

I frantically searched through the mass of bodies. Everything was a blur. I looked back toward Kaitlyn and watched her face morph into a worried grimace. It was time to go after him. None of us were supposed to separate. Certain I could catch him, I bellowed, "You two stay together. I'll find him." Without waiting for their response, I jumped off the back of the truck and ran toward the gas station where I'd last seen him.

Running down Mt. Shasta Boulevard, I bounced through the crowd of people.

"Slow down there, kid. You're going to hurt someone," a grumpy, old man shook his cane at me. I slowed down long enough to whisper, "Sorry," before I continued to jog toward the downtown area.

Next, I spotted a crowd of cheerleaders, ready to climb onto the fire truck. I found myself weaving through their high kicks and toe touches.

"Jenna!" A voice bellowed from behind me. "Jenna, here!" I turned to see a black SUV with tinted windows driving beside me. As its window slowly vanished, the image of a furry hat and coat appeared in its place. With snowflakes sticking to my lashes, I squinted to see who the voice belonged to. "Do you need a lift?" I was surprised to see it was Daemon.

"Oh, hey, Daemon," I panted as I continued to jog, "Are you here for the dash?"

"Zomething like that. Hey, you zeem to be in a hurry. Can I take you zomewhere?"

That's when I spotted Caden's plaid flannel. "Nope," I shook my head." I see who I'm looking for. Besides, you can't get through the barricades." I pointed toward the south boulevard. "You'd better go that way."

Daemon's mouth drew into a serious line. "Very well. Have fun whiz your date tonight, huh?"

"Thanks. I will," I waved. "I'll catch up with you later, if you still want to work on the project." Afraid I might lose sight of Caden, I smiled and didn't look back. Though I'd seriously wished for a pair of yak tracks right about then, I poured on the speed, finally catching him down by the Italian restaurant.

As soon as I was within reach, I tugged at his shoulder. He whipped around, nearly giving me a heart attack from his rapid movement.

"Holy crap, you scared the hell out of me."

"Good!"

"Good?"

"Maybe it will wake you up to the reality of this situation."

"What situation?"

"He could still be out there, Caden. What happened to sticking together? You know damn good and well we aren't supposed to go anywhere alone. You took off like a bat out of hell. What happened back there?"

"I was sick of it. That's all!"

"Sick of what?"

"I just wanted to have fun today and people are trying to force me to drive, force me to ride with old lady carolers, jump my shit for stuff beyond my control ... I just want to have a good time for once, okay? We need to move on with our lives. I don't want to think about it anymore. I don't want to be reminded of it. I don't want anything to do with it. I just want peace. I want to watch the parade, go do my good deeds for the dash, and enjoy a traditional family Christmas. Is that too much to ask?"

That's when I finally realized that Caden was overwhelmed. He had been in constant protective mode and he needed a break. Looking around at all the people and feeling the Christmas spirit assured me that we were in a safe place. We could let our guards down there.

I nodded, "You're right. That's why we're down here. We need to give you that Christmas." I continued to talk him down and try to make him feel better.

"Thanks."

"For what?"

"For letting me vent. For sticking by me even when I'm an asshole. For making sure that I'm going to be okay. You're a great friend. I don't deserve you."

"You'll make it up to me," I giggled, nudging his shoulder. That's when I felt the buzzing in my pocket. "Hang on a sec." I pointed to my phone. "I've got to take this. It's Ty." I raised my eyebrows wondering what in the world he was doing calling me.

"Go ahead." Caden turned away and looked toward the parade.

"Hey, Ty," I answered, curiously.

"Hey. Are you someplace you can talk? Sounds loud in the background."

I covered my open ear with my hand and nodded, "Uh huh."

"Caden told me he was taking you tonight."

"Oh, really?"

"Well, I don't want to bother you. Actually, my little brother asked me to call. He was admitted to the hospital yesterday. Complications with his diabetes."

"Oh, no."

"Listen, do you think you'd be able to drop by and see him? He has to stay another night, and it meant a lot to him last time."

"Yeah, I think so."

"You sound distracted. Maybe I shouldn't have called."

"No, we just got down to the dash. Remember, you were going to come with me?"

"Yeah." He quieted, sounding almost disappointed that I'd replaced him. "Look, I don't want to ruin your date with Caden, but I really need you tonight. Maybe you can get him to come back up here with you."

Before I knew what I was saying, I answered, "Maybe. I'll try my best." What was I thinking? I knew Caden wouldn't give up the dash. I didn't even have a ride back. Clearly, Ty did something to my brain that stripped me of all logical thought.

"Well, if it doesn't work out, I'll try to find another way to take his mind off Christmas in the hospital."

The words "I really need you tonight," left my mind scrambling for a way to get home. I fell silent, thinking of ways to get up to the hospital to help him.

"Are you still there?"

"Sorry." I knew my tone hadn't come out right. It sounded more cold than compassionate.

"Look, Jenna, I know I had to break our date. I can tell you're pissed at me, but I'm calling for Aiden. You know he still keeps your picture pinned to the roof of his bunk bed," he chuckled. "If you don't want to come because I'm here, I get it."

Clearly, my silence was sending the wrong signal. The last thing I wanted was for Ty to think I didn't want to be around him. Nothing could have been further from the truth.

"I'm going to try, okay?"

"Thanks."

"If I can't get back up there, give him a hug for me."

I hung up the phone and turned back to Caden.

"Everything okay?"

"It's Ty's little brother. He had some complications with his diabetes yesterday. He's still in the hospital. Looks like he's going to be there overnight." I explained my history with Aiden and how we'd grown close at summer camp. If I could do anything to help on Christmas Eve, I wanted to be there. Caden seemed sympathetic to the situation, but the bottom line was I didn't want to let him down by bailing on him. Not to mention, I didn't drive.

I turned to him, "What should I do?"

"It's going to be okay. I'll tell you what. We'll either let you take one of the store trucks or find T and Brody to get you back up to the hospital. Don't worry about the dash. They can always put me on an open team. There's usually a handful that needs to pick up an extra person. Let's get you up there and help your man."

"My man, huh?"

"It's obvious you like him," he chuckled, "… and after hearing him in the locker room on Friday, I'm pretty sure he's wishing he was here with you."

"But he broke our date."

"He didn't want to. Trust me."

"But, his family? Come on. What kind of an excuse is that?"

Caden shrugged. "The kind that's too lame to make up. He likes you, Jenna."

"No way."

"Yes, way. Why do you think I've been messing with him so hard?"

The smirk on his face started to worry me. "I know you haven't been dispelling any of the rumors, but what else did you do?" I questioned.

"Just helped my best friend a little. Figured I owed you after how selfish I've been. I've been a little deceiving about us being more than friends, and I'm sorry. I set him straight during our locker-room chat."

My cheeks warmed when I imagined what he could have possibly discussed with Ty. "Don't worry, I didn't say or do anything to embarrass you."

"You sure love messing with people." I smacked his arm. "Especially me right now."

"Believe what you want," he smirked, "you'll thank me soon enough."

Brody and Kaitlyn pulled up to take me back to town. "Just a minute guys. I've got to do something really quick." Knowing they always had great mystery bags during the holidays, I hurried into the gift store behind me and bought one for a tween boy. Thankfully, it was a quick purchase and they hadn't left without me. Before I hopped into the waiting truck, I ran over and gave Caden a hug. "Good luck tonight. Hope they get you on a good team."

"Don't worry about me," he smiled. "I'm feeling kinda lucky." I nodded and thanked him again.

As we pulled away, Caden hollered, "Go get him!"

Although I knew he was joking, his last command had my forehead pooling with tiny beads of sweat. The possibility that things might be looking up for Ty and me, sent my hopes soaring. I couldn't help but think back on the times we'd hung out last spring, at camp, and flirted in the halls. It was quite a revelation finding out the reason things had been so on-and-off again were because my best friend needed me around more than he cared to admit. I couldn't believe he'd been the one leading everyone to believe we were together.

Before I got too hopeful about a romantic Christmas Eve, I had to remember Ty had called me for his little brother. He hadn't said anything about wanting to hang out with me. Either way, I was going to be there for Aiden.

I held up the cute Christmas package, twisting the bow into curls before I slid it into my purse. I hoped it held something that would brighten Aiden's night. In case something happened that prevented me from getting to the hospital, I decided not to call first. To me, surprises were always better than disappointments.

Thanking Kaitlyn and Brody for the ride, I wrapped myself in my pea coat and pulled my purse over my shoulder.

"Let us know if you need us to pick you up," Brody called, watching until I was inside.

Having been there several times that year, I knew exactly where to go. Straight to the nurse's station to find Aiden's room number.

When I got there, the station was nearly empty, manned only by one nurse who wouldn't turn around. After clearing my throat, she mumbled, "Be with you in a minute."

"Thanks."

That's when I caught sight of Ty making his way across the hall with large thermoses. Mid-hallway he stopped and looked at me.

"Hey," he grinned as he glanced around and then looked back to me. "I thought I saw you."

One grin and I was mush. I could see the twinkle in his sky-blue eyes all the way from the nurses' station. The way his dimples popped sent my heart racing. My throat went dry. It was one thing to fantasize about Ty, but it was another to see the breathtaking human standing in front of me. I couldn't help but blush as my heart pulled all the blood from my chest and shot it straight to my cheeks. I wanted to look away, so he couldn't see the sudden change in my coloring. Instead, I found my eyes drawn to his athletic figure. His chiseled jawline. The definition in his neck and chest. And I certainly couldn't help but notice the bulge of his biceps beneath his thin sweater. Those drinks must have been heavier than they looked.

It took everything in me to act casual when he began to walk toward me. "You made it. Is Caden with you?"

"It's just me." I held out my arms, trying to play it cool, "Surprise." Thank God my pea coat was thick enough to cover my trembling. I was literally at war with the geyser erupting inside of me. It was all I could do to steady my voice. I couldn't let him see the effects of his presence. As nervous as I was, he seemed exceptionally composed. How was he so calm? I didn't see red in his cheeks or hear an earthquake in his voice. Clearly, Caden had misunderstood Ty's feelings for me during their locker-room chat. Damn it. He had me worked up again over nothing.

"Well come on then," Ty tilted his head toward the door. "Our little star is in here."

When I walked through the door of the crowded room, Aiden sat up and smiled. "You brought her! Hi, Jenna," he waved the arm of the little, stuffed lab I bought him on his last trip to the hospital.

"Anything for you, pal," he winked at Aiden.

So, I was his anything. I could've been a video game for all he cared, as long as it made his little brother happy.

"Everyone, this is, Jenna." Ty smiled as he held his arm out to introduce me. "Jenna, this is everyone." He made the same motion toward all the people.

"You know my parents, Don and Michelle, I'm sure. This is the rest of my family. Uncle Trevor, Auntie Leora and my cousins, Jacob, Maddie, and Izzy." He looked at me again and raised his eyebrows. "My family." Saying the word, "family," he mimicked the same shiny smile I'd given him in the hallway last Friday when he broke our date.

Clearly, my reaction had affected him more than he'd let on. He wasn't lying. He really did have family in town. I waved to everyone, "Nice to meet you all."

After the formalities had ended, I couldn't help but notice the way Aiden looked at me. I was there to visit him after all. "If you guys will excuse me for a second, I have someone I'm here to see." I plopped down on the bed next to him. "How's it going, little man?" I asked.

"Feeling better, now. Guess I had too many cinnamon rolls for Christmas. We couldn't get my blood sugar down."

"Are they getting you fixed up?"

"Doctor said he's pretty sure I'll get to go home tomorrow."

"Just in time to open presents."

The room grew silent. I could tell Ty's parents were stressed about the timing of Aiden's hospitalization. "Speaking of presents, I got a mystery bag for you down at the dash." I pulled the bag out of my purse. "Let's see what's inside."

Conversation picked up around the room, with smiles and

encouragement for him to open his gift. Aiden's face lit with amusement, as he took the bag from me, untied the bow, and stuffed his hand inside. He giggled as he left it there wiggling his fingers, so we could see the sides of the bag popping. He was playing with us, trying to kill us with anticipation. Finally, when Ty told him to get on with it, he pulled out a silver frame. Inside was an autographed Buster Posey trading card. The same one I'd hidden away with my treasures each time my family was uprooted.

"Did you know?" he gasped. "I've been trying to get this one!" He climbed out of the covers and began to jump up and down on the bed.

"Slow down there, Tiger." Ty grabbed him and looked at me. "Thanks, Jenna. You really know your way to this kid's heart." Ty set Aiden back down on the bed and he crawled onto my lap and gave me a hug. "Now if you don't mind, I'm going to take your favorite girl. I need her help with something."

"Will you bring her back?"

"It's your bedtime, kid. You'd better get to sleep so Santa can do his job."

"I'll tell you what," I leaned into him and whispered in his ear, "if you're still here tomorrow, I'll come back and visit. Deal?"

"Deal."

Chapter Twenty-Six

Shades of Jenna

A S WE WERE WALKING OUT OF THE HOSPITAL, TY LEANED INTO ME, close enough that I could feel his words on my cheek. "I'm sorry. I didn't even ask if you wanted to come help. If you're willing, it's going to take a lot of work to make the magic happen."

It was only the slightest brush of his chin against my shoulder, but I almost crumbled from the roller coaster of impulses that twirled through my chest. I knew that even though a wrecking ball had just been released on the inside, I had to play it cool. For all Ty knew, he was the reason I had just cut my time short with Caden. When it came to the dating world, it put him one up on the leaderboard. The fact of the matter was he broke our date, and I turned around and sacrificed my night to help him. It almost felt desperate. The last thing I wanted was to give him the upper hand. I shrugged nonchalantly, "I've cleared my schedule."

Ty grew quiet, "Yeah, sorry I pulled you away from your date."

He'd opened another opportunity for me to leave him guessing about mine and Caden's relationship, and that was one more card I was willing to hold on to. "No worries. It's not like you had to twist my arm or anything." When his face lit at my response, I clarified, "I adore Aiden." It was all I could do to stop myself from saying, almost as much as I adore you, but I wouldn't dare speak the words out loud.

"Well, thanks for lifting his spirits. His reaction to seeing you was more than I could've hoped for. You made his night."

"It was my pleasure, really. He's a great kid. But if there's anything more I can do, I have a few hours."

Gratitude laced his expression as he looked into my eyes. His smile lit his face enough that I could see the slight shake of his head. "You're really up for this?"

"Anything to help a friend on Christmas. You name it."

As he pursed his lips and his eyebrows pinched together, I could tell he was reviewing his mental checklist. I'd never seen concentration look so hot. I was hoping he'd speak soon before I melted into a pool of mush right there in front of him. "Well, I have a few things I promised my parents I'd help with, but if you're really into working a Christmas miracle, there is one thing Aiden asked for that Santa couldn't quite deliver on."

"What's that?"

"A puppy. They're kind of hard to come by this time of year. I've had a few leads, but nothing solid. You know of any?"

By the chuckle he released as he shook his head, I could tell he was joking. But in fact, I did know of a breeder. Roger and his wife had a litter of labs, and I had been waiting to get my puppy since October. It wouldn't be hard to put in a call to see if my pup had any brothers or sisters available. "As a matter of fact, I do. Let's hope they aren't all spoken for."

"You're serious?"

I took out my phone. "Watch this."

Roger answered right away. I turned away from Ty in case it was bad news. Unfortunately, all the puppies were promised. At first, it seemed the only thing I could do was tell him I had no luck. However, as I chatted with Roger, my mind began to search for another solution. There was clearly a Christmas puppy available. It just happened to be mine. For the slightest moment, the thought crossed my mind that I could give it up. I dismissed it at first, but the thought kept circling back around. Spring would be busy, after all. I had senior project stuff, softball, and vineyard duties. The more I thought about it, the more I realized the timing for me to take on a puppy was terrible. Aiden really would be a better caretaker for my puppy, and I could always get one from the next litter. More than anything, if it meant making my little friend's Christmas, I would be okay with the sacrifice. Nobody needed to know it was supposed to be my puppy. I decided I could wait.

"We got one!" I grinned after I hung up the phone.

Ty shook his head, "You're unbelievable. How did you pull that off?"

"Ancient Chinese secret," I giggled. "My friend, Roger, is going to meet us at the vineyard in a couple hours with the puppy. He was a little surprised to see him off a couple days early, but super excited to get rid of the crazy, little booger he had available. Those little rascals are starting to drive him crazy."

As we walked toward the parking lot, I continued to tell Ty all about the pups, leaving out the fact that Aiden's puppy was supposed to be mine. I didn't want him to feel uneasy about taking the one I'd been waiting for. I wanted him to feel nothing but joy at giving his brother the one thing he wanted most. By the time we got to the parking lot, Ty was silent. We stood in front of his truck as he stared at me shaking his head.

"Everything okay?"

"It's more than okay. It's just …"

"Just what?"

"The rumors about you are true."

"Rumors!" I sighed, "Which rumors this time?"

A grin lit his face as he whispered, "The ones that say you're really good at getting out of pickles." He pulled me into a thankful hug and released me as he chuckled, "I don't know how you pulled that off, but thanks, Pickle."

My heart threw in a few extra beats. Not only had he just pulled me into his strong arms, but he had used my nickname. On purpose. The memory attached to the way he started calling me Pickle, after he rescued my top that night, unleashed a thousand butterflies. It was like we were right back in that moment. The rush of heat that filled my cheeks was in stark contrast to the cool night air. It left me shivering.

I couldn't let him see what his hug did to me. I looked down at my feet. "Alright, we've got two hours. What've we got to do?"

"We've got to hurry, that's what." Ty popped the trunk of the car next to us.

"What are you doing?"

"I need to grab a few things from my mom's car."

As I watched him pull an endless number of bags and rolls of wrapping paper from the car, I ran over and held out my hands. "Right behind you. Let me help."

"Never pegged you for such a good assistant," he said as he laid the rolls across my arms and hung a bag of gifts from my wrist. "You always seem to be so …"

"So what?"

"In charge."

I almost laughed at the idea that he found me bossy, one trait that I was sure he could identify with. "I'm actually a pretty good team player."

"We'll see about that," he laughed. I must have looked like a Jenga tower as I peeked through the tiny peephole he left for me. "Let's see if you've really got what it takes to wrap with the big boys."

"So, tonight's my tryout, huh?" I giggled as I carried the bags and rolls over to his truck.

"Girl, you already made my team the minute you showed up at the hospital. I'm just working on what position to put you in."

It was an intense drive to Ty's house, as I mulled over his suggestive comment. The minute I slid into his truck, I analyzed every position he could possibly put me in. Coupled with the smell of his cologne wrapping itself around me, my tummy was nearly squeezing itself through my throat. I could see him watching me struggle through the corner of his eye. A new grin lit his face every time a fresh wave of adrenaline coursed through me. The way he looked at me with every rush, told me he noticed.

"What's so funny over there?" I finally asked as he began to chuckle.

"I didn't know there were so many shades of Jenna."

My neck and cheeks scorched as the blood pulsed to my brain. I began waving my hand in front of my face. I needed to roll down the window and quick. "Are you cold-blooded or something?" I asked, trying to distract from the reality that he had just taken a sledgehammer to my internal thermostat. "It's like Death Valley in here." I reached for the dash to turn off the heater.

Before I could spin it all the way to AC, his hand met mine as he chuckled, "What happened to you being cold? It's December. It ain't the truck heater, Pickle."

It was hard to hide the reaction of what sitting near him in his truck did to me. To make matters worse, he had just called my bluff. I had to say something. Do something before I passed out from the heat. Thankfully, I was wearing layers. I began to tug my sweatshirt over my head, accidentally exposing a bit of my belly.

"Whoa! Slow down there, girl. We're just gonna be wrapping a few gifts."

He was really having fun watching my temperature soar. "You really know how to get a girl flustered. You know that?"

"Good to know. Flustered looks cute on you."

The minute he said it looked cute on me, I decided flustered would be my new favorite emotion. Before I could get the last word in, we pulled up in front of his house. Finally, I could get the air I needed. I reached for the door handle, ready to fly from his truck and find a pile of snow to cool off in.

"Hold up," he stopped me as he jumped out of the truck. "Don't go anywhere."

After pulling my sweatshirt back over my head, I looked up to find him standing outside my window. He was waiting to open the door for me. "After you."

"Do guys still do that?"

"Only the ones who want to see another shade of their favorite girl." He held his hand out and gently took mine to help me step down. Once I had both feet on the ground, he slid his hand under my chin and inspected what he'd done to me. Smiling, he whispered, "Let's call that one bubblegum." And there with my face resting in the palm of his hand, I found myself mush again.

No sooner did I remember to breathe, then Ty pulled his hand out from under my chin and placed a super-sized bag of toys in my arms. "Time to get to work."

When we got in the house, we laid all the wrapping paper out on the floor beside the gifts. He sat on one side. I sat on the other. The tape and scissors in the middle. Still coming down from my bubblegum high, I sat speechless, focused on the gifts in front of me. We took turns cutting, taping, wrapping, and tying bows. When I finally had the nerve to look up and see what he was doing, I noticed he hadn't even finished his small pile of gifts.

"What're you doing?"

"Watching you."

"I see that. You've been doing it a lot tonight."

"Can't help it," he mumbled. "I mean, it's a good excuse to get out of wrapping."

With the way I'd just caught him staring at me, I couldn't help but wonder if I had started to earn my own slash on the scoreboard. I was suddenly gifted the boost of confidence I needed to play back. "Well, you'd better start helping or you're going to have to explain this to your parents."

"Explain what?"

"That the reason Aiden's gifts aren't wrapped is because you have a staring problem," I laughed and smacked him with a roll of wrapping paper.

"I have a what?" Before I could react, he'd snatched the roll of wrapping paper from my hand, rolled it toward the couch, and wrestled me to the ground. His hold on me was strong enough to let me know that even at his weakest, this boy could take care of me if I ever needed him to. But at the same time, he was gentle enough that I knew he was playing. We rolled and twisted back and forth in the middle of the living room until we stopped suddenly and stared into each other's eyes. Too intensely. Too soon. It had created an awkward situation that neither of us was ready to face.

That's when I giggled, "You have a staring problem." Then I pushed myself into him, wrapped my leg around the back of his, and flipped him over. I could feel his body tense when he wound up pinned beneath me. "Gotcha," I breathed as I rested on top of him.

By reversing our positions, I hadn't done anything to relieve the intensity between us. If anything, our sensitive contact, had increased the problem. Again, our stares met. All either of us could do was breathe heavily through our exaggerated grins.

"We need to talk," he finally breathed, as he lifted me from the top of him and set me down.

There it was. I knew things were about to get serious. I took a deep breath.

"What's up with you and Caden, really?"

The tension was thick, and the way he'd just felt beneath me, made me believe what Caden had said was true. Ty really might like me, and this could be the only chance I ever got to set the record straight. It was time for him to hear the truth from me. "He's my best friend. He's gone through a lot with the accident and Peyton, and I've just tried to be there for him. That's all."

"Does he like you? Like, like you, like you?"

"God, no. He's like my brother." I laughed before I turned serious. "Don't believe the rumors."

"It's just … when I talked to him about you, he didn't say anything to make me believe otherwise."

I knew they had talked. Caden had told me all about it. What I also knew was that Caden wasn't setting him straight because if he did, he'd likely have to start sharing. He wasn't ready to drive on his own. And he had just lost Peyton. He was lonely, and I was his crutch. However, now that he had asked, it was my opportunity to find out a little more … from Ty's perspective.

"So, you talked to him about me?" I smiled.

"Maybe."

"Well, maybe I talked to him about you too."

His eyes twinkled as his grin began to show the dimples on his cheeks. "You did, huh?"

"And, it seems my best friend thinks it's rather funny to play with our insecurities."

"And what might those insecurities be?"

I was stumped by his question. The fantasy I'd been dreaming about for so long, could actually be coming true. I didn't know if I was ready to tell him. Ready for possible rejection. I needed to get out of that conversation as quickly as possible and give myself more time. I needed water. I needed air. I needed anything but to let him know that *he* was my insecurity. The only one I couldn't seem to shake anyway.

He finally broke the silence. "It's me, isn't it?"

I couldn't help but gasp. Quickly, I looked down at the floor to try and cover the shock of him calling me out.

Those were the moments I lived to avoid. The ones that left me vulnerable. Exposed. Not knowing how he'd feel about it, there was no way I could admit that I'd liked him since the previous baseball season, even before we were counselors together. He had to know I was attracted to him. He'd caught me spying on him in the locker room, we'd danced together at Homecoming, and if he knew I was into him, he never acted on it. He had plenty of opportunities to like me back. I refused to tell him with my own mouth that I'd been resisting a secret crush since last spring.

He tilted my chin, "Look at me." I looked him in the eye and knew he could see right through me. There was no way I could hide the way I felt. His grin let me know I'd been caught. Not only that, but he didn't seem to mind that I liked him. "Pickle, don't worry. When I look at you, it's like looking in a mirror. I know exactly what you're thinking. You're thinking I might not like you back. You're questioning yourself, wondering why, if I liked you, I haven't made a move. Jenna, we've been playing the same game, and I think it's time for one of us to be brave. It's time to tell you the truth. I've liked you for a long time. A really long time. The last thing I want to be is your insecurity."

I swallowed the lump in my throat. He started to lean into me. For the millionth time that night, everything inside of me contracted and twisted. I could almost feel his lips when he set his forehead against mine and shook his head. "I could kiss you right now, but I'm not going to."

I breathed a sigh, "You're not?"

I felt his head shake, no. "I don't want our first kiss to be like this."

I couldn't believe what I was hearing. Ty was thinking about a first kiss. With me.

"After Christmas, when everything settles down. I'm going to take you on a real date and give you a real kiss. The kind you won't forget."

I couldn't stop the fireworks from spiraling through my chest. I'd never had a guy set a special date just to kiss me. The anticipation of knowing that Ty's lips would soon touch mine was unexplainable. Blood rushed from my heart and gushed to every extremity of my body, only to be stopped by the thin layer of skin that trapped it below the surface.

Feeling the heat rise all over my body, he pulled his forehead from mine and smiled as he studied the new shade of my face, "Berries. Just like the ones on Christmas holly."

Chapter Twenty-Seven

Surprises or Secrets?

THE LAST GIFT HAD BEEN SET UNDER THE TREE AND THE FINAL stocking had been stuffed. It was time to go pick up Aiden's Christmas puppy. Anxious to get out to my house and meet Roger, Ty clutched my hand to pull me off the ground. The feeling of his strong, warm hand holding mine sent another tidal wave of blood coursing through me.

Always the over-thinker, my mind searched for what to do after I was on my feet. We had just entered new territory. A place where lingering touches may or may not be wanted. Once I was standing, I couldn't help but wonder if I should keep holding on to him. The Lord knew I didn't want to let go, but I didn't want to make assumptions. I began to unfurl my grasp, but was stopped when Ty's fingers wrapped more tightly around mine.

"Not so fast," he grinned. "You're not getting away from me this time." I couldn't help but tremble, especially once I knew he was going to kiss me in the near future. I was sure any nearby scientist could've easily read the P waves on their seismometers. He had to have felt it too. He was holding onto me in the epicenter of my own personal earthquake. "On second thought, hop on." He pulled me onto his back. "I'd hate to see you turn into Bambi out there on the ice."

With the little strength I had left, I wrapped my legs around him and held my breath as he carried me to his truck. As I pulled into him, shielding myself from the frigid night air, I memorized the way our bodies moved together. Each bounce of his step. Each tightening of his arms. The warmth of his body heat dancing with mine. I reveled in the way he felt against me. Warm. Strong. Protective. I could have clung to him all night.

When he opened the door and gently slipped me onto the seat, I was disappointed to let go. It was too soon. The separation from his hold, combined with the fragrance of his truck left me light-headed. It was hard to focus on anything but the warmth he had just transferred from his body to mine. I could still feel the comfortable embrace of his phantom arms carrying me. I had to force myself back to reality. Settling into the passenger's seat, I shut the door and buckled my seatbelt.

I hadn't noticed him get into the driver's side until he cleared his throat. When I turned toward him to see what he was doing, his eyes roamed from my head to my feet. Quickly, he looked up at the ceiling of the cab and then back to me with a humorous grin. Again, he glanced at where I was sitting and quickly poked his finger down onto my seat belt release.

I couldn't help but wonder if he was going to make me get out. "What're you doing?"

"You're in the wrong seat."

I looked around the cab. Clearly, I was in the right seat, he'd just set me there. That's when his hand came across my lap and gently pulled me into him until my leg rested against his. "That's better."

The first few minutes of the ride, I wondered what I'd gotten myself into. Jefferson guys were notoriously decent drivers, yet Ty seemed to have a few issues in that department. It wasn't the smooth ride I'd expected from such a seemingly coordinated guy. In fact, he could've used a little practice with his turns. With each

219

swerve around an obstacle or corner, I ended up millimeters closer and a lot more nervous.

At the rate I was being pulled into him, we could have very well shared the driver's seat by the time we neared the vineyard. There wasn't enough space for an atom to fit between us. At the last stop, he looked down at me and grinned, "Punch."

"You think I'm going to hit you?"

"No," he laughed. "It's your shade of pink right now."

That's when I realized every point of contact I shared with him was on fire. My knee. My thigh. My hip. My arm. My shoulder. All pressing into him. My face was probably glowing. Just when I thought I was going to need a firehose, he asked, "You need me to turn the air conditioner up again?"

The amusement in his expression told me he'd been reining me into him on purpose. When we finally stopped in front of my house, he turned toward me and whispered, "That was a little too fast. Kinda wish you lived a few more miles away. I'm not going to lie. I hope you enjoyed that ride as much as I did."

"If riding the Scrambler on a winter road is your idea of fun, sure," I joked.

"Don't go anywhere," he opened the door and slid out. "You're coming with me." Carefully, he pulled me through his side of the door and slid me onto his waist. Chest to chest. Heartbeat to heartbeat. I looked over his shoulder as he carried me away from the truck. There I was for the second time that night, being held by the boy of my dreams. I pulled my arms around his neck and rested my chin on his shoulder, again concentrating on the bounce of his steps and the rising and falling of his chest. I was just beginning to completely melt into him, when I noticed the same black SUV Daemon was driving at the dash. It was parked outside my front gate.

"Oh gosh," I flinched, pushing away from him.

"What is it?" He held me at arm's length and looked at me,

"Too much, too soon?"

"No, nothing like that."

Ty stopped walking when Daemon's voice rang out from up ahead, "Jenna, I've been waiting for you." He was waving something in front of him.

I took a deep breath then whispered in his ear, "I need down. I've got to see what he wants."

Hesitantly, he slid me down the front of him. I could tell that Daemon's presence at my house so late at night wasn't sitting well with Ty either. "Listen, if you need me to help you get rid of that guy, I'm right here."

I squeezed his hand. "Thanks," I whispered. "Be right back."

As I turned to walk away, Ty pulled me back to him and half-laughed, half-whispered into my ear, "And I thought I had to worry about Caden."

It was cute the way he tried to break the tension, but I couldn't hang back and flirt. I had to go make sure, once again, that Daemon knew where he stood with me. "Funny," I winked and playfully thumped him on the arm before walking over to see what Daemon had recovered.

My body tightened as I left Ty and headed toward the SUV. Walking toward him, I could feel the annoyance growing in the back of my mind. He had been finding more and more reasons to interact with me lately. At first Daemon showing up here and there, seemed cute and harmless, but it was starting to feel a little off. I couldn't believe he was at my house. I didn't know what I could have possibly dropped at the dash that was so important he needed to drive all the way to the vineyard to deliver it on Christmas Eve.

"I zee you've found yet anozer guy to zpend the night whiz," he grumbled in Ty's direction.

I knew at some point I was going to have to tell him his behavior was inappropriate, but I didn't want to address his obvious jealousy before I knew what he had to return to me. Trying not to sound irritated, I questioned, "What're you doing here on Christmas Eve? Shouldn't you be with your host family?"

"They're back home waiting for me. But, right now I have zomething that belongz to you." He swung what looked to be a dog leash in front of him. It was too dark for me to see. "You dropped zhiz at the dazh."

When he shined his phone light on the dangling object, I couldn't believe what I was looking at. It was my pink, camo lanyard with the flash drive and house key that I'd been missing. "Holy crap, where was that?" I gasped.

"It dropped out of your pocket while you were running. Juzt after you zent me around the corner. I ztopped to pick it up."

My mind halted. Something wasn't adding up. My entire outfit was brand new. In fact, there weren't even pockets in my leggings or sweater. The only place the lanyard could have been was inside my ski jacket, but that hadn't seen the light of day in weeks. Not since it took a backseat to my basketball warmups. There was no way my lanyard was on me at the dash.

"What? You don't believe me?" Daemon asked, trying to break the silence. Judging by his question, he must've known I was wondering where he'd really found the lanyard. "Check it out for yourzelf." He handed it over. "A little appreziazion would be nize."

He was right. Maybe it stuck to me while I was riding with the Woodleys. I didn't know. I couldn't come up with a logical explanation, and I didn't have time to. Daemon was just trying to help. Obviously, he was nice enough to drive all the way out to my house on Christmas Eve. I didn't have the heart to tell him he was creeping me out by showing up everywhere I went. That could wait.

"Sorry, it's just been a long night." I shook my head, still mystified as to how the lanyard ended up in Mt. Shasta. "Thanks. I owe you."

"You keep zaying zhat." He pointed at me and winked as he

clicked his tongue. "Don't worry, zomeday zoon I'm going to collect."

I took a deep breath. I wasn't sure I wanted Daemon collecting on anything.

"For right now, a hug would be nize."

When I went to put my arms around him, Ty walked between the two of us. "Not so fast, pal. The only guy hugging this girl from now on is gonna be me."

Fire lit Daemon's eyes as he cocked his head, "For now, anyway," he smirked before he got into his car and sped away.

Ty nodded toward the tire marks where Daemon had just peeled out. "There's something odd about that guy. What was that all about?"

I shrugged and whispered, "Unhealthy crush?"

"Do you think we set him straight?"

"Well," I grimaced, "I think you did. I sure could have used you sooner."

"You've got me now and that's what matters."

His words seared themselves into my mind. I had him? Was I being blessed with some kind of Christmas miracle? I'd seen Hallmark movies where unattainable wishes came true, but I'd never experienced it myself. When I left for the dash that evening, there was no way I would've ever imagined ending up with Ty, the very person I was trying to forget. The thought of fulfilling a Christmas wish pulled me back to reality. I'd almost forgotten I was in the middle of making Aiden's come true. I looked down at my watch. It was almost ten o'clock. We'd kept Roger waiting. I grabbed Ty's hand. "We've got to get Roger back to his family. I think he's been here for a while."

Because it was dark, I led the way. I knew Ty had been there last spring to practice on my field, but we were going to an area of the vineyard that was off the beaten path. He clung to my hand as I tugged him beyond the cellar and down to the warehouse.

"I never knew there was so much to this place."

"Yeah, there are a few things we kind of like to keep secret."

"So, it's okay that I'm here?"

"Oh, yeah. My parents trust my judgment on who to share my secrets with."

As we continued to walk, Ty grew quiet. He must have been thinking about my private life at the vineyard. Who I allowed to come. Who I chose to share my space with. "So, Kaitlyn and Caden obviously know about this place."

"Parts of it, yeah."

He seemed intrigued by my response. "Really? Not all of it?"

"Nope. A girl can't give away all her secrets."

Again, he grew quiet. I could almost feel his concentration. "Interesting."

"Not until she finds the right person to share them with, anyway."

"So, you still have secrets you haven't shared with anybody?"

I raised my brows and pinched my lips, "Not a soul."

With amusement lacing his tone he chuckled, "You're telling me, after all these years of being the gorgeous Jenna Bailey, stand-up comedian, athlete extraordinaire, the right person hasn't come along yet?"

His compliments left me flustered. I'd never had anyone as insanely handsome as Ty tell me I was gorgeous. Looking up at him I smiled, "I can't be sure."

He released the hold he had on my hand, then slipped his arm around my shoulder and pulled me into him. The warmth of his breath gave me goosebumps as he whispered into the top of my head, "So, how does one become worthy of getting to know you, Ms. Jenna? Secrets and all."

Excited that Ty could be the key to unlock them, I grinned, "Stick around and you might find out."

By the end of the conversation, we stood outside the door of the warehouse. It was time to get the puppy. Roger, holding a bundle in his arms, smiled and greeted us as we walked inside. I could see the furry, little, black nose sticking out of the baby blanket. Roger's face lit up the minute I approached and gave him a hug. "This is my friend, Ty."

"Nice to meet you," he nodded.

Roger looked back at me and grinned, "All these weeks you've been coming to visit this little one and you decided tonight's the night you couldn't live without him?"

"He's a Christmas gift."

"Well, I'll be darned." He shook his head, staring back and forth from Ty to me and back again.

"This girl sure is full of surprises. Must be someone mighty special. I swore this was going to be your best friend one day."

Ty turned toward me and raised his eyebrows, whispering, "surprises or secrets?" I felt his grin against my ear. I knew he was onto me and I didn't want to strip the joy away from the gift by making a big deal about my sacrifice.

"Uh, Roger. Can I take him? There's someplace he needs to be."

He held the bundle out to me. As I took the puppy, I whispered in Roger's ear, "I'll explain later."

"You must be one special guy," Roger winked at Ty.

He looked back at Roger and shook his head, "Nope. I'm just the lucky one."

Then he moved behind me and wrapped me in his arms as he whispered into the top of my head. "But I promise you, I'm going to do everything I can, to be the special one. The one that's worthy of all your secrets. Thank you, for giving up your Christmas puppy, Pickle. I'll never forget it."

Chapter Twenty-Eight

Christmas Games

RATHER THAN SEEING SUGAR PLUM FAIRIES DANCING IN MY HEAD, my dreams the night before Christmas took me on a trip down memory lane. I couldn't help but wonder why the Ghost of Christmas Past looked exactly like Ty, but as long as I had power over my dreams that night, I was determined to keep him as my personal tour guide. Something about him being near me was comforting, and though he'd had no place in my early childhood history, I wanted him by my side through the scenes that were about to unfold. He wrapped his arm around me as we began the journey back to a Christmas long ago.

We stood outside in the snow looking through the window of a small, cozy cabin near the big castle. Smiling at the quaint holiday memory, I noticed a six-year-old me on the ground near Mason and Nikolai. It was the afternoon of Christmas. The parents had gathered in the other room while the three of us sat on the floor beside the Christmas tree. Nikolai had a new game board and we were making up our own version of chess. It was my job to collect all the dead pieces the boys killed in their battle to be the last king standing.

My job was more than cemetery caretaker, however. I was Nikolai's secret ally. With each move he was about to make, Nikolai would look to me, and each time, I would nod in approval or shake my head, no and signal a better move. I played my part well, never allowing Mason to see my cues. Nikolai however, was not so subtle.

"Why do you always look at her like that?" Mason asked.

"Like what?" Nikolai shrugged, knowing full well that every move he made depended on me.

"Like the whole game revolves around her."

"Because it does," he said matter-of-factly in his strong Russian accent. Then mumbling quietly he continued, "She's my queen."

Mason looked at the pile of his dead pieces that I was guarding in front of me, then looked to all of Nikolai's still standing on the board. When he finally realized how badly he was being beaten, he stood up and flipped the game upside down. The remaining pieces scattered and rolled across the hardwood floor. "No fair. It's two against one." He looked back and forth between the two of us. "You cheat!" Nikolai hopped to his feet and pushed his chest against Mason's.

Still standing outside the window next to Ty, I remembered how my heart pounded while my stare bounced from one friend to the other. As I watched myself in that moment, I realized I had betrayed my friend. At six years old, the only way I knew to fix the mess I'd caused was to gather the scattered pieces and apologize. As I crawled around on my hands and knees collecting rooks and pawns, Mason's thundering voice cut through the tense room, "She was my friend first!" I looked up just in time to see Mason push Nikolai to the ground and storm out the door.

I knew Mason's feelings were hurt, but I was under Nikolai's spell. There was something about him that demanded my help. He was such a sad and lonely little boy. Aside from the time our dads worked down in the cellar together, Nikolai was isolated from everyone his age. Unfortunately, his family was far too busy to notice, or too cold-hearted to care how his secluded life at the castle vineyard affected him.

Mason's family, on the other hand, showered him with love and attention. He was the center of their universe. They took him everywhere and introduced him to many friends along the way. Besides me, he had a group of embassy kids that he was quite close to. When there was an opportunity, he always chose them over Nikolai. In fact, the only time they played together was when I begged Mason to come with me.

In my mind, Nikolai needed me more than Mason did. I was his only friend and the only one who could get his pouty lips to smile. For that reason, I had grown protective over him during our stay in the cabin near the castle. I was his closest ally and the only one who truly saw him for the brilliant and loyal friend he was.

Ty's ghost directed my eyes back to the scene. I cringed as I watched Nikolai's father peek around the corner. Nikolai was still sitting, frozen from the shock of being knocked to the ground. "I tought I heard somefing."

Their eyes met, as his father shook his head in disbelief. "Are you really my son? One day you will learn to stand strong and tall against your enemies. Now get off the ground, you idiot. You're embarrassing me!" He shook his head as he disappeared around the corner.

My heart sunk as the six-year-old me kneeled beside Nikolai. "Are you okay?"

Grinning, he nodded, "My first fight over a girl. You are so worf it."

I remembered how much I loved him as I stared at him on the ground, so weak and vulnerable. His thoughts weren't on his father's harsh words. They were on how brave he was to make me his queen. I swept his fine, brown hair away from his forehead and stared into his big, blue eyes. Knowing how he'd put himself on the line to make me his ally, I thanked him for claiming me as his queen.

Again, I was aware of Ty's presence as we stood and watched a little me tug Nikolai to his feet. No sooner was he up, then Ty pulled me to another room at the castle. I recognized the room right away. I'd seen it so many times in my recurring nightmares, only this time I wasn't in the house. I was standing outside the window looking in. I was a little older in this vision. It must have been closer to spring. My father had just swept me off my feet. He was taking me away from the big party. My heart raced as I remembered the feeling of my father's strong, trembling arms holding onto me tightly. Lit by the moon, I memorized the dire look on his face and noticed the sweat trickling down his temple. As the intruder alarm began to grow in intensity, we ran quickly away from the castle.

I stood and watched the memory replay with Ty. I remembered how late it was that night. The party lasted far past my normal bedtime. As we fled the castle, I struggled to see the path beneath my father's feet. Finally, my eyes were drawn to an illuminated window glowing in the darkness. My father had paused beneath it to adjust his hold on me. In all my other dreams, I'd never gone that far or seen that much.

But that night's dream was lucid. I forced myself to remember what came next, and what came next tugged at my heart. It was little Nikolai. He stood with his face and hands pressed against the window. Tears streamed down his cheeks as he waved goodbye. Bouncing up and down against my father's strong chest as we ran toward our car, it was all I could do to hold my hand steady enough to wave back. "Goodbye," I whispered.

My father's steps quickened as the sounding alarm intensified. Ding. Ding. Ding. The incessant noise was so loud, so clear, almost clear enough to be real. The farther we ran, the stranger the tone became, until suddenly it morphed into the sound of my chiming phone. The scene before me vanished as I opened my eyes to new messages.

Kaitlyn:
We have a gift that's addressed to both of us. You coming by soon? I can't open it without you.

Ty:
Mornin', Pickle! Merry Christmas! :)

Caden:
Is it any surprise that T got the biggest gift? You've got to get over here and check this out.

I looked at the clock. It was already seven. Having the ghost of Ty with me all night to witness one of my secrets was unsettling. Though I knew it was completely illogical, it felt so real that I couldn't help but wonder how he would react to the memory he'd just seen. I wasn't ready to share it with him. Not outside of sleep anyway. I had to shake it off and remind myself it was just another nightmare. In reality, they were still my secrets. My secrets to keep all to myself.

At least it seemed like I was gaining some control over what I dreamed. I'd never been able to press past the party before, but last night's dream let me know that Nikolai had seen me wave goodbye. It brought some comfort to know he saw us escape. That was new.

Still, Ty's appearance in the dream had me unsettled. I couldn't help but wonder why suddenly my past was overlapping my present. Regardless of why, I had no intention of thinking any further on it. If my parents found out I was having new nightmares, I'd be back in therapy for sure. I had to refocus, take a quick shower to clear the sweat, and get out to the living room before my mom dragged me out of bed by my toes. As I slipped on my robe and headed for the shower I sent off a couple quick texts.

Me:

Kait! Merry Christmas. I'll come to town as soon as my parents release me from holiday jail. Traditions, you know?

Me:

Merry Christmas, buddy! Hope Aiden likes the puppy. Did he name him yet?

Me:

Cademan, you know good things come in small packages. Maybe they're gonna surprise you. :P

I tossed my phone on the bed, slipped on my basketball warm-ups, and headed out to the living room. As expected, I found my parents sitting on their recliners sipping coffee and eating pastries.

"Cinnamon roll?" my mom tipped her plate to show me her traditional Christmas breakfast.

"Nah, I'm ready to get started here." I rubbed my hands together, scanning the small pile of gifts under the tree, "Lots to do today."

If my mom's expression didn't say it all, she let me know exactly what she was thinking. "It's Christmas. You're not planning to leave, are you?"

I wasn't up for the boredom that came with holiday tradition at the Bailey house. Board games, Christmas carols, and fireside chats were all great when I was ten. At some point, my parents had to realize that I had grown up. It was a lot of pressure being the only child. It was up to me alone to break my parents' hearts and let them know I was done being a kid. I wanted to have fun without the guilt of messing up Christmas for my parents. I needed to figure out a way to let them down easy. Maybe find some kind of diversion to distract them from the fact that I wasn't lying around with them all day watching movies. I brought up the idea of having the Woodleys over. After all, we always had plenty of food and wine.

Thankfully, they were happy to have guests. I'd never thought of it before, but maybe they had outgrown the childhood stage of Christmas too. Excitedly, I tore into my gifts, knowing that as soon as I was done, I was going to get to hang out with my friends. Quickly, I scooped up the wrapping paper mess and stuffed it in the burn pile, then ran and gave both of my parents tight squeezes. I thanked them for each of my new treasures and the thought they'd poured into the gifts. After making sure they knew how much I loved and appreciated them, I carried the small stack to my room and laid it on my bed. At the dip of the mattress, my phone screen lit up, showing me I'd missed a few texts while I was away.

Kaitlyn:
Where are you? You know you're killing me here.

Caden:
My parents say we're headed to your house today. Get your ass over here and see what I got!

Ty:
Buddy?

Knowing I'd see the twins soon enough, I ignored the first two texts. My attention was focused solely on the one from Ty. Buddy? I stared at the text. One word, but the question mark carried so much meaning. Did he want me to think of him as more than a friend? I held my breath, knowing I was about to find out.

Me:
What would you like me to call you?

Ty:
I can think of a few things.

Me:
Pal?

Ty:
A little too close to Buddy, don't you think?

Me:
I'm at a loss here. :/

His responses came in three-minute waves. Enough time to keep me on edge. It was irrational that the simple act of texting Ty over what to call him had my nerves pulsating. I was literally sweating through the foundation I was trying to apply when the phone chimed again.

Ty:
How about …

Ty:
boyfriend? :)

The blood rushed straight to my head, leaving my texting fingers frozen. Blankly, I stared at the screen. I didn't know how to answer him without putting my ego on the line if he was messing with me. At least the slowly antagonizing pace of our last few texts had bought me some time to think about it. The more I thought about it, the more I doubted he was serious. I couldn't imagine Ty being the kind of guy to ask a girl out over text. His response called for wit, which had all but escaped me. Based on the lengthy intervals of our previous texts, I had about two minutes and thirty seconds to get it back. Thankfully, he didn't wait that long before he let me off the hook.

Ty:
Scared you, didn't I? I'm just playing, Pickle. I'm not the kind of guy to ask a girl out over a text.

The brief shot of disappointment soon turned to excitement. I was spot on about his character, and I was worth more than being asked out by a text. The mini-burst of adrenaline from his response was strong enough to reignite my cleverness.

Me:
Phew! You were about to lose style points. I'd never accept a textposal. ;P

Ty:
Nonetheless. I know I had you going. Hey, would you mind taking a selfie right now? I'm looking forward to seeing your new shade.

I glanced over at my mirror to see he was right. My face had turned a new shade of berry. How did he know?

Ty:
Let me guess. You're checking your color right now. On second thought, hold that selfie. You need to get over here quick. I've got to see this face to face.

Me:
What makes you think I'll be this color in fifteen minutes?

Ty:
I know you. And I have something to ask you.

Ty:
In person.

No witty comebacks. Nothing. All I knew was Ty was going to see that shade. Feeling the way I felt after his text, there was no way I was going to lose it anytime soon. In fact, for all I knew, he may have changed my skin color permanently.

Ty:
No need to text back. I know you'll be here. Just make sure it's before ten. Aiden will be coming home soon and I want to see the look on your face when he gets this pup.

I threw my phone on the bed and stared in the mirror. Time was running short and I had to get over to Ty's before I went to the Woodley's. They'd understand. I decided to lose the braids and style my long, blonde hair into loose curls. I lightly dusted my blue eyes with a subtle shade of neutral minerals and brushed my thick eyelashes with a couple coats of black mascara. I painted my lips a berry pink, and topped it off with a tiny hint of blush, just enough to cover the real color I knew Ty was about to bring out in my cheeks.

I was almost ready when I decided to change from my basketball warm-ups to my black sweater, jeans, and boots. I looked in the mirror, satisfied with my Christmas morning look. Game on, I thought to myself. I had done all I could do to my one hundred and fifteen pound, five-foot-four frame. I hoped it was enough for Ty. Enough for him to repeat the word "boyfriend" in person.

Chapter Twenty-Nine

Make You Miss Me

NERVOUSLY, I ROUNDED THE LAST CORNER ON THE WAY TO HIS house. Had I actually eaten breakfast that morning, I may have lost it. After putting the car in park, I pulled down the rearview mirror. My cheeks had refilled themselves with the shade of pink Ty had brought on earlier that morning. I couldn't stop thinking about our texts and how he was certain I'd be showing up at his house any moment.

He must have known me better than I knew myself. If anyone had ever asked me if I'd be rushing over to Ty Connelly's house on Christmas morning at his request, I would have answered, "When pigs fly." The joke was on me, I guess. There I was sitting in front of the modest, two-story home, just around the corner from the Woodley's. I checked the sky for flying swine, then took a deep breath to calm myself as I stepped out of the car.

If my stomach wasn't already tumbling through its own floor routine, it threw a quadruple handspring back tuck when I was grabbed from behind. "I knew you'd be here," Ty whispered into the back of my ear. The sensation of his chest gently pressing against my back, sent the rest of my tummy soaring for the big finish … double layout with a half twist for the landing.

Even though my gut had just completed an Olympic-worthy

tumbling passage, I decided to play it cool. "Well, I couldn't miss seeing Aiden get that puppy."

"So, you're just here for Aiden, huh?" Obviously amused, he continued, "My invitation to talk in person had nothing to do with it?"

I shook my head again and giggled, "Nope."

Maintaining his hold around my arms, he walked behind me. Keeping our stride perfectly in sync as we walked toward the house, he raised his arm slightly to bring his watch into view. "Well, looks like we have a few minutes before the reason for your visit gets here. Do you think we can talk?"

At my nod, he stepped in from behind, and timidly cradled me in his arms. He didn't move, but glanced over my shoulder and into my eyes almost as though he was checking to see if it was okay for him to hold me. I grinned, thankful his arms began to secure around me. I may not have made it the rest of the way otherwise. The newness of his strong, tender touch shook me to the core and stripped me of my steadiness. He pulled me in tighter as I trembled beneath his embrace. Not wanting to be vulnerable so soon, I was thankful when he misread my body's response to him.

"You're shivering. Let's hurry and get you inside," he whispered in my ear as he slid his feet beneath mine, walked me up his stairs, and through his front door. I could tell Ty had done some work since the night before. The gifts were nicely stacked around the tree, and spiced apple cider candles glowed around the room. I started to walk toward the couch when he grabbed my hand and redirected my destination.

My heart raced as we broke the hallway barrier and stopped at the third room on the left. I had never been into a guy's room before, and to be in this particular guy's room was almost more than my heart could take. Standing at the door, I took in the full, room-sized trophy case. In front of me, there was a huge canvas mural with pictures of him playing baseball. Another wall held all his trophies and framed award certificates. The third wall must have been his study space. It held a large desk with a stack of books, pamphlets, and an oversized mirror with pictures tucked into the frame.

"Can I take your things?"

I nodded as I slid my purse from my arm and handed it to him. As he walked across the room to hang it on his wall hook, I wandered toward the desk. The pictures that hung around the mirror weren't what I would have expected from one of the most talented athletes in high school. I thought there might be candids of old girlfriends, parties, or sports action shots, but all I saw was photo after photo of Aiden and him camping, hiking, rafting, and horseback riding.

As I worked my way around the frame, surprisingly my eyes caught sight of a familiar picture. It was a wallet-sized trading card of me in eighth grade. I was still in braces and wearing my catcher's gear. I hadn't remembered giving it to him until just then. It was the only picture stuck to the frame that wasn't of him and his little brother. I smiled as I pulled it off the mirror and read the back.

Hey, Ty,
Save this pic. One day it'll be worth millions.
Haha, Jenna.

"Hehem," he cleared his throat, as he lightly pressed his chest against my back. "Do you know how close of an eye I've had to keep on that picture over the years? All my friends wanted to be millionaires, I suppose," he chuckled, "or, maybe it was because you looked super hot in those braces. Either way, it's mine. You're not getting it back." He took the picture from me and stuck it back in its place on the mirror. Then, he took my hand and pulled me over to his bean-bag chair. He plopped down and pulled me on top of him.

"So, I've been thinking about this for a while now, what I was going to say, what I was going to do, how I was going to get you to consider letting me call you my girl."

"Your girl?"

"Come on, Pickle. You had to have known how long I've liked you."

I hadn't been expecting him to dive right in. Not the minute he got me through his bedroom door. I paused before I asked, "How long, exactly?"

"You saw the picture," he looked over toward the mirror. "You caught my eye the minute you moved into town."

He had to be messing with me. Ty had plenty of girlfriends between the time I got to town and the moment he just brought me into his bedroom and pulled me onto his lap. I couldn't help but wonder if he had a box of other girls' junior high pictures somewhere. Did he pick those out of the box before he invited them over too? I tugged at his navy-blue bean bag. I couldn't figure out where else to look to avoid letting him see my confusion. Maybe the picture thing was his sure-fire plan to get the girl. If it was, it was a good one. The fact that he'd kept my picture after all those years made me feel pretty special. Like my face was worth holding onto.

I could feel him growing uncomfortable as we sat in silence. Knowing the ball was in my court, I had to come up with a way to find out more. "Why didn't you ever say anything?"

A small grin played at his lips. "You know me, I like to play it cool."

I spun around to face him, "For five years?!?"

"Alright, maybe I was scared"

I couldn't help but find what he was saying humorous. Ty was anything but scared. Especially not of me. I'd seen the girls he'd dated, and they could have each had their own month in the Sports Illustrated swimsuit calendar.

I shook my head, "Not buying it. I've seen the girls you've dated. You weren't scared." I couldn't help but giggle.

"Pickle, I don't know if you realize this, but you're intimidating as hell. You should hear the way the guys talk about you in the locker room. Not a single one of my friends has ever gotten a date out of you."

I had to stifle the grin that was trying to play at the corners of my lips. I really was proud of my record with the boys of Jefferson. There was only one guy who I'd ever wanted to put any kind of time into, and I wasn't going to settle for anyone else.

Ty studied my face before he continued, "Besides, I wasn't ready for you yet. It would've been like trying to get drafted to the majors without playing little league first. I had to practice. Make sure I was good enough. I couldn't just jump into something when I didn't know what I was doing. I wanted to know I had everything right before I got up the balls to go for the girl I really wanted. You."

My heart's dam broke as every blood cell in my body sprinted directly to my face. He shifted me onto one leg, so he could look me in the eyes. "I'm ready now ... if you are."

I could see it in the way he studied my reaction. His brows raised, his eyes locked on mine, the way he swallowed the lump in his throat. He was serious. He really had been practicing for this. For me. I tried to catch my breath so I could answer.

He spoke again. This time his gravelly voice was low and whispered. "Do you want me? The same way I've been wanting you?"

Ty was the only guy I'd wanted since I started high school. I was sure he knew that. After all the months of spying and trying to get him to notice me, I couldn't believe it was finally happening. He had fallen for me. I felt the happy tears start to build. I knew if I spoke, my voice might not break through the quivering. All I could do was thread my fingers through his and nod my head, yes.

He put his hand under my chin and wiped the solitary tear that rolled down my cheek. "So, will you be my girl, then?"

"Yes," I blushed.

He bit down on his growing grin, as he pressed his forehead against mine. Rather than the kiss I was expecting, he whispered, "Champagne pink, the best color yet."

The heat traveled from my cheeks and burned into the place where our heads rested against one another. He must have felt the sudden change in temperature. "I didn't know champagne pink was a hundred degrees," he chuckled.

I could have kissed him right there. In fact, I would have kissed him right there had we not heard the loud voices booming down the hallway. He pulled me to my feet. "We'd better get out of here. Don't want my parents to think ... let's just go." He grabbed my hand as we ran down the hallway to the laundry room where the puppy was waiting. Ty handed me a baby blanket. Quickly, I wrapped the pup as we slipped out the back door and jogged around to the front.

We stood at the front door only long enough to catch our breath before we gave three loud knocks and swung it open. "Ho, ho, ho," Ty bellowed as we walked into the foyer together. Peeking around the corner, Aiden was already under the tree sorting through his gifts. There was a tower sitting in front of him and he was studying which one he was going to open first. His eyes lit up the minute we walked toward him. "Think you missed one," Ty smiled.

"Ty! We didn't think you were home!" he rose from the ground and ran toward us. "You brought Jenna!" Just then his parents walked around the corner.

"Oh, good morning, kids. Hi, Jenna!" His mom walked in and gave me a hug. "Thanks for helping Ty last night." Then she leaned into me and whispered, "He told me you were the one who wrapped everything." As she pushed against me, the puppy whimpered and shifted beneath the blanket.

The sound didn't go unnoticed. Aiden cocked his head and grinned, "What's that?"

"You caught me." Ty chuckled. "I have more than Jenna here." He took the bundle from my arms and held it out to Aiden. "Santa asked me to take care of this for you until you got home. Careful now, you don't want to hurt it."

Aiden quickly peeled the blanket away from his whimpering gift and looked up in disbelief. "You brought me a puppy?" he jumped up and down. "My own puppy?"

"Slow down there, kid. He's not a stuffed animal. This one's the real thing," Ty gently warned.

It filled my heart to watch Aiden bouncing around the room, cuddling his new, black lab. After the shock of getting his puppy wore off a bit and he thought to share, we all sat down in a circle, patting the ground and calling to him, "Come here, boy!" Each time he pranced around the circle deciding on a lap, he tripped over his own feet. We couldn't help but fall in love with the clumsy, little bundle of Christmas joy. We found it hysterical that no matter what we did to get him to come to us, each time we set him back in the circle, the pup chose to run to Aiden.

I was so happy that I'd made it to Ty's house that morning to witness my little guy's immediate attachment to Aiden. Watching them together showed me I couldn't have made a better sacrifice. Clearly, the pup had made it into the right family. It was meant to be.

"Will you help me name him, Jenna?" Aiden asked. "Something cool?" He held him up to my face, so I could give him Eskimo kisses. "Maybe, Eskimo?"

As he licked at my face, I couldn't help but giggle. "Well, that's cute, but kind of wintry. Maybe you should go with a name that's special all year long. Something that will warm your heart through every season."

"And what warms your heart?" Ty asked expectantly.

There was no way I was going to give him a flirty response, especially not in front of his family. I looked back at him and grinned, "Baseball." He knew he'd embarrassed me by trying to expose my feelings in front of his family.

"You know what warms mine?" he asked.

I couldn't imagine what his response was going to be after my smart-ass remark.

"The shade of red covering your face right now."

I buried my face in the puppy, pretending like he was attacking me. There was no way I could look at his parents at that moment.

"That's it! I know what's warm, loves baseball, and is red all over!" Aiden laughed.

His dad chuckled, having clearly guessed the answer to Aiden's riddle, "Clever, son."

"What is it?" his mom asked.

"Mom. They're warm, red, and love baseball … The Red Sox!"

"Good one!" I laughed handing the puppy back to Aiden. "But, what does that have to do with naming this little guy?"

"That's it. It's going to be his name. Red Sox Connelly. But I'm gonna call him Sox for short."

I couldn't help but love his awkwardly cute name. It was my favorite baseball team after all. After we tossed Sox around a bit more, it was time for me to go. I could feel my phone buzzing in my pocket and knew I'd ignored the messages long enough. "I've got to get over to the Woodley's. They're waiting for me."

I said my goodbyes to Ty's family before he grabbed my purse and walked me outside. "I need to talk to you about something."

Intensified by the freezing December air, my insides twisted as I thought maybe it was time for our first kiss. "Okay?" I looked at him, wondering why his tone had taken such a serious turn.

"I'm not going to be able to see you for a couple weeks."

It was difficult to process what I'd just heard. I had just gotten him. School was back in session the next week. I hoped it was nothing serious. "A couple weeks? Are you okay? You're not sick or anything, are you?"

"Nothing like that," he grinned, shaking his head. "My dad and I are going on a college tour up the West Coast. He thinks we might be able to get some scouts to come up here and watch me play this season. He made up a bunch of highlight tapes of me pitching. They're actually pretty cool."

"That's super exciting." I couldn't help but be happy for him, but in the same turn, I was sad for myself. We had just begun a relationship and I wouldn't see him until well into the next year. "But ..."

"I know, Pickle. You're thinking I should've waited to ask you to be my girl. But, there's no way I wanted to leave town thinking all these other guys would be going after you while I was away. After listening to them in the locker room before vacation, I had no doubt you were their New Year's resolution," he chuckled.

I was never good with flattery or compliments. I didn't know what to say. "Well, since I'm off limits to everyone else now, who's going to keep me company while you're gone?"

"Oh, we'll be talking. It's going to be like I live in your pocket. Here, let me see your phone."

I looked at him questioningly, as my frozen fingers worked to pull the phone from my pocket. When I finally managed to get it, the screen lit with messages, reminding me that I was in a hurry to get to the Woodley's.

Ty held out his hand patiently waiting for the phone. I hoped Caden hadn't messaged me anything questionable. Sometimes he did that just to get a rise out of me. "What're you doing?" I shivered. My body was no longer resisting the chilly morning air.

He fiddled with it for a few seconds and handed it back without saying a word about Caden's texts. "I just shared my location with you, so you always know where I am. I'm just checking to make sure it worked. See." He held up my phone and showed me a dot with a picture of his face and a radiating circle. "You won't even miss me."

With my teeth beginning to clatter I joked, "Nope. Not even a little."

He grinned and gave me a hug. "Sorry I've kept you so long. You're freezing," he whispered into the top of my head. "There's something else I should share with you before you go." He pulled his sweatshirt over his head and immediately slipped it over mine.

"But, you always wear this one. Won't you need it for your trip?"

"Keep it. It looks good on you ... and hopefully, it will make you miss me just a little."

Dazed by the smell and the warmth, I could barely think let alone speak about just how much I was going to miss him. I wrapped my arms around him and simply said, "Thank you."

"You can share yours with me too." He looked down shyly. "If you want."

"My sweatshirt?"

"No, silly. Your location."

I had to think about it. I didn't want to be tracked like a chipped dog, but the way he looked at that moment, I wanted to. It could come in handy. "Okay." Then I added playfully, "Just so you don't text me in class or during practice or anything. I know how hard it's going to be for you to stay off the phone with me."

As we stood there exchanging locations, my phone began to ring. It was Kaitlyn. "I'd better go."

"Come here, you." Ty took me into his warm arms and held me until I could barely breathe. Finally, when he was ready to let me go, he pressed his lips to my forehead. It wasn't quite where I'd expected our first kiss to land. When I looked at him questioningly, he shook his head. "Not yet, Pickle. There's a time and place for everything. You'll know when we're in that place. I've got a plan. I promise." He opened my car door and helped me slide in. "Thanks for making my Christmas dream come true."

"Your dream? At some point, I thought I might run out of dandelions, birthday candles, and shooting stars. Guess nothing compares to the magic of a Christmas wish." Before he could say another word, I gave him a quick wave and drove away, hoping I didn't give him enough time to see the pink fill my cheeks.

Chapter Thirty

Paranoid?

I GRABBED THE STACK OF GIFTS FROM THE CAR AND HEADED AROUND THE block to the Woodley's. When I pulled up in front of the house, there was a brand new, shiny, black Dodge diesel draped in a big, red bow. Based on where it was parked, I knew exactly whose Christmas gift it was. Caden had talked about that truck for as long as I could remember. I couldn't wait to get into the house and see his reaction to his childhood dream come true. I balanced the gifts in my arms as I trudged my way up the snowy sidewalk. Thankfully, Kaitlyn opened the door at the same instant I rang the doorbell. I had to give it to her, the girl had instinct. It was as though she knew I was going to need help with the tower of gifts.

As she lifted the boxes out of my arms, I spotted Caden sitting on the couch holding his phone up to his face. His grumpy expression told me I had taken way too long to get there. I knew he relied on me to help keep his spirits up, and that's exactly what I intended to do on Christmas. He hadn't flinched since I walked in the door, so I knew I was going to have to pull him out of his funk. "I brought gifts!" I began to walk toward him.

That's when Kaitlyn stepped between us. Apparently, she had a more pressing issue than cheering up her brother. "I've been waiting for you to open this one with me." She lifted a shiny box to my face and shook it. "I think it's from Peyton!"

The excitement in her voice confused me. I couldn't help but think back on the way Peyton had gone crazy after the nearly fatal crash. She was so angry with all of us, especially Caden. She had suffered a debilitating psychological trauma. One that needed more than a small-town counselor to get through. We hadn't heard from her since she dropped out of school and left town to go to therapy. Not a text, phone call, update, nothing. "Peyton? She got us a gift? Seriously? I thought she blamed us for everything."

Kaitlyn shrugged, "Well, she's been in counseling. Maybe she's had a breakthrough."

My mind shifted to the memory of Peyton's breakdown in her bedroom. It was the day I took Caden to give her his Christmas gift. It tore me up to remember what zombie-Peyton had put him through. She screamed and threw things at him, shattered his beautiful snow globe against the wall, and then told him he made her sick. I didn't think he'd ever be the same after what she put him through. I blamed myself for taking him there. I should have known better. The guilt I carried from that day was probably the biggest reason I felt responsible for keeping his spirits up. And just then, staring at the package that Kaitlyn held in front of me, my heart hurt for him once again. She had sent us a gift and given him nothing.

"Glad she's had some kind of breakthrough," Caden grumbled from the couch. I knew it killed him to see his sister so excited to hear from Peyton. I looked over to see him still distracting himself with his phone. I wanted to tell Kaitlyn to be a little more sensitive, but before the words came out, I heard paper ripping.

I looked up just in time to see her confused expression. "This looks … interesting. What is it?"

She held up a matryoshka doll. "It has my name written on it. I thought this gift was for both of us."

I knew what it was the minute I saw it, though it was clear

Kaitlyn had no idea what it was. Of course, she'd never seen mine. I kept my Russian treasures on a hidden shelf in my closet. I thought it was an insightful choice of gifts coming from a girl who knew relatively little about my life before Jefferson. I decided to open up about my collection. I guessed I could let one harmless secret slip. "It's a nesting doll. I have a collection of them at home. My parents bought them for me as gifts from Russia. They give me a new one every year for my birthday."

At first glance, I caught sight of the red handkerchief and blonde hair. Oddly, it looked identical to one I had at home. My first thought was to call my mom and see if it was still on my closet shelf. "Look inside. They come in sets," I directed Kaitlyn.

When she popped it open, a small slip of paper drifted to the floor. Caden crawled over and picked it up.

As he huddled near the couch clutching the paper, Kaitlyn held the two dolls side by side, studying their likeness. "Oh, this one has your name on it." She handed me the smaller doll. There was no question, it was my name scrawled in fancy script.

As we looked over the intricate designs of our dolls, Caden finally decided to hand the slip to Kaitlyn. "Here. Looks like you dropped something." His tone confirmed that he was upset, but it didn't stop her from reading the note out loud.

"Please accept this gift as my most sincere apology. Remember me when you wear them. You'll always have a piece of my heart. ~P."

Kaitlyn raised the doll once again to study it. "How do you wear something like this? I'm not following."

I giggled through my explanation of how there were several dolls tucked inside of the larger ones. Then I held mine next to my ear and shook it. "Yep. There's something inside." I opened my doll, to find another, and then another. When I popped open the tiniest doll, silver shined through a layer of wrapping.

As we peeled away the tissue, we discovered a set of charm bracelets. One read "Best" the other, "Friends." Inspecting them, I knew exactly which one was for whom. Kaitlyn's held a guitar, swimmer, and beaver. Mine held a catcher's mitt, basketball, and something that looked like a building.

"I'm not sure what this is." I held it up to Kaitlyn. "Do you know?"

"Looks like some kind of castle."

I couldn't help but feel happy that Peyton's sense of humor had returned. Therapy must have been working. "A castle? That's funny. She always joked that I was a spoiled, little princess. Here," I held out my arm, "help me put it on."

Distracted by the gift, it slipped my mind that we weren't being sensitive to the fact that Caden was watching us admire our new jewelry. I was quickly reminded when he barked, "Glad to see you reconnected with P!" He emphasized the P with a popping sound. "See you later," he pushed away from the chair.

"Sorry, Caden. We didn't think…"

He cut off our apology, "It's all good. I'm working on someone new."

He stormed out of the room, obviously trying to get away from the fuss we were making over our new jewelry. I wondered what he meant about working on someone new, but turned my attention back to the shiny bracelets. On closer inspection, I'd never seen anything quite like them. The charms were bulky and round. Nothing I'd seen at the mall, that's for sure. I couldn't help but wonder where Peyton got them. And the castle. The more I looked at it, the more it resembled a place that had been seared into my memory, a place from my childhood.

It was at that moment I found myself questioning the entire gift. The dolls. The bracelets. I grew uneasy, wondering just how coincidental it was that the castle charm she'd included on my bracelet looked like the Kremlin. Was there some significance to the gift that I might be overlooking? My thoughts began to flood with possible explanations. Maybe Peyton had seen my Russian treasures and decided to unbury my past to pay me back for hanging out with Caden. I knew it didn't make sense that she was being so nice all of a sudden. Or were the bracelets from her at all? When Kaitlyn told me she thought they were from Peyton, I didn't question it. It was signed P, after all.

For the briefest moment, the thought crossed my mind that they could be from another P, but I pushed the thought away instantly. I knew I was being ridiculous conjuring up such impossible scenarios. The previous night's dream about Christmas past must have been filling my head with insanity. It was probably just a regular, old castle. I was being paranoid. It was distracting from the happiness I should have felt at Peyton's progress.

I decided not to make an issue of it. There were many things I still hadn't shared with Kaitlyn about my past. Things I was definitely not ready or willing to bring up on Christmas day. But as much as I tried to dismiss the paranoia, my brain had a mind of its own. It forced my hand to discreetly pick up the little slip of paper and read it for myself.

The handwriting was dark with wispy letters and twirly tails, unlike anything I'd ever seen from Peyton. However, it was signed with a P, or maybe it was a D. The fancy lettering made it nearly impossible to tell. There was only one way I could think to find out. I would have to text Peyton and thank her for the gift. Her response would tell me everything I needed to know.

Chapter Thirty-One
Swimsuit Model

T HOUGH MY MIND WAS REELING, I WAS THANKFUL THAT I HAD A lot of practice at hiding things. I stuffed my suspicions away and focused on the impending ski trip we were going to take up to Mount Ashland. We were stoked that the parents were getting together while Brody, Mason, the twins, and I would all head up for a day of skiing.

As we drove up the interstate, I couldn't help but feel for Caden, who had decided to let Brody take the wheel of his new truck. With every twist and turn on the snowy road, his face turned a lighter shade of green. The surrounding vehicles seemed to agitate him as well. Brody had commented several times on a car that had been on our tail. Each time he did, I watched Caden's eyes in the rearview mirror. Each glance was followed by tensing muscles in his forearms as he tightened his grip on the armrest and handle.

I couldn't help but wonder if he was thinking of the last time he drove. The time he went over the embankment and into the river. It wasn't until we pulled off the side of the road to let him empty his stomach of Christmas breakfast, that I actually saw the tailgating car that was making him so nervous. At first glance, it looked a lot like the one Daemon had driven to my house the night he helped me with my project.

When we pulled over it passed so quickly, I couldn't be sure. I could only make out the blur of a solo driver whizzing by. The thought of him traveling the interstate alone on Christmas, made me realize how lucky I was to be in America, surrounded by my closest friends. I couldn't imagine how it would have felt to be in Daemon's shoes, left alone through the holidays in a foreign country.

It was a fleeting thought as we pulled up to the ski park and got out. The snow coming down in buckets reminded me that there was going to be a lot of fresh powder on the mountain, something I had a bit of a rough time skiing through. Having lived in the city while all my friends were learning to ski, I was still relatively new at snow sports. I could definitely handle groomed runs, but powder took an otherworldly kind of strength to jump through. The kind that did not come from a cinnamon roll. I knew I'd have to grab something more to eat soon, but I wanted to check it out first.

When we got up top, the powder hit me at the thigh. Even though we tried to hang with the boys, by the time we got through the first run, both Kaitlyn and I were sweating and exhausted. I was right, I was no match for ungroomed runs. At one point I literally took my skis off and chucked them down the hill. When the boys saw our frustration, they let us off the hook. They wanted to hit the terrain park and we wanted to split off and tail the groomer. We made plans to meet later, promising not to separate.

After a short break in the lodge to power up with some food and hot chocolate, we went back out to catch the lift. On the way up, we had a short conversation about Caden, Peyton and how we hoped therapy could get them through the aftermath of the wreck. I still hadn't heard from Peyton. She'd never responded to my text thanking her for the beautiful gift. As we talked, I pulled my bracelet out of my glove, to look once again at the uniquely beautiful charms. That's when I heard someone shouting.

"Jenna! Kaitlyn!" It was a male voice that sounded like it came from a lower chair, but muffled by the whipping wind, I couldn't tell who it was. I spun on my seat to see if I could see who was yelling.

As I squinted to see through the blasting snowflakes, I spotted a guy riding solo on the lift behind us. He was dressed in neon pink and black and wore a matching joker hat. When he noticed I'd turned around, he waved his pole wildly. "Hi, zhere!" he yelled once more.

"It's Daemon," I turned to Kaitlyn, giggling. "That must have been him who passed us on the road. I thought I recognized his car."

When the lift approached the end of the cable, we slid off the chair, skied down the short path, and stopped at the top of the run. "Should we wait for him?" Kaitlyn asked.

I had to think about it for a minute. I hadn't exactly been planning to run into him during vacation. But then again, it was Christmas. "He is alone. It would be nice."

Before it was even decided, he skied between the two of us, grabbing our shoulders and snowplowing to a stop. "I didn't realize you'd be up here today," he grinned, struggling to gain his balance.

Trying to hide the annoyance that he had just run over my skis, I grimaced, "Last minute thing. Are you with your host family?"

He looked around. "No, zhey took off to zpend time in zhe zun. I wanted a white Chriztmaz, zo zhey let me ztay home."

As annoying as his constant appearances were becoming, I felt bad for him. "You can take a run with us," I lifted my gloved hand and set it on his shoulder. "Nobody should be alone on Christmas."

He glanced at me for a brief second when a strangely familiar expression brightened his blue eyes. It was almost like deja vu, but I couldn't place when or where I'd seen it. It was almost as though he felt it too. Then quickly, he looked away, "No worriez. I'm not alone now."

His quirky awkwardness melted my heart. Being a rescuer, I

had a weakness when it came to leaving anyone alone on the holidays. Clearly, Kaitlyn hadn't found the same soft spot for him that I had. "I kinda have to pee. How about you two go and I'll catch up with you," she grinned.

She must have forgotten we weren't supposed to separate. Obviously, Daemon's presence had clouded her judgment. "Okay!" I yelled to her disappearing figure. I needed to catch her, so I turned to him and quickly demanded, "Follow me."

As we skied down the run, it was obvious that we weren't going to catch Kaitlyn anytime soon. Daemon's problems didn't stop at getting off the lift. He had a hard time staying on his feet, period. The first time he fell, I stopped in front of him and smiled. "I zhink it waz a rut." The second time, "A znowflake got it my eye." By the third time, he wasn't the only person involved. He skied right over the top of a heavy-set guy who was sitting off to the side of the run.

"Holy shit, you douche bag. These are new skis!" The huge guy shook his fist as he skied past.

"Awe, leave him alone! It's not like he meant to." I skied back to Daemon and reached out to help pull him to his feet. His cheeks flushed red. "Don't be embarrassed. It happened to all of us when we started." He took my hand as I pulled him back to his feet.

"Hey, now zhat I'm ztanding, could we get a zelfie? I need a picture whiz zhe girl who juzt zaved me from zhe abominable znowman," he laughed.

I felt bad for the guy. I had to do something to make him feel better. "Sure." I slid my glove off and slipped my phone from my pocket, then stood close to Daemon as I snapped the picture.

That's when he noticed the bracelet that dangled from my arm. "Ziz iz zooo beautiful." His gloved hand gently came to my wrist and slowly turned it back and forth as he inspected the shining charms. "Oh look. It'z zee Kremlin." I must not have done a good job of hiding the surprise at his mention of the Kremlin. He paused and swallowed, "I went zhere wiz my program before I got here." A distant look overtook his expression before he asked, "Where did you get zhis?"

The change of his tone as he continued to hold onto me brought an uneasy feeling. I wondered how Ty would feel about him touching me so admiringly. I wanted to be nice, but at the same time, I didn't want to send any mixed signals. I needed my hand back. Beginning to pull away, I told him it was a gift. "It's from my friend. She gave it to me for Christmas."

"She?" His voice sounded oddly high pitched as he held on a little tighter.

"Peyton. You might remember her. She went to our school first quarter."

Finally deciding to release his hold, he continued to stare at the dangling charms. "Aww. Zuch a zweet friend. The Kremlin. What a zpezial plaze. It'z known for its miraculouz powerz to protect from enemy invazion."

My suspicions had just been confirmed. It wasn't just some princess castle. Daemon thought it was the Kremlin too. Rapt in thought, I almost didn't notice when he bowed before me. I had no idea what he was doing, but I almost started laughing. Just then, an unexpected knock on my helmet distracted me from the embarrassing gesture that I didn't quite know how to deal with. Caden had found me.

A little startled by his sudden thump, I gasped, "What are you doing here?"

"Apparently, I'm here to teach Daemon some new moves," he laughed.

Embarrassed that Caden had caught him in the middle of his bow, Daemon began to fidget and back away. "I'll catch up whiz you later. Oh, wait. Text me zhe picture. I want to zhow my hozt family."

"I don't have your phone number."

"Oh, yez, I put it in zhere for you at zhe barn danze. Let me check juzt to make zure."

Not wanting to endure the awkwardness of the moment any longer, I handed him the phone. "Very good. It'z zhere. Zhankz, Jenna. I'll zee you at zchool next week." He looked toward Caden and grunted. "By Ca-don."

As we watched him tumble his way down the hill, Caden roared with laughter. "I can see why Coach hasn't let him race yet." Then he clamped his lips together and grinned, "You took a selfie with him! What's he going to do with that? Post it on Facebook? There goes your chance at Winter Court!" he continued to tease.

He was messing with me so hard I was ready to shove a snowball down his pants. "I'm just trying to be nice. It's Christmas. He's away from his family and I wanted him to feel like he had someone. Have a heart."

"Speaking of hearts. You know who's in his?"

"What are you talking about?"

Again, he began to snicker with the kind of snorty laugh that told me he'd been keeping something from me. "You know he's totally into you, right?"

And that's when he let me in on a little secret he'd been keeping. He was doing his homework on the bus before his last ski race when he'd caught an eyeful of Daemon's background picture. He told me I was his wallpaper photo, but I wasn't buying it. I'd worked with him on his laptop and his background was definitely a scene from Rocky Balboa.

As I argued with him, he clarified, "Not his laptop background. His phone."

Just thinking of the possibility that I was the lock-screen photo on his phone made me cringe. It was a little awkward thinking of a picture of me traveling around in Daemon's pocket. My face twisted into a grimace, "I don't believe you. You're just messing with me again."

"If you don't believe me, ask Lennart. He saw it too."

"Lennart?"

"Yeah, our German exchange student. The really smart guy in our physics class. You know he thinks Daemon is weird too. It's not just me."

I didn't know why I wanted to defend him. Especially when I was really beginning to believe I was his lock-screen picture. I huffed and rolled my eyes. I didn't know if I was trying to convince him or myself. "It's just his culture. You should give him a chance. He really helped me out with the whole heritage thing."

"So, it doesn't bother you?"

"What?"

"Having your picture on his screen?"

I began to shake my head back and forth. I tried to play it cool, not wanting Caden to know I was affected. Though I was curious, "Well, what picture is it?"

Through a big, toothy grin, he quipped, "Oh, just one of you in your swimsuit," he snorted. Then quickly, he bent down to strap back in. Without looking up to see my face, he chuckled, "Race you to the bottom," then he stood up and pushed off. My mind was blown. I was Daemon's personal swimsuit model. The question was, how was I going to handle it?

Chapter Thirty-Two

The Bodyguard

THE WEEKS FOLLOWING CHRISTMAS BROUGHT A NEW PEACE OF mind that none of us expected. Vacation had ended, and basketball was back in full swing. It was the morning of our first weekend practice in preparation for Championships, when I stopped by the Woodley's. I wanted to catch Kaitlyn before her music rehearsal, so I could see how things were going with her and Brody and keep her updated on my news about Ty.

Boyfriend stuff wasn't something we liked to relay through text. She'd have to see my face and hear my voice to know all the ways Ty affected me. The way my tummy contracted when he whispered in my ear. How my body betrayed me every time I tried to hide the color he brought to my cheeks. The way his humility overrode his sexy confidence to create the most endearing conversations. I couldn't wait to talk to her.

Unfortunately, the heart-to-heart chat I'd been hoping for still wasn't in the cards for Kaitlyn and me. That morning at the Woodley's was crazy as usual. Caden, once again, was arguing with his mom about driving to snowboarding practice, and once again I got thrown in the middle of it. My ability to play on his stories was a little help in getting him out of the drive, but just as his ride down to the bus was resolved, the police showed up at the door with some important news.

Over vacation, Pistol's body had been found by a group of snowshoers. To the surprise of the investigation team who had searched the river for weeks, it was wedged between two boulders near the edge of a forested area. The police were still baffled by its distance from his truck. The snow had covered any evidence of how he had gotten so far from the scene of the accident. They weren't sure if he'd been dragged by an animal, a person, or if he'd possibly crawled there before he passed.

Whatever the case, his body was found without any weapon, and there was no evidence of residue on his hands. That contradicted our theory. There was definitely a gun involved during the chase. The bullet holes in Caden's truck were proof of that. The fact that the weapon used to make them could not be tied to Pistol, left the investigation wide open.

Thinking about the discovery of his body stirred a lot of emotions. It was tough to think about the death of an eighteen-year-old, especially in an accident we'd all been directly involved in. We felt terrible for his family, and for the situation in general. There was a tinge of guilt, wondering if we could've done anything differently. At the same time, that thought brought back anger. No. Pistol was responsible for all of it. It was premeditated. The proof was in the bottle of Jack Daniels he'd left in Caden's truck before he chose to play chicken with him on the snowy highway. There was nothing we could have done differently. The accident was definitely beyond our control.

And with that thought, came relief. Relief in knowing Pistol Black was no longer out there hiding. The fact that he was gone allowed us to finally let our guards down and go back to our lives, the way they were before the accident destroyed us. Kaitlyn picked up the guitar again and began writing and singing. Brody hit the gym and started working more with Mason at his ranch. Caden had sworn off Jefferson High girls. He had made the south county his destination for snow sports and dating, and someone down there definitely seemed to have him wrapped around her little finger. It made my heart happy to know everyone was getting back on track.

Without needing to attach myself to the twins every minute, I got a little bit of my independence back, and I was able to focus on two passions of my own, sports and Ty. With only a week of practices left, basketball was coming to a close. I knew we would be headed to Championships, but coming out of our small school league, our season would likely stop there.

I was okay with that. It meant I could start gearing up for my first true love, softball. I needed to get ready for Abby's sixty-five mile an hour pitches, and the best person to help me with that was going to be Ty. He didn't know it yet, but as soon as he got back, he was going to make me the best catcher our small town had ever seen.

Ty was still away on his college trip, but he was never far from my thoughts. Every night I snuggled into his oversized sweatshirt and every morning, I stuck him right back in my pocket so I could carry him around everywhere I went. I looked forward to evenings when I learned of his newest campus visits, which ones had the country feel he liked, and which ones had way too much concrete. He was ecstatic that he'd found a few Division 1 schools that were interested in watching him play. I got nervous for him just thinking about the possibility of scouts scrutinizing his every move, but I knew I was the right person to help get him dialed in.

High school baseball wouldn't start for another month and I convinced him to practice with me during the pre-season. I knew that with every slider, curveball, and changeup he threw, I'd be that much better to catch for our all-star pitcher. I couldn't wait for the chance to work on all Ty's pitches and get his fastball up to lightning speed. It stoked the fire inside to think that I was going to be the catcher on the other end of his throws. I could barely stand the anticipation of practicing with him, but our plans would have to wait for just a few more weeks. Until then, my sights were set on basketball championships. Thankfully, Ty would get back just in time to see the big game.

"'Scuse me." My heart jumped when I heard his voice. Looking up from my homework to see if my ears were deceiving me, I saw Ty making his way through the center aisle on the bus. It was the first time I'd seen him off the screen since he'd left for his college tour. I closed my notebook and shoved it into my backpack before he got back to my seat.

"This seat taken?" I could smell the peppermint of his Colgate smile, as it shined down on me. When our eyes met, my stomach tied itself in a bow, leaving me almost as nervous as the night he held me for the first time. I really hadn't expected to see him on the bus after he'd missed so much school. Between the surprise of him standing in front of me, and the butterflies batting their way up my throat, it was hard to find my voice.

I finally shoved out a whisper. "They let you come?"

"I'm only here in case someone gets injured. Tradeoffs," he shrugged. "My trip was totally worth it."

The guys got a little mouthy as the line began to back up behind him, "Fish or cut bait, Connelly!"

He eyed the open spot beside me. When I finally realized he was waiting for an invitation, I patted the seat. A grin lit his face, "I thought you'd never ask." Again, my insides tumbled as he slid against me. We hadn't been that close since Christmas. Suddenly, having him so near heightened my senses. Though we were barely touching, I felt the warmth of his body transfer to mine. It carried the spicy fragrance of fresh cologne, paired with a hint of peppermint. He must have just taken a shower. The combination of his scent and light touch completely reignited the fire he'd started the night we were wrapping Aiden's gifts. I looked down, afraid he might actually see the flames reflected in my eyes. I still didn't have much control when it came to my body's reaction to him. It was something I definitely needed to work on.

"Come here, you." He slid his arm around my shoulders and pulled me into his strong chest. "I missed you so much."

As I slid my hand onto his knee and laid my head on his shoulder, I inhaled a deep breath and closed my eyes, absorbing everything about him. His scent. His embrace. The rise and fall of his chest. I had been resting against him all of thirty seconds when I sensed the staring. It reminded me that we were in public and up until then, nobody had seen us together. None of our teammates, not the cheerleaders, not even the statisticians knew we were officially a couple.

When the whistles and comments started, the heat began burning in my throat and quickly clawed its way into my cheeks. "Don't listen to them," he whispered into the top of my head. But I didn't want to make a scene. That night was about a championship game, not broadcasting our new relationship. I pulled away and sat facing forward. Ty shifted in his seat, then his hand came under my chin and turned my face toward his. He leaned in and whispered, "I missed that too."

"What?"

"The color you turn when you're embarrassed. It's watermelon," he smiled and pressed his lips to my forehead. He held his kiss long enough for me to hear another train of whispers make their way from the seats behind us. Again, I pulled away.

"You okay?"

"I just. I don't want you to look whipped or anything. You kind of have this untamable image thing going. It works for you."

"I don't care what anybody says." He shook his head excitedly, "I want the whole world to know about us." That's when he stood up, "Hey everyone." He looked around the bus. "I'd like to introduce you to someone. Some of you call her Jenna. Some of you call her Captain. Hell, some of you even call her the one who got away. But from now on, you can call her Ty's girl. That's right team." He held up my hand, "I finally caught her."

"Took you long enough, man!" Timmy hollered from the front of the bus.

Tycen followed with, "Five-year fishing trip, wasn't it?"

Peels of laughter roared around us as some of the guys made their way back and gave both of us high fives.

"Alright, alright, everyone take a seat," Coach Bennett stood up and smiled at us, "Congratulations," he winked before he turned around and sat back down behind the bus driver.

The only guy on the bus who didn't seem happy was Daemon. His lips turned down as he raised his eyebrows and tried to smile. Then he shifted his head and rested it against the seat in front of him. I could tell he felt bad, and wondered if I should talk to him. He must have thought that in the time Ty was away our relationship had fallen through. He had asked to carry my books around school a few times, all of which I politely refused. I tried to show a lack of interest, but maybe I hadn't done a good enough job. A text came across my phone.

Daemon:
I'll miss you. :(

I'd have to get back to him later. Before I could respond, Ty pulled me onto his lap. "How's that? Everybody knows now, so you're free to use me as a couch, pillow, whatever you want."

Wiggling into him playfully, I smiled, "Best chair I have ever sat in."

"Glad to oblige ... especially for such a fine, little booty," he cracked.

I flipped around and gave him a playful tap before I worked my fine, little booty off his lap, curled my legs up on the seat, and pressed into his chest. We snuggled that way all the way to the game, his back to the window, me lying on his chest. He was warm and comforting. It was calming the way his breathing flowed with mine. We meshed like waves meeting in the ocean. Where his chest rose, mine fell. It lulled me into a dreamy state.

"And I missed this." I breathed him in and closed my eyes.

"What?"

"The way I feel when you hold me," I whispered.

"Get used to it, cuz I don't plan on letting you go."

The security of his arms tightening around me gave me the comfort I'd been needing for as long as I could remember. I had never felt anything more consuming than what I felt for him in that moment. I snuggled into him, taking in the fragrance of his spicy cologne. His scent caused a firestorm of fluttering inside me. I slipped my fingers through his and pulled him tighter around me. I could've stayed wrapped in his arms forever. Unfortunately, the bus ride was only two hours.

We must have fallen asleep. In what seemed like no time, the bus came to a stop and the doors flew open. We both jumped when Coach stood up and addressed the team, "Alright, we're here. They're changing out busses so grab everything and take it with you."

I felt around my seat and made sure to grab my gym bag along with all my gear. "Here, let me get that." Ty took the bag from my hand. "I can watch it for you while you play."

After handing him my bag, I slipped my backpack over my shoulders. The fact that my earring caught on the shoulder strap reminded me that I was going to get called off the court if I didn't remove my jewelry. "Wait a sec," I tugged on the strap that was hanging over Ty's elbow. I took my earrings out and my charm bracelet off and slipped them into the pocket of my bag. Looking up at Ty, I grinned, "No jewelry. I usually forget."

"I can watch it, if you want," Daemon walked up the aisle behind us. "Juzt cuz you boz have to play."

"Thanks anyway, bud." Ty patted his shoulder. "I'm benched tonight. I can take care of my girl's stuff."

With Coach shouting for us to get a move on, I barely caught Daemon's face morphing into a sad grimace before I turned around and walked down the aisle.

We were the first game of the tourney, and the competition out on the court was intense. The crowd was roaring, and the Hurricanes definitely lived up to their name. They were huge, fast, and left us spinning. We rolled through our arsenal of set plays, and despite switching our offensive tactics, we had a really tough time getting around their defense. We were denied nearly every shot. Our average five-foot-five heights were no match for the towers of power that dominated us leading into the second half. I was panting like a dog when the buzzer blared through the gym, signaling halftime.

Before I left the court to the locker room, I spotted Ty making his way through the bleachers. With his tight t-shirt and athletic pants, it was hard to take my eyes off him. A couple feet away, Daemon stood with his back to me. I found it odd that Ty was rushing toward him. Though my team was calling me to get off the court, I couldn't stop watching what happened next. Ty quickly approached Daemon, then shoved him down on the bench and grabbed what looked to be my bag.

That's when Daemon's hand came down on the other strap. Back and forth they jerked the bag until with one last tug, it flew back into Ty's chest. In the arm farthest from Daemon, he held the bag, while pushing him back down to his seat with the other. He looked over his shoulder and appeared to be threatening him as he carried the bag with him into the locker room. I couldn't believe what I had just witnessed. There was definitely a story there that

I'd have to find out about later, but both of us were due in our respective locker rooms. Me, to get an earful of the "You're Sucking Tonight, Bailey" speech, and Ty to get ready for his own game.

After the third quarter, I was done. We were behind by thirty and Coach knew it was time to let the second string take their part in the game. I took my place on the bench and grabbed my water bottle. Slunk down in my seat, I couldn't watch. It was going to make me puke to see one more swish by the opponents. Rather than watching the massacre, my eyes were drawn to Ty, who was warming up on the opposite court. Instead of sinking the shots like he normally did, his eyes kept moving back up to the scorekeepers table where Daemon sat keeping stats. I could see their skirmish escalating. There was a war of death glares, firing between the court and the bleachers, and I couldn't help but feel like I was caught right in the middle of it.

It was a good thing Ty wasn't going to get to play. Clearly, his focus was more on Daemon than the game. I couldn't imagine what had happened with my bag to get them both in such an uproar. Ty definitely had too much confidence to feel threatened by him, and Daemon, I'm not sure he'd ever be man enough to take on Ty. Looking up to see Daemon's face, maybe I was wrong. He looked vicious as he cast down dominating, threatening glares. It was a side of him I'd never seen before. For a moment, he didn't even look like Daemon. He actually looked like someone out of a nightmare.

My heart flipped when the buzzer sounded and we had to go congratulate the other team. I wasn't ready to take my eyes off the boys. Unfortunately, it wasn't my choice. I had to get to the locker room and get the last of the season's lectures over with.

The pep talk was much longer than I'd expected. We'd just been chewed up and spit out by the new North State Champions, and thankfully rather than tearing us down, Coach tried to make us feel good about our season. It was a heartfelt goodbye to the seniors, and with much effort on his part, a strong passing of the torch to the juniors. There were a lot of stories shared and tears shed. In the end, we didn't make it out of the locker room until halftime of the boys' varsity game. The buzzer had just sounded, and the mob of guys was lining up.

As we headed out of the locker room, I glanced up at the scoreboard. Their game wasn't going much better than ours had. Too bad they weren't letting Ty play. He could have made all the difference. Down by 28, it didn't look like they had a prayer for a comeback. We passed each other on our way to and from the locker room. Pulling away from the mob of players Ty cautioned, "Please stay away from that guy." He quickly glanced up at the bleachers and then back toward me. "I've got to talk to you about him."

It didn't sound like a jealous warning. It sounded like he was concerned about something. When I glanced to the place where Ty's eyes had just directed, Daemon was still sitting at the scorekeepers table. He was watching our brief meeting down on the court. An unsettling feeling came over me. At least with him stuck at the table, he'd be easy to avoid. I'd just grab my bag and head back to the locker room to shower and change. Maybe I could hang out there for a bit until the game was almost over.

The problem was, I couldn't find my bag. Ty had done something with it. Since he was benched, I slipped into the row behind him so I could discreetly ask for it back. There were things in there I needed, namely a bra and underwear. I didn't want to sit in my sweaty sports bra and uniform the rest of the night.

I leaned forward, "You mind telling me where my bag is?" I whispered.

Without looking back, he simply said, "Yeah."

I knew Daemon had him ruffled, but I was the owner of the bag. I didn't understand why he wouldn't tell me where he put it.

"You need it now?" He finally asked.

"Kinda. It has some stuff I need."

"Yeah, apparently it had something Daemon needed too. He was digging through it earlier."

I didn't know what he'd want with my bag, but the thought of Daemon's hands all over my underwear kind of freaked me out.

"Seriously?"

"We'll talk about it later. I'll help you get it after the game. Stay by me, huh?"

Though I wanted to shower and change, I couldn't argue with him. Something wasn't sitting right with me. Ty wasn't one to play games. By the tone in his voice, it wasn't jealousy. He was really bothered by Daemon. Whatever was going on was more of a threat than an unhealthy crush.

Chapter Thirty-Three

Same Story, Different Devil

TY STOOD OUTSIDE THE LOCKER ROOM DOOR WHILE I QUICKLY slipped on the clothes and jewelry I'd been waiting for. When I was done, he wrapped his arm around my back and escorted me out to the area where the teams were waiting to load the bus. Both teams had been destroyed and the mood was quiet and somber. Too quiet to ask about what was going on without being overheard by the rest of our teammates.

We stood back and waited for Daemon to enter the bus before Ty took me by the hand and helped me up the stairs. Since he was near the front, we looked for an open seat in the last row far from his earshot. As we walked by his seat, I felt him tug at my wrist, "Jenna," he whispered. "I juzt want to talk to you."

"Hands off," Ty slid in between us and escorted me away. "You okay?" he asked as we settled in the seat at the back.

Daemon was stronger than I thought. I rubbed the place on my wrist where he had just grabbed me. Instantly I realized where I should've felt my bracelet, I felt only bare skin. I began to work my fingers up my sleeve, but still felt nothing. A wave of adrenaline hit me. My bracelet from Peyton wasn't there. I checked my other wrist to see if I'd worn it on the other side. Nothing.

"I think I dropped my bracelet." I turned to Ty. "I put it on in the locker room and now it's not there." I held my wrist to show him.

"Did you have it when you got on the bus?"

"Yeah, I'm pretty sure. I didn't notice it was gone until just now. Maybe it came off when Daemon tried to stop me."

Without another word, Ty stood up and marched down the aisle. It was dark so I could barely make out what was happening. When he returned, he held up the bracelet. "Found it, Pickle."

"Where was it?"

"With Daemon. Listen, there's something I need to talk to you about."

"Yeah?"

"I don't know what it is about this thing that he's so attracted to, but while you were down on the court, he was rifling through your bag. I spotted the bracelet just as he lifted it out. I made it across the bleachers just in time to get it back. Pissed him off though."

I was baffled to think Daemon tried to take my bracelet out of my gym bag. He really did have a weird obsession with me. Or maybe it was the bracelet? I hugged Ty and thanked him for getting it back. "I think he likes this charm." I flicked the castle. "He made a big deal over it at the ski park." I sat and stared at it for a minute. It was so intricate in its design. "Maybe it's worth money," I joked.

Ty paused a moment and then grew serious, "Or, maybe it just reminds him of you. Next thing you know, he's going to be taking the hair out of your brush," he warned.

"Gross!" I shuttered, "Don't joke like that."

"I'm not kidding." And he wasn't. His tone grew even more serious. "There's something disturbing about that guy. I don't know what it is, but something's a little off with him."

I found myself reflecting on the way Kaitlyn and Caden spoke of him. They were not Daemon fans at all. "Everyone keeps saying that."

"Maybe it's time to listen." Ty was getting to know me well

enough that he could sense my unease. "How 'bout a change of subjects, huh?" He took me into his arms and ran his fingers through my hair. "We get to start practicing tomorrow. You think you can catch my fastball?"

I sat up and looked at him. "If anyone can catch your balls, it's me," I patted his chest and grinned.

"Well, I'm looking forward to that," he grinned back before he grabbed me and pulled me into him. "So, we know your favorite team is the Sox. You ever seen them play?"

"You mean in real life?"

"Yes, in real life, silly."

"Nope. But my dream is to see Fenway someday. To step out onto the same field where baseball legends like Babe Ruth actually played. Oh, yeah, and I want to stand during the seventh inning stretch and sing 'Sweet Caroline.'" I paused and smiled. "One day."

"Yep. One day." I could almost feel his wheels turning as we sat silently next to each other dreaming about a trip to Fenway. My ringing phone broke the silence.

"I should probably get that. Nobody ever calls." I peeled myself away from his warm chest and reached into my pocket. Caden's name and picture lit up the screen. "It's Caden," I whispered.

"Hey, Caden." I held my hand over the phone and joked to Ty that he didn't need to be jealous. He chuckled, assuring me that we were way past that hurdle. I turned my attention back to the waiting conversation.

"Hey. Where are you? I need to talk to you."

"I'm on the bus."

"You're still coming back from the game?"

"Uh huh."

There was a brief pause, but I could hear his muffled voice on the other end of the line talking to someone. "Damn it. He's on there with her."

"Caden, what is it?"

"Sorry. Are you alone?"

"No. I'm sitting with Ty," I smiled at him.

"Can I talk to him?"

"Sure. I guess."

"He wants to talk to you," I shrugged, handing the phone to Ty. As he spoke to Caden his hand came over my leg and pulled me closer to him. The serious tone he took paired with his short, quick responses had me wishing I could hear what Caden was saying. "I won't. I will. Got it. *You're* going to pick him up? *You're* okay with driving?" I felt the muscles in his forearm tense as he sat straight up and looked toward the front of the bus. "We're just pulling into town. Yep, I'll wait for you. Yeah, I'll make sure she stays with me. Got it. Yeah. We can meet at my truck. It's in the senior parking lot."

Caden sounded worried. It wasn't like him to call. He usually texted. I couldn't help but wonder why he chose to talk to Ty and not me. Feeling snubbed I asked, "What is it? Everything okay?"

"Not sure. Caden has something he needs us to see."

"Why couldn't he just talk to me about it?"

Ty got quiet. "I guess it's something he has to show you. He just wanted to make sure I stayed with you till he gets here. He's swinging by to pick up Brody first."

The bus pulled up in front of the gym and everyone began to flow out. Some left in cars and others had parents waiting for them. My car was parked across the street near Ty's truck, but he asked that I stay with him until Caden got there with Brody.

"Caden's driving?" I swallowed the lump in my throat knowing something serious must have taken place to put him behind the wheel. Maybe they'd misidentified Pistol's body and it was time to put our guards back up. That possibility was always lingering in the back of my mind. I couldn't imagine what else it could be.

By the time we got to my car, mostly everyone had cleared out of the parking lot. I opened the door and tossed my stuff in before

273

locking it up and rejoining Ty. "After you," he easily lifted me onto his tailgate and then hopped up beside me. I shivered. The chill in the air amplified my anxiety induced trembling. I had no idea what could have been so important that I couldn't go straight home after the game. It must have been something big.

Caden's truck came from around the corner lighting the parking lot. I could clearly make out the silhouettes of Caden and Brody, but there were two more shadows in the back. Kaitlyn's messy bun identified her right away, but there was someone else. Maybe Caden wanted to introduce us to his new girl after all.

They pulled up next to us and the doors flung open. Caden and Brody jumped out first and moved around to open the back doors for the girls. After Kaitlyn, a springy, little country girl with curly, brown hair bounded to the ground. I took a second look just to be sure my eyes weren't deceiving me. I was shocked when I recognized her as Avery Black. I'd known her from swim team. She'd competed against Kaitlyn and me for years, but she didn't live in our town so I hadn't seen her since the previous summer. After everything that had happened, it floored me to see her with Caden. Confused, I couldn't help but wonder if he knew she was Pistol's little sister. I couldn't make sense of it.

"What's going on?" I questioned. "What's Avery doing with you?"

"You're not going to believe this." The group moved into a circle around me. "We've got to show you something. Then we're headed down to the station."

Avery handed me a journal, "This was my brother's."

I didn't want to touch it. I wanted nothing to do with anything that belonged to Pistol Black. I pulled my hands away. "What would I want with this thing? Outside of being Kaitlyn's best friend, I had nothing to do with him." I turned to Avery. "Sorry, I don't mean to be insensitive." Her expression was covered in disappointment.

Seeing the tension grow between us, Caden stepped in. "This

whole mess, Jenna. It wasn't what we thought it was," he said. "I mean part of it was. Pistol had a problem. He was in rehab trying to fix it. He wasn't after us. Look!" He set the journal in my hand. "You've got to read this."

"Why me?"

"Because. It has everything to do with you."

I swallowed the lump in my throat as I took the journal and began to read.

November 25

It's the middle of the night. I'm drenched in sweat. I can't sleep. The last two months have been re-playing in my mind. Tonight when he came to visit, it brought everything back. I can't believe the crap I've done. What the hell was I thinking? I wasn't. The alcohol scrambled my brain. It fueled my jealousy. It amped my anger. It turned me into a monster. If I could go back, I never would've done it. This place has brought me clarity, but along with that, I think I just inherited an even greater nightmare. Living with what I've done. I loved her. I loved her more than anything. I still do. Next to my little sister, she's the only one who ever saw the good in me.

I know I was in a messed up frame of mind the night of the homecoming dance. The night he pulled me aside and offered me my ego back. It was jealousy. I was pissed off about Brody and her. I felt like they'd made a fool of me. All I wanted was revenge. Maybe I wanted to scare her. Pay her back for the way she made me feel. I don't know. I was too drunk to know what I was thinking. But how? How did it get so out of control? Helping him plant cameras? Watching? Stalking? How could I have done this? For a little cash, some booze, and a few pictures here and there? Why didn't I question him more? For weeks, I let him turn me into his puppet. Telling me what to do with that screwed up accent of his. What the hell did he want with her friend anyway? I can't believe the nerve he had showing up here, asking me to go with him. What is his obsession? Something doesn't feel right. I didn't like the look in his eyes tonight when he told me he was going down to see her. I don't trust him. Not one bit. I've got to go down to that river and make sure they're okay. All of them. I owe them that much.

Shaking by the end, I nearly dropped the journal. "I don't get it. Am I?"

"The friend," Caden barked. "He's stalking you, Jenna. It's Daemon. He used Pistol to get to you. Him being everywhere is no coincidence. He knows every move you make."

"It doesn't make sense. It's just a high school crush," I rationalized.

As soon as the words left my mouth, a rush of warnings came racing back. My missing wallet. The lanyard with my information.

Even the lingering smell of Fritos and Peanut butter invading my car. It was him. I could feel it. He really had been stalking me.

Ty must've read the worry on my face, "I told you he was off. We've gotta get down to the station. You're riding with me. Leave your car here." He slipped his arm through mine and tugged me toward his truck. Looking over his shoulder he yelped to the others, "Meet you guys down there." Sweaty and trembling, he had to help me climb into his cab, while the twins, Brody, and Avery got into Caden's truck to lead the way.

Caden had just started to pull out when I noticed a second set of tail lights at the far end of the parking lot. Had that car been there the entire time? We thought we were alone. Clearly, we weren't. Just as we began to follow Caden, we heard the squeal of tires and looked up to catch a little, black car speeding out the gated entrance. "It's him! That's his car," I squeaked.

Caden must have spotted him in his rearview mirror. Before I could process what he was doing, he spun around and sped toward the north entrance.

Ty flipped around too.

"But the police," I squeaked.

"Caden's following him. I'm not letting them do this without me."

Our trip to the police station had just turned into a chase through the back roads at the north of town.

We were about three miles down Shasta River Road when we spotted the black car sitting in the brush. It was barely visible. The lights were off, but we could see that the driver's door was open. It looked like Daemon had abandoned it and fled on foot.

"Careful!" I yelped as we pulled up behind Caden's truck and all three of the guys got out. Caden and Brody first, followed by Ty. I looked around cautiously before I jumped out too. Ty was already on the passenger's side waiting to take my hand. After escorting me to Caden's truck, he slipped me into the cab with

Kaitlyn and Avery.

"Stay here and lock the doors," he panted before I watched him jog toward Caden and Brody. We all huddled together.

"What should we do?"

"Call the police. Right now. They need to get here before something really bad happens. The boys obviously aren't thinking this through."

Just as I was getting ready to dial, a thump on the window next to me sent my heart into my throat. I spun around to see Daemon. He was trying to lift the handle.

"Jenna, it'z not what you zhink."

I backed away from the door toward the other side of the truck.

"Give it to me!"

I shook my head, no.

"Go away, Daemon!" Avery yelled. "You've already done enough damage."

"Hello, I have an emergency!" Kaitlyn's voice yelped from the front seat.

He began lifting the handle wildly as he pounded on the window. "I zaid give it to me. It'z not what you zhink!"

"Yes, Shasta River Road," her voice sounded through again. "Hurry!" she screamed as we watched Daemon draw a knife from his pocket.

His eyes grew wild as he held the knife to the door handle. The squeaking of metal pierced the cab of the truck.

"What's he doing?"

"He's trying to pick the lock."

"Stop, Daemon!" I screamed. "Just go away! There's nothing in here that belongs to you!"

Light began to flood the window and the sound of screeching metal disappeared. We all scanned every direction, spinning to check each window. Our panting was causing them to fog.

"Where is he? Where is he?" We all spun back and forth,

pivoting in our seats. Panicked, I tried to smear enough of the fogged window to see out. A couple feet away, I could make out silhouettes running toward us. It was the boys, lit by the flashlights on their phones. I rolled down the window.

"We heard you screaming," Ty shouted. "Did you see him?"

"He was just here," I gasped.

"Keep searching, guys. He's close."

We rolled up the windows and double checked the doors to make sure they were locked as the boys made their way back toward the river. Huddled together, we scrambled for theories about where Daemon was and what we thought he was doing. Clearly, he was off his rocker to think I was worth the kind of trouble he was going to be in when they found him. Cameras? Stalking? Persuading Pistol to help him? What could possibly be so enticing about me, that he was taking such extreme measures to keep me under a microscope?

At the squeal of tires we lost it again. I whipped around to see who it was but couldn't see through the foggy windows. There were no lights or sirens, nothing to indicate that the police had arrived. I cleared another circle from the window and peeked through. Pushing my head against the glass, I squinted to see out. It was too dark, too still. We sat a few seconds in silence when unexpectedly a fist came up and pounded on the window. If I didn't have a neck to cage it, my heart would've surely jumped out of my body. My hand came to my chest to hold it in place until I figured out how to slow it down.

"Let me in!" It was Caden's voice. I pulled the lock, pushed the door open, and saw the other boys running up behind him. "He just took off! That was him in the car! We've got to go!"

Ty took my hand as I jumped to the ground and we ran to his truck. Caden's engine roared to life, followed by Ty's. He was just getting ready to shift it into gear when a police siren sounded and blue and red lights pulled up in front of us. They had just missed him, but in the same turn, they were stripping us of any possibility of catching him.

I threw my head back into the seat when a voice sounded over the speaker. "Step out of the vehicle." What were they doing letting him get away? I hoped they didn't think we were the problem.

"I called!" Kaitlyn screeched. "It's not us." The boys held their hands up in the air and shook their heads.

"You're going to lose him! He just left!" Caden bellowed, pointing to the highway.

Slowly, we lowered our hands as the officers moved toward us. It took us nearly five minutes to explain the situation. How we were headed to the station when we noticed him. "It's all on file. There's an ongoing investigation. This is new information." Caden held Pistol's journal. "We didn't know Daemon was a part of it until tonight. Listen, you've got to get a hold of the officers on this case. Here." Caden dug into his wallet and pulled out the business card the detective had given him after they pulled his truck from the river and discovered the bullet holes. "This guy knows everything."

The police officer looked at the card and immediately called the station. After a few minutes, they put out an APB on the little, black car. We didn't know which direction it had gone, but hopefully, with the massive search, they would find it soon. The problem was, there were a lot of hiding places in our neck of the woods. Forests, mountains, rivers, old mining shafts. If he ditched the car and fled on foot, it could take years to find him.

We took out our phones to see if we could find a picture to give the officer. At least that way they would have an image to go from. As we scrolled through every photo we'd taken since school started, we all came up empty. There wasn't a single picture on our camera rolls. Even the selfie I'd taken with Daemon on Christmas Day had vanished. I searched for his contact to find the picture that way. It was gone. I couldn't help but panic, knowing he had just texted me on the bus. Did he erase his contact when he was digging through my bag? I was at a loss. We all were.

The one thing I did know was we were back to our new normal, living life on guard. Only this time I had pulled in Ty. Same story, different devil. I could only hope the police could find him and return him to the hell from which he came.

Chapter Thirty-Four

Addicted

OVER THE NEXT FEW WEEKS, WE WERE CALLED INTO THE STATION several times. After we'd turned over Pistol's journal, we were asked to recount everything we remembered about the Christmas tree hunt and the horrific situation that unfolded down by the river. We even revisited the night at the cabin. The boys had always given us a hard time about thinking someone was in there, but after reading Pistol's journal entry, the possibility that it had been Daemon looked extremely likely.

The police were still working to verify their suspicions. They had a tough job on their hands. Just like his contact information in my phone, everything had disappeared. There was no sign of him anywhere. When the police went to the school to pull up his file, they discovered there were no transcripts for Daemon in their system. In fact, they couldn't even find a record of his host family or evidence of him being tied to any exchange program. We knew he was a genius when it came to manipulating technology, but he'd taken his hacking skills to a whole new level. All of the information the school's system once held, had been erased. Addresses, phone numbers, contact information. All of it was gone.

It seemed he'd removed himself from the face of the Earth. Unfortunately, Daemon's wasn't the first disappearing act we'd lived through. We all knew he was still out there somewhere. Though he was out of the picture for the time being, we couldn't be sure how long it would be before he resurfaced. The question was how did we go about our lives until he was found?

We'd done our share of hiding and we weren't willing to run again. We knew how to live under the radar and we were fully prepared to use our resources. Since Daemon was young and likely in over his head, the police thought he might have been scared off for good. However, my parents suspected it may have been more than a high school crush gone wrong and called in a highly experienced professional. Someone who had worked excessively in international investigations. Mason's dad.

After hearing the details, he wanted to come in person to monitor the situation and make sure safety and security were handled properly. Within a day of the call, he flew in, promising to stay with us for as long as it took to make sure we were okay. With an added security team and Isaiah staying at the vineyard during the investigation, we all felt a little more at ease. I was confident the necessary protection was in place to carry on with my high-school plans.

Weeks had passed with no signs of Daemon. All of us had begun to fall back into our normal high-school routines. Miraculously, the spring-like weather came early. It allowed me to get a jumpstart on practice. Because the snow had melted away, the infield had dried out, and the grass could be maintained, every day provided a new opportunity to practice with my favorite pitcher.

I remember the first day I brought Ty onto my private field at the vineyard. He hadn't been there since the previous year when the high school field had flooded. Since then, Roger had added a few improvements. He'd rebuilt the backstop, added a dugout, and put some bleachers outfield by the first base line.

All the wood we used was brought in from a nearby ballpark that was in the process of being rebuilt. We wanted to give it that old stadium feel. My last project had been to paint the backstop green with white lettering that matched Fenway's. Across the back-stop, I had stolen my favorite quote from the Cardinal's catcher, Yadier Molina. "I don't always throw base stealers out … Ohh, wait! Yeah, I do." I got a kick out of that saying, and I knew my visitors would too.

"Pretty confident, aren't we?" Ty smiled as he ran his hand along the quote.

"I can hold my own."

He looked me up and down and grinned. I could tell he thought I was in over my head when he paused and cautioned, "Well, base-balls are a lot smaller and faster, but I'll go easy on you." He paused for a moment and grimaced. I could tell he remembered the last time he used that line on me it didn't go over so well.

"No need. I'm not afraid of your tiny balls, Connelly," I winked as I stepped behind the plate. "Been bruised by bigger balls than yours." I began to back away. "Let's see what you've got."

Ty shook his head as he walked toward the mound. I knew I'd amused him with my humor about the size of his balls, but I intended to show him that I could handle any size he wanted to throw at me.

I held my mitt out as I watched him wind up for the first pitch. I could almost count the threads as it was lacking heat and came straight down the line. I knew I was going to have to show him that it was okay to throw a little harder. I stood up and winged it straight to his chest.

"Damn, girl!" He pulled his hand from his mitt and worked his fingers in and out, clearly trying to lessen the sting of my throw. After shoving his hand back in, he wound up and released his sec-ond pitch. Again, it was soft, but this time I had to dive two feet to the left to snag it. I promptly signaled that it was inside and giggled. "Am I making you nervous? Try that again."

His next pitch was an out-of-control fast pitch that was high and outside. I literally jumped like Tigger to snag it. The pitches he was throwing certainly weren't going to catch a scout's eye. He hadn't thrown a strike since we started. I decided to call a meeting, just like I would have if it was Abby having an off day. I stood up and met him at the mound.

Setting the ball in his hand I said, "Look at me."

His eyes met mine. I could see a glimmer of something I'd never seen in him before. Uncertainty. Nervousness. He was going to have to toughen up. That kind of weakness would never do for the level of baseball he was trying to prepare for.

"I need you to do something for me, Connelly."

"What's that?"

"Breathe. Calm down and focus on my mitt." I held it up to his face. "Don't take your eyes off it." I moved it left to right. "I said, don't take your eyes off it." Then I moved it again in a circle. This time his eyes followed. "Now, forget the fact that I'm a girl and throw that damn ball like you would if you were in a game." I thumped him on the head with it and started to walk away.

"But I don't want to hurt you," he called out.

I stopped in my tracks and turned toward him, then ran my hands down my sides and smirked, "This body is a machine. Ain't nobody gonna hurt this girl. Besides, it's not a pitcher's job to worry about their catcher. It steals all the fun out of the game." Then I put my mitt up to catch the ball. "Here, we'll start close then work our way back, just like we used to in ponytail," I giggled.

The ball came at me with a little more force than the pitches he'd thrown at full distance. Then we took a step back and did it again. We winged the ball back and forth, increasing the velocity as our distance grew. Faster, stronger, harder, until I had him up to speed. There was a point when I actually felt like my fingertips were going to break, but there was nothing he threw that I was willing to let pass by. With as much fun as I was having, I didn't care if I ended up black and blue all over. I jumped, dove, rolled, and sprinted. I had become a human magnet and the ball was my iron.

As my catches grew wilder and more dramatic, his confidence in me grew. The more challenging the pitch, the better I liked it. He wasn't holding back anymore. In fact, he had me on a baseball high.

By the end of our first practice, I was addicted. Addicted to the look in his eyes before he released the ball. The way his muscular thighs contracted as he executed each windup. How his face twisted into a cute grimace as he concentrated on my mitt. Not only was I addicted to him physically, but the chemistry between us was palpable. There was a rush that came with catching each of his different pitches, like with each new throw, he was giving me another part of him.

The true high came when I realized I could predict the kind of pitch he would throw and exactly where it would arrive. I'd never experienced anything like it with my other pitchers. It made it even more fun when I began giving him signals, and he delivered on each one. It was almost like we had a secret language. Each delivery was so smooth, there could have been an invisible track between the two of us and that ball.

It was the best practice I'd ever had in my life, and I'm pretty sure he felt the same way. After I caught his last pitch, he ran to where I was still standing at home. His face was beaming as he picked me up and spun me around. A fire ignited in my core as he slowly slid me down the front of him to set me back on the ground.

"Now I see what they've been talking about," he smiled down at me.

"Yeah?"

"I guess seeing is believing."

"You haven't seen anything yet. Thanks for the warm-up practice. We'll keep working on your speed," I chuckled to myself, knowing damn well I'd never been pushed so hard in my life. And though I could barely stand on my own two feet, I didn't want it to end. "This really was fun. Thank you." I smiled and looked up at him through my masked eyes.

The way he looked at me with such admiration made me want to rip my face mask off right then. He'd been killing me by withholding our first kiss, and I was about ready to take matters into my own hands. The stillness between us grew as I stared into his eyes and silently waited for him to make a move. Then slowly, I began to lift my mask from my face as I leaned into him.

His hand met mine, stopping the mask from unveiling the rest of my face. "Almost, Pickle, but not like this." He slid it back in place, "You'd better keep that right there so I don't blow it. I've got big plans for us. Patience."

My chest contracted in disappointment. What could I do? I took a deep breath and huffed. I was too tired to fight him on it. He could tell I was frustrated when he took my hand and leaned into my mask, "You'll thank me later."

I didn't want to appear desperate, so I lightened the mood. "Well, it better be worth the wait," I raised my eyebrows up and down, then topped it off with a sideways grin.

"Oh, it will be. Just give it time."

Speaking of time, we needed to get home. The sun was setting on an already chilly evening. I was getting cold and we were both exhausted from the two-hour practice. Ty snuggled me into him as we walked up the path. Not wanting to separate, we stood at the front door wrapped in each other's arms. When security finally interrupted us to make sure I was okay, we decided to meet after school again the next day. And we did. Again. And again. And again. The rest of the week, until it was time for our regular season to start.

Chapter Thirty-Five

Show Me What You Got!

"I HOPE YOU'RE READY FOR TONIGHT," TY SIDLED UP BEHIND ME IN the hallway. "I think I finally got it right."

"What?"

He leaned over and whispered, "You'll see." I could feel his grin against my ear as he pulled away and left the scent of his peppermint gum to fill me with the same warm, tingly sensation it always did.

"A few more details, please!" I called out and waved as he headed down the hall.

Looking over his shoulder he shouted back, "Dress warm. I'll be at your place just before sunset."

The twinkle in his eyes and the humor in his voice told me he was planning something that was going to steal another piece of me. He had done that a lot lately. At school. Out on the field. Riding in his truck. I didn't know it was possible for someone to own another's smile, laugh, and heart the way Ty did mine, but with each of his words and each of his thoughtful actions, I willingly handed over another piece of myself. I'd never been so unguarded. I hadn't even kissed him yet, but something told me the second I did, he would own me completely.

It was tough watching him walk away. It was all I could do

to stop myself from sprinting down the hallway to pull him back to me. I was beginning to need him like the Earth needed rain. The more time we spent together, the more I missed him when we were apart. He consumed my every thought. The only time I could suppress my urgency to have him near me was when I was behind the plate. Even then, he was there. Living in my mind. Telling me where to put my mitt, where to play, how to move, how to be the best. Practicing with him, being with him, loving him, were the best decisions of my life.

My heart flipped as I watched the front of his truck pull up next to my walk. It was time for whatever he'd been keeping from me that day. I could barely contain my butterflies when all six-foot-three of him jumped out of his truck. As I watched his lean, muscular body wrapped in a snug t-shirt and blue jeans saunter up to my doorstep, I couldn't help but think of him as a gift. He was wearing his Red Sox ball cap and white, toothy grin when I opened the door and greeted him.

"For you." From behind his back, he pulled out a small bouquet of sunflowers wrapped in burlap. Knowing they stood for adoration, the bright, yellow flowers instantly put a smile on my face and stole the breath I'd been holding since he walked in. After thanking him in a quiet whisper, he gave me a hug and continued, "I got special permission from your dad to keep you out just a little later than usual since we'll be staying on the property."

"We will?" I was surprised to hear we weren't going out. I had suspected he might take me mudding. I'd heard a bunch of the baseball team was going out to the valley and assumed he might want to take me too.

"Yep. Looks like you're all set too. Your outfit is perfect."

I looked down at my boots, leggings, and long sweater. Warm enough for the cool spring air, but not too casual. Considering most of the time I was in athletic gear, I had a little fun dressing up for a special night with my guy. I even went the extra mile and wore my hair down in loose curls. He leaned into me and whispered, "I'm not used to seeing you without your mask and twisty hair thing you do." I felt him take a deep breath against my ear before he continued, "You're absolutely stunning. Shall we?" He held out his arm and I draped mine over his.

"Our chariot awaits." He chuckled, mimicking a fairy tale prince.

When he walked out the front door, Roger was waiting in the Ranger. "Hey, kid!" he greeted me. "You're in for a treat tonight."

As much as I wondered what Roger had to do with our date night, I couldn't help but feel excited for whatever Ty had planned. Clearly, he'd put a lot of thought into whatever it was. He'd even ditched the baseball mudding party to be with me. Though it was still out of view, I began to smell the freshly cut grass wafting up from below. I breathed in the spring air. The soft breeze that evening, combined with the warm sensation of snuggling next to Ty, had my insides turning cartwheels. As we approached the crest of the hill that overlooked my baseball field, there was a subtle glow. The setting sun had never cast such a beautiful glimmer on my field before. When we were in perfect position to see the entire valley below, Roger pulled to a stop.

Looking down from the top of the hill, I took it all in, awestruck by the vision before me. At first there looked to be hundreds of fireflies dancing in the darkening sky, but on closer inspection it was the flickering of hundreds of mason jar candles. As evenly spaced as a perfectly stitched quilt, they lined the baselines and circled the pitcher's mound. Against the fading light of the early evening sky, they shined like a diamond.

"Do you like it?" his voice finally broke through my

mesmerized stare.

"Wow," I whispered. The sight took my breath away.

"And this is where I drop you off," Roger said as he let us out. "Be back later to pick you up." He waved and pulled away.

As we made our way toward the field, even more surprises came into view. There was a blanket covering the pitcher's mound. Next to it sat a wicker picnic basket, a bottle of sparkling cider, and two champagne flutes.

I wrapped my arm around the back of him as my eyes focused on the beautiful display in front of me. The warmth crawled from my chest, and instantly I suspected a new shade covered my cheeks. Slowly, I turned toward him, speechless. Silence filled the night air. I couldn't believe the hours of planning and preparing Ty had done. Taking in a deep breath, I whispered, "You did all this for me?"

He pulled me closer into him, not taking his eyes off my flushed cheeks, "Of course. I had to do something to bring this color back." He rubbed the pad of his thumb across my cheek and grinned. He already had my laugh and my smile. And with this night, I knew without a doubt, he would have the rest of my heart.

It was so much. He had saved all of it for my favorite season. My sacred place had become home to a thousand candles glowing on the infield, all surrounding a beautiful picnic dinner. Overwhelmed, I looked down so he couldn't see the tears building behind my eyes. I didn't think I was worthy of that kind of effort. Until Ty, I had always been a third wheel. The funny one. The one who could never truly let someone in because of her secrets.

But that was all about to change. No one had ever made me feel more special than Ty did at that moment. He had proven that I was worth his effort. Knowing I meant so much to him, awakened emotions I hadn't felt for a very long time. Vulnerability. Need. Desire. I tried to hide the tears, but they snuck their way down my cheeks. Slowly, he lifted my chin and his eyes studied mine. "I'm hoping those are happy tears," he whispered as his thumbs dried the wetness from beneath my eyes. I nodded my forehead against his as he held me tightly. "I was happy to do this, Pickle. It's not every day that two hearts share the same favorite place. Come with me. There's more."

He took me by the hand and walked me toward the pitcher's mound where his mitt was waiting. "Go ahead, grab your mitt." He directed me toward home. When I looked over, I saw it there. My pink mitt was sitting on the plate.

"What're you planning here?" I giggled. "It's too late for practice."

"This isn't practice, Pickle. It's the game … and I'm throwing out the first pitch."

Whatever it was, I was into it. I jogged over to pick up my mitt.

"Careful with it!"

Careful with a glove? Hah. My mitt was indestructible. It had seen eighty-mile an hour pitches and come through like a champ. When I started to put it on, I noticed a streak of silver shining through a small opening in the web. I turned the mitt over to see that inside the pocket sat a silver chain. It held the charm of a baseball mitt with a ball in the center.

My jaw slackened and I drew in a breath. It was the cutest necklace I'd ever seen. Just as I lifted it from the mitt, Ty jogged up behind me.

"Let me help." He took it from my hand and stepped into me to clasp it behind my neck. I shivered as he gathered my hair to the side and laid it over the front of my shoulder. I could feel him working behind my neck, when he leaned into me and whispered. "This is to let you know that you caught me. And just so you don't forget it, I had it engraved on there. It's kind of hard to see in the dark."

I held the charm up to the moonlight and turned it back and forth. There it was, engraved on the baseball, in all capitals, CAUGHT ME. "I love it. Really."

"Well, good. I love that you love it. I'll tell you what. Now that the first pitch is out of the way, let's have some dinner and then continue our game. Sound like a plan?"

We walked back to the blanket on the mound. There, we huddled close while Ty fed me cheese and crackers and we sipped sparkling cider. There was comfortable silence as we devoured the tasty picnic dinner and enjoyed watching the stars begin to pop up in the night sky. When we'd finished the pressed Italian sandwiches he'd tied neatly in strings, he pulled out yet another surprise. Chocolate covered strawberries.

"Did you have this catered?" I asked, amazed at how picture perfect the contents of the basket had been.

"Can't a guy have more talents than throwing a ball?"

I studied his face. I could see the twinkle in his eye, lit by the light of the glowing mason jars. Then with a flirty urgency, I looked at his plump lips and suggested, "That's yet to be determined." He knew exactly what I was talking about.

"Guess that's my cue to get on with our game." He stood and held out his hand. After lifting me to my feet he challenged, "Race you to first!" then he took off to the base without looking back.

When we got there, I had to ask, "What's this all about? You can't get to first unless you earn it. We didn't even hit the ball."

"This is my game. My rules. Look down."

When I looked down, there was a Chinese takeout box. I squinted my eyes and tilted my head. "What's this?"

"Open it."

When I picked it up and opened it, it was filled with fortune cookies. "I believe you want this one," he stuck his hand in the box and pulled out a cookie. "Go ahead, break it open." When I did, I pulled out a long, white slip with a handwritten message.

~For every base we visit tonight, a special memory awaits.
I hope you enjoy the journey as much as I've enjoyed ours.~

"The fortune cookies." I was touched that he thought of Kelsey Creek Camp. I remembered thinking that he had a crush on another girl the entire time. Lucky for me, she turned out to be his cousin. "Camp was one of your special memories of us?"

"I couldn't take my eyes off you. You didn't notice? It wasn't a coincidence that my cabin was always bussing tables while yours was doing meal prep."

"Seriously?"

"And now that I'm being honest. The scavenger hunt? Yeah, I set it up so I could get some time with you."

"It's not tradition?"

He shook his head, no. "Really, Pickle? You think the directors are going to send a teenage boy off with some hot girl in the middle of the night to look for a tackle box full of unnecessary items? Not on your life."

I could feel myself blush again. Thankfully, this time it was too dark for him to see. "Your idea?"

"My idea." He took the box from my hand and set it back on the base. "I think it's time to hit second." This time, he held my hand and ran with me.

Before I could jump on the bag, he stopped me mid-air and gently pulled me back to him. "Hold up. This one's breakable." When I looked down I saw a CD case. I picked it up and looked it over. It was labeled, "Our Greatest Hits." I felt myself grimace in confusion. "Stay here." He took the CD from my hand and ran toward the dugout, where it looked like he'd set up an old boom box. As he started back toward me, I heard the music begin. It was "I Don't Dance" by Lee Brice.

"Now you can step on the base." He lifted me onto the bag, took me into his arms, and we began to sway to the song. "You know I never danced with a girl until Homecoming, right? You were my first."

I looked at him puzzled, until I thought back on that night. He'd sent every girl away who had come up to him. I was the first girl who he danced with. At least that night I was. "You mean to tell me, you never danced with anyone but me? Not even before Homecoming?"

"That's what I'm saying. I always had two left feet. You were the first one I didn't care about stepping on. It meant I could be close to you. Touch you. And damn girl, did I want to touch you." I saw his bright smile widen in the moonlight. We continued to dance in circles until the song came to an end.

"Third base time." His smile lit up his face. "This is the one I'm most excited about. This is what made me fall in love with you."

I froze in place, blown away that he'd just admitted to falling in love with me. "Damn," I heard him whisper under his breath. "Come on," he pulled me down the baseline toward third. I hadn't noticed it when we passed on the way down, but sitting on the base was an oversized gold box with a red bow. From the looks of it, it was moving. I couldn't help but giggle as I watched the box bounce from one side of the base to the other.

"What's that?" I laughed as I bent over to listen to the sound of little claws scratching at the inside of the box.

"It's something we'd better get to fast. Roger just brought it down. I thought you might've spotted him."

"What in the world?" I bent down and pulled off the top. As soon as I lifted the lid, a little, black lab pup grabbed the edge by his paw and toppled over onto the dirt. The box rolled over the top of it and came to rest just outside the baseline.

"Oh, my gosh. Where did you get him?"

"Roger's been searching ever since you gave up Sox for my

little brother."

We watched the tiny, little guy make his way toward the mound. Clearly, he needed to release some boxed-up energy. He ran so fast he nearly tripped over his two front feet. We finally caught up with him after he came to a stop at Ty's mitt. That's when he tried to grab the ball from the pocket. His mouth was still so tiny, he could barely fit the ball inside. "Look! He already likes baseball!" I giggled, as I tried to get the ball from him. He was barely holding on. "Come here, you little rascal." His sharp, puppy teeth had snagged the stitching, and I was struggling to pull it away from his mouth.

"Need help?" Ty kneeled beside me chuckling at the sight of the ball dangling from the side of his mouth.

"I've got it."

"He sure is a feisty one. Maybe you should call him, Firecracker."

I couldn't help but laugh as he jumped around with the ball stuck to his face. I was finally able to calm him down enough to get it loose. "I've got a better one. Something that has to do with baseball, or baseballs I should say."

"What's that?"

"Stitches."

"For a name?"

"I think it's cute." I patted my lap. "Come here, Stitches." Without hesitation, he came running, and went straight for the ball. That confirmed it. He was a baseball dog through and through.

"Do you think he'd want to join us at home?"

"I think he might like that."

I tucked Stitches under my arm as Ty took me under his, and walked me home. This time, the plate was empty. I looked down. "Looks like we finished our journey."

"Oh, girl. This journey is far from over. I have one last thing to give you."

"But you've given me so much already. The necklace, the dance, the puppy. I haven't given you anything."

"That's it. It's your turn."

"My turn?"

"There's something you've been trying to give me for months, but I hadn't proved I was worthy. Hopefully, tonight I changed that. And now, if you're still willing to give it to me, I'm ready to accept it."

He took the puppy from my arms and set him down at our feet. Then he lifted me onto the front of him and held my face to his. "We're at home plate, Pickle. Your favorite place on the field." He rested his forehead against mine and whispered against my cheek, "It's your play."

Even though it was just a whisper against my lips, the feel of his breath tickling the corner of my mouth had my heart pounding and my palms sweating. I couldn't hold back any longer. His arms slid beneath me as I secured my legs tighter around his waist. Then I leaned into him. If he wanted me to be in charge, I was certainly willing. I'd waited for him for months, and now was the time. I breathed in as I carefully set my mouth against his, and pulled his bottom lip into mine. The gentle tug and tiny nibble I'd always wanted to try, left him grinning. The new feeling of his lips against mine sent tingles to every nerve ending in my body. I was literally pulsing inside. I couldn't restrain myself from leaning back into him.

I decided to start off slow, with an innocent kiss. It was sweet the way our lips swept before we pulled away. The newness of the intimate connection left us both grinning, but he could tell I was holding back. "Come on, Pickle. Show me what you got," he whispered to me. That's when I decided it was time to let go and hand over the control.

"You're the pitcher," I whispered back, "take charge."

"If that's the way you want to play." He leaned into me and gradually pressed his mouth to mine, gently separating my lips to work his magic. The first time his cool tongue brushed mine, the butterflies soared. He must have felt it too. His kiss deepened and his hands began to explore the small of my back. Those same butterflies that he'd unleashed with the first brush of his tongue, worked themselves into a swirling cyclone. My heart raced. My breathing quickened. My entire being was a bundle of hot, pulsing nerve endings. Standing on home plate, clinging to the front of him, I was all in. Every ounce of my being.

I didn't know how things could have gotten any better, but what came next left me breathless. As we kissed, his hands slipped beneath my thighs to cradle me, and we began to walk. The friction of my body against his as we moved through the breezy night air, heightened the ecstasy I was already feeling. I clung even tighter and didn't let go, not of his neck, his waist, or his lips. The easy movement of his step, and strength of his hands, mixed with his passionate kiss had my belly twisting and my chest exploding. I'd kissed a few boys in my day, but none of them ever felt like that.

It was so easy with Ty, our mouths moved in perfect rhythm. I was completely intoxicated by him, the natural ease of our movements, and the comfort of his embrace. We had come to a stop on the mound. He slowly pulled away so he could set me on the blanket. Lit by the glow of the mason jars and the stars in the sky, I watched his silhouette come down beside me. He snuggled in close, pulling the blanket around us. It was only seconds before he came in next to me and sprinkled tender kisses up my neck until he reached my ear. My skin was on fire from the tiny trail of nibbles he'd left along the way. The thumping of my heart was soon drowned out by his soft whisper tickling against my ear. "Now that's how a first kiss should be. Standing under the stars on our favorite field. Our very own field of dreams."

Chapter Thirty-Six

Worth a Try

I T HAD BEEN A WEEK SINCE OUR DATE NIGHT AT MY FIELD AND I STILL couldn't stand to spend a minute without him. His first kiss was so highly addictive that after multiple encounters with those lips, I still couldn't get enough. Unfortunately, Ty and I had our own schedules and our own sports that didn't allow for us to spend as much time together as we wanted. With each separation, I itched to have him back beside me. In my arms. Breathing the same air. It was a yearning that left me thinking about little else.

That afternoon was no different. Since my practice ended early, I wandered straight to the boys' field to see if I could catch him in action. I snuck in behind the visitor's dugout and made my way behind the backstop, where I dropped my practice bag, curled my fingers through the fence, and watched my guy wind up.

The pitch was straight down the line. I could almost feel the breeze sweep my forehead as the batter swung, missed, and the ball went right through the catcher. From where I stood, I didn't anticipate that I'd have to protect myself. I jumped away, thankful that my lightning quick reflexes saved my fingers before the ball smashed into the fence in front of me. Ty caught sight of me watching and cocked his head slightly to acknowledge I was there. I gave a tiny wave, which was met with a wide smile.

Looking down at the ball which had come to a halt in front of the backstop, I wondered how Jesperson could have possibly let that pitch get through. Not only how it got by him, but why he still hadn't gotten to the ball. Was he sick? As he jogged back to retrieve it, I realized the face under the mask wasn't who I'd expected. I thought he looked a little bulkier than our first-string catcher. That's when I remembered Matt had broken his femur in a mudding accident the night Ty ditched the team for our date. He had mentioned that they were trying to find a suitable replacement. Judging by what I'd just seen, this was not the guy. In fact, they might have done better if they hit up Senior Little League.

Things got worse from there. Passed balls. Dropped balls. Short throws to second. The guy couldn't even get to a bunt. He kept cursing at his gear and twisting it back into place, whining that he couldn't see or move in it. It was becoming all too clear that the team didn't have a prayer if this was Jesperson's replacement.

I felt sorry for Ty. His senior season would determine his future in baseball, and it was going to be hard to shine when the guy behind the plate couldn't catch a ball if Ty walked up and set it in his hand. I continued to watch the disaster unfold before me, when Ty finally walked off the mound and headed over to Coach Pine.

Both of them turned to look at me. Ty extended his hand in my direction as Coach folded his arms and shook his head, no. Judging by the intensity of their body language their exchange was morphing into a small argument. I began to wonder if I was causing some kind of problem by showing up at practice. Coach had always been so nice to me when they were practicing at my field. Was my being there his problem, or Ty's?

Thinking I might be making them nervous by standing behind the backstop, I picked up my bag and started to walk away. That's when I heard Coach's voice, "Bailey! Stop!"

Immediately, I stood in place and looked around to see if there were any other Baileys in the area. Then turning back in his direction, I pointed to myself. "Me?"

"Yeah, you. Get over here."

I slung my bag over my shoulder and jogged toward the dugout. Standing face to face with Coach Pine, I apologized for being a distraction behind the backstop.

"You're fine, Pickle," Ty smiled. "It's not you."

It was a relief to hear it. "Then what's up? I don't want to interrupt your practice more than I already have."

"I need you to get behind the plate," Ty directed.

I wasn't sure if I heard him correctly, "Huh?"

Coach Pine was great at reading minds. "You heard him correctly. Connelly here, seems to think you can improve our practice," he grinned. I knew all about that dimpled smile from watching his amusement when students did stupid things in his science class. Things like catching their hair on fire by bucking the ponytail rule. Or fainting from directly inhaling chemicals when he'd told them not to. That was the smile that grew when students paid the price for not following his advice. Those dimples told me this was one of those times.

I understood his hesitation. He'd never seen me play. He was always tied up with the guys. If it was anyone else, I'm sure he would have put his foot down. But, after loaning him my field last spring, he knew he owed me a shot. He decided to humor us.

I offered him an out. "Are you sure you don't want to try one of those other guys?"

Ty was quick to respond. "That's the problem. We have. All of them. Caden was our last shot, but we need him at shortstop."

When Coach glanced over to see Smith kicking the helmet down the baseline, he shook his head. "You're worth a chance, kid." Then he set the ball in my hand, "Even if you've only played softball."

There was that comment again. The same one that I'd heard the whole time I was growing up in the sport. "I know, I know, we play with bigger balls," I smirked as I turned the tiny ball in my hand.

"Look, kid. You don't have to do this. It's probably a bad idea to throw you out there with the varsity boys."

"Yeah. I am just a girl."

I watched Ty's face pull into a humorous grin. This was my opportunity to show Coach Pine what a girl could do with a baseball, just like I'd shown Ty. I could tell by his saucy grimace that he was ready for me to put on a little show. I held up the ball like I'd never seen one before. "I guess I could try." I turned my face sideways and batted my eyelashes.

"Well, we don't have any other options, so show us what you've got, doll," he yawned.

Did he just yawn? After an insult like that, my feisty side reared its head. "Let me get on my gear." Sarcastically, I turned to Ty so Coach could hear, "Go easy on me, huh? We wouldn't want Coach to worry about you hurting me." I winked at Ty, knowing damn well he was going to throw with everything he had.

He wanted to play games? I could play games. The first thing I pulled out of my bag was my brush. I held it up so Coach would make sure to watch me brush my hair into a perfect ponytail. I even took the time to grab a ribbon and tie a bow. Then I winked before pulling my helmet and face mask on. Next, I pressed my hands into my breasts, plumping them together before strapping on my chest protector. I watched the coach pull his hand up over his eyes as I listened to the guys chuckling in the background. Then, I extended my leg and pointed my toes to carefully slide my first shin guard into place. Then seductively, I smoothed my hands over my bottom and hips to make sure no extra fabric was bunched under the straps.

By that point in the show, a couple of the guys started to bring their mitts down over their crotches. That's when Ty turned to his fielders and shouted, "Awe, come on! Seriously, guys?" By the time I had my gear on, the boys had all crouched into position out on the field to hide whatever was going on behind their mitts.

"Let's take a few warm-up pitches, just to make sure she can catch a baseball," Coach shouted. "Don't hurt her."

Ty looked over and nodded toward the coach, then lobbed the ball to me. Right into my mitt. I lobbed it back to match his speed. The second pitch came a little faster. I caught it easily. We repeated the warm-up until he looked satisfied. "Batter up!"

It was time to play ball. I couldn't wait to put all our signals into practice. We were going to take out our first batter together, and Coach was going to know I helped. His first pitch was a little high and outside. I think the boys were impressed that I got it. The next one was low and inside. Again, I snagged it. Then a curveball. A slider. Fastball. All three strikes, with no passed balls. The second batter popped a foul outside the third base line. Instantly, I flung my mask off and sprinted to the dugout to get under it. Right into my mitt. Chatter started building among the guys. "She's got speed."

"She can actually catch, guys."

"Who knew?"

"But can she throw?"

Ty walked the next batter, so I knew I needed to watch the runner on first. He looked awfully cocky as he wagged his booty back and forth with the leadoff. I knew he was going to try to steal on me as soon as the next pitch left Ty's hand. I could feel it. I was ready for it. The pitch was released, the batter swung, I snagged it, and winged it straight into Schuler's mitt at second, where he tagged the runner out. "Damn, girl!" he pulled his hand from his mitt and shook it. "I wasn't expecting that."

There was a shift in Ty's energy after I threw the runner out at second. Clearly pumped from what he had witnessed, he became a pitching machine, throwing nothing but strikes. Since nobody could hit off him, the coach had to place runners on the bases to set up some defensive plays. He wanted to test me to see if I knew where to throw the ball. It was my opportunity to truly prove that I knew what I was doing. I threw the runners out at every base, nobody could slide under me at the plate, and I even showed them how I earned my nickname, Pickle, when Caden got a little cocky and tried to steal home.

At the end of the practice, the boys gathered around to meet me with high fives and a pat on the back. Even Coach came up to me with a humble grin and congratulated me on the way I handled myself out on the field.

"Do we get to keep her, Coach?" Bennett asked.

Then Cadola piped in, "Yeah, the girls can get another catcher. She's ours."

"Well, actually, boys, this girl's mine." Ty pulled me into him and smiled. "And can I just say, I told you so?" He smirked at Coach.

"You sure did."

As the boys started making plans for my future in baseball, I couldn't help but feel a bit overlooked in the decision. I was just supposed to help out with practice. Sure, it was fun playing with them for a day, but I wasn't sure I wanted it to be a permanent gig. There were certain things that came along with being on a baseball team. Things girls didn't deal with. Sweaty Boys. Locker room talk. Naked shower booties. The thought of the boys' locker room sent my memory back to the day I snuck down the restricted hall to spy on Ty. I found it to be the most pleasant thought I'd had all afternoon. I didn't think twice when I popped off with, "Count me in." Before I could retract my words, I closed my mouth. Crap. I wondered if I'd just opened a can of worms. "If they let me switch teams, that is."

A dominating look came over Coach Pine's face. "Oh, they're going to let you. I didn't make this team what it is by settling for less than the best. You definitely belong here, if you want to be." He set his hand on my shoulder, "I would've never believed it if I hadn't seen it for myself. Go figure, Jenna "Pickle" Bailey is our ticket to Championships."

Since she taught at the high school and heard the story first hand, my mom got the inside scoop on how it all played out. There was a bit of a battle with my coach, but in the end, Pine snagged me for his team. Knowing the girls were going to have a mediocre season at best, they decided to pull up the JV catcher. She was already pretty aggressive and giving her an extra year at varsity would push her to stardom by her senior year. Apparently, me changing to baseball would also give Jefferson High the opportunity to have at least one team represent them in League Championships. I could only hope I didn't let them down.

The next several weeks were a whirlwind. We were on a winning streak. Having beaten the three top-seeded teams in the league, we were second to none. I had become one of the two faces of JHS baseball. Our image as Jefferson's dynamic duo, decorated posters that hung in the student union and plastered the hallways. We got a couple of radio spots together to promote our home games. We were even slathered all over the team's social media pages. From the local newspaper to the Channel 10 News, our story had garnered a lot of attention.

I could have never imagined what would come from joining the boys team. Baseball fans everywhere couldn't get enough of the star pitcher and the faith he'd shown his softball catcher girlfriend. We'd gotten so many shares on video clips highlighting our play. Scouts from teams Ty hadn't even visited started showing up at the big games. They had to be impressed by how much he'd improved since last season. He was stronger, faster, and had a lot more tricks up his sleeve. He credited me for that, but I knew he was just trying to share the limelight. Little did he know that living life in the spotlight was the last thing I wanted.

None of us thought that our stepping onto the baseball field together would have drawn the kind of attention it did, and I had to hide the fact that my local celebrity had my entire family on edge. Isaiah worked overtime with his technical team to clean up anything that could be linked to my residence. Security was also with me whenever I had to run an errand or do anything by myself. There were a few times when my parents actually considered an extended stay at the ranch, just long enough to get through the season so people would forget about me and we could go back to being anonymous.

I had to beg them to ride it out at the vineyard. The fact that Isaiah was there and we'd strengthened our security was just enough to keep us there. For the time being anyway. If Isaiah had detected anything, we would've picked up and left immediately. It was a highly sensitive situation and I couldn't tell any of my friends. It was the hardest secret I'd kept since moving to Jefferson, and I knew it could blow up at any minute.

I had to put on a brave face and act unaffected. Sometimes that was more difficult than others. But most days, I didn't have time to even think about the reality of the situation. One thing I learned was that varsity baseball took a lot more commitment than softball. The practices were longer and harder. Our schedule was packed with games that were double the distance from home. Sometimes we didn't get back till two in the morning.

The only thing that differentiated my crazy life from the rest of the team were the secrets I had to keep. I always had a security guard "uncle" waiting to pick me up. Also, my parents required that I kept my phone hidden in my shin guard when I couldn't carry it in my pocket. Just like the rest of my teammates, I barely had time for homework. There was no time for socializing. Thankfully, I had student government with all my friends. It was the one place we could actually catch up.

It was the day before Championships in Trinity, and Ms. Morrill wanted us to make a bunch of signs to hang on the bus. As we walked through the door, she handed each of us poster boards and told us to have fun with them. Scattered around the room were cups filled with red, gold, and black paint. I scanned the floor for an open spot to make a poster for Ty. The first person who caught my eye was Chelsea. I'd just as soon use my own blood than share red paint with her. Next, there was Tiara, yeah, that wasn't going to happen. In the back corner, Kaitlyn was kneeling with her back to me. She hadn't seen me come in, but thankfully, there was an open spot next to her.

"You coming tomorrow?" I smiled as I sat down beside her.

"With you and Caden on the same team? I wouldn't miss it for the world. Brody and I are going to drive over with my parents." She stopped painting for a second and looked up, "Nobody can believe this you know. You're a legend. A girl on the varsity team?" She laughed as she finished marking my number four on the jersey she'd painted.

"It was luck. Right time. Right place. Right guy." Ty really stuck his neck out for me and I wanted to give him credit for his part in getting me on the team.

Clearly, Chelsea had an issue with the two of us. Her eyes landed on mine at the mention of Ty. As she watched me through the corner of her eye, she whispered into Tiara's ear. Though the rest of their crew had matured over the course of our senior year, the two girls were still into playing the mean girl game. They hadn't forgotten about the night I tossed them both into the wishing pond at the hospital and took every opportunity to get under my skin. As I watched them paint signs for everyone but me, I sensed they were holding out till they came up with just the right pun for mine. I was actually looking forward to seeing how creative they could be. I was ready for whatever it was. What I wasn't prepared for was how long they could stare at me without breaking eye contact. I'd had enough.

"What are you looking at?" I snapped.

"Trying to figure you out, that's all. Like, how many guys score on you every game?" They started to giggle.

"Why don't you look at my stats?"

"Um, I don't think the team keeps those kinds of records," she fake coughed into her hand, "if you know what I mean."

"No. I don't know what you mean."

"How cute. You think we're talking about the game." Chelsea snickered, "We're talking about the bus rides home in the dark."

Tiara continued, "We've heard Ty's a team player."

"Yeah, like he doesn't mind sharing his … equipment."

They were certainly getting a kick out of themselves insinuating that I was the play toy on the bus rides.

"Ignore them. They're not worth it," Schuler came up behind me. "Pickle, you know why you're on the team. You're the best and there's nothing those two can say or do to change that." He shook his head at the girls with a disapproving look and walked back to the front of the room.

Embarrassed that the hot second baseman had heard their crap and stuck up for me, the girls re-focused on the posters they were painting and didn't look up again.

Needing a distraction, I directed my attention to Kaitlyn. I filled her in on the perks of playing on the boys' team. It was nice to catch up, since we barely saw each other with our crazy schedules. That's when I remembered I hadn't gotten many details on the upcoming game. "So, you're definitely coming to Championships?"

"Yes. I told you that when you sat down. And Brody. And Avery. And Mason. We're all coming to watch our superstars."

"And then afterward, we can all go out to celebrate our win!" My excitement was smothered by the uproar that was arising behind me. When I turned to see what was happening, I was surprised to find one of my softball girls ripping a sign from Tiara's hands. She was backed by two of my old teammates.

Kaitlyn nudged me, "I think you need to read that poster before the softball team destroys it." Taking a moment to prepare myself, I inhaled a deep breath and walked over to read the sign. It was just as I'd suspected. They were holding out on making mine until they could come up with something demeaning. I thought I'd prepared myself, but the minute I saw what they'd written, my face instantly filled with heat. They had chosen the phrase, "**Hey, Boys! You can always score with #4.**"

Knowing there were still girls in this world willing to tear down others was a tough pill to swallow. Especially girls like me, who had broken a gender barrier. Though I was pissed off thinking that they were mean-spirited enough to actually hang that sign on the bus for everyone to see, I knew they weren't going to get away with it. I could sense everyone in the room gathering behind me. I was like the head pin in a bowling set up. If they wanted to mess with me, they were going to have to take us all. There we stood, the twenty-plus kids in my class, in a standoff with Chelsea and Tiara.

"Enough is enough," Lexi shouted.

Then Cadence joined in, "Your bullying isn't welcome here!"

"Yeah, it's not funny. You mess with her, you mess with all of us."

I heard the sign rip, followed by a crumpling sound. It was Ms. Morrill, standing on a chair so she could be seen. Apparently, she was supporting our protest against the bullies. "We've got your back, Jenna." Then she pointed to the door, "Get out of my class, girls. True leaders don't pull mean stunts like that. As far as I'm concerned, you're off student council. I'll let the office know you're on your way."

I watched the color leave their faces as they inched their way toward the exit. I looked around at the angry mob in back of me. For the first time in my life, I wasn't standing alone. I didn't have to say a word. My classmates had done it for me. There was a cosmic shift in the school that day. We had become one. For the first time, I felt protected. Like I was no longer a target. None of us were.

Chapter Thirty-Seven

The Big Game

"IT'S GONNA BE A HOT ONE GUYS. MAKE SURE TO GRAB YOUR water," Coach reminded us as we began to unload the bus at Trinity. I shoved my gear into my bag and slung it over my shoulder before making my way off the bus and into the heat of the midday sun. The pep busses had arrived before us, and the mass of fans they'd brought from Jefferson High had formed two long lines, creating an aisle between our charter bus and the field. I was happy to see my parents, Isaiah with Mason, the Connelly's, the Woodleys with Avery, and the rest of the crowd holding signs. They whistled, hooted, and snapped pictures as we made our way through.

As I jogged in the middle of the pack and headed from our friends and family toward our opponents, I could sense the stares and hear the whispers coming from the crowd. Apparently, my reputation had preceded me. Before I set foot on the field, a cute, little snack-shack girl galloped up to me. Wide-eyed, she pulled a pen and paper from her apron and whispered, "Will you thign thith pleath?" Through her missing front teeth, I could barely understand the words she spoke. I couldn't help but giggle when I finally realized she wanted my autograph. I didn't realize my local celebrity status had reached Trinity. I bent down and gave her a hug before

I signed, "*Home is where the heart is. ~ xoxo~ J. Bailey.*"

Pigtails bouncing, she jumped up and down excitedly before running back to the snack shack, waving the paper wildly to all the ladies inside.

"Let's go, Bailey! We're taking the field for warmups."

My attention shifted away from the snack shack and back to the field. It was time to focus. As I jogged out to the plate, I could hear the banter in the home dugout. "This is the team with the girl!"

"We've got this, boys!"

"They don't stand a chance." Though the last comment was barely audible, I realized it came from a player looking directly at me.

The cutting comments fueled my determination. Those players had no idea who they were talking about. The banter continued as we warmed up. Knowing I was going to prove them wrong soon enough, I kept my cool, but could tell someone else was losing his. Ty moved away from the mound, balling his fist. It wasn't hard to anticipate where he was headed, so I sprung to my feet, and jogged over to stop him, "Don't listen to them."

"But they're being assholes."

"Do you know how many scouts you have out there watching you today? They're not just looking at your skill. They're also watching how you handle yourself. I've got my big-girl panties on. Don't worry about me," I winked. "Block it out, Connelly. Focus on this mitt. Got it? We'll let our talent speak for itself."

He nodded with a half grin, then I spun him around and sent him straight back to his position to finish our warmups. We only had two minutes to wrap it up before the home team reclaimed the field.

Before Championships, I had discussed with Coach whether I wanted to bat during such a high stakes game. I had a decent average, but I knew that I couldn't send it sailing the same way some of the guys could. Thankfully, our league allowed us to use a designated hitter for any position, and we were going to use one to take my place in the lineup. That way I wouldn't have to mess with my gear in between innings and we could get a real slugger to take my spot.

It was a great decision. The boys were on fire. After three base hits by Bennett, Cadola, and Schuler, Robinson cleaned house with a grand slam. It didn't end there. Ty got a triple, and Caden drove him in with a homer of his own. The last two runners brought our first inning total to six.

There was an eruption of hooting and hollering when we stepped out of the dugout. I looked over my shoulder to see my family, Isaiah, and the gang cheering wildly on one side with Ty's family close by. Aiden was holding his puppy and waving a sign that said, "**I won't keep calm. My brother is the pitcher**." The stadium bursting with the color of signs, balloons, and streamers, had me pumped to take the field for the first time that game. I knew it was time to prove myself. I had to look just as aggressive and strong as the guys. I would not be the weakest link. When Ty took his warm-up pitches, I made sure to blast them back at him to show I was ready for anything he wanted to throw at me.

And, he definitely proved he trusted me with some tough pitches. Sinkers, cutters, curveballs. He was putting it all out there. The offense couldn't keep up. He struck out the first two batters with flair. When batter number three stepped up to the plate, he watched the first two strikes sail by. "Not taking his crap," he grumbled, as he wagged his bat back and forth and ground his back foot into the dirt. Ty must have wanted to save the third out for me. He put it in a little low, but I instantly saw Mr. Cocky's bat was too far out front on the upswing. When the bat met the ball, it went sailing about twenty feet straight up in the air. I raced under it to snag it for the third out. Three up, three down. Not a bad way to start.

The next several innings we had to fight a little harder to keep Trinity from scoring, but it gave Ty a chance to prove what he was made of. I couldn't believe how well he was doing in the sweltering sun, but he was pulling through like a champ. I was also getting in a few good plays of my own. When the sole batter, who was able to get a base hit, tried to steal third, I threw him out easily. I couldn't help but look into the home dugout to see how my play had affected their insolent attitudes. Apparently, it knocked the wind out of their sails. They were awfully quiet compared to the way they came onto the field first inning.

As Ty put away one after another, the game was completely in our favor. With each guy he retired, the crowd roared louder. The girls began lining the fence, jumping up and down and screaming. At one point, a pink bra flew out of the bleachers and landed at Ty's feet. We had to stop the play, so he could pitch it back into the crowd. Watching how Chelsea, Tiara, and CJ fought over the flying bra, I didn't want to think about what might be next. I shook the image of them shredding his jersey and pawing his chest from my mind. I had to focus, but with the midday sun beating down on me, it was getting harder and harder to do.

By the fifth inning, the sweat began to trickle beneath my jersey and pool at the backs of my knees. Between jumping for foul tips, throwing out runners, and catching for an increasingly aggressive pitching style, I had been playing so hard that my body was beginning to rebel against the heat. My full gear was stifling hot. I needed some relief. The minute the team came off the field at the top of the sixth, I found a shade tree outside the dugout. I bent over and put my hands on my knees, straining to catch my breath.

That's when the adorable, snack-shack girl headed my way again. Carrying a large cup with what looked to be a sports drink, she shyly said, "I brought you thomething. A cute boy bought it for you."

I smiled at the thought of Ty's timing. He knew exactly how to take care of me. "And the cute boy didn't want to bring it over here?"

She shrugged her shoulders, "I don't know. He gave me a dollar to bring it to you. Maybe he wath embarrathed to do it himthelf?"

The way she interpreted his feelings showed her sweet innocence. If I wasn't in such a rush to get re-hydrated, I would've explained to her about Ty and me, but as woozy as I was, I simply
smiled and thanked her. It didn't matter why he hadn't brought it
to me himself. I was dying of thirst, and happy to have the gift of
an icy, cold drink in my hand.

Watching her retreat to the snack shack, I chugged the blue
liquid, then headed back. I got to the dugout just in time to pull my
helmet on for the bottom of the sixth, then ran behind the plate
and crouched into my ready position. I still felt a little off from
the heat, but thankfully we were so far ahead in the game it took
a lot of pressure off me. I convinced myself that if I could just get
through one more inning, it would be smooth sailing.

But it wasn't. Halfway through the inning, I started feeling dizzy. The sun was blasting through my mask, causing sweat to drip
from my forehead. I had to work twice as hard as I usually did to
keep my balance and focus on the ball coming into my mitt. I swore
I was starting to suffer from heat exhaustion. At one point, I began
to lean forward to keep from falling into the umpire. When I set
my mitt down on the plate to catch myself from falling forward, he
actually stopped the game to have me scoot back. Ty noticed me
struggling and called a meeting.

"You okay, Pickle? You look like you're a little tipsy back there."

"It's the heat. It's making me so dizzy. I can barely focus on
the ball."

"Coach!" Ty waved him over to talk.

"You two are doing fantastic. What's up?"

"I think Jenna might need to cool down. She's losing her balance, and I don't want to hurt her."

I was stronger than that. I knew I had some fight left in me.

Coach looked back and forth between the two of us. "We've
got one more out until the end of the inning. You got one more

batter in you, kid?"

I knew I could do it. I would do it. Even if it took everything I had. I gave him a thumbs up, then nodded to Ty. "Let's hurry up and get him out."

I held my mitt in place, knowing Ty was going to put the ball right there. I had to let him work for me. I moved my mitt slightly and signaled him to throw a curve. He did. Strike one. Next up, we got him with a sinker. I paused for a second to flip my mask and wipe the sweat from beneath my eyes. I had to stand up and walk in a circle before coming back to crouch behind the plate. I prayed for a third strike, so I could get off the field before I embarrassed myself. Thank God, Ty delivered. He put him away with a fastball. A fastball that nearly knocked me on my seat. I was pretty wobbly by the end of the inning.

Stumbling off the field, I was thankful for my designated hitter. It meant I'd have a few minutes to get myself together. I made my way to Coach and asked if I could go to the bathroom to throw some water on my face.

"You okay to go alone, Bailey?" He looked around. "I don't have any ladies here that can go with you."

"I'm fine. I'll try to get back before the bottom of the seventh."

"Take your time, kid. You're looking a little pale. Hey, Smith!" He turned to Greg, "Start gearing up in case Bailey doesn't get back in time." Then he turned back to me, "Don't worry, kid. We've already got this game in the bag. There's no way they're going to catch up, even if he drops every ball," he chuckled.

I grabbed my bag and started to head to the set of bathrooms just outside the park, near the soccer field. I needed a little privacy and didn't want to wait in line at the stadium bathrooms. At least I wouldn't have so many eyes on me. I knew everything I did made a story those days, and having to cut out of a game a little early to splash water on my face, wasn't one I wanted to make the news.

As I walked through the grassy field, my legs continued to

grow heavy. I pulled myself along the chain link fence, trying not to lose my balance. Who knew 325 feet was so far away? Poor center fielders must be pooped by the time they got all the way out to their position. My legs shook and sweat raced down my back. It was becoming more and more clear that I was in worse shape than I'd thought. Another blue drink would've been good right about then. I looked over my shoulder to the snack shack, noticing when I turned my head back toward the bathroom my vision was dominated by white streaks. As I approached the brick building, the trees began to blur and the sights and sounds around me began to slowly fade. I couldn't stay on my feet another second. I slithered down onto the sidewalk to feel the cool concrete against my skin.

With nobody around, I closed my eyes. The buzzing grew stronger in my ears until it drowned out every other sound. Somewhere in the back of my mind, I knew I shouldn't be sleeping, but I couldn't force myself to get up. My body was rebelling against me. Against what I had put it through. All it wanted was to cool down. To shake the dizziness. To dream. I tried to roll onto my side, so I could push myself up, but again I was denied. It was no use. Unable to move, my body was holding me captive right there in front of the girls' bathroom, forcing me into an altered state of consciousness. There was no choice but to stay on the cool, hard ground. It was time to let go. Time to rest.

Images began to form behind my eyes. Images of me running the bases. *I heard the crowd yelling as I rounded third and began to run home. I was too far down the baseline when the catcher got the ball and headed toward me. I sensed the third baseman right behind me. Damn it. I couldn't believe I'd gotten myself into a pickle during the championship game. Maybe I could fake him out. I took a step back and then jolted forward. He was too quick. He threw the ball to the third baseman, who returned it instantly as I started forward again. Endlessly, I ran forward and backward until I was dizzy. There was no escape.* "You need thome help?" I heard a whisper tickle my ear.

It was the little girl's voice, pulling me to the surface. "Sthay there." I fought between getting out of the pickle and trying to open my eyes. I needed to wake myself up. There was a real ball-game happening behind me, and if I didn't pry myself out of the dream I was going to miss the rest of it. Unfortunately, my body wasn't ready to release me just then.

I felt arms beneath me but was still unable to open my eyes. Thank God someone had found me. They would carry me back to the game. To my waiting team. My parents. My friends. My legs dangled and my arms hung as I felt myself being hoisted over a strong shoulder. I wanted to help my rescuer take some weight off, but I couldn't bring myself to move. I had lost all control.

"You'll be alright. I've got you, Jenna." That voice. Even through the haziness, I swore I recognized it. But it was different somehow. Not as soft. The accent was harder than I'd known it to be in the past. It spoke again. "You'll be okay. This won't last long. I had to do it. For your own good."

I felt the weight of my body sink into a cool leather seat and heard an engine roar to life beneath me. As we gently pulled away, the shifting of my heavy body clued me in that we were moving. Knowing something was wrong, I struggled to open my eyes. I thought he was going to carry me back to the field. What was I doing in a car? I fought the buzzing. The darkness. I fought to come back to life. I still couldn't move, couldn't see, but I could hear.

"I need your bracelet. Where is it?" His hand came down on my wrist. Did I even have it on? I was too disoriented to remember. Then I felt his fingers travel up my arm and move quickly to the other. I couldn't process what he was doing until he sighed with what sounded to be relief. "At least he can't find you that way."

Can't find me? At his terrifying words, my mind flashed to one person. Adrenaline spiked inside of me, wiping me of my last conscious thought. It was all too much. The buzzing increased, and the darkness settled in once again.

Chapter Thirty-Eight
The Last of the Secrets

THE POUNDING INSIDE MY HEAD HAD GROWN SO INTENSE IT FORCED my eyes open. Staring across the blurry, wooden surface, I realized I was no longer outdoors. A flannel shirt that had shielded my face from the dusty floor was drenched in a pool of sweat. As I scanned the room, the dizzying trails of light made it difficult to comprehend what I was looking at. There was a small, faded sofa, covered with a plastic tarp. It sat just in front of an old, wooden table with a broken chair. Or was it two chairs? I couldn't tell. Everything was still spinning. Even the cedar walls seemed to be moving. The unceasing motion was enough to make me nauseous. Needing to find a place to relieve the swirling, blue liquid that was clawing its way up my throat, I worked to roll over and force myself onto my hands and knees. I had to find someplace to go. Someplace to release the poison inside of me. But where was I?

As I pushed myself to my unsteady feet, I noticed an old, dirty sink. Webs had formed between the counter and handles of the faucet. The brown, crusted, muck that was stuck to the inside, gave me just the push I needed to release the contents of my stomach. Over and over again I heaved, until all that was left was a wailing sound. As I stood at the sink gagging, cool relief came in the form of a washcloth that had been placed against my forehead.

It was accompanied by that voice. But again, it was so different. The accent was harder, yet more natural than the French one I had come to know. "It's okay. You're okay. You'll feel better soon."

I used the washcloth to wipe my mouth before I bravely turned around to acknowledge my captor. At the sight of his face, a course of adrenaline pounded its way through me, forcing me to stumble backward against the counter. Wide-eyed, I took in the sight of him, as he stood there staring over my shoulder. His expression looked distant. Faraway. Confused. Like he'd made a mistake. Gone too far, and he didn't know what to do or how to fix it.

I needed to capitalize on his obvious error in judgment. Maybe if I could get him to understand what a crazy mistake he'd made, he would take me back home. "What the hell have you done, Daemon?" I panted. I couldn't imagine what had been going through his mind to steal me away from my baseball game and bring me to God knew where. What kind of a person was hidden under that awkward French facade? If I could put on a brave face and speak boldly, I thought I might be able to talk my way back to safety. "What were you thinking? You know they'll come looking for me! The whole stadium knows I'm missing."

"Idiot!" He grunted as he curled his fist and gave himself a quick blow to the side of his head. He stared back at me and took a deep breath before he released a low growl. His angry tone re placed my confidence with alarm. Something had changed in his expression. A change that told me if I didn't get out of there quickly, it might be the last place I'd ever see.

Frantically, I began to sidestep around him, trying to make my way to the door.

"Don't go!" He lunged toward me as I began to run down the steps.

I jumped, just before his hand grabbed for my ankle and missed. An eerily familiar path with moss-covered trees and giant ferns stretched out before me. As I picked up speed, I could hear rushing water drawing near. The intensity of dashing through the forest, scared out of my mind, was like deja vu. My memory flashed back to Thanksgiving. Truth or Dare. Running with my friends by my side. The only difference was this time I was alone. There was nobody to run to. Nobody knew I was there.

Thankfully, it was still twilight. I could see the twigs protruding from the path and the streaks of color from the newly-blooming wildflowers as I whizzed by. That's when the camp came into view. I knew this place. I could see Mule Bridge in the distance. Still running, I looked over my shoulder to see where I'd been. That's when my shoe caught something that slammed me to the ground.

The bellow of his voice grew louder. As the pain shot through my leg, I scrambled to my feet. It was too late. He had me in his arms. "You need" he tugged me in tightly, "to come back," he hoisted me over his shoulder, "to the cabin."

My worst nightmare had come to life. I kicked and screamed as he trudged back toward the creepy cabin up the hill.

"You're not going to get away with this," I cried, pounding on his back.

"You had better hope I get away with this," he replied.

Again, I kicked and wildly pounded at his back.

"Just stop, okay?" he grunted. "I'm trying to save you. You need to let me!"

I stopped long enough to think about what he was saying. "You're trying to save me? From what? The only one around here I need saving from is you!" I began to scream. "Help! Somebody help me!" Daemon was a lot stronger than he looked. Carrying me in one hand, he brought the other over my mouth to silence me. Still weak, nauseous, and now broken from the fall, he had a hold on me that I wasn't likely to break free of.

"You don't understand." He continued to walk, "I'm not who you think I am."

Nearly suffocating from his hold over my nose and throat, I

couldn't respond. "You don't recognize me, do you?"

I shook my head back and forth beneath his firm grasp.

"It's me, Jenna."

I bit his finger, and in the brief second he pulled it from my lips, I yelped, "Daemon!"

"No." He shook his head and slid me to the ground in front of him. Wrapping me firmly in one arm while he held his other hand even tighter to my mouth, he groaned, "Take another look."

I looked up at the towering boy in front of me and focused on his scruffy face. His blue eyes. His brown hair. He was Daemon alright.

"Don't you recognize me?" He leaned in closer. "It's me, Jenna."

There was a long pause as I continued to study my insane captor.

"I'm not Daemon ... I'm Nikolai."

Nikolai? I stiffened beneath his arms and jerked back to study his face once again. My Nikolai? "I don't understand." My voice was muffled beneath the palm of his hand.

"Promise me you won't scream and I'll let you talk." His pleading eyes stared at me, begging for my consent.

I nodded, agreeing that I wouldn't scream. Rather, I whispered, "Nikolai? What? How? Why?" I couldn't believe who I was seeing. It was him. Why hadn't I recognized him before? He had the same round, blue eyes, but his hair had slightly darkened, and the softness of his baby face had grown into sharp angles. He was tall with lean muscle, a far cry from his childhood physique. I studied him, wondering how he had found me thousands of miles away, and why he had put in such great effort to get to me.

I knew he had read the confusion on my face when he spoke, "Quickly, come with me. I need to explain, and I don't have a lot of time."

He slid me down onto my feet but kept his hand around my waist to guide me back to the creepy cabin. The firmness of his hold told me he didn't quite trust that I wouldn't run. Still not sure that I could trust him either, I pulled away and tried to put some space between us. He held me more firmly as he guided me up the steps and set me down on the covered sofa.

Sitting silently, I watched him pace around the room before he finally stopped in front of me and spoke, "It's my father, Jenna. He sent me here to take care of this mess once and for all."

A vision of Nikolai's father instantly darkened my mind. It was the foreboding figure of the angry winemaker who always screamed at his son. The same man who taught him to sling knives and ditch baseball for strategic war games. The last time I saw him was the night of the party, leaving through the back door with the broken lady. My God. It had just clicked. In my dreams, I had never been allowed to see his face. But in that moment, I realized the guy in the black gloves wasn't just some random guy … it was Sergei. The dominating figure of every childhood nightmare I'd ever had was Nikolai's dad. My nightmares weren't just memories. They were warnings. Premonitions. Nikolai's father had killed Olivia, and now he was after me.

I began to claw my way backward on the couch, but was tripped up by my feet tangling in the plastic tarp. Nikolai's dad knew where I was. I couldn't help but think back on how he'd snapped Olivia's neck and hidden her body away in a wine barrel. I was next. Only rather than an extravagant, Russian castle, this dark, dingy cabin would be the last place I'd ever see.

"Hold still!" he whispered as I kicked at the tarp. "I need you to hear me out. Please! I promise I don't want to hurt you. Just give me a chance to explain." Kneeling beside me, he pressed his hand against me to slow my kicking legs.

"I'm trying to help you. You're in more trouble than you know. When your family fled from my country, you left a wake of destruction you couldn't imagine. My family paid a great price for your impulsive departure. Your father was the source of the grapes we needed, and the one with the expertise necessary to complete the winemaking process. Without him, the deals could not be carried out. When my father couldn't deliver on his promises, we were raided, battered, and stripped of everything. It took him years to rebuild his empire and restore our honorable name. He's held a bitter vendetta for years. You are the key to regaining his rightful place in the organization. It was my job to find you and bring you back to him. The bait for your father. And after all the suffering I went through, I wanted to do it … until you changed my mind."

I looked at him, trying to comprehend what he was telling me. I knew my father had helped his Sergei back in Russia, but that was years ago. I couldn't help but wonder how stealing me could bring any kind of honor back to some Russian winemaker I barely even knew. It all sounded so unbelievable. "I don't understand. This is crazy. I'm just a teenage girl who lives in the middle of nowhere. Vendetta? Bait? What is he, like some kind of Mafia boss?" I shook my head questioning his absurd story.

His deep breath and twisted grimace told me the answer. I was spot on. All the hiding. The secrets. It made so much more sense. We weren't just running from some bat-shit-crazy winemaker. We had fled the Russian Mafia. My heart sped up as I choked out, "Start from the beginning."

"Your father. Mason's father. They ruined us. We knew we had to bring you back to fully restore the operation. To make things right. Your fathers hold the secrets to our livelihood. More than that, you are a dangerous little girl. You saw something your last night at the castle that could be the final nail in the Vasiliev coffin. We've been looking for you for years. And since Isaiah has been putting on pressure, the situation has become … urgent."

Again, the image of Olivia's broken body flashed before me. It wasn't the way I'd wanted to go, but there was no escaping it … not unless I could get Nikolai to help me. I had to act calm. I needed to hear more. To see if I had a prayer in hell of escaping the nightmare playing out right before my eyes.

"We had an idea of your location, but waited it out until we knew for sure. For a few years, it seemed you had disappeared from the face of the Earth. It wasn't until the day you popped up on the internet, that we got the confirmation it really was you. When we saw Mason's picture with you, there was no longer any question. That's when we set our plan into action. My father created an alias and sent me to your high school to pose as an exchange student. I was to wait until the time was right to bring you back to my father."

It was hard to stomach. Creating that social media profile was what drew him here? How could I have been so reckless and irresponsible? I felt my jaw slacken as I tried to pull in a breath and hear him out.

"It was trickier than I thought it would be. You were never alone. Your sports life is unending. Your friends are constant. And I don't even want to mention the thick security at your house. And Roger. I could've taken out that bastard myself. So frustrating. I tried to break into your world in any way I could. I'm sure you noticed I showed up everywhere you went, but I still couldn't get you alone. I'd almost given up until Homecoming. That's when I thought of a way in. I found the one person who was too drunk and stupid to know better. That night, when Kaitlyn dumped the drunk cowboy for Brody, he became the ideal puppet. An accomplice. A decoy."

I thought back on the homecoming dance. The night I was so entranced by Ty that I barely noticed what was going on with Kaitlyn and Pistol. But it was true. That was the night everything changed. She'd dumped Pistol at the dance and gone home with Brody. Someone had broken into her room. Shredded her stuffed animal. Torn up her pictures. Was it Pistol? Or was it Daemon … Nikolai?

"After I planted the camera in her room that night, I had him wrapped around my finger. He was obsessed with watching her in her room. It was really quite genius if I do say so myself. Pistol couldn't get enough. He wanted more. Thinking he was spying on Kaitlyn, he helped me with the rest of the cameras so I could watch you until I had the time and place to take you away. He had no idea how much he was helping me," Nikolai laughed as he reflected on how he'd manipulated Pistol. "It was too bad he slipped up, really. I almost felt bad having to hide his body the night he came back here to tell you about me." His eyes drifted away before they looked back on me. He shrugged his shoulders, "Oops. Didn't mean to tell you that part."

"Pistol? You're the one who killed him?"

"Oh, no. His stupidity killed him. I simply sat on the side of the road waiting for him to come back down to the river. I still needed that damn truck. My shots were only meant to scare him to a stop. If he'd had any kind of sense about him, he would have held to the road. His panic is what put him over the cliff that day."

"Dragging my best friend with him!" I screamed. "You're a crazy bastard!"

I was having a tough time processing what he was telling me. He was the one who planted the cameras, stalked us day in and day out, manipulated Pistol, caused the car wreck that devastated all of us, turned Peyton into a zombie, and damn near destroyed Caden. I wanted to hurt him for what he'd put my friends through. What he'd put me through. And now, he had me alone in the cabin. There was no telling where this was going to lead. I wasn't sure if I wanted to hit him out of anger or fear, but I clenched my fists and started to raise them to his face.

"Calm down, Jenna," he grabbed my hands. "Listen. There's more." A new gentleness covered his expression. "Look at you. You care so deeply about your friends. That's what draws me to you."

I struggled to pull away when he brought his hand to my face. "You're the most beautiful girl I've ever known. Being around you made me remember how much I loved you when we were kids.

You were the only one who ever stood up for me. Complimented me. And you still did. At school. At the ski park. To your friends. The more time I spent around you, the harder it was for me to think about what I was sent to do. Jenna, I fell for you all over again. I'm not going to hurt you. I still love you."

I closed my eyes and took a deep breath. His words were like a punch to my throat. I could barely speak through the anger and pain he'd inflicted. "Love me? If you loved me, you wouldn't be doing this. You wouldn't have hurt my friends. You would've gone back to Russia the minute you figured it all out!"

"You don't understand. I can't go back without you."

"Why now, Daemon? Nikolai? Whatever the hell your name is? Why did you choose the most important game of the whole season to drug and kidnap me?"

"I know the timing is not desirable, but he's coming. I am no longer trusted to finish this job. I knew that the minute I saw your bracelet. He sent it, Jenna. The Kremlin charm? It's exactly the tracking device he'd use. It showed up after we spoke on the phone. I knew he heard it in my voice that I could never hurt you."

As he leaned into me, the door slammed open and both of us reflexively swung our heads in the direction of his deep voice. At the sight of the heavyset man in black, I scrambled from the couch and crawled under the table. My God. It was him. In living flesh. The man from my nightmares. The cold-blooded killer. Adrenaline shot through my chest as I drew back farther against the wall.

"Father?" he gasped. "How did you know where to find me?"

"It wasn't hard. Have I taught you nothing?"

Nikolai ducked in time to miss the little black object his father threw at his head. "I've been tracking you for weeks. I knew you couldn't be trusted to see this through." He took a few steps closer to Nikolai. "You had one job, and you failed me. Now move away so I can take care of this myself." He swept past Nikolai, shoving him to the ground as he walked toward my hiding place. Before he got close enough, I scrambled out from under the table and crawled to the door. Meanwhile, Nikolai had shuffled across the floor in time to grab his father's leg and slow his advance.

Nikolai was pinning his father to the ground when he yelled out the open door, "Run, Jenna! He'll kill you!"

"Bastard!" I looked over my shoulder to see Vasiliev kick his son in the mouth before prying his leg from his grasp. I was overwhelmed with confusion when he retreated back into the cabin allowing Nikolai the chance to escape.

"You can't have her, Father! I'm not letting you take her!" Nikolai jumped to his feet and began to run toward me. As he neared, I could see his twisted jaw and the blood running from his mouth. I had to stop, just long enough to help him. When he got near enough that I could see he was in pain, I pulled him behind a large cedar, and put my hand on his face.

"Look what he's done to you." I couldn't help but remember that Christmas in Russia after we played chess. The Christmas his father had found him disgraceful for being knocked to the ground by Mason. All the times he put him down. Called him names. And now this? Did he have any love for his poor son at all? As I fixated on his dislocated jaw, and the sorrow I felt for my long-lost friend, I'd forgotten that his father was still hunting me.

Without a word, Nikolai suddenly pulled me around to the back of him, facing us toward the cabin. His father had spotted us. He stood there silently, gun drawn, glaring. It was the stealthiest move I'd ever witnessed. He was ten feet in front of us and I hadn't even seen his approach. But there he stood, looking back and forth between Nikolai and me.

"Point proven." He raised his gun.

It all happened so quickly I couldn't take it all in. I heard the crunch of wheels on gravel from the driveway behind me. With one hand, Nikolai shoved me to the ground. At the same time, I heard an echoing of blasts. My ears began to ring. Bang. Bang. The sounds came from in front and in back of me. I couldn't keep track of where the shots were coming from. Nikolai had dropped beside me, struggling to crawl to my side. "Stay down," he whispered. "I'll protect you." He propped himself on top of me, shielding me from the raining shells.

When there was a break in the gunfire, I tried to nudge him off me, whispering back, "Are you hurt?"

There was no sound. No movement. "Nikolai," I cried. "Are you okay?" His body was growing heavier. I scooted from beneath him, just enough to look him in the eyes. His head lay on my lap while he looked up at me. He took in a deep breath as a tear streamed down his cheek. "Nikolai. You're bleeding." I held my hand to his chest, trying to stop the blood. He swallowed the lump in his throat, taking one last breath before he whispered, "You'll always be my queen." Then, he looked at me one last time before his eyes closed.

I tried with everything in me to stop him from bleeding. I heard the stampede of feet thundering behind me. "Help!" I cried. "It's Nikolai! He needs help!"

I looked up just in time to see Isaiah with his gun. "Is it safe?" Ty's voice hollered from behind me. Isaiah walked toward the lump that was Vasiliev and booted him in the face. "That one's for my Olivia," he screamed. No movement. He kicked him again, "And that one is for the poor kid over there who never had a chance."

Then he looked back toward Ty, "It's safe."

Isaiah had taken him down. In a heap of blood and bodies, I sat wondering how I had gotten into this position. My parents and all my friends ran over and kneeled beside me.

"Daemon?"

I shook my head. "Nikolai," I whispered.

Everyone looked so confused. Everyone but Mason, whose face took on a whole new expression. "You're kidding me." I shook my head, no.

"He needs help," I cried. "Look at him!"

Isaiah came down beside us and put his ear to Nikolai's mouth. He felt for a pulse and moved his hand down to his chest. Shaking his head, he whispered, "It's too late," then he wiped the final tear from Nikolai's cheek. "I knew this day was coming. Damn it." He lifted his body just enough for me to slide my lap out from under him. "We need to leave him here." He stood up and kicked the dirt.

As a swarm of patrol cars pulled up, officers jogged to the scene. Watching the commotion around me, all I could think about was how things would have ended so differently had my friends and family not shown up. I trembled at the thought of my near miss. My family closed in on me and Ty pulled me into his chest, where I sobbed uncontrollably. "How did you know where to find me?"

"The phone in your shin guard. You shared your location with me before my college tour, remember?" He brushed the hair from my face and brought his lips to my forehead. I took a deep breath and let it go along with the flood of tears I had been holding.

I should have been angry for what Nikolai had done. For him coming to America with the intention of taking me back to his father. My mind told me to hate him, but looking down at his lifeless body, the one he had sacrificed for me, all I could find in my heart was forgiveness. Forgiveness for my friend who never stood a chance against the evil terror of his father. A friend who died in my place.

Chapter Thirty-Nine

Commencement

THE NEXT MONTH WAS A WHIRLWIND OF CLASSES, REPORTERS, explanations, and investigations. It was a bit overwhelming, but at the same time, I finally began to feel what it was like to really live. Take it all in. Unabashed. Unbridled. Unveiled. I was no longer hiding from my past. Baseball had finished. We had finals under our belts, and graduation was upon us. It was time to say goodbye to the school I'd called home for the last four years.

The last thing to do was make it through the hour-long ceremony. It wasn't something I looked at with dread, but excitement. I sat with my cap, gown, and flower lei looking out at the crowd, waiting anxiously to get commencement started. Bubbles began to drift through the air, and cheers roared from the stadium as a beach ball dropped into my lap, sure signs that our class clowns were ready to get the show on the road. Quickly, I popped the ball back to Caden's row. He stood up and gave it a good spike right into the back of Mr. Pine's head. Thankfully, he had a sense of humor and just rolled it back to the band which was waiting for its turn to play "Pomp and Circumstance." As the ball rolled to a stop, the principal called my guy to the mic.

His senior year, Ty had studiously snuck past the rest of us and earned the honor of first in the class. He was to give the

Valedictorian's address. Still mesmerized by his every action, I watched him move to the front of the crowd and begin to speak. His baritone voice had me entranced from the first line. As he went on talking about growing up in Jefferson, our small community values, and the roles each and every one in the crowd had played in our successes, I was caught off guard when he invited me up to the podium.

"I'd like to give a special thank you to this girl, right here." He looked at me. "You all know her as Pickle, the girl who stole my heart when she stole home plate. But to me, she's just my best friend. Without her on the other end of my pitches, I wouldn't have found the success I did this year. She showed me what it meant to be brave, take risks, and live every moment like it could be the game changer. So, thank you, Jenna. You wrote the perfect play-book for my senior year." He tapped my shoulder. "Oh, yeah, one more thing," he looked back at the crowd. "I couldn't leave this stage without saying something I've been waiting to say to her for a long time." He leaned over and whispered in my ear, "You okay?" I nodded, yes. He straightened up and pulled the mic from the stand. "I just wanted to tell you in front of everybody here, that I love you." He turned back toward our class. "I love her."

I smiled and leaned into the microphone. "Guess what?" I raised my voice so everyone could hear, "I love you too."

"You hear that, boys? The girl from the trading card is mine!"

The crowd began to laugh and cheer when he grabbed me by the waist and spun me around. Then he carried me off the stage and kissed my cheek before he set me down in front of my chair. "See you after we turn our tassels."

The next half hour was a dream. Looming above all the speeches and special awards was the fact that Ty had declared his love for me in front of a thousand friends and family. It wasn't until Kaitlyn stood up and walked toward the platform that I regained focus. As I sat in the front row watching her play her guitar and sing the farewell song she had written, I couldn't help but think that all the pieces were finally falling into place.

One story, through the seasons, woven together by a place we called Jefferson. I thought of the pool deck where we met for the first time. The fun times we'd had. The classes we'd sat through. The parties. The bonfires. The battles we'd fought. The friends we'd made together, and those we had lost. Her song was a beautiful reminder that we had traveled a deep and rich path to get to this point. Faces and memories flashed through my mind. Each one carving a special place in my heart. Even the ones who'd been so hard to deal with, were a valuable lesson that I wouldn't have traded. They made us stronger and prepared us to take on the world. The last line of her song brought our journey to an end:

"So through the years and through the tears,
friends I hope you know,"

Her voice softened as her eyes filled with emotion,

"I'll carry you inside my heart,
everywhere I go."

Sniffling filled the stadium. It was time to say goodbye. Each of us had been holding a balloon with a message to our departed friends. When the song ended, we released them and watched them soar into the blue sky. As I watched two hundred red strings dancing to new heights, I thought back on the sacrifices Pistol and Nikolai had made, and whispered, "Thank you for saving me and all my Jefferson friends. Godspeed."

For the first time since I could remember, I was no longer captive to my past. None of us were. There was a sense of relief knowing there were no more secrets. Secrets that not only consumed our lives, but stifled them. Somehow the feeling of sadness and loss was a little less in that moment. Watching the tiny dots ascend from view, opened my eyes to the reality that there were no longer limits. Not for our fallen friends and not for us. The seasons at Jefferson High were behind us. We turned our tassels as we faced the sun and cheered for the future.

Epilogue

I RAN TO PICK UP THE PHONE. I'D BEEN WAITING FOR HIS CALL FOR TWO weeks and he was finally able to talk.

"Hey there, superstar."

"Pickle! Are you in town?"

"Sure am."

"We're still set for tonight, right?"

"Got my new Connelly jersey on and everything. Thanks, by the way, for the special delivery. It's a perfect fit."

I could hear the relief in his voice when he told me he'd send the car over to pick me up around three.

"I'll be waiting."

"I'm so excited, Pickle. You have no idea!"

"Oh, I think I have a pretty good idea. I'm feeling the same way. Can't wait to watch you tonight."

"Can't wait to finally play with my good luck charm sitting behind the plate again."

"Behind the plate, huh?"

"Got to keep an eye on my gorgeous girl during the game. Plus, it wouldn't feel right to have you anywhere else."

"God, I love you."

"Love you too. See you soon."

We hung up the phone so I could finish getting ready for our first date since spring training. It was opening day and Ty had flown me out to Boston for his first season game as the starting pitcher. Excited to finally see Fenway Park for the first time, I pulled my hair into my Boston ball cap and buttoned my new jersey. Turning my back to the mirror, I looked over my shoulder, "Connelly's Catcher," it read. He'd even gotten my high school number "4" on it. The thought that he'd actually touched my new Red Sox jersey brought back the warm, tingly feeling of being near him. It was the closest thing I could imagine next to being wrapped up in his arms. I couldn't wait to wear it to the game.

It was hard to believe that after just two years of college ball, Ty had been drafted to the majors. My favorite team, nonetheless. Though I was still studying sports medicine at Stanford, and the separation had been challenging, we hadn't gone a day without face messaging, writing, or talking on the phone. But today, something felt different. More exciting. It was almost as though the electricity was palpable. My nerves were stinging by the time the buzzer rang to call me down to the hotel lobby. I took a deep breath as I shoved my lucky mitt into my bag and headed down the elevator. I couldn't imagine Ty would actually have time to warm up with me, but he wanted me to have it there.

The driver smiled as he introduced himself as Tommy and then escorted me to the luxury car. "I've been instructed to take you on the scenic tour," he said as he opened the door. My heart smiled in response. Ty knew me so well. He knew I'd want to see as much of the historic city as possible.

My senses reeled as I took in the excitement of downtown Boston. As we drove through town, I memorized every sight. The historic buildings. The Irish pubs. The swan boats. The old fire station. Dunkin' Donuts on nearly every city block. The driver checked his watch and cleared his throat, "There's a lot more, but it's time to get you to the stadium."

I could barely catch my breath when the old brick building with the green doors and Championship banners came into view.

My dreams were turning into reality. In just moments, I would be walking through the entrance of Fenway Park. And not just to see any game, but to watch my Ty take the mound.

He had planned a special pick-up for me on Lansdowne Street. Wally, the green monster, was to meet me there and escort me into the stadium before the guys took to batting practice. It was still way too early for the crowds to form, so it was a quick exchange. Only seconds after the driver left me at the designated spot, a golf cart pulled up with the team mascot. He waved me over. To my surprise, Ty popped out from behind him. Before I could even process that he was right there in front of me, he jumped out of the cart and swept me off my feet. After twirling me around until we almost fell from dizziness, he set me on the ground and looked me up and down.

"You weren't kidding. It does fit perfectly. Can't wait for everyone to see you in it. We'd better hurry up and get you to your seat. I'm expected out on the field in a few minutes." He put his arm around me and pulled me onto his lap as he sat down. As we pulled away from the crowd, I turned to face him.

"I can't believe you broke away from the team to get me. Wally would've taken care of me, you know."

"Yeah, looking at you in that jersey, I don't trust him alone with you," he winked. "I'm gonna make sure you're right where you belong before I get back to the boys."

As he walked me through the sparse crowd, which likely consisted of other players' special guests, I could see why Ty had insisted that I come early. He'd wanted to escort me to my seat himself. Even with the handful of fans who had been admitted early, he was being pulled and tugged at for autographs. Being a good sport, he smiled for the photos and signed the autographs, before giving me a quick kiss and telling me the real one would come in a bit.

Again, my nervous curiosity spiked when a mischievous grin played at his lips. With the added twinkle in his eye, I wondered what he was up to. I watched his cute, baseball booty jog down toward the field as he looked over his shoulder one last time and waved. His dimples shined when he realized exactly what I'd been looking at. He stopped momentarily and shouted up to me, "Red Sox Red!"

"What?" I lifted my hands to question what he was talking about.

"The color of your cheeks before your first game as my ..." he turned around and kept running before he finished his sentence.

His what? I had to give it to him. Ty always kept me guessing. I wasn't surprised he'd noticed the color he'd brought to my cheeks. They were practically on fire. I could feel the heat sticking around this time. Fueled by the anticipation of watching him pitch in his first major league game as a starter, I had a feeling the color wouldn't be disappearing for a while.

He took the mound for warmups. I had seen him play in college and knew he was good. However, the guy warming up in front of me was an entirely new player. I had no idea what he could do with his body. He was like Zeus throwing lightning bolts. As they whizzed by, I could almost hear the pitches from the stands. I was glad that I was no longer the one who had to try to catch those fastballs. He had definitely risen to the next level, and I was in the perfect place to watch him show his talent. Right behind the plate. Exactly where I first fell in love with him.

Mesmerized by watching him, I hadn't even noticed the crowd fill in around me. Every seat was filled except for the few empty ones surrounding me. I wondered if Ty was being overprotective again by creating a barrier of empty seats. I giggled, enjoying the extra arm and leg space he had generously provided.

The Red Sox had taken their positions. They were just beginning to set up for the national anthem when Wally appeared with a cart full of Ty's family and my parents. Giving me extra tight hugs and greetings, they unloaded and filled in the empty seats around me. That's when Wally held out his hand and motioned for me to join him down on the field.

"It's okay," Aiden said. "You need to go quick. Here, you'll need this." He picked up my bag and handed it to me. "It's got your mitt, right?"

My head was spinning. I was surprised to see our families, but even more surprised that I was being summoned down to the field by the cute, green mascot. Shaking, I took my mitt from my bag and followed Wally down to the field. There, Ty was waiting with a huge grin plastered across his face.

The announcer came over the speakers. "Ladies and gentlemen, tonight we welcome a new pitcher to the Red Sox family. As a special request, he will be throwing out the first pitch of the game, and has asked for a very special friend to join him on the field for the first catch. Please welcome to the field, Mr. Ty Connelly, and his favorite catcher, Ms. Jenna Bailey.

The crowd roared as I hesitantly stepped out on the field. Shaking, I slid my mitt onto my hand and leaned into him. "Go easy on me, Zeus. I watched the lightning you were throwing before the game." His small chuckle and sideways grin let me know he was humored by his new nickname.

"No worries. I'll put it right in there. I really need you to catch this one," he whispered, then sent me behind the plate.

As I sat there nervously anticipating my one and only catch on a professional field, by a professional pitcher, I had to remind myself that this was Ty. My Ty. The guy I had caught for a million times. He would never do anything to embarrass me or hurt me. I knew he was going to make a pitch I could definitely catch. But before he did, I watched him take the microphone.

"Hey, Pickle. I know you weren't expecting to be out on this plate today, but having you there has been a dream of mine for as long as I could remember. You're the reason I'm here today. You believed in me. You stood by me. You are the one who got me recognized. I'm not sure I'd have had half the attention I did senior year if I hadn't had the only girl in the state behind the plate for a league championship game. My success is your success, and I want the whole world to see what an amazing catcher you've been for me. You ready to catch my first Major League pitch?"

I nodded my head, yes, and waited in anticipation as he walked to the mound and started his wind up. The crowd began to cheer wildly as the ball came over the top and headed straight for my waiting mitt. It was much slower than I'd expected. I could almost see the threads spinning their way toward me. I could actually see lettering on the ball as it hit the pocket. The crowd cheered even more wildly as I stood and held it in the air. Then bringing it back to my eyes, I inspected what I'd seen. It was no ordinary baseball. It had a metal clasp and small hinges. When he saw the confusion come across my face, he jogged toward me, took me by the hand, and guided me back to the mound.

He took the baseball from my hand and slowly lowered himself before me. Down on one knee, he looked me in the eyes and smiled. Then he glanced over his shoulder to the big screen and said, "Pickle, look out toward center field. There's something out there I need you to see."

Overwhelmed with emotion, I looked over his shoulder to the big screen blaring against the darkening sky. It read, "**Ms. Jenna Bailey, will you be my forever catcher?**" It was hard to catch my breath and stop the tears from blurring the vision before me. My handsome pitcher, down on one knee, opening the baseball that held a beautiful diamond ring.

"Marry me?" he whispered.

I pulled him to his feet, jumped into his arms, and buried my head in his strong chest. Without saying a word, my lips found his. With more love and passion than I'd ever felt, I kissed him so hard there was no way he wouldn't know my answer. The crowd went wild when he finally pulled away and slipped the beautiful ring on my finger.

"I take that as a yes?"

"Yes! A million times, yes! Forever and ever, yes!"

Ty Connelly, Fenway Park, baseball, diamond ring. I was engaged to my best friend. My pitcher. I took it all in. There was no way anything would ever top that night. Top my life. I stood right there on the field of my dreams holding tight to the best thing that had ever happened to me. Would ever happen to me. Ty Connelly was my dream. He always had been, he always would be, and from that day on he was my teammate for life. My forever pitcher.

The End

A Message from the Authors

When we first started writing *When Fall Breaks*, our dream was to write books as gifts for our own children. However, as the stories came to life, a message started to form. We realized, being teachers, we witness difficult situations our students face every day. It is our hope that reading our stories will help teens make connections and seek help from professionals when needed.

Our first story, *When Fall Breaks*, dealt with underage drinking and substance abuse. Our message at the end of that story provided The Pathway Program as an available resource for help. We'd like to offer that information again. If you know of a young person who may need help, The Pathway Program is available by both phone and via the internet. You can call and talk to a representative Toll Free at 1-877-921-4050 or visit them on the web at www.thepathwayprogram.com. If you are a teen and find yourself struggling with drinking or substance abuse, please reach out to a parent, school counselor, teacher, youth pastor, or friend. As teachers, we are always open to help our students get the help they need. It doesn't matter if you were a former student, current student, or didn't even have us as a teacher. We care about all of you.

A second issue we addressed in *When Fall Breaks* was how teens and young adults struggle with domestic violence. This can happen to people of any race, age, sexual orientation, religion, or gender. Sometimes it starts out subtly and intensifies without the victim realizing how bad it has become. If friends are warning you that they see signs of control, verbal, or physical abuse, please listen. Many abusers are masters at manipulating their victims and making them feel like THEY are the reason for the incident. It's NEVER okay. It is NOT your fault. If you or someone you know is in an abusive relationship, there is confidential support out there 24/7. Please visit the National Domestic Violence Hotline at www.

thehotline.org. Teens can go to www.loveisrespect.org, or call 1-866-331-9474, to speak with someone privately. It's a confidential online resource available to help young adults prevent and end abusive relationships.

As a follow up to the severe incident that occurred in our first story, *The Dead of Winter* focused on an issue that is extremely serious and often undiagnosed. It is called Post-Traumatic Stress Disorder (PTSD). This disorder is a mental health condition that's triggered by terrifying events. Some people have either experienced or witnessed catastrophes that may cause them to have flashbacks, nightmares and/or severe anxiety. The teen characters in *The Dead of Winter* lived through such traumatic events and did not receive the attention needed right away. Please do not ignore the symptoms of Post-Traumatic Stress Disorder. Get help if you are having a severe reaction such as nervousness, fear, and even guilt after experiencing a traumatic event. If you believe you are experiencing PTSD, reach out to a professional. They can help you restore a sense of control in your life. Post-Traumatic Stress Disorder can happen at any age. You are not alone. Please visit the National Center for Posttraumatic Stress Disorder (NCPTSD) at www.ptsd.va.gov or call (802)296-5132. It is a confidential online resource available to help adults of any age.

Our third story, *Secrets of Spring*, allowed us to highlight another common issue that many students face today. Internet safety. As middle school teachers, we have found that our students are joining social networking sites at a very young age without awareness of the dangers. Also, many online gaming sites have chat rooms where predators have easy access to vulnerable minors. It's easy to get swept up in the addiction of building on-line relationship and sharing information that could pose a threat to one's safety. Even posting pictures can be a security risk if the location feature has not been disabled. It's important to be aware of what you're posting and who you're making friends with. Jenna's fictitious account was just one way to draw attention to an ever-growing problem. There are several great websites one could visit to become educated on internet safety. One site we'd like to share with you is childrescue-network.org. Get educated. Be smart. Don't share information with strangers.

Secrets of Spring addressed another serious problem. Underage drinking, even in moderation, is extremely dangerous. While under the influence, it's not uncommon to make poor decisions that could put yourself or others at risk. Also, the dangers of mind-altering drugs being slipped into drinks is a growing problem. You should never leave a drink unattended or accept a drink from someone at a party. The drugs people slip into these drinks can cause memory loss or an altered state of consciousness. Please visit www. futuresofpalmbeach.com/womens-health/victim-spiked-drink   or call (866) 817-0766 for more information.

Acknowledgements

Thank you to everyone who had a role in making our third book come to life. As you read our story, you'll realize it's not just about sports. It's about the bonds between people we love. That is why we'd like to dedicate this book to our families. We know that in writing these books, we've given up countless hours with our families. We promise it's your time now.

To our BETA readers, thank you for the time you put into helping us. Sarah, Darlene, Karen, Candy, Heather, Jenna, Kaitlyn, Sandy, and Macy, we value all your advice and direction. To XxId Editing, thank you so much for your keen eye and honest input. This book would not have been the same without you.

To our formatter, Stacey Blake from Champagne Formats, we can't thank you enough for making the interior of our book beautiful. You have created masterpieces with all three of our novels. Your designs blend together flawlessly, and we can't thank you enough for the beauty and magic you continue to produce.

To our amazing bloggers and everyone else who has shared positive reviews, supportive words, and blessed us with your friendship, we are forever grateful for your continued support and presence in our lives. You have added so much joy to this experience. We can't thank you enough for putting our books out there.

About the Authors

Julie Solano has lived in far Northern California, nearly her entire life. She graduated from CSU, Chico, where she majored in Psychology and minored in Child Development. She later went on to Simpson University where she obtained her multiple subject teaching credential. Julie enjoys life in the "State of Jefferson," where she lives with her two children. As a family, they spend their time tromping around the Marble Mountains and Russian Wilderness. They also take pleasure in water sports, snow sports, off-roading, campfires, and living it up in the great outdoors. When she's not with her family, Julie spends her days teaching next door to her co-author, fellow prankster, and partner in crime, Tracy. The most recent of their crazy adventures was to take on the challenge of writing this series of novels about what life is like in their neck of the woods.

Born and raised in Northern California, **Tracy Justice** is a wife, mother, and full-time teacher. She graduated from CSU, Chico, with a Bachelor of Arts Degree in Liberal Arts. One of her fondest memories growing up was herding cattle in the Marble Mountains with her family. She enjoys spending time with her family and friends, riding horses, running, hiking, swimming, and of course reading. After some encouragement from Julie, she decided to add "Co-author" to her ever growing bucket list. She never knew how much fun it would be to write a book with her best friend. She hopes you enjoy reading their third book in the "Seasons of Jefferson Series" as much as she enjoyed writing it with Julie.

Julie and Tracy hope you enjoy reading their stories, which were inspired by their small town, rural upbringing, and the personalities of their four children.

Remember to visit Julie and Tracy on Facebook, Twitter, and Instagram.

www.facebook.com/JT-Authors

twitter.com/jt_authors

instagram.com/jt_authors